NO JUDGE, NO JURY

A DS JACK TOWNSEND NOVEL

ROBERT ENRIGHT

*In loving memory of June Enright,
My NJ. x*

CHAPTER ONE

It's surprisingly easy to murder someone.

As the calm, spring night hung above the trees, Asif Khalid was still unconscious. The man was in his early fifties and dragging him from the back of the van had been a struggle. The combination of being a doctor and a father of three meant Khalid had shunted exercise down his list of priorities, and his flabby body had been difficult to move while deadweight.

But it had been moved.

Step by step, the Executioner had dragged the limp man from the van, and through a gap in the bushes that stretched for miles around the farm in Cadmore End. The leafy village was five miles away from the bustling town of High Wycombe, but it could have been hundreds more. What was the stark difference between the two? Narrow country roads, lined infrequently with the odd, quaint-looking cottage, the small village was as nondescript as they came.

Which was why the Executioner had chosen it.

Nothing happened in Cadmore End.

Certainly not murder.

With leather-clad hands, the Executioner had pulled the unconscious doctor through the wire fence he'd snipped the day before, and then, with his hands clutched under the doctor's arms, had dragged the man towards his death. The mud was moist from the spring showers that had scattered across the day, and with the rich soil of the farm primed for the crops, the Executioner's boots plunged down deep as he'd shuffled with his captive. Khalid's heels dragging through the mud.

All the way through two fields under the starlit Friday night sky, until he'd made it to the small cluster of trees in the field. There'd clearly been more of them, forcibly removed over time, but a few remained. Their wiry, thin trunks reaching up and splaying their branches out like fingers.

And they'd chosen one that was just as wide as the man they intended to kill.

Just a tree.

Tonight, it would be so much more.

A firing post.

Khalid was slumped against his restraints, his hands pinned above his head, strapped to the tree by a series of tightly pulled cable ties. The plastic was digging into the skin, causing a trickle of blood to slither down his arms. A few metres away, his captor was assembling a tripod, pushing out the base and standing it steadily on the soft mud. As he placed the camera into an extended holder, he caught a glimpse of himself on the small screen of the device.

The dark clothes.

The hood.

But most importantly, the mask.

Covering his skull from the back of his neck to underneath his chin, the thick leather mask was a fearsome sight. The leather clung tightly to the skull, and although there were small openings for his eyes, it was the thick, white stitching that stood out. Jaggedly stitched across the front of the mask was a white cross slashing diagonally across the entire face.

It was a symbol.

One they would remember.

One they would fear.

Beneath the leather, the Executioner felt his lips crease into a cruel smile.

Beneath the leather, he felt invincible.

It didn't matter who he was underneath.

A law-abiding citizen or a criminal.

A god or an immortal.

The mask made him untouchable.

It made them the living, breathing embodiment of justice.

And as he locked the camera in place, he felt the surge of injustice that had led to this point jolt through his body like an electric current. Feeling his gloved hand tighten into a knuckle-whitening fist, he clicked the button, and the powerful ring light affixed to the tripod illuminated the scene before him.

Khalid murmured slightly, slowly regaining consciousness. That quickly shifted to panic, and, within seconds, the mild-mannered doctor was screaming for help, straining against the cable ties until the pain became too much.

'Please,' Khalid said through anguished breaths. 'Please. Whatever…t-t-this is…Whatever this is about. Just let me go.'

The Executioner said nothing, refusing to turn as he adjusted the camera. His body was bathed in the light, shielding them from Khalid's vision.

'What is this about?' Khalid yelled. Tears trickled down his face and disappeared into his neat, grey beard.

Still no response.

Khalid pulled once more against his cable ties, but the plastic sliced through another layer of skin and he fell back against the trunk in agony.

More blood flowed.

More tears, too.

'Please…I have a family.'

Khalid's pitiful pleas fell on deaf ears, and the Executioner pressed the *record* button on the camera and then turned. Crunching across the grass, the Executioner stepped from the blinding light, and Khalid's eyes widened in fear.

The mask had the desired effect.

There was no pity or mercy within the Executioner. Even if he'd searched his soul for it, they'd have been searching forever. While Khalid was, without question, an honest doctor and a loyal family man, he still needed to pay for his actions.

For the injustice he'd been a part of.

But, as the Executioner's eyes bored through the mask and locked onto the snivelling, cowering man strapped to the makeshift firing post, it was evident Khalid didn't know of his crimes.

Didn't know of the pain and the suffering he'd caused.

Didn't know what had marked him for death.

The Executioner looked up to the sky at the stars and knew that this was the point of no return.

This was the beginning of the crusade.

The mask turned back to Khalid, who wept through his sharp, panicked breaths. His mind raced to his family. His wife and his children, all of whom would undoubtedly be worried about his disappearance.

He closed his eyes and thought of them.

In the glow of the ring light, the Executioner stood ten feet from Khalid, who was held against the tree by the blood-soaked cable ties. Slowly, the gloved hand reached into the black jacket and pulled from it a Glock 17 handgun.

There was no trial for this man.

Khalid would pay the ultimate price for his participation.

Without skipping a beat, the Executioner lifted the weapon expertly, drawing it up to his eyeline and locked onto his target.

No judge.

No jury.

The sentence was death.

The gloved finger pulled back the trigger, and a horrifying blast echoed through the night sky, causing a flutter through the surrounding trees as birds scattered in panic. The bullet blasted through Khalid's forehead, ripping through his brain, before exploding out the back of his skull and embedding into the wooden trunk. Blood and brain matter showered the surrounding grass, and the doctor fell limp, swaying gently against his restraints.

With no emotion, the Executioner pocketed the weapon and walked calmly back towards the camera, the mask in full view of the lens. Somewhere in the distance, a dog was barking, and the low hum of the M40 traffic rumbled.

But all was calm.

A sense of justice had washed over the night, and carefully, the Executioner went about dismantling the tripod, before heading back through the dark fields, and back to the normal life everyone believed he lived.

And as the murdered man swung against his restraints behind him, the Executioner headed off into the darkness with two thoughts racing beneath the mask.

His first murder had been surprisingly easy.

He hoped the rest would be, too.

CHAPTER TWO

'Dad. Watch this.'

As Eve took a run and jump, she hit the trampoline and, to Jack Townsend's amazement, his daughter nailed a perfect front flip. As she landed it, her friends cheered and then they bounced away, leaping from trampoline to trampoline as they swept across the park. As he watched her gracefully leap around, Townsend couldn't believe his daughter was now nine years old.

How did that happen?

Time had a funny way of racing past without you realising, and Townsend knew he needed to stop sometimes to appreciate the moment. It had been a long road back to rebuilding a relationship with his daughter, and watching her laugh and giggle with her friends was a luxury he refused to take for granted.

Not after what they'd been through.

Years under cover in some of the most dangerous organised crime gangs in the country had put his and his family's lives in danger.

The 'make good' from the Merseyside Police Service in

making him a detective sergeant by way of an apology for the heinous betrayal of his operation handler.

The two years he spent stuck behind a desk being given busy work just to keep him out of the way.

When the opportunity had arisen almost a year ago for him and his family to relocate from Liverpool down to Buckinghamshire, it could have been the death knell to his frayed relationship with them.

It turned out to be the greatest thing that had happened to them.

Although he was shunted into the Specialist Crimes Unit of the Thames Valley Police, DS Townsend soon found himself on the hunt for a serial killer within his first week. The haunting experience built a bond between himself and the rest of the SCU within days, and upon the successful arrest of the killer, Gordon Baycroft, Townsend not only proved himself to his team but also to himself.

He'd found somewhere to belong.

His boss, Detective Inspector Isabella King, soon saw what he was capable of, but whether she liked it or not, he looked to her for guidance throughout. Especially over the course of the winter months, when a slew of staged suicides were pieced together to reveal the blood-thirsty revenge plot of Gemma Miller, who'd targeted those she felt had contributed to her father's suicide.

During the hunt for the vengeful daughter, Townsend had taken his eye off the ball more than once, allowing Gemma's rampage to continue and resulting in two more deaths.

That was something he would have to live with.

This is the job.

A job that had also seen Townsend piece together the murder of Jamal Beckford, which left the victim's abused wife a widow and her son now facing life imprisonment for killing him.

Just a kid.

This was the job.

Townsend shook the memories from his head and scanned the garishly bright trampoline park for his daughter and soon caught Eve and her friends scurrying away from one of the staff members, who seemed tasked with the sole purpose of limiting the fun as much as possible. As the grumpy steward waved them away from the ball pit, Jack turned to see his wife, Mandy, deep in conversation with the other parents. Beautiful as ever, she stood casually, charming the group with another story as she effortlessly made friends with them. She was the polar opposite to her husband, who, despite trying his best to be outgoing, had too much baggage to really open up to people.

He had his family.

He had his team.

That was enough for Jack.

But Mandy always amazed him with how easily she found common ground with strangers, and he knew she was making an effort to befriend the other parents for their daughter. Since moving Eve away from her school and home back in Merseyside, Mandy had been instrumental in getting her settled in her new surroundings. The village of Flackwell Heath was a world away from the urban maze that was their former city, and her village school was a quarter of the size of her previous.

Everything felt quainter.

Less hectic.

But Mandy had thrown herself in, despite starting a new job, and was already a vital part of the PTA, as well as ferrying Eve to all the extra-curricular clubs they'd signed her up for. A few had fallen by the wayside, but as evident by another perfect somersault, she'd found her passion in gymnastics.

As she landed, Eve scanned the trampoline park until her eyes found Townsend's, and she smiled.

So did he.

'She's getting good, isn't she?'

Mandy's voice cut through the thumping pop music that was hammering from the speakers, and Townsend spun to his wife.

'She's not bad.' Townsend beamed proudly. 'She reminds me of a young Jack Townsend.'

'Bollocks.' Mandy laughed. 'Like you could ever do a front flip.'

Townsend wriggled his eyebrows, and then to his wife's loving amazement, he ran across two trampolines, leapt, planted both feet on the trampoline and pushed himself up into the air.

The front flip was atrocious.

He barely rotated.

And to a howl of laughter from his wife, and a barrage of giggles from his daughter and her friends, Townsend landed on his arse before bouncing awkwardly onto his back. He sat up, smiling.

'See,' he said proudly.

A shrill whistle blew a few feet behind him, and a scrawny teenager marched over to read him the riot act, but Townsend just waved him off and headed back towards his wife, as his daughter called from behind.

'You're so embarrassing, Dad.'

'Get used to it, Pickle,' Townsend called back, winking to his wife. The other parents had shuffled over, and in light of Townsend's goofy behaviour, had seemingly let their own guard down around him.

Sometimes he forgot that being a tough, Scouse detective could be a little intimidating to some.

'Nice one, Jack.'

'That was hilarious.'

'I didn't know you were an Olympic gymnast.'

The banter flowed quickly, and Mandy rolled her eyes as her husband suddenly became the centre of attention.

'All right, Max Whitlock.' Mandy joked. 'Why don't you go and get us all some coffees?'

Townsend took down the orders, slid his trainers back on and then headed back towards the front of the trampoline park. Beside the door, a staircase led up to the café, which overlooked the park itself, and offered parents a little respite from the mayhem. Townsend smiled politely to the other parents in the queue and then ran through the order again in his mind. As he did, he caught a glimpse of himself in the reflection of the cake display and smiled.

The grey was starting to show in his hair, especially around the sides, much to Mandy's delight. She said it made him look a little more *seasoned*, and with the tinges of grey that had now peppered his thick stubble, Townsend certainly looked like a man in his early forties. It was why he was even more committed to his daily run and workout, to ensure he kept energetic enough not just for his job, but so he could dazzle his family with his trampoline skills.

As he re-established the light parting in his otherwise dark hair with his hand, Townsend finally approached the counter and began to relay the coffee order to the slightly panicked teenager on the other side. Just as he gave his final choice, a familiar voice cut in.

'And an oat milk caramel latte, please.'

Townsend sighed and turned to see the beaming smile of DC Nicola Hannon. Despite her smile, he knew something was off.

Not only because they'd accosted him at a trampoline park on his day off, but because with Hannon was DS Michelle Swaby, and her permanent state of positivity had been replaced with a frown.

Townsend sighed and then turned to the two other members of the SCU.

'Let me guess…you're not here for a bounce, are you?'

'Sadly not.' Hannon looked out over the park. 'Looks like fun, though.'

'It is.' Townsend nodded. 'A really great place to get away from work, you know?'

Hannon and Swaby shared a look of guilt, and Townsend felt a little bad for forcing that upon them.

'The guv sent us,' Swaby piped up. 'We're on.'

Townsend sighed.

With civilians surrounding them, Swaby wasn't going to give him the details of the incident then and there. Not only was it not for the ears of the public, but if anything, the last year had shown him that news spread across social media like the bubonic plague. Detective Superintendent Geoff Hall, the man who ran the Thames Valley Police Station, had made it very clear he didn't want anything said in public anymore.

Townsend couldn't have agreed more.

'It's Eve's birthday,' he said with a shake of the head. He looked over the railing towards his family and locked eyes with Mandy, who'd obviously seen Hannon and Swaby arrive.

Reading the situation.

Without hesitation, her gorgeous face broke out into a stunning smile, and she nodded to her husband.

This was the job.

Townsend finished paying for the order, told the staff where to send the coffees and took his to go.

Seconds later, he, along with the other two members of his team, were marching through the brisk, spring morning towards Swaby's car, heading towards whatever had sent them searching for him.

As Townsend dropped into the passenger seat, sipped his coffee, and watched the trampoline park disappear in his wing mirror, he knew one thing.

It wasn't going to be good.

CHAPTER THREE

A spring chill carried on the wind, whipping up and around Detective Inspector Isabella King and she pulled her jacket tightly around her slight frame. As she stood in place, she took a long, thoughtful puff on her vape before tucking it into her pocket, let the smoke out with a sigh and headed towards the chaos before her.

Nothing like a murder scene to wake you up on a Saturday morning.

Unfortunately for King, it was just one of many over her two decades as a police officer, ranging from her time in CID for the Met, all the way up to her current position as head of the Thames Valley Police Specialist Crimes Unit. There'd been a multitude of obstacles along the way. The underlying sexism and racism that still existed in the world. The never-ending feeling of self-doubt. The venomous breakdown of her marriage to Detective Chief Inspector Marcus Lowe, who just so happened to head up the CID function in the same police station as her.

But she'd overcome them all.

Her team of Townsend, Hannon and Swaby had delivered when it mattered most, and over the past year, had solved and closed two of the most notorious murder cases the county of Buckinghamshire had ever seen.

Obstacles were there to be overcome.

That was something she'd always believed, and it was why, despite always echoing at the back of her mind, she knew she couldn't have a drink. It had been four months since she'd revealed to her team that she was struggling with alcoholism, an addiction she'd finally confronted when the murderous Gordon Baycroft had accused her of betraying the women he'd brutally murdered.

Lauren Grainger. Natasha Stokes. Michaela Woods. Irena Roslova.

All four of those women had deserved better.

From life.

From her.

That was eight months ago, in the middle of the summer, and King had promised the four deceased women she would give up the drink and get her act together. That promise was pushed to its breaking point during the winter, when Gemma Miller's blood-thirsty quest for retribution piled up the bodies and terrified the town.

Jason Gallagher. His wife, Rachel. Penny Durant. Connor Davis.

Four equally flawed people, all of whom were killed at the hands of a woman who blamed them for an insidious rumour that had broken her father's will to live. It had stretched not only King's resolve but also the bond between her and her team, but when it mattered most, when King had been sitting with a drink in front of her, they came through.

And she'd told them everything.

Now, facing another murder scene and the potential turmoil that followed it, King knew that *that* voice would creep up again, urging her to give up her willpower and succumb to her addiction.

She couldn't allow that happen.

Wouldn't.

Not when those eight names were tattooed to her memory and as she gazed at the body hanging lifelessly from the tree trunk, she readied herself for a ninth. Throughout her career, which spanned over two decades, King had seen plenty of dead bodies. Had hunted several killers. But those eight victims had met their grisly end while she'd been responsible for the investigation.

And that was a responsibility she would never let go of.

The field was scarce beyond the murder scene, with a light fog still eerily hanging over the wet grass beneath her feet. The country roads that weaved around the farm were empty, although the odd vehicle did slow as it passed, eager to see what was happening. SOCOs were spread across the crime scene, wrapped up in their body suits as they tried their best to salvage any evidence from the elements. A few metres away from her, the swiftly erected tent flapped against the wind, obstructing the murder scene from the road beyond. Inside, the ever-reliable PC Kevin Boyd was sitting with the young farmer who'd stumbled across the dead body on his early morning walk. Despite his gruff demeanour, Boyd was one of the best uniformed officers in the Thames Valley Police, and although she wouldn't tell him, King was pleased he was first on scene.

His partner, PC Simon Walsh, had recently followed the same path as King and transferred across from the Met. King didn't know the man, but as he stood by the cordon with a scowl on his face, his expression matched the rumours that he was a 'cantankerous old git'.

But he was here.

As was she.

Because a man named Asif Khalid had been brutally murdered.

King took a few steps towards the corpse, her eyes

searching him for any signs of struggle. The wrists were drenched in blood, the skin peeling from the deadweight of the body pulling against the cable ties. Beyond the gruesome bullet hole that dominated both sides of his skull, it looked like Asif had been completely unharmed.

Boots crunched on the grass behind her, and King turned to see her team approaching. Although her instinct was to smile at the sight of the three people she trusted the most in the world, the situation dictated she just nodded her greeting.

'Guv,' Townsend said in his thick, Scouse accent.

'Jesus,' Hannon said, blowing out her cheeks. Her eyes were glued to the dead body. 'I guess we can rule out natural causes.'

The attempt at levity fell flat and King clicked into gear.

'Asif Khalid,' King said with authority. 'Fifty-three years old. Our killer left his phone and wallet, meaning whoever did this wanted us to know who they'd killed.'

'Could just have been sloppy?' Swaby offered.

'This doesn't look sloppy,' Townsend said, stepping forward, his eyes scanning the crime scene.

In the eight months he'd been working for King, she'd realised Townsend's approach was a little less orthodox than most detectives'. But he had a natural eye for detail, and although sometimes his train of thought thundered down irritatingly irrational tracks, she was experienced enough to know a good detective when she met one.

It was her job to make him great.

'What d'ya think, Jack?' King asked, stepping slightly to the side.

'This wasn't a murder. It was an execution,' Townsend said coldly. 'It was planned. Meaning whoever did this knew how to get access, knew when and where Mr Khalid would be—'

'There are no tyre tracks,' King cut in. 'But there are some boot prints in the mud SOCO have been able to lift, and what appear to be heel marks, too.'

King pointed to where a few red flags had been pinned into the mud a few metres from them. Swaby instinctively walked across the step plates that had been laid out by the SOCOs, eager to take a look.

'He was dragged?' Townsend turned to her with an eyebrow arched.

'That'd take some effort,' Hannon said. 'Dragging a fully grown man through a few fields? Reckon our killer is a man?'

'It's likely,' King agreed. 'But we can't rule out anything yet.'

'We can rule out accidental death,' Hannon quipped again.

This time, it drew a smile from King. She knew Hannon's way of dealing with the gruesome side of the job was to try to lighten the mood.

'Nic, get back to base and start trawling through the CCTV. Check the houses and buildings on the roads leading towards the field to see if they have any security or doorbell cameras. Something might have been triggered.'

'On it, guv,' Hannon said with a nod. She hid her appreciation as well as she hid the pain in her back. The bitter chill of the spring morning was causing her injury to flare up. As Hannon headed off back through the field, PC Boyd emerged from the tent and greeted Townsend with a meaty handshake.

'Scouse,' he said with a nod.

'Detective Scouse,' Townsend replied, drawing a grin from the gruff officer. 'How's our farmer?'

'Shaken,' Boyd said with a sigh. 'Young kid is barely out of his teens. His family run the farm, and he was out on the usual walk and he sees this. Poor lad.'

'Have you taken his statement?' King asked.

'Yes, ma'am,' Boyd replied. 'Didn't hear any gunshots either, but the family home is a few miles that way so…'

'Okay.' King looked around the scene. 'Stay with him and let him know we'll need him to come down to the station for a few more questions. We'll also need to speak with everyone who has access to this land.'

'Guv,' Swaby called out. She was squatting down by the flags surrounding the boot prints. Her short blonde bob was hanging over the rims of her glasses. 'Check this out.'

King burst forward, striding to her colleague with purpose. As Townsend was about to follow suit, PC Walsh approached, the sleeves of his shirt rolled up to reveal old, faded tattoos.

'Ah, Townsend. Meet PC Walsh,' Boyd said, stepping aside so his partner could extend a hand. Townsend took it. The grip was as firm as he expected.

'Nice to meet you,' Walsh said, his voice laced in a Cockney accent.

'Likewise,' Townsend said with a nod. Walsh's eyebrows raised with surprise.

'Scouse?' Walsh asked and then turned to Boyd. 'Ah, this is the fella you were telling me about…'

Townsend turned to Boyd with confusion, who was smiling.

'Yes, mate.' Boyd turned to face Townsend. 'Walshy here used to box for the Met. I told him you were pretty handy.'

'Only when I have to be,' Townsend replied modestly and then took a step to the side. 'Back to work, eh? Nice to meet you.'

'Likewise.'

Townsend stepped away from the two uniformed officers, who trundled back to their posts. King had joined

Swaby in the squat, their eyes scanning over the grass as Swaby pointed her fingers.

'Everything okay?' King asked, looking up.

'Yeah.' Townsend rolled his eyes. 'Just a quick 'boys' meeting' with the lads. You know how it is.'

King scoffed and shook her head.

Swaby beckoned Townsend downward.

'Check it out.' She pointed to the markings in the mud. 'Three-pronged. Faint indentation from each one to this central post.'

Townsend looked at the markings in the mud and then back to Swaby, who seemed pleased with herself.

'A tripod?' Townsend asked, and stood up again. King followed, and the two of them looked back to the tree, where Khalid was now being cut down from his restraints. Erecting a tent around a tree had proved a tricky task for the SOCOs, and although they had been able to shield the murder from the public road beyond, Khalid's body was still visible as the team prepared to send him to Dr Mitchell. They both knew what she'd find.

A clean bullet wound to the skull.

Most likely, some form of drug in his system to render him helpless.

But that wasn't what they were thinking.

Swaby stood and said out loud what was racing through their minds.

'You think whoever did this filmed it?'

Their silence said everything.

They realised at once this wasn't just an execution.

There was something more at play.

Before King could order them back to the station to start digging, Townsend spoke their worries into existence.

'I think this is more than just a murder.'

CHAPTER FOUR

The Saturday morning roads were starting to fill up as they navigated their way back from Cadmore End, with King guiding her car through the small village of Lane End on the way back to the town centre. Townsend took a moment to point out to Swaby that on his first day in the job, he'd chased a small-time drug dealer called Dean Riley through the small estate in the village. With the Eden Shopping Centre looming over the town centre, King approached the Magic Roundabout and joined the slow procession of traffic, before turning towards High Wycombe Police Station. As they rounded the mini roundabout facing the Rye, a sombre silence filled the car.

They all remembered what happened there last summer.

The death of Lauren Grainger.

And Baycroft's attempt to provide DI King with the same fate.

Had it not been for Townsend, King knew she would have faced the sharp end of his blade and bled out in the mud. It was why she trusted her DS completely, and it was great to see the same bond being forged between

Townsend and Swaby. Gemma Miller's misguided vendetta had taken her to within minutes of murdering Swaby in her own home, but once again, it was Townsend who'd intervened in the nick of time.

Despite his penchant for saving the lives of his team members, King hoped it was the last time he'd ever have to.

As they exited the car, a few of the other officers who'd been rostered for Saturday threw an inquisitive eye in Townsend's direction. The usual white shirt and tie had been replaced by his casual clothes, and it made him stick out like a sore thumb. With his broad physique filling his black polo shirt, Townsend marched through the back entrance of the station with his team and headed up to the SCU office. Hannon was already at her desk, her eyes glued to the screen and a Chocolate Hobnob in her hand.

'Anything?' King asked as she strode into the room. Hannon shook her head and pressed herself against the back support affixed to her chair.

'Nada,' Hannon said sorrowfully. 'Like you guessed, there was little in the way of CCTV, and the nearest traffic camera is over a mile away. I've got uniform canvassing the houses for home security videos, but considering there are so many windy roads to the farm, it's a needle in a haystack.'

'Well, they used one of them, so keep looking,' King said as she headed towards her office. 'I need to speak to Hall.'

King's team offered her a pained smile. Detective Superintendent Geoff Hall was a respected figure within the Thames Valley Police, and his watchful eye over the High Wycombe station had been seen as one of the reasons for its rise in reputation. Despite the original political reasons for King's appointment in charge of the SCU, Hall had received plenty of praise for putting the team together. He was a firm but fair leader and was the personification of an iron fist in a velvet glove.

He'd been there for King, too.

Before her team was aware of her struggles with the bottle, Hall had pulled her out of the firing line and had even been by her side when she ventured into an Alcoholics Anonymous meeting for the first few times. Although he wasn't officially her 'sponsor', she knew that Hall would be there for her if things ever got too rough.

But he'd insisted that she couldn't let it get that far.

Not when the town was so quick to turn on the police the second the media began to paint them in a darker light.

Despite the station's strict 'no smoking' policy, King closed the door to her small, private office at the back of the SCU hub, and took a long puff on her vape.

Disturbing Detective Superintendent Hall during his Saturday round of golf wasn't encouraged.

Telling him there had been a violent murder was unlikely to be appreciated, either.

With one final fruity puff of encouragement, King put her vape into her desk drawer and then lifted her phone. After a few rings, it connected.

This is Detective Superintendent Geoff Hall of the Thames Valley Police. I am unable to take your call right now. Please call the front desk on...

King waited for the pre-recorded message to end.

'Hello, sir. It's DI King. We've got a body. Call me when you get the chance.'

King hung up and looked out through the blinds of her office. Swaby had taken her usual spot on the desk next to Hannon and was dipping her own biscuit into a fresh mug of tea. Behind the two women, Townsend stood, his powerful arms folded across his chest, and the three of them were in deep conversation.

King felt guilty that they were there on a Saturday morning.

They all had families and home lives they were fiercely protective of and loyal to.

Happy, loving homes.

Yet here they all were.

Without question.

Without hesitation.

King felt a swelling of pride in her chest and used that to fuel her next movements. Hall would undoubtedly call back and demand results, but until that happened, she needed to take control of things. She needed to start guiding the investigation and start collating an evidence trail that could at least give them a direction to chase.

Right now, they had a dead body and nothing else.

No killer.

No motive.

No real idea of what was coming next.

She clicked a few times on the mouse of her computer and sent a document to the office printer.

King pulled open the door and walked back out into the SCU, knowing all eyes were on her. Without a word, she marched across to the glass board pressed against the far wall and then wheeled it out into the centre of the room. Then she headed to the printer and lifted the A4 picture of Asif Khalid she'd printed and stuck it to the centre of the board. With a firm slap on the glass, she turned to her team.

'Right...Asif Khalid was murdered last night.' She looked at each of them. 'He was taken out to the middle of nowhere, tied to a tree, and shot through the skull. We have no evidence beyond a few muddy footprints, a potential tripod and our victim's identification. Uniform are canvassing the nearby houses, and a FLO has been assigned to the Khalid's home, where we need to go as soon as possible. This man right here is the priority. And we have two questions we need to answer and answer fucking quickly.'

She looked at the photo of Khalid, the stern face taken from his driver's licence. Then she turned back to her team, her eyes encouraging an answer.

'Who killed him?' Swaby offered, and King clicked her fingers and pointed at her.

Townsend pushed himself off the desk and placed his hands on his hips before laying out the second question.

'And why?'

CHAPTER FIVE

As Townsend stepped away from the urinal in the gent's bathroom, he approached the row of regularly cleaned sinks and held his hands to the sensor. Lukewarm water poured out from the tap, and he combined it with a few sharp presses of the soap dispenser. After a thorough wash, he dried his hands of the soapy remnants, before cupping another handful of water and splashing it to his face.

He was tired.

It had been nearly five hours since he'd rushed away from his family to jump two-footed into a murder investigation. It was part of the job, and while his girls understood that, Townsend always felt a sense of guilt when he had to step away. His relationship with Eve had been rebuilt since his long stint undercover, and ever since they'd moved to Buckinghamshire, it had blossomed into the most precious thing in Townsend's life.

She understood why he would have to leave.

It didn't make him hate it any less.

With a frown, Townsend scorned himself for being so selfish. A father had been found executed in a field and he was annoyed he couldn't stay at a trampoline park.

Three daughters had just lost their father.

A wife had been widowed.

A man had been killed.

Keeping things in perspective, being called away from a loving family to do some good in the world wasn't the worst thing in the world, and Mandy would be the first one to tell him that.

Ding

His phone buzzed along with the sound of a message arriving, and Townsend felt his heart thump as his wife, once again, had seemingly read his mind.

Taking Eve shopping and for lunch. Might go cinema, too. Go get 'em, babe Xx

Townsend smiled. His thumbs found the heart emoji on his phone and he felt better as he sent his brief reply. She was right.

He had work to do.

Just as Townsend turned to open the door to the gents', it swung open, and DCI Marcus Lowe marched in like a man on a mission. The door almost caught Townsend in the face, and he stumbled back a few steps, causing Lowe to chuckle.

'Fuckin' hell, Scouse.' Lowe smirked. 'Don't piss your pants this close to a urinal.'

'Sir.' Townsend nodded respectfully. Lowe reciprocated and then rushed to the urinal to relieve himself. As he let out an audible sigh of relief, Townsend rolled his eyes and pulled open the door to leave.

'Heard you caught a fresh one?' Lowe called out with an inquisitive raise of the eyebrow. Townsend stepped back in, as Lowe zipped himself up and headed to the sink. He stared at Townsend in the mirror as he washed his hands, and Townsend just shrugged. As head of CID, Lowe was seen as one of the jewels in the crown of the Thames Valley Police. It had also helped foster an ego that had seen him collide with Townsend from the moment he'd stepped through the station door. Most of it was simply bravado, with Lowe having a small following of officers and detectives who hung on his every word.

Lowe was the stereotypical alpha male.

Tall. Handsome. Brave. Relentless in his pursuit of justice, but also just as conniving when it came to the political side of the job. It was a side Townsend would never allow himself to be drawn in to, and the fact Lowe had used his sway to effectively demote King to the SCU after the breakdown of their marriage would always be a point of contention between the two.

The SCU was supposed to just be a small unit in the basement, assigned the busy work until King eventually broke and left the service.

But King had survived. And not only that, she'd built a team that was now a respected branch of the Thames Valley Police. Lowe had tried to scupper their progress a few times for his own gain, but after being introduced to Townsend's boxing glove last year, he'd taken a step back. Lowe's grudging respect for Townsend had expanded to the entirety of the SCU, and although the relationship between Lowe and King would never extend beyond amicable, it was a marked improvement from the volatile one that had existed previously.

'Yeah, it's early days...' Townsend finally offered, not wanting to say too much. Lowe smiled appreciatively.

'Look, Jack, I'm not going to try to steal it from you.' Lowe chuckled as he pulled a paper towel from the holder and dried his hands. 'But if you guys need some assistance, give me a shout. We've got a bit of capacity.'

'Thank you, sir.' Townsend turned to leave.

'Remember, we've got court this week,' Lowe called after him, his voice tinged with sadness. 'Tyler's day is finally here.'

Townsend felt his stomach drop.

As a detective, all Townsend had wanted to do was the right thing and come to the right conclusion. Tyler Davis was the first time he'd wished he'd been wrong. When the body of Jamal Beckford had been found in a car park, all evidence pointed towards his past life as a gang member. But Townsend soon pieced the puzzle together, and Tyler was arrested for the murder of his stepfather.

To protect his mum from abuse.

The guilt of that moment, where Simone blamed Townsend for condemning her son to a horrid future still haunted him, and Townsend tried his best to push her screams to the back of his mind.

Lowe could clearly see what was going on.

'This is the job, Scouse,' he said with a reassuring pat on his shoulder. 'It kicks you in the dick. It infects every part of your fucking life, but at the end of the day, you caught a killer. No matter his age or his reasoning, Tyler took the law into his own hands. We'll do our best for him, but don't beat yourself up for doing a good job.'

It was moments like this that Lowe became a mystery to Townsend. Throughout the entire investigation into Beckford's murder, Lowe had shown Townsend why he was so respected.

He might have been an egotistical prick at the best of times.

But Lowe cared.

Townsend took a breath and pulled open the bathroom door.

'Thanks, sir,' he said sincerely. 'I'll make sure I'm ready.'

'And remember, Jack. If ever you fancy a change of scenery…'

The offer had been extended once before, and Townsend once again politely declined. CID was an enticing opportunity, and there was no doubt in Townsend's mind that learning beneath Lowe's branches would further his own career.

But Townsend was proud to be part of the Specialist Crimes Unit, and his loyalty, forged under the pouring rain against the murderous Gordon Baycroft, was to DI King.

Leaving the team would never be an option.

As they stepped out of the bathroom, King looked up from her phone and her face dropped when she saw Lowe.

'Marcus,' she said firmly.

'Izzy.' He smiled politely. 'Let me know if you need any help with this one, okay?'

Townsend looked to his boss, who frowned a little.

'Thank you,' she said and then turned to Townsend. 'We need to go.'

Lowe headed off back towards the CID office, while Townsend picked up the pace to keep up with King, who was already halfway down the stairs. It wasn't until she'd stepped outside into the car park and retrieved her vape from her pocket that Townsend had managed to fall in step with her.

'You all right, Guv?'

'I just spoke to DS Ramsey,' King said, referring to the Family Liaison Officer already on site. 'She said the family are, understandably, in turmoil. So if we can keep the little boy's meetings to a minimum, that would be great.'

Townsend didn't rise to the dig.

During their hunt for Gemma Miller, King and Townsend's relationship had been strained by his bourgeoning respect for Lowe, a man who'd broken King's life in more ways than one. The two of them had put it behind them, but King had made it clear that she wasn't comfortable with Townsend and Lowe's new-found level of respect.

'He was just telling me about court this week,'

Townsend said as he opened the passenger door of King's car.

'Tyler?' King asked as she took a puff. Townsend nodded. A sense of responsibility washed over her. 'Just make sure you do what you always do, Jack.'

She winked at him, and Townsend felt a smile crack across his stubble-covered jaw.

'Also…' Townsend began as they both dropped into their seats and King fired up the engine. 'Lowe's been less of a dick recently.'

'I know,' King agreed. 'It's annoying.'

A mutual chuckle echoed in the car as they pulled away, and both detectives were grateful for the brief moment of levity. Especially as they were heading to a devastated family home, to gather anything they could to help explain why Asif Khalid had been brutally executed.

CHAPTER SIX

'Mrs Khalid. We are so sorry for your loss.'

King's manner with victims and their families was always tactful, and Townsend offered a solemn nod of agreement. Shreena Khalid tried to force a smile, but her bloodshot eyes failed to hold back more tears. The woman, like her husband, was in her early fifties, and had taken care and pride in her appearance over the years. Her hair was nicely cut, and years of yoga and spin classes had kept her in fantastic shape. Townsend looked around the family home and was impressed.

The four-bedroom house was positioned near the top of one of the many hills in Downley, and the two expensive cars on the driveway had given an indication to the wealth within. The sofas were of the finest quality leather, and the other furnishings were equally expensive. Asif Khalid had been a doctor for nearly three decades, with nearly half that time running his own private practice in Beaconsfield.

He'd built a fantastic life for himself and his family.

Yet here Townsend was, watching as his boss told a heart-broken woman that her entire life had been shattered.

This is the job.

The door to the front room opened, and DS Rebecca Ramsey appeared with a tray, two cups of tea and a cold water, and she placed it on the glass coffee table between the two sofas. Upon their arrival, Townsend and King had been greeted on the driveway by the Family Liaison Officer, who'd given them an overview of the mood in the house. Understandably, it was one of devastation, and as she'd calmly relayed that information to King, Townsend once again marvelled at how calm Ramsey was in these situations. A FLO was an underappreciated task within the service, as they were the shield between the dedicated team trying to solve the crime and the broken victims who would grow restless with every passing minute. But their role was so much more than that. The FLO was still a police officer, and they juggled being that conduit with undertaking their own investigation. They were tasked with noting down everything about the family, from the comings and goings to the general behaviours of everyone connected, all while slipping seamlessly into the background.

It was a tough gig. One of the toughest.

And Ramsey was tough.

'Do you want me to stay, Shreena?' Ramsey asked softly, her voice juxtaposed with her stern appearance.

'No. I'll be fine.' The widow's voice cracked as she feebly responded. King led Shreena to the sofa and sat down beside her, taking her hand with her own and cupping it.

Townsend took a seat opposite.

'The girls are lost,' Shreena offered. She sniffed back a few tears. 'I don't know what to say to them.'

Shreena broke down, sobbing wildly into the sleeve of her jumper, and King put a comforting arm around her. Townsend fidgeted awkwardly in his seat.

What could he say?

There were no words that could fix the damage that had been done, and even a promise of justice would hardly feel like compensation.

This entire family had been brutalised.

After a few moments, Shreena's sobs softened, and she sat up, taking long, deep breaths.

'I'm sorry,' she said.

'Don't be.' King shook her head. 'Mrs Khalid, what has happened to your husband and your family is truly horrible. DS Townsend and I are doing everything we can to find out what led to this atrocity.'

'Please, call me Shreena,' the widow said as she dabbed her eyes. 'Who would want to kill my Asif?'

'That's what we're going to find out,' Townsend said reassuringly, as he leant forward. 'Shreena, do you know of anyone who might have wanted to hurt your husband?'

The question seemed to take Shreena by surprise.

'My Asif? God no.' She shook her head. 'My husband was a good man, detective. A loyal husband. A doting father. You couldn't have dreamt of a kinder soul. And you must know he was a doctor?'

'Yes, we do,' King confirmed.

'He was much more than that. His patients loved him, and he was a true pillar in our community and the community around his practice. He was there last night…'

'Where?' Townsend asked as the new widow tailed off.

'In Beaconsfield. There was a charity auction, and he was involved in the planning of it.' Shreena dabbed her eyes once more. King and Townsend shared a look, and Townsend made a note to investigate the event further. 'I knew it was going to be a late one for him, and potentially messy as he went by taxi, so I didn't wait up for him. Besides, the girls and I were on a round trip to pick my eldest up from Lincoln. She goes to university up there. Studying medicine.'

The mother's pride was clear, and King offered a warm smile.

Inside, it hurt her to know she would never feel it.

'Is that why you didn't report him missing?' King asked softly. Shreena blinked back tears and nodded. King progressed. 'What about this morning?'

'We all slept in. The girls were shattered from yesterday, and so was I. Asif usually went for a run on a Saturday morning, so there was no point in setting an alarm,' Shreena said sadly. 'I just assumed he'd gone out, and then there was a knock at the door and…'

She tailed off again, her grief taking over, and King squeezed the woman's hand.

'I know this is hard for you, Shreena. I do.' King assured her. 'But these first hours are crucial.'

Shreena nodded and took a few deep breaths. Townsend shuffled forward in his chair.

'Did your husband ever mention any issues he was having at work?' he asked calmly. 'As a private practice, would there be charges and payments that could potentially cause problems? Were there any issues around that?'

'Not that he mentioned.' Shreena shook her head. 'I don't want to sound like a snob, but those who booked in with my Asif did so because they had the money to.'

'Were there any changes to his routine?' Townsend continued. 'Any differences in behaviour? Anything that stands out as worrying?'

Again, she shook her head.

'And he never said anything about a problem with a patient? Or a patient's family?' Townsend probed. Unintentionally, he and King had slotted into their roles of comforter and inquisitor. 'Anyone who might have held a grudge about a misdiagnosis or been angry about their prescription?'

Shreena's eyes began to water once more as she shook

her head. King helpfully pulled a packet of tissues from her pocket and handed them to her.

'Thank you.' Shreena dabbed her eyes on a tissue. 'He never said anything to me if there was anything. Doctor/patient confidentiality was something he took very seriously. But my husband was such a loving man. This just…it doesn't seem real?'

As Shreena cried into the tissue, King shot an approving nod to Townsend as she comforted her.

'I know,' King began. 'But it is real, Shreena. Someone has murdered your husband. My team is working through all the physical evidence from the scene, as well as exhausting every resource we have to piece together the events of last night. If you don't know of any issues at work, who does?'

'Jenine.' Shreena looked up. 'His secretary. I have her number here.'

'Last name?' King asked, looking at Townsend, who had his notebook ready.

'Carlisle.' Shreena sniffed as she handed Townsend her phone. 'Lovely woman. She's worked for Asif for years.'

'Thank you,' Townsend said, as he took the number. 'Does she or anyone else have any financial stake in the practice?'

'Oh no. My Asif owned the whole thing. Worked his whole life for it.' The pride in her voice pushed slightly over her grief, and she seemed to find a second wind. 'But Jenine has worked for him for years. She'll know if there were any issues he hasn't told me about.'

'We'll make sure to speak to her.' King assured her. 'Do you have access to your husband's diary at all?'

'His work diary? No, he kept that away from home.' Shreena stood with a renewed sense of purpose. 'But his satchel should be upstairs in his study. It will have the keys to the practice and his notebook in it. Give me a second.'

King gave Shreena an encouraging smile as the woman headed to the door, and she pulled it open. Instantly, the sound of sobbing echoed through, and Townsend's heart broke at the sound of it.

Deesha and Minal were both sat in the kitchen with Ramsey, weeping at the loss of their father. The girls were thirteen and fifteen respectively and should have been looking forward to returning to school the next day.

Now they were dealing with the horrible truth about how dark and unfair the real world was.

Townsend thought of Eve, and the idea of being pulled away from her again caused his knuckles to whiten as he clenched his fist. A seething rage was slowly slithering through his body, and the need to find justice for the Khalid family intensified. King stood and headed to the doorway and then loitered at the bottom of the stairs. Townsend followed her but held back in the doorway. One of the girls looked up from the table and down the hallway and caught his eye.

Townsend offered her a nod.

I'll find out who did this to your father.

The girl tentatively lifted a hand and gave a feeble wave, and Townsend gently waved back.

Upstairs, Shreena was arguing with her eldest daughter, Nikki, who was screaming that the police had no chance of finding the killer. As a first-year student at university, Nikki had come back for the weekend, and judging from her mother's angered response, had seemingly adopted some more activist views on the state of the police service.

King looked at Townsend, who raised an eyebrow in agreement.

Why had Nikki come back this weekend?

What was her relationship like with her father?

The shared wavelength of the detectives was broken as

Shreena's footsteps echoed down the wooden staircase but were softened slightly by the luxury carpet runner that snaked up the middle of them.

'Sorry about that,' Shreena said with a hint of embarrassment. 'My daughter is just grieving.'

'No need to apologise.' King held up a hand. 'It's a horrible time for everyone. Is that the satchel?'

'Yes, it's my Asif's.' Shreena held it tightly in a heartbreaking hug. 'It has the office keys in there. His notebook. The passwords to his accounts are in there. He was never too good at remembering them…'

Her voice trailed off as another wave of sadness crashed over her, and King reached out and placed a hand on her shoulder.

'Shreena, we will do everything we can to find out who did this to you and your family. DS Ramsey will be here for whatever you need. Okay?'

Shreena blew out her cheeks as she tried to stay strong.

'I have to be strong,' she said aloud. 'For them.'

'We'll be in touch,' King said as she gently squeezed the shoulder. 'Just look after each other.'

Shreena nodded as she blinked back more tears, and King turned and waved to Ramsey who was watching from the kitchen doorway. Townsend turned to follow, but then looked back to one of the grieving daughters, who was still looking at him.

He nodded to her.

A confirmation that he'd do everything he could to try to give them back something that was taken from them.

Not their father. That was impossible.

But hope.

Hope that, despite the very recent events, the world wasn't an entirely dark place.

As the two detectives headed down the driveway and back towards King's car, they could feel the tension leaving their bodies. It was always harrowing to see the devastation an act of violence could leave in its wake, and as they approached the doors on each side, Townsend finally spoke through gritted teeth.

'I couldn't imagine being taken from Eve,' he said angrily. 'And sometimes, knowing that I've given up my time with her to see that much pain, it makes me hate this job.'

King looked back to the house. At the landing window, above the front door, the eldest daughter was staring down at the two detectives. King held up a hand to wave to her, but the curtains quickly closed.

King turned back to Townsend, who seemed genuinely upset by the situation.

'This job takes more than it gives, Jack.' She pulled open the driver's door. 'But we can at least give that poor family some peace.'

Townsend joined King in the front of the car and blew out his cheeks. He looked up at the house once more, keeping his eyes locked on it as he spoke.

'So what do you think, guv?' Townsend asked. 'They all seem pretty broken by what's happened. Which is understandable…'

King pressed the ignition button, and the engine roared to life.

'I think we have a lot of work to do.' King followed Townsend's gaze to the house. 'And remember, Jack, until we know otherwise, everyone is a suspect.'

The two detectives pulled away and headed towards Beaconsfield, completely oblivious to just how disturbing things were about to get.

CHAPTER SEVEN

Their first port of call was the social club, where the charity event had been held the night before. King had let Townsend take the lead when they spoke to the caretaker, who was overseeing the clean-up. The posters were still on the wall, and a big, cardboard thermometer which showed the donation totals was still proudly displayed at the front of the dancefloor. The man was as helpful as he could be, but as he hadn't attended, he wasn't able to divulge much.

He didn't know how drunk Khalid had been, nor who he'd sat with. Helpfully, though, he provided Townsend with a confirmed list of guests for the event, along with the staff list. Townsend assured the caretaker he'd been a great help and then sent the list on to Swaby to follow up with them with the help of a few uniformed officers. With CCTV already acquired and with Hannon, Townsend and King thanked the man and then headed off to Khalid's surgery.

The search of the office had been swift, with King making the executive decision to take the laptop that was closed on Dr Khalid's desk, along with the notepads beside it. Aware that there would be an avalanche of red tape when it came to the confidentiality of medical records, King assured Townsend that given the nature of the crime and perpetrator they needed to identify, the warrant she would acquire retrospectively would cover it all.

Sometimes it was easier to ask forgiveness than permission, and with the clock ticking and the urgency of the situation, King decided getting her knuckles wrapped would be worth it.

As they drove back down the M40 from Beaconsfield to the Handy Cross Roundabout in High Wycombe, Townsend checked in with Mandy. As always, his wife was understanding and judging from the excitement in Eve's voice in the background, his family was enjoying their 'girls' day', which had now evolved into a potentially expensive shopping spree. As Townsend said his goodbyes, he hung up the phone and then looked glumly at the woodlands that sped past the window.

'Everything okay?' King asked.

'Huh?' Townsend turned to her, lost in his thoughts. He gathered them quickly. 'Oh, yeah. Fine.'

'I know being called in on a Saturday sucks, but—'

'This is the job.' Townsend cut her off and then held up an apologetic hand. King smiled in agreement.

'This is the job,' she finally repeated, and then the two of them remained in comfortable silence, the case occupying their minds. The day seemed to be getting away from them, and Townsend tried his best to make sense of it all.

Who was the person behind the mask?

Why had they killed Dr Khalid?

Why the farm? Khalid had no links to the farm itself, and the background checks of the farmers so far had shown no links between the two.

Why was Khalid abducted, transported, strung up and shot? If the killer just wanted him dead, they could have done it in the car park. That horrible feeling in Townsend's gut continued to grow.

As his head began to spin, Townsend shook it clear and turned to King. Her eyes were fixed on the road ahead, but Townsend knew her well enough by now to know she was following the same train of thought. King glanced to the side, aware her colleague was looking at her.

'How are things with you?' he finally asked. 'You still—'

'Sober?' King cut him off, as she pulled off the motorway and headed up towards the monstrous roundabout. 'Yep. It's never easy, but I'm working through it. Day by day.'

'Well, if you ever need an ear or a moan—'

'Oh, trust me. You'd know if I needed a moan.'

That ended that conversation, and although Townsend didn't mean to pry, he didn't want King to face her problems alone. The last eight months had brought them closer together, as a team and as people, and the last thing Townsend wanted was for his mentor to suffer in silence.

DI King was the most brilliant detective he'd met.

But even brilliant people had demons, and although she'd made the team aware of them, she was still a closed book at the best of times.

Townend's mind went back to the investigation, and he found himself thinking out loud.

'Why a tripod?'

'Huh?' King didn't take her eyes off the road.

'The tripod,' Townsend repeated. 'Swaby wondered if the killer filmed it.'

'It's a possibility.'

'But why?' Townsend frowned. Something wasn't

sitting right. His gut was telling him they'd only scratched the surface.

'Well, that's the million-dollar question, isn't it?' King said with a sigh. 'Maybe it's their trophy?'

'As morbid as it might sound, guv. I fucking hope so.'

The two shared a worried glance as King eased her way through the traffic towards the town centre, and ten minutes later, the duo were marching back through the station, towards the SCU office. Hannon was seated at her desk, locked into whatever she was doing, and she barely noticed them return. Across the room, Swaby was pinning photos to the murder board, having spent the morning collating as much as she could from the farmhouse and the staff responsible for the running of the farm itself. She hadn't drawn anything to raise suspicion but was adding every detail she could to the board as she built a collage of crime scene images underneath the picture of the victim. King headed straight to Hannon, who startled at her presence.

'Sorry, guv. Away with the fairies, there.'

'Any luck?' King asked, looking at the myriad of CCTV images on Hannon's screen.

'Still no needles.' Hannon shrugged as she reached for a biscuit.

'Put a pin it for now and boot this up.' King handed her Khalid's laptop and then the notebook. 'The logins are in there. Get yourself familiar with the systems and try to get access to his most recent appointments. I need to know who he's seen over the past few weeks and scour his notes for anything that might indicate an issue. Also, cross reference his patient list on the PNC and see if anything comes up. I mean anything. Even if someone hasn't paid a parking ticket on time. I want us turning over every stone of every person who's been at the doctor's surgery over the past few months. Any new patients. Any patients that have left – find out why.'

Hannon nodded, trying and failing to hide the weight of the task at hand. King offered her a comforting smile.

'If anything leaps out, pass it on to uniform to chase up. Just keep on top of it. While we're out, Swaby, you dig into the involvement with the charity. I want to know what the event was about, Khalid's level of involvement and PNC the guest list.'

'No worries, guv,' Swaby said, still working on the murder board. King walked across to join her. Hannon sat, laptop and book in either hand, and turned to Townsend.

'Are we allowed to do that?' Hannon asked. 'You know…look at patient records?'

'The guv will handle any problems that end. You're good.'

Although he technically outranked Hannon, Townsend never saw himself as a superior in anyway. But it had become clear to him that the rest of the team saw him as King's second in command. His word seemed to fill Hannon with a degree of confidence, and she went to work, sorting cables and clearing space on her messy desk to set up the laptop. Townsend left her to it.

Technology wasn't his strong suit.

Everyone had a role to play within the team, and over the past eight months, the entire SCU had naturally fallen into place. Hannon's strengths were her attention to detail and ability to get to grips with almost any software. She had, in essence, become their tech wizard. Swaby was a seasoned detective who could be relied upon to dig through the dirt, put in the hours, and slog through the paperwork to keep things ticking over. King was a natural leader.

But Townsend?

He was the wildcard. His lack of true detective experience and grizzled past meant he didn't think like most detectives. He could connect the dots on a case, surprisingly quicker than most seasoned veterans, and he attributed that to his rough upbringing in Toxteth along with his years spent walking the beat and infiltrating the criminal world as one of their own.

King saw him as an asset.

Lowe did, too.

Townsend settled down at his seldom-used desk and began his enquiry into the gun used to shoot Khalid. A shell casing had been found at the scene, and from that, they were able to ascertain that a Glock 17, the most popular handgun in the world, was the likely murder weapon. From there, Townsend began searching through the PNC for any recent firearms crimes and known individuals with links to gun crimes. That would be the start of a long search into cross referencing those names with the list that Hannon would pull from the doctor's software.

So transfixed was he to the screen he didn't see the looming presence beside him.

'Stare a little harder, son, and your eyes will go square.'

The authoritative tone belonged to Detective Superintendent Geoff Hall, his voice bellowing as he marched through the door to the office. His colourful, chequered jumper and beige pants indicated he'd come straight from the golf course, and the thunderous frown that dominated his brow told Townsend that Hall valued his Saturday game.

'Thanks, sir,' Townsend replied, standing to attention.

'Keep at it, son.' Hall marched past him and approached King. 'DI King. What's the story?'

King brought the detective superintendent up to speed, walking him through the murder board and highlighting the key parts of the investigation so far.

A middle-aged doctor executed with a single bullet to the skull.

Footprints and a potential tripod.

A broken and devastated family who all had alibis that DS Ramsey had corroborated for them.

King also brought to his attention the potential issues with the medical files on Khalid's laptop, but Hall waved them off, assuring them any obstacles could be sent his way. He might have been a demanding man, but Hall certainly had the back of everyone under his watch. As he digested the entire situation, he folded his arms over his flabby belly and sighed deeply.

'What a mess,' he finally said with the shake of his head.

'We're doing our best to clean it up, sir,' King assured him, before turning to Townsend. 'Jack, get hold of Jenine Carlisle. We need to speak to her as a matter of urgency.'

'On it, guv,' Townsend said, marching to his desk. He dropped into his chair, booted up his laptop and got to it. Hall stood to the side, watching the team in action.

'Good work so far, everyone. But let's get this solved and sorted as quickly as possible. I'll get our media team prepped for a statement before the journalists start bombarding social media with misinformation.'

'That might be a little too late, sir.'

Hannon's voice piped up from her desk, and she looked up, her eyes wide with worry. Instantly, King strode across the room to her, followed by Hall and Swaby. Townsend also stepped across, peering over the group at her screen.

'What's this?' Hall demanded, waving at the screen.

'A local journalist has posted on social media saying they've been sent this from the killer.' Hannon hovered the mouse over the link on the journalist's post. 'Should I click it?'

She looked up to King, but Hall's wide eyes told her the answer.

She clicked it.

A grainy, black-and-white video began to play, and Townsend's gut began to churn as the dread of the situation worsening started to grow. Despite the flickering filter that had been applied to the footage, it was clear it was of the farm the team had visited earlier that day. An unease fell upon the room, as slumped against the tree, with his hands bound above his head, was Dr Asif Khalid.

Unconscious, but still alive.

'We need this taken down,' Hall spat angrily. 'Now!'

Swaby rushed out of the room, heading down towards the cybercrime unit of CID, as the rest of the team kept their eyes glued to the screen. Ever so slowly, Khalid began to stir.

Then the video went blank.

A message appeared on the screen.

The execution of Asif Khalid will premiere at 5 p.m. By the hand of The Executioner

Then the video ended.

'Fucking hell,' Hall said as he pulled his phone out of his pocket. 'I need the IP address of where that video was posted from.'

'Do you think it's real?' Hannon said, turning to King.

King looked to Townsend, who stood stoically, his muscular arms folded across his chest.

They were both thinking the same thing.

It was very real.

Hall demanded they move hell and high water to find that address and get the video taken down before he dashed from the room, already managing the avalanche of panicked phone calls hitting his phone.

The view counter on the post was increasing rapidly.

It was being shared.

People were commenting their morbid excitement.

They had just over two hours until the promised video would play.

Townsend's gut had settled.

He was no longer concerned things were about to *get* worse.

They already had.

CHAPTER EIGHT

It was the second time that day King had made the journey out towards Downley. She'd called DS Ramsey the moment the terrifying video had ended to ensure the Khalid family was informed and that she'd be over as soon as she could. Her team was working tirelessly, aided by the rest of CID in trying to locate and remove the feed, but as there'd been no update on their success, King was working on the assumption that the worst was about to happen.

Dr Khalid's murder would be broadcast for the world to see.

With Townsend doing his best to make contact with the deceased's secretary, King was hoping that Jenine Carlisle would have a nugget of information that would tie the whole situation up in a bow.

Wishful thinking, but it was good to have hope.

When she arrived, she took a quick second to check the social media channels. As expected, the video link was being shared at an alarming rate, with the morbid curiosity of the public allowing it to gain traction. People whose entire sense of self-worth was predicated on engagement were sharing it across every platform they could, with the overriding message being that the police could do nothing to stop justice.

Somehow, Khalid was already being painted as the villain of the piece.

The murderer was, to King's disgust and dismay, the hero.

Anonymous posters, with no information, were happy to hide behind their keyboards and throw their support behind such a violent killer without any understanding of their motives. Vile rumours were spreading regarding the nature of Khalid's "crimes", all of which had been discounted upon the search of his laptop and internet history. But that didn't fit the narrative of the trolls. The majority of the country had long since lost faith in those in charge of it, and the systems put in place to protect them. The anonymity provided by the internet allowed those with a chip on their shoulder to voice that disdain. But by doing so, they were only spreading the dangerous idea that the Executioner was a force of good.

That the Executioner was brave enough to extract real justice.

It made King sick to her stomach.

They couldn't be more wrong.

King's trip to Downley took in a quick pit stop at High Wycombe Hospital, where Lady Luck finally smiled upon her as she found an empty bay in the usually overflowing public car park. She hurried across to the main building and strode through towards the morgue. Unfortunately for King, the drab, crumbling building was a place she knew too well, and without even thinking, her autopilot took her towards Doctor Emma Mitchell's domain. The pathologist was usually a ray of sunshine in an otherwise gloomy profession, but when King arrived, the doctor was a little disappointed Townsend wasn't in tow. Such was Mitchell's exuberant manner, that King wasn't sure if her attraction to Townsend was legitimate or just a light-hearted way to make her colleague squirm.

But this time, with the news of the impending video adding a real urgency to the case, Mitchell's usual positivity was noticeably absent.

'Pretty straightforward, this one,' Mitchell said dryly, as she peeled back the sheet that had hidden Asif Khalid's corpse from the world. She pointed to the bullet hole that had ripped through his skull. 'Cause of death was a bullet through the right frontal lobe that exited through the base of the skull, severing the spinal cord. It would have been instant.'

'So this *is* a murder?' King said, feeling dumb at stating the obvious. But had Khalid suffered a heart attack in the panicked seconds before his death, then there is always a chance some smarmy lawyer would try to get this bastard off on a technicality.

Sometimes the legal system didn't quite make sense.

'No signs of a heart attack,' Mitchell said, pulling her gloves on tight. 'Despite the man's shape, his organs were all in pretty good nick. No medical issues there. Although he did have his appendix removed.'

'Time of death?' King pressed. Time was of the essence.

'Judging by the state of the body, the wound and the decomposition...' Dr Mitchell paused as she cast her expert eye over the corpse. 'I'd put the death somewhere between midnight and one o'clock this morning.'

'That tracks,' King said. 'A young farmer found him this morning just before eight. But at least it narrows our timeframe for the CCTV.'

'Sounds like a shit start to a Saturday for that young man.'

A smirk spread across King's lips. Mitchell always had a way to lighten the darkest of rooms.

'He was out last night at a charity event,' King said, before trailing off to allow the doctor to take over.

'Stomach contents show a good meal and a fair bit of alcohol,' Mitchell confirmed. 'But, more interestingly, there was a high, concentrated dose of Diazepam in his bloodstream.'

'Antidepressants?' King asked and Mitchell nodded. 'His wife didn't say anything about his mental health, nor were there any prescriptions on his medical records.'

'Look here…' Mitchell pulled the skin on the side of Asif's neck tight, revealing a visible puncture mark. 'With the amount in his blood, I can say with some confidence that it was injected into him.'

'He was drugged…' King stated and then felt the anxiety build. 'Any signs of sexual abuse?'

'None. Thankfully,' Mitchell confirmed.

'Any DNA traces?' King asked hopefully.

'Nope.' Mitchell shook her head glumly as she pulled her gloves off by the fingers and threw them in the waste bin by the wall. 'Not one jot. Nothing under the fingernails. Not so much as an eyelash anywhere. Whoever did this was clean and concise.'

'Anything else?' King asked wearily. The journey hadn't been for nothing, but it hadn't been filled with revelations.

'Full tox reports should be back some point this afternoon. I'll send them straight across to you.'

'Thanks, Emma. Appreciate it.'

King turned to leave, when Dr Mitchell called after her.

'Tell Jack I miss him.'

At least King got to leave the hospital with somewhat of a smile.

But that quickly faded as she waded through the afternoon traffic towards Downley, knowing she was heading into a potentially hostile environment. She'd called the rest of her team individually for updates, hoping against hope that one of them had found something significant. But as expected, all of them had come to same conclusion.

Whoever had done this, had done this expertly.

Just a few hours before, she'd promised the Khalid family she would do everything to bring Asif's killer to justice. Instead, the killer was mocking them by sharing their act of violence with the world.

They had drugged and killed the man in cold blood, and the police had no leads to go on and as she hadn't had any updates, no way to take the link to the video down. As she pulled her car to a stop a few houses down from her destination, she was racked with an overwhelming sense of guilt.

The Khalids had gone through hell all morning and afternoon.

And that was only the start of it.

As she gazed at the clock on her car dashboard, King knew that in less than half an hour, Asif Khalid's final moments would become public knowledge. She took a few deep puffs on her vape stick, pushed the longing desire for a glass of wine to the back of her mind and stepped out of the car. As she approached the front door, DS Ramsey pulled the door open and stepped out, a look of concern across her usually stoic face.

'Ma'am,' she said quietly, as she pulled the door until it nearly closed. 'Any update?'

'I'm afraid not,' King replied.

'It's not good in there.' Ramsey looked over her shoulder. 'Nikki, the eldest, is kicking off. I've absorbed the brunt of it, but she's been banging on about you getting here. Just as a warning.'

'Appreciated,' King said with a grim nod. 'But if I were in her shoes, I'd have a few choice words for me, too.'

Resigned to her fate, King stepped in through the door

and addressed the Khalid family in the front room. The two youngest were sitting with their mother, huddled on the sofa, while Nikki unloaded with a barrage that King did her best to negotiate.

But what leg did she have to stand on?

Just hours before, she'd told the grieving family that their patriarch's murder would be investigated as a priority, yet here she was, begging them to not look at the video of his final moments. The situation was slipping through her fingertips, and by the end, a tearful and exhausted Nikki cut her to the core and then stomped out of the room.

'You're fucking useless.'

That was her sign off, and as King and Shreena called after her, Nikki burst from the room and thundered up the stairs. Ramsey was on hand to follow her, but King heard the very audible slam of the door and clang of the lock.

'I'm sorry,' Shreena offered feebly, but King held up her hand.

'She's upset,' King reasoned. 'It's understandable, given the circumstances. What I came to tell you was this is our top priority. All hands at the station are working on trying to locate and disable the feed of the video and in doing so, we should be able to trace it back to whoever is behind this.'

King flashed a glance down at her watch: 16:57.

Three minutes.

No updates.

As she glanced up, the resigned look in the widow's eyes told King that Shreena was on the same train of thought.

There was no stopping it now.

'Right, what we need to ensure is that there is no access to the video in this house,' King said firmly, trying to appear in charge of a helpless situation. 'All phones, tablets, laptops—'

'Already done, ma'am,' DS Ramsey interrupted, stepping in from the door. 'Figured it was the best thing to do.'

'Good job.' King nodded, then glanced at her watch. Any second now, the video would go live, and their case would go from a murder enquiry to a national scandal. Every journalist and media outlet in the country would be on to them about how they allowed a murder to be broadcast to the public, and all eyes would be on their investigation.

Hall would have a conniption fit.

Her team would be worked to the very edge of their sanity.

But worst of all, the Khalid family would have to live with the very real fact that the entire watching world had watched Asif being murdered in cold blood. 17:00.

The entire house fell deathly silent.

Shreena wrapped her arms around her daughters who still sat either side of her on the sofa.

King's phone buzzed.

Townsend.

Just as she went to answer it, an ear-piercing scream echoed from upstairs, and King and Ramsey instinctively burst from the front room and thundered up the staircase. From behind the locked door of her bedroom, Nikki Khalid was screaming in blind panic, and King thumped wildly against the door, asking her to unlock it.

Somehow, her instructions made it through, and Nikki hauled the door open, pushed past the two police officers and buried her head into her mother's chest who had followed them upstairs. Ramsey shot a concerned glance to King, and then turned to the family, as King stepped into the young student's room.

It was messy, as expected, and the walls were lined with posters of the latest indie bands and cliché life quotes. On the desk beneath the window was a laptop. The screen was lit up with the imagery King found familiar.

It was the farm in Cadmore End, and the grainy footage showed Asif Khalid's body slumped forward, straining lifelessly against the restraints.

Nikki Khalid had just witnessed her father being executed.

But what caused DI King to freeze and feel every single muscle in her body go tight was what followed.

The black-clad figure, a silhouette against the light behind the camera, slowly lowered his gloved hand, and then strode towards the camera. As he approached, the terrifying mask he wore became visible.

Black leather, with a white cross crudely stitched from corner to corner.

It was an unnerving sight, and King could feel her phone buzzing in her hand once more but couldn't draw herself away from the screen.

She was looking at the person she was hunting.

The Executioner.

The camera faded to black, and then four terrifying words slowly appeared on the screen, and King felt a chill of terror dance down her spine. A fear that even surpassed the image of Gordon Baycroft, lunging towards her with a knife.

A message that would stir up the public, and one that told King that this was only the beginning.

Justice has been served.

CHAPTER NINE

The entire High Wycombe Thames Valley Police station had been brought to a standstill. All eyes had been on the website, which had provided a morbid countdown to the five o'clock premiere of the video. The SCU had been chasing every potential lead, supported heavily by the uniformed officers, while CID were hunting for the IP address, but cybercrime had quickly poured water on that fire.

Whoever had set it up had been as meticulous with their digital footprint as they had been with their execution.

The video link was being run through a randomised algorithm that was bouncing the IP address from country to country, randomising its location every few seconds. Pinpointing it was out of the question, which meant any hope of taking the video down evaporated with every move.

It meant the world was going to witness a murder.

As the clock ticked towards five, DSI Hall emerged through the door to the SCU, his phone attached to his ear and his face contorted in a stressful scowl. He was trying to control a narrative that was beyond his reach, and Townsend watched the man struggle to control his temper.

DCI Lowe also made his way into the office, a sense of dread overwhelming his usual self-confidence.

Townsend stood behind Hannon, his arms folded across his chest and his eyes glued on the countdown clock. They'd been unable to make contact with Jenine Carlisle, which had sent suspicions spiralling, but a deep dive into her life hadn't raised any flags, so far. Townsend had made it clear that didn't exonerate her from the investigation, and that speaking with her was a top priority. Then, it was back to the grind, with everyone shifting through the breadcrumbs, trying to find a trail.

One minute to go.

King had messaged to say that Mitchell had little information for them but a few things to add later, but by now, King was no doubt tackling one of the most difficult conversations of her career.

Everything had devolved to chaos.

Thirty seconds.

Hannon shot a worried look to Swaby, her inexperience bubbling up and Swaby rested a reassuring hand on her shoulder. They both looked to Townsend for guidance, but all he could do was set his jaw and keep his eyes on the screen. He had tried to reach King, but understood she was occupied.

The countdown came to an end.

Instantly, words began to appear on the screen.

'Sir,' Townsend called to Hall, who marched over and ended his call.

Lowe also stood, hands on hips, his eyes burning with fury.

Asif Khalid's decisions have led him to this point. The court of law cannot be trusted...

Townsend shifted uncomfortably on the spot as he read the ominous message.

Therefore, there will be no judge...

No jury...

The entire station had fallen deathly silent.

Just execution...

The video then kicked in, with Townsend instantly recognising the farm he'd been whisked away to that morning. There, strapped to the tree trunk, was Asif Khalid, the middle-aged doctor slowly coming to as whatever anaesthetic had worn off. But it wasn't Khalid who Townsend's eyes were on.

It was the Executioner.

The figure, dressed head to toe in black, stomped across the grass and then stopped ten feet from Khalid. The doctor was clearly struggling against his restraints. The bright light bursting from behind the camera lit the scene in a stark glow. Without hesitating, the murderer reached into his jacket and pulled a gun.

Khalid squirmed, and the Executioner lifted the weapon expertly to eye level and held it steady.

Hannon looked away.

Swaby shook her head in disgust.

Townsend stood, feeling a combination of dread and helplessness.

The gloved hand pulled the trigger, and instantly, Khalid's head snapped back as the back of his skull blew away.

It was over in a second.

As the man's body dropped limp and strained against the ties around his wrists, Townsend felt guilt at the horrifying end Asif Khalid had met.

A lone message filled the screen.

Justice has been served.

'Motherfucker,' Lowe uttered under his breath, doing little to hide his clear anger.

Townsend lifted the phone to call King, but there was no answer.

Hall marched out of the room, barking orders into his own phone as he tried to wrestle some control of a situation that had just escalated beyond a crisis. Lowe followed, muttering angrily about their inability to track the IP address.

But it didn't matter.

It was out there now.

The cesspool that comprised the majority of the internet would have already copied and shared the video to the point where it now belonged to the Web. The statement had been made, and by the rapid sharing and the continuous streams of comments, it had been heard loud and clear.

The police were given a deadline they couldn't hit, and in doing so, had allowed a man's murder to be televised.

The Executioner's form of justice had become legend.

The video feed ended, and Hannon slumped back in her chair.

'You okay?' Townsend asked, his eyes locked on the now-black screen.

'No,' Hannon said firmly. 'I'm pretty far from okay.'

'You heard from the guv?' Swaby asked, and Townsend shook his head.

'Not yet. Keep going through those records and try to get a name. We need something,' Townsend said. He turned towards the door and as he did, Hall barged back in, his face showing the visible signs of stress.

'This is a fucking disaster,' he said curtly. 'At least the video is down.'

'Not really, sir,' Hannon said, not looking up from her

screen. 'About a million engagement farmers recorded it and are now sharing it online.'

'Engagement what?' Hall snapped.

'Engagement farmers. People who literally post anything online for clicks and engagement.' Townsend shook his head. 'Sad people.'

'Well, I'll get CID to track each and every account that shares that video until it's taken down and whatever fucking laws on sharing harmful material we can twist will be twisted to the maximum for every fucking one of them. You all focus on the matter in hand. Catch this bastard,' Hall said firmly. He sighed and rubbed his eyes. It was the first time Townsend had ever seen the man show even a modicum of vulnerability. Hall was a dominant presence within the station, and although he commanded respect in every room in which he entered, it was through his tact and handling of people. Not fear.

But now, as the two men stood in their casual clothes, both ripped away from their idyllic weekend plans, neither one of them had anticipated the way the day had panned out.

A man murdered.

The execution televised.

Hall's phone began ringing again, and he blew out his cheeks and looked at the screen.

'The mayor,' Hall said with a grimace. 'Townsend, get hold of King. Tell her to get back here as soon as possible. We need something to find the sick fuck who did this.'

'Yes, sir,' Townsend said, as a sense of pride swirled through his body.

Hall was looking at him to hold down the fort.

So were Swaby and Hannon.

Despite being instrumental in the capture of two serial killers since he'd arrived in the team, Townsend still battled with a daily bout of Imposter Syndrome. But now, with the crisis spiralling out of control, and a renewed confidence bestowed upon him, Townsend was ready to get to work.

'Fuck.'

Hannon's voice cut through the noise, and Townsend spun back to her. Hall lowered his phone and joined him, and they slowly approached her desk, where Hannon's eyes were glued to the screen.

More writing appeared on the webpage.

This is only the beginning.

Townsend felt his muscle tense.

More justice will be served. By the hand of The Executioner.

Hannon drew a hand to her mouth in horror.

Hall stormed to the doorway, almost colliding with Lowe who was checking that the rest of the team had seen the warning. The renewed sense of purpose that had emanated within Townsend had swiftly dissipated and been replaced with a genuine fear of what was to come.

This time, they were being given a head start.

The Executioner would strike again.

Swaby was already on the phone, using her contacts at other stations to hunt down any potential missing persons reported, but Townsend doubted she'd get anything tangible. Hannon was checking the databases for similar.

How do you stop an announced murder when you didn't know who the victim was going to be?

Townsend rubbed his eyes with the palms of his hands, dropped down into his seat, fired up his laptop and navigated to the social media platforms that were quickly filling up with posts pertaining to Khalid's murder.

Shock.

Praise.

Fear.

Excitement.

None of it surprised him, and Townsend found the first post that had taken a still image of the Executioner's mask and he hit print. Then, with a burning hatred building within, he rushed to the printer, collected the printout, and slammed it onto the middle of the murder board.

The Executioner.

'Who are you?' Townsend uttered quietly.

As he stared at the horrifying mask of the murderer, Townsend felt his phone vibrating in his back pocket. He pulled it out, saw it was DI King, and went to answer it. As he did, he threw a quick, concerned glance across the room to Hannon's desk.

Her screen was still on the untraceable link.

The words of warning were still on the screen.

Somebody had been marked for death.

They just didn't have any idea who.

CHAPTER TEN

As Townsend blinked open his eyes, the daylight was already cutting through the curtains of his living room, and he pushed himself up from the sofa. His entire spine ached from an uncomfortable few hours of sleep, and as he collected himself, he knew the house was empty. On the coffee table in front of him was a stone-cold cup of tea and a note from Mandy.

Didn't want to wake you, so have taken Eve out. Whatever you're facing today, just know we are proud of you.
Love,
Your girls
X

Townsend managed to smile at the note, grateful by the continuous understanding his family showed for his career. The guilt he'd felt for abandoning them at the trampoline park had dissolved the moment Mandy had messaged him the day before, and had since been replaced by the heavy guilt of allowing the public to witness a murder. He'd stayed at the station until King had returned from the Khalids' house, and her recount of the trauma the video had caused the family made Townsend yearn for his own.

Not only had that poor family been faced with the tragedy of having their father and husband murdered, but they'd relived it through the sickening video the Executioner had posted.

The three children had watched their father squirm and plead for his life.

Shreena Khalid had witnessed her soul mate wiped from the world.

All at the hands of, as Hall had labelled, a psycho.

But Townsend didn't believe that for a second. Nor had King.

They'd spent a good hour in front of the murder board, their eyes locked on the mask of the Executioner and had concluded that there was nothing crazy about the killer. Their sense of justice was clearly warped, but the perpetrator was anything but.

Cold.

Calculated.

Efficient.

Lowe had been in to update them that despite the cybercrime's best efforts, there was just no way of tracing back the IP address for the video link, meaning the Executioner had gone to great lengths to ensure their plan went off without a hitch.

It meant that the countdown to the promised second execution wasn't just a timer for them to act.

It was a doomsday clock.

King had sent Townsend home just after midnight, dismissing his protests and reiterating that the best way to help and to seek actual justice for Asif Khalid was to face things with a clearer mind. Swaby had left a few hours before to help her husband with the kids, and Hannon, clearly traumatised by the heinous video, had been excused shortly after that. Despite his stubbornness, Townsend knew King was right, and the two of them headed back to their respective homes to rest.

Townsend stood and stretched his back out and hurried up the stairs, pulling off the clothes he'd slept in and he hopped into the shower. A few minutes later, he was brushing his teeth and convincing himself that the thickening stubble around his strong jaw could wait for another day.

His appearance was hardly high on the list of priorities.

Townsend darted to the bedroom and changed into a pair of black jeans and a white shirt, and as he ran down the stairs, he threw on a tie with minimal care. Two minutes later, he was headed out to his car, a black bomber jacket wrapped around his frame and a single slice of buttered toast between his teeth. Before he pulled off the drive, he caught a glimpse of himself in the rear-view mirror.

His wet hair was messily pushed into a side parting, and the bags under his eyes were evident of a lack of sleep.

But he had a job to do.

The road from Flackwell Heath towards the town centre of High Wycombe was lined with schools, both public and private, and Townsend impatiently sat in the backlog of traffic that blocked the single lanes. On the radio, the morning host was waxing lyrical about a reality program he'd never watch. In fact, Townsend couldn't remember the last time he and Mandy had sat together and watched anything, just the two of them.

Or even been for a night out.

Despite her unwavering support and understanding for his job, Townsend couldn't help but feel he was taking his wife for granted. Mandy never complained when he was back late, or, like the day before, he had to skip out on Eve's birthday. His job was a crucial one, especially when there was a masked murderer on the loose, but it wasn't his only one.

He was needed at home.

By both Eve and Mandy.

As he navigated the once dreaded Magic Roundabout with minimal fuss and then turned into the High Wycombe Police Station car park, Townsend made a mental note and a solemn vow to show his family just how much they meant to him. And holding onto that thought was what was going to get him through what he was certain was going to be one of the most intense days of his career.

It started the moment he walked through the corridor, as DCI Lowe called out his name as he bounded down the stairs two at a time.

'Morning, Scouse,' Lowe said, adding a little too much force to the slap to Townsend's back. A needless display of machismo. 'You get enough beauty sleep?'

'There aren't enough hours in the day for that,' Townsend quipped dryly. 'You not been home yet?'

Lowe shook his head.

Despite his monstrous ego, there was no denying that Lowe was dedicated to the job.

'Not yet. Not sure if King's got hold of you, but she's over at Jenine Carlisle's.'

'Already?' Townsend felt a twinge of guilt. His boss had more than enough on her plate, and he'd assured her that he and Swaby would follow up with Khalid's secretary that morning.

'She was back here a few hours after you left.' Lowe shrugged. Despite spending all night at the station, the DCI seemed full of energy. Townsend wondered how comfortable the sofa in Lowe's office was. 'You know what she's like.'

Townsend wasn't sure if that was a compliment or not.

'Any other updates?' Townsend asked, changing the subject.

'Beyond everyone trying to clean up the shit that came spraying out of the fan? No. But whoever set up that IP knew what they were doing or found someone who did.'

'You think there's more than one person behind this?'

Townsend's question stopped Lowe in his tracks and the DCI rubbed his bearded chin in contemplation.

'Possibly. I mean, I wouldn't rule it out. Not until we know more.' Lowe continued walking again. 'The cyber team is working round the clock, so you never know, we might get lucky.'

'You reckon?' Townsend asked dryly. They both knew the answer to that.

'Unlikely.' Lowe shrugged as the two marched through the corridor. 'But we need to do what we need to do.'

Townsend thanked Lowe and then stepped into the SCU office, where Hannon was already hammering her keyboard. Before Townsend could even speak, she held up a coffee.

'Thought you might want this.'

'You legend,' Townsend said as he gratefully took it. It was still warm, and he took a long sip. 'How long you been here?'

'A few hours,' Hannon said glumly. 'I don't know about you, but watching someone get a bullet put through their skull had an impact on my sleep.'

'Yeah, I didn't get much,' Townsend offered, as he looked over her shoulder. 'How you getting on?'

'Needles. Haystacks. Bullshit.' Hannon groaned. She reached for a biscuit but scrunched an empty packet. 'Oh, for fuck's sake.'

'Anything we can go on?' Townsend asked, diverting her attention back to the case. He took another sip of his coffee.

'Maybe. A Mr George Callis had an appointment with Dr Khalid last week. Nothing out of the ordinary, but he does have a few hits on our system for drunken violence.'

'Hmmm...' Townsend grunted sceptically. 'This doesn't feel like the work of a drunk.'

'And we also have a Mrs Beverly Ballard, where Khalid has made a note that she was aggressive towards him for refusing to increase her prescription to sleeping pills.'

'Anything about being violent?' Townsend asked, his eyes lighting up slightly.

'No. But she did need to be escorted from the surgery.' Hannon read from the screen but then turned to Townsend. 'Unless she's a power lifter, I'd be hard pressed to see her carrying Khalid through two fields on her own.'

'Anger and revenge do crazy things to us,' Townsend said. 'Plus, she might have had help?'

'Want me to get uniform to bring her in?' Hannon asked. Townsend pressed his tongue against his lip and then turned to the murder board. The picture he'd printed of the hideous mask stared back at him, the white cross a symbol of the Executioner's murderous intent. More photos had been added to the board, all of it building out their case, but none of it forging a path towards their killer.

Or to stopping the next murder.

'Yes,' Townsend finally ordered. 'We've got fuck all else to go on right now, and King said we need to do what we need to do. And right now, we need to start eliminating as many reasons this has happened as possible.'

Hannon nodded and picked up her phone. Footsteps echoed behind him, and he turned to see the usually jovial figure of Swaby enter the office. Like everyone else, the morose atmosphere was weighing down on her as well.

'Morning, Jack,' she called across to him. 'You okay?'

'No,' Townsend said, his eyes still glued to the board as she joined him.

'Same.' She sighed as she folded her arms beside him. 'Where's the guv?'

'She's at Jenine Carlisle's.' Townsend shook his head. 'She's out there, trying to find out what the hell is going on.'

Swaby looked up at Townsend, whose jaw was set and his eyes burning. She patted him on the arm.

'We all are, Jack,' she said softly.

'We've got a masked killer showcasing their murders to the world…' He tapped the photo of the masked killer. 'And a ticking clock to another on the way. Lowe said CID have no hope of tracking the link, Hannon has found scraps going through Khalid's notes, and beyond a few unruly patients, we've got nothing tangible to go on. So far, we've been able to eliminate an awful lot of people from the doctor's surgery and the charity event, and I'm still looking into the employees of the farm. But right now, nothing that can link anyone to this murder.'

'Follow the evidence. That's what King says,' Swaby said. 'So let's just keep going and keep eliminating.'

'Uniform are on their way to get Mrs Ballard,' Hannon said, cutting into the conversation. She turned to Swaby 'Morning, Michelle. Strap in, it's going to be a long, shit day.'

Hannon comically crunched her empty biscuit packet and tossed it into the bin. Swaby leant down, rummaged in her bag, and pulled out a fresh packet of bourbons and waggled them slightly.

'Not totally shit.'

Townsend felt a small chortle leave his lips.

Hannon was right.

It was going to be a long, shit day.

But at least they'd get through it together.

CHAPTER ELEVEN

There was nothing worse than the feeling of failure.

As a detective sergeant in the Thames Valley Police, Townsend knew there was an expectancy, coupled with a responsibility that would always weigh heavily on his broad shoulders. The uniformed officers faced their own set of pressures, ones that he respected and at times, often pined for.

They were the response.

They were the ones who would head blindly towards an emergency call, putting their lives on the line every day they strapped on their vests and proudly placed on their hats. They attended, without hesitation, to any call, and although budgetary cuts meant they were often light on the ground, every officer who wore that badge did so with bravery.

They didn't know what was at the other end of the call.

They didn't know if the crime would escalate.

If the situation was hostile.

They received the call, fired up the siren, and headed off to try to take control of the situation.

The pressures he faced were different.

He'd taken the long road to get to this point. Years undercover had sapped away at his mental state and the bond with his family. Years rebuilding those broken bridges along with soul-destroying years spent trapped behind a desk in Liverpool, only adding more truth to the idea that his detective title was nothing more than an apology. But ever since his transfer to Bucks, and his assignment to the Special Crimes Unit, Townsend had finally found his footing as a detective.

He'd stopped serial killers.

Found justice and peace for those affected.

With that came a certain level of expectation, especially from those higher up the food chain. After the Khalid video went viral, all eyes were on the SCU, with Hall making it clear he was holding off the wolves at the door.

They needed a result, and they needed it quick.

With the eyes of the town and soon the nation upon them, failure really wasn't an option.

But it was all they were finding.

Beverly Ballard had been more than willing to come to the station, and she was delivered by PCs Boyd and Walsh, who offered a few grim, pessimistic views on the ongoing case. Townsend had thanked them sarcastically and then spent the next thirty minutes questioning Ballard.

That's all that was needed.

She was more than happy to admit to her poor behaviour at Khalid's surgery, but her remorse for treating him so badly had been genuine. She spoke openly about her addiction to sleeping pills, and how she'd been trying everything in her power not to return to rehab. She was a slim, pretty woman who hardly seemed capable of lifting an overweight man. Hannon's flippant comment about being a power lifter had swum through Townsend's mind at that point, but he filed it away, pushing it beneath the rest of the negativity he was trying to push away from the front of his mind.

Ballard had an alibi for Khalid's death.

Due to her insomnia, she'd reached out to a close friend and the two of them had ventured to the cinema in town. Ballard had taken in the latest horror movie, and was able to pull up the e-ticket that had been sent to her email. Townsend assured her he'd follow up with the cinema itself, ordered her not to go anywhere until they'd been in touch, but beyond that, it seemed pointless to keep her any longer.

After organising for Boyd and Walsh to drop her home, he tasked them with heading to the cinema to clarify her story. When they called him back within the hour to confirm her alibi checked out, Townsend blew out his cheeks with frustration. It had felt like a waste of time, but he knew he was doing what needed to be done. His investigation into the murder weapon was also proving fruitless, as unsurprisingly, the firearms offenders in the area weren't the sort to have access to a private doctor. However, a man in Khalid's position was under less monitoring from the NHS and could be a target for criminals wanting to keep their real names off the radar, their crimes under wraps and their injuries even more private. So far, the doctor's legitimate finances and lifestyle matched perfectly – with a level of luxury but a healthy amount of historical debt to account for it. He certainly wasn't spending any ill-gotten gains, but it was an avenue Townsend would need to venture down at some point. The searches into reported stolen firearms had also come back empty, and Townsend was now putting the call out to other departments to see if anything had landed on a random desk somewhere.

It was a slog.

But it was imperative.

They had to eliminate as many possibilities to arrive at the eventuality, but once again, it felt like failure.

The warning the Executioner had plastered on their untraceable link had been connected to the screen on the wall, and with every second that ticked by, Townsend felt the pressure growing.

Khalid's death had come without warning.

Another had been signposted in advance.

King had been pulled into a few crisis meetings with Hall, Lowe and other higher-ups, all of them pushing their own political agendas to the front of the line, but all of them had the same conclusion.

The Executioner needed to be found.

What had irritated King more than usual was that Lowe had been fairly reasonable and had offered further support from his team should the SCU require it. She knew that had been due to his burgeoning relationship with Townsend, but also, and most annoyingly, it was because her ex-husband was happier in his new relationship.

He'd moved on completely.

Being a prick to his ex-wife didn't seem to hold any appeal anymore.

Hall had made a suggestion at getting in some expert help to try to connect some of the dots, and despite biting her tongue and nodding along, King couldn't help but feel it was the first sign of his wavering faith in her and her team's ability.

The clock was ticking.

Everything came up empty.

That feeling of failure continued to grow.

King's visit to Jenine Carlisle had been relatively fruitless. The secretary was, understandably, in a state of shock at the news that her longtime employer had been brutally murdered, and King once again leant on her near limitless empathy to help her through the news. Once Jenine had managed to calm herself, King asked her the necessary questions.

But the secretary couldn't offer anything of substance.

She corroborated the instances of conflict Hannon had found but denied that they were too serious. There were no issues with money within the business that she knew of, and just like the recently widowed Shreena, Jenine only spoke of Asif Khalid in glowing terms.

One of the good guys.

Finally, Jenine provided all the necessary times and numbers to confirm that she and her husband had spent the weekend in the Cotswolds, celebrating their anniversary, and King quickly confirmed those upon her return to the station.

It was another necessary tick off the list, but not one that brought them any closer to catching Asif Khalid's killer.

Or finding out who would be next.

The pressure of another execution depending on their ability to piece together a puzzle with so many missing pieces inevitably exploded when King angrily threw her phone at the wall after hitting another dead end. Townsend stepped in, calmed her down, and assured her they would find the sick mind behind the mask.

They all needed a clear head.

They were running on empty.

King agreed, and the last thing she needed was the last of her resolve to fritter away and for the alcohol to flow again. Hannon had been checking every available video to try and track the killer's movements, from traffic cameras to video doorbells. Swaby had been elbow deep in the background checks of everyone associated with the farm, whilst Townsend had been delving into the financial history of the victim, Asif Khalid.

The team was covering every base.

Turning over every stone.

But they hadn't found anything.

Lowe had a night team looking across the final few leads they had, with strict instructions to notify King if they found anything. Although nobody in the SCU office was religious, the best they could do was to head home, grab a few hours of sleep, and pray that somehow one of them made a breakthrough.

King dismissed her team, and Hannon made a dry comment about the puppy that she and her partner, Shilpa had recently purchased, before heading to the door. Swaby walked out with her, heading home to her own responsibilities.

Begrudgingly, Townsend accepted her orders and headed home with a slim hope of spending time with his girls. Alone in the SCU office, King perched on the edge of Hannon's desk, arms folded, and her eyes locked on the murder board.

The haunting image of the Executioner stared back at her, mocking her with the surrounding photos of Khalid's murder scene.

In the back of her mind, King's self-doubt was begging for her to walk out of the office, turn onto the high street and find the nearest pub.

A glass of wine would calm you down. Just one.

But one would turn to two, and two would turn to a bottle, and in doing so, King would unravel eight long months of hard work.

But she still headed out of the office, and she did turn towards the high street.

Fifteen minutes later, she was sitting in an AA meeting, reaffirming her strength and sobriety and making silent promise after silent promise that she wouldn't lose her resolve.

Over the past year, eight people had been murdered within this town.

Another one this past weekend.

If King and her team were going to stop that hitting double digits, then she needed to be at her best.

Even if that best wasn't good enough.

CHAPTER TWELVE

Despite the recent upturn in weather as the world headed toward Easter, the early Sunday morning still brought with it a brisk chill. A thin layer of moisture coated the grass that Hannon trod under her hiking boots, and she often wondered if she was getting old before her time.

She was still only twenty-six years old, yet here she was, out before 6 a.m., wrapped up in her walking clothes, alone with her thoughts. At home, her partner, Shilpa, was still in bed. Their relationship had fallen into the comfortable routine of every long-term coupling. The romance hadn't faded, far from it, but the initial spark that drew people together and often manifested in regular trysts between the sheets had evolved into a genuine bond that made itself known through regular shows of affection.

Holding hands as they ventured out into the town centre.

Shilpa picking up a packet of Hannon's favourite biscuits when she was at the shops.

Leaving a cup of tea on the side table before heading out to work.

As Hannon blew out her cheeks and stopped at the top

of the muddy hill, she paused to catch her breath. Their relationship had faced a few hurdles over the past year or so. Hannon's reluctance to come out as homosexual to her parents had been understandable but ultimately misguided and once they'd confirmed their relationship, her mother and father had embraced Shilpa into their family. That seemed to trigger Shilpa's desire for a family of her own, but after several long and arduous discussions, Hannon managed to convince her that now wasn't the right time to heap that much responsibility into their lives.

They were both striving to build their careers, and the idea of one of them carrying a child for nine months, then taking a stretch of time to get to grips with parenthood, wasn't something either of them was ready for.

It was certainly in their future, but right now, Hannon was laser-focused on her job, and eventually, Shilpa was happy to put their parental aspirations on hold.

But now, as the sun was casting a beautiful glow across the rolling fields as it began to peek through the clouds, Hannon wondered how much that was true.

'Fudge! Here, boy!'

As she called out, Hannon scanned the nearby shrubbery, the small Cavapoo came bounding from the bushes, his fluffy face damp from the plants and his eyes wide with excitement. The compromise on parenthood was dog ownership, and considering the number of times Hannon had had to scrub urine from the carpet or been woken in the night by anxious howling, she wondered if they'd really made the right choice. But as Fudge rushed to her, any inconvenience soon evaporated, and she waggled a ball in front of her canine companion before hurling it across the field.

He was gone in an instant.

Despite the constant dog-adjacent interruptions to their routine, Shilpa was adamant that Fudge was good for them, especially Hannon. The back injury she'd sustained while walking the beat, at the hands of a drunken lout who'd assaulted her, had always been an excuse for Hannon to not put her fitness first. But her natural body clock, thanks to nearly a decade within the police, meant she was up before dawn and the morning walks with Fudge had become a daily staple.

It got her out and about, got her breathing in the brisk morning air and meant most days, she headed to the station with a spring in her step.

But not today.

Not when the call came in a little before seven to say that a woman had been reported missing by her husband, and uniform had found her car sabotaged in the car park where she worked. King hadn't said it explicitly, but Hannon knew she needed to get a wriggle on, and she fastened Fudge's lead to his collar and then dragged him, unwillingly, back down the hill and hurried back along the final stretch that they'd marched that morning.

By the time she'd arrived at the office a little before eight, Hannon was already longing to return home. The haunting video of Khalid's murder had shaken her more than she'd let on, although Shilpa had sensed that was the case.

So, seemingly, had the rest of her team, and King, Townsend and Swaby had quietly asked how she was doing. As the youngest in the team by over fifteen years, Hannon could have taken it as patronising, but she never did. Her colleagues were older and more experienced, both in profession and life, and over the past eight months they'd been a collective, their bond had grown strong and they'd fallen into almost family-esque roles.

King was the head of the team, the matriarch, and watched over them all.

Swaby was the caring older sister, who was always on

hand with a wise comment and a backup packet of biscuits.

And Townsend was like the older brother she never had and had proven twice over the past eight months that he was willing to run headfirst into a weapon wielding murderer to protect his team.

Watching a man being executed had shaken them all, some more visibly than others, but what hung over them like a darkening storm cloud was the promise of more to come.

That the Executioner had only just begun.

'Maureen Allen,' King said loudly as the rest of the team were congregated in the office. She made a show of slapping the glass board, where an image of an older woman was now displayed. The wrinkled face was full of life and happiness, a snapshot from a holiday picture that King had lifted from Facebook. 'Her husband reported her missing in the early hours of the morning. She works at the supermarket in Loudwater. According to Reggie Allen, she sometimes joined the rest of the team for drinks, so he didn't report her missing until this morning.'

'He didn't try to contact her?' Swaby asked, notepad at the ready. 'Seems strange to go a whole evening with no contact.'

'Apparently, she was pretty useless with her phone.'

'Apparently?' Townsend said, raising an eyebrow to match his sceptical tone.

'That's what we're going to find out,' King said with authority. 'Nic, we should have the CCTV footage from the area as requested. So crack on and do your thing. I'm talking the finest of toothcombs. Michelle, dig deep. If there is any connection between Maureen Allen, a sixty-two-year-old supermarket assistant and a fifty-three-year-old doctor, I want you to find it.'

'On it, guv,' they replied in unison, before sharing a smile.

'Jack, you're with me,' King ordered, sliding her arms through her jacket sleeves. The AA meeting had given her a renewed sense of control and purpose, and she was adamant that this missing woman wouldn't undercut it. 'Let's go.'

'Lead the way,' Townsend said, gesturing to the door as he grabbed his jacket from his chair.

As they headed to the door, Hannon rocked back against the back support of her chair and called out after him.

'Jack, grab us a coffee on the way back, would you?'

She had a wry smile on her face.

She knew he hated asking for her order.

'Really?' He sighed. 'Fine.'

'Oat milk caramel latte.' She wrinkled her nose. 'You can tell him it's for me if you like.'

Townsend gave her a lazy salute and disappeared out of the office. Hannon swung back in her chair, as Swaby, as she tended to do when it was just the two of them, put the radio on to provide a little background music. Hannon was an expert at blocking it out, and considering Swaby loved to hum along with pretty much every song, she didn't see the need in denying her friend that modicum of joy.

Especially when joy was in such short supply.

With a sigh and a sense of dread throbbing through her like a secondary pulse, Hannon began pulling up the CCTV footage that had been sent through and she sent out a silent promise to Maureen Allen that she would do everything she could to bring her home safely.

To stop her from being the next victim of a horrifying video that would haunt Hannon for the rest of her life.

CHAPTER THIRTEEN

Sometimes people look exactly how you thought they would.

On the journey over to Bourne End to the Allen residence, Townsend built a picture of what Reggie Allen would look like, and when the designated FLO had introduced them, it felt like they'd already met. Reggie was in his mid-sixties, and he wore a bland, ill-fitting shirt and trousers combo befitting a man of his age. He was slightly portly, a lifetime of good food and regular drinking, and it also showed on the raggedness of his wrinkled face. A light, white fuzz gently coated the top of his head like a dandelion, and he respectfully stood as the two detectives were led into the living room of his family home. The three-bedroom house was just off Bourne End High Street, which was only ten minutes away from where Townsend himself lived, and he'd stopped a number of times at the local coffee shop when running errands on this side of the town.

'Mr Allen,' King said softly as she took his hand. 'I'm DI King, this is DS Townsend…'

She stepped aside to allow Townsend to shake the man's hand. A firm grip.

'How you holding up?' Townsend asked. His accent always seemed to catch people off guard.

'My son went to university in Liverpool,' Reggie said, ignoring the question. 'Great part of the country.'

'I couldn't agree more,' Townsend said with a warm smile.

'Shall we sit?' King offered, and the three of them took their places on a long corner sofa, which was comfortable enough but showing signs of wear and tear. King sat beside Reggie, while Townsend sat across from them on the armchair. As they sat in silence for a few moments, the detectives' eyes fell upon Reggie, who suddenly looked a lot smaller.

'What a mess,' he said, shaking his head. 'My poor Maureen.'

'Mr Allen...' King began.

'Reggie. Please.'

'Reggie,' King began again. 'First off, let me say that we have every available officer doing everything in our power to locate your wife. While the specialists at the station do their bit, DS Townsend and I have some questions.'

'Absolutely.' The man seemed genuinely keen to help. Townsend felt his suspicion easing. King continued.

'When did you report that your wife was missing?' King asked. A simple one to start off with.

'About two thirty this morning,' Reggie said, scratching his fluffy head. 'I woke up in the middle of the night and she wasn't next to me. She hadn't answered my calls before I fell asleep last night...'

'And that didn't alarm you?' Townsend cut in.

'A little. But it's happened before,' Reggie said sincerely. 'Look, Maureen is a woman who loved life. Loved people.

She spent thirty years as a teacher, but retirement wasn't for her. She loved talking to and dealing with people, that's why she got her job at the supermarket. They usually headed to the Old Queen's Head sometimes when they handed over to the night shift, and she was always up for a drink and a laugh with them. Kept her young.'

'And that was where she was last night?' Townsend probed.

'I assumed so.' Reggie shrugged. 'She's pretty rubbish at answering her phone. Much to our kids' annoyance, she didn't really put much stock in having one.'

'And there isn't somewhere else Maureen could have gone?' King pressed. 'A friend's, perhaps?'

Reggie shook his head.

'She always came home. She liked going out, but she hated sleeping anywhere that wasn't her own bed.' Reggie blew out his cheeks. 'And when the other officers said they found her car still at the car park, I knew something was wrong. I can feel it in my gut.'

'What makes you say that?' Townsend asked. He had a gut feeling the man was telling the truth, but that didn't matter.

Not until they could prove it.

'Because I've been with my wife for over forty years. Our whole lives have been intertwined, and I know how she thinks and acts. If everything was fine, she would have been home late last night.'

The man's voice cracked, the first signs of his genuine fear peeking through, and King reached out and placed a hand on his forearm.

'I know this is difficult, Reggie. But we just have a few more questions.'

King asked them methodically, and Reggie answered them as openly as he could. He couldn't recall his wife having any altercations with anyone.

Nobody who'd threatened her.

Or scared her.

No worrying interactions with colleagues or customers.

A marriage that long and that happy was built on trust and communication, and for all intents and purposes, Maureen Allen was just a cheery older woman who people loved to have around.

Reggie had been at home all night, watching the football with a few beers, and that was confirmed by his neighbour, who he'd spoken to when taking out the empty bottles to the bin.

Their children lived miles away, with families of their own.

Reggie had answered all their questions as helpfully as he could. Unfortunately, as they said their goodbyes and headed back to their car, the answers didn't offer much. King dropped Townsend off at the coffee shop on the way back, and he joined them in the office ten minutes later, with a cardboard tray containing four cups of piping-hot coffee. The team gave their thanks, and King asked them for an update.

Swaby seemed a little downhearted, as despite her best efforts, there wasn't a single shred of a link between Maureen Allen and Dr Asif Khalid. There had been no medical records that linked them, and the woman had never been registered at his private practice, nor any of the NHS surgeries he'd worked at before he took his business private. They'd crosschecked their credit cards to see if they'd crossed paths on a personal level, but nothing there, either. She'd also checked any links between Maureen Allen and the farm where they'd found Khalid's body, but there was none to be found.

Hannon had reviewed the CCTV of the evening before and found Maureen's abduction. They watched and grimaced as the elderly woman inspected her tyre, and then foolishly trusted the man who approached her.

So it was a man. That much they could confirm.

But he was clever enough to keep his face obscured from the nearest CCTV camera, and Swaby gave a small gasp as he wrapped an assumed chloroform-coated rag over Maureen's face and dumped her in the back of the car. Then, within seconds, the man had brought a van up beside the car, transferred Maureen into the back of it, and sped out from the dark, empty car park.

It was chilling to watch.

But Hannon had done a little further digging, and although the number plates were different, she'd been able to identify a van of a similar make and model on a CCTV camera in Beaconsfield the night that Dr Khalid had been taken. She ran both sets of plates and both were reported stolen.

'Great work, Nic,' King said. It was their first proper lead. 'Get the message out. I want every officer looking for that van. Have we been able to track her phone?'

'It's off, guv.' Hannon shook her head. 'No way of tracing it beyond where she was taken.'

'Damn it.' King sighed. 'Keep digging.'

As Hannon went to work, King wrote the make and model of the vehicle on the murder board, and then let out a deep sigh.

It could have been nothing.

But it felt like something.

And considering they were chasing shadows before, being able to identify the Executioner's method of transport would close the net, even by a few inches. It was a modicum of hope, one that could lead them to Maureen Allen in time. In the pit of his stomach, Townsend doubted that, and as he looked to her photo that was now on the board, he thought back to the worry on Reggie Allen's face when they'd left him.

He was just a terrified husband who had no idea how much danger his wife was truly in.

But before he could suggest to King that they explain the situation to him, Hannon's outcry of dismay meant he wouldn't have to.

'Nic?' King turned, concerned.

'Another post on the link,' she said, her eyes widening. The screen on the wall had been connected to the Executioner's untraceable website, and sure enough, the words were presented for the team to see.

King felt her stomach turn.

Townsend felt his knuckles whiten with anger.

The execution of Maureen Allen will premiere at 5 p.m. tomorrow...

By the hand of the Executioner.

Townsend and King looked at each other and shared the same word.

'Fuck.'

CHAPTER FOURTEEN

It's surprisingly easy to kidnap someone.

The Executioner had done it twice now, and both times were a walk in the park. Gone were the days when people would look around as they walked, greeting people with a warm smile and a hearty hello. Nowadays, thanks to the rise of social media and the constant sense of dread pedalled through the actual media, people locked themselves away. They avoided eye contact at every opportunity, and when travelling on public transport, the Executioner was astounded by how fearful people were. Obviously, he travelled without the mask, but even then, people would turn away if eye contact was made.

People were afraid.

For no reason other than that was what they'd been conditioned to be.

With Khalid, the Executioner had simply watched for days to put together the man's routine, and had made plans to snatch the doctor away in the car park of his practice. It wasn't until the Executioner, *sans* mask, had headed into the doctor's surgery to make a fake enquiry about signing up, an even easier opportunity than he'd planned presented itself. He'd given a false name to the friendly, middle-aged woman behind the desk, and then enquired about the latest appointments possible.

There were flyers on the reception desk for a charity event that Friday, which, as he was looking at them, the receptionist helpfully said that Doctor Khalid would be attending.

Kidnapping Khalid was as simple as telling him his taxi home had arrived, leading the slightly inebriated doctor out into the dark and empty car park, and drugging the man before bundling him into the van.

Maureen Allen had been even easier.

Sitting in his van in the giant car park surrounding the supermarket, the Executioner watched as waves of customers ascended upon the doors, returning several minutes later with bags of groceries and other needless purchases. The later the evening progressed, the darker the car park became, and with Maureen's registration number memorised, it was easy to find her car and puncture the tyre.

Soon, the lights of the supermarket began to turn off, and the last of the staff began to filter from the building. Maureen got into her car, reversed, and quickly stopped. With a smile across his face, the Executioner watched as Maureen hopped from the car, discovered the flat tyre and became irate with stress. As she tapped on her phone, the Executioner pulled the van around, parking in the row behind her.

He watched as one of the other staff members stopped, wound down their window, and Maureen explained the situation. The colleague didn't offer to help, another sickening display of selfishness that someone like Maureen would be all too familiar with.

One that would cost her her life.

With a smile on his face, the Executioner wound down his own window and leant out.

'You okay?' His voice was chipper and helpful. Maureen startled, looked up and then felt relief.

'Oh, sorry,' she said with a smile. 'I've got a flat tyre. I was just about to call my husband to get the recovery service out.'

'Ah, you don't want to go through them. They'll take hours.' The Executioner pushed open the door and stepped out. 'Is it a flat?'

'Yeah. Not sure how.'

'You have a spare in the boot?' He carried on walking towards her, and she turned to the boot of the car, unaware of the cloth in the approaching hand. The rest of the car park was empty. It had taken less than ten seconds to wrap the cloth around her face and then drop her into the backseat of her car, before the Executioner had swiftly returned to the van, pulled it up beside Maureen's car, and transferred her across.

Simple.

Another kidnap with minimal fuss.

However, Maureen's execution wouldn't be as straightforward as Khalid's.

Not if the Executioner wanted to send the message as intended.

When Maureen had woken from her enforced slumber, she'd found herself bound and gagged in the rented garage. A single lamp had been switched on to allow her to see her surroundings, but beyond the grey van that had been used to transport her, there was little else. Her screams were muffled and tears pointless. The Executioner knew that the hunt for the next victim was well underway, and when Maureen was reported missing, they'd be doing everything in their power to retrace her steps.

To try to save her from the inevitable.

They would be in touch with the husband, treating him with an undeserved suspicion until they found the CCTV footage of the grey van. That would give them false hope, until they realised the number plates had been replaced, stolen from a car registered in Maidenhead.

While some of them would be on that wild-goose chase, others would be trawling through the CCTV of the supermarket from the previous day, in a pointless exercise to see who may have been a threat to the woman. They would also look through the staff records, trying to find any shred of hope they could cling to.

Anything that would drive someone to kidnap the woman who'd been marked for death.

But it would all be in vain.

When the Executioner finally appeared before Maureen, she'd wept uncontrollably, yet all the masked figure did was raise a finger to his masked lips and place a bottle of water and a sandwich before her. Ironically, it was from the very store from which she'd been abducted. The Executioner once again gestured to keep quiet, and then threateningly displayed a Bowie knife, making the implication very clear as to what would happen if she made a noise.

When the gag was removed, Maureen was deathly silent, and the masked captor held up the bottle of water for her to drink, and then roughly fed her the bland cheese sandwich.

Then the gag went on again, and minutes later, as the Executioner left the lock-up, Maureen Allen was cloaked in darkness.

The process continued through to the morning, with the Executioner feeding her dry toast in the morning, and the rest of the bottle of water. She'd watched as he loaded the van with long, thick beams of wood, ignoring her completely as she finally lost control and urinated in her underwear.

The Executioner paid her no mind.

Her captor seemed focused on the task at hand, and after loading the van, the Executioner turned, injected her neck with a syringe, and soon everything blurred before falling to black. The Executioner had caught her before she tumbled sideways onto the concrete and then had lifted her limp body into the van, plonking her beside the neatly stacked apparatus of justice.

The police had less than twenty-four hours before the video of Maureen Allen's execution would hit the web, but they'd find her much sooner.

And when they did, there'd be little doubt in their mind as to what had happened.

And that evening, as the van stood stationary in one of the parking bays of High Wycombe Train Station, the Executioner kept his eyes on the road leading back towards the city centre. There was no chance of a traffic warden at this time, as the other cars that were dotted across the station had the luxury of free parking until the morning. Less than a five-minute walk from the police station, it was almost cruel how close they were physically.

But mentally, they couldn't have been farther.

The media were all over it, as every newspaper in the country was now running the story of a crazed person in a mask, murdering people and posting the video online. They were painting the Executioner as a psycho, but they couldn't be further from the truth.

Within the next few hours, they would understand that.

The country would see his work.

Would be forced to understand how true justice worked.

Asif Khalid had at least been afforded the luxury of a

private death. Alone, afraid and shivering with fear in a field, the doctor had met his end intimately.

Maureen Allen wouldn't be given the same send-off.

The timing had to be perfect.

Eight trial runs had been done, and the Executioner had the process down to a fine art.

Fifteen seconds to place the tripod and press record.

Eighty-two seconds to construct.

Nineteen seconds to place the guilty in position.

Seven seconds to drop the blade.

It would all be accomplished in just over two minutes.

The impact would last a lifetime.

In the back of the van, he could hear the weak, desperate moaning from Maureen as she awoke from her enforced slumber, and the Executioner looked at the clock on the dashboard.

Nearly midnight.

The city centre would be deathly quiet, with the drinkers in the string of pubs that dotted along the streets kicked out over an hour ago. High Wycombe boasted a tremendous shopping centre, but offered little in the way of nightlife, save for the seedy Paradise Bar tucked away in the backstreets, and its repugnant regulars who would've been in attendance.

Perhaps one of them would stumble across his handiwork first?

The Executioner took a deep breath, ensured his mask was close to hand, and then slid the van into first and pulled out of the station car park.

With the city finally asleep, he guided the van towards the centre and got ready to shake it to its very core.

CHAPTER FIFTEEN

All hands to the pump.

That had been the silent agreement between every single member of the Thames Valley Police, as the hunt for Maureen Allen had taken full priority. The Executioner had thrown down the gauntlet, challenged them to stop them from delivering their grisly promise and every single member of the SCU and beyond were working to meet it head on.

But they had nothing.

PCs Boyd and Walsh had reported stopping four vans matching the description that King was clinging to, but all they'd received were ear bashings from impatient tradesmen who were just going about their business. Being stopped, questioned, and then made to wait while those answers were verified had made Boyd and Walsh less than popular, but something told Townsend that neither man particularly cared. They were both too long in the tooth, both too experienced, to be offended by an ear bashing, and should the worst come to the worst, both men were more than capable of handling themselves.

But the clock was ticking, and Townsend could feel his,

and the rest of the team's patience, beginning to wear thin. Hannon was working through every van-hire company in the county, trying to match up bookings of the hire vans to correlate with the model and timings of the deaths.

Townsend was trawling through insurance records, seeing who had a van insured or declared SORN that could possibly lead them to the killer. Swaby wrapped her checks on the staff at the farm, ticking their names off the list alibi by alibi, and then dived in to help him.

Everything felt like a blind alley, and as evening began to fall, Townsend glanced up at the clock with frustration.

Less than twenty-four hours until the video would be made public.

Which meant Maureen Allen's execution was fast approaching.

King had spent the majority of the trying to find a connection between any of the names on the guest list for the charity event and Maureen Allen, pulling at every thread possible to find a link. Anything that could lead them to her.

To save her.

As she hit brick wall after brick wall, she checked in with the FLO assigned to the Allen household, where the mood had swiftly changed. Reggie had, understandably, morphed into a ball of fury, angrily chastising the FLO whenever she tried to initiate a conversation. It was the fear and anger talking, and King knew, deep down, that his terror was correlated with their inability to find his wife.

She took it on the chin.

When she'd returned to the station, Hall marched right to her office and made little attempt to conceal his frustration at how things were going.

A man had been executed.

The public had been presented with the footage.

The team were chasing their tails trying to catch the

killer who'd signposted that they'd kill an innocent woman in less than a day.

'A shitstorm's coming, Izzy,' he'd said with a grunt. 'And I'll do my best to keep it from your door. But you need to find this woman. Fast.'

Like with Reggie's anger, King took Hall's warning on the chin and tried to rally her team, but as the evening bled into night, she watched as they were beginning to run on empty.

The sharpest minds cut through the thickest fog, and so King sent them all home. Townsend led the protests, but King made it clear and would liaise with the night shift within CID to keep her abreast of any developments. It was probably worth throwing a few scraps to Lowe and his team, especially as he'd been sniffing around the table for them.

Promising to return at the crack of dawn, Townsend left, leading Swaby and Hannon as they reluctantly followed her orders.

None of them spoke as they headed to the car park.

By the time Townsend made it home, he was ready to drop, but a smile fell across his face when Mandy greeted him in the hallway, wrapping her arms around him and holding him for a few moments. She'd seen the update online, that another murder was imminent, and she could tell just by looking at him that it was taking its toll.

As he checked in on Eve, who was wrapped up in her bed amongst an army of cuddly bears, Mandy whipped him up a quick bacon sandwich and after he demolished it within a few bites, she followed it up with a cold beer.

They sat together for a while.

Their fingers locked.

The room quiet.

Townsend asked her about her day, but five minutes into the conversation, he could feel his eyes dropping, as the fatigue flooded through him like a broken dam. Mandy led him upstairs, and he was asleep before she'd finished brushing her teeth.

The rumbling of his phone snapped him awake, and Townsend shot upright in the dark and turned to the bright light of the screen.

DI King.

Within minutes, he was dressed, and he shuffled quietly out of the house to his car with that overhanging guilt of absence rearing its head once more.

Both Mandy and Eve were asleep.

And it had been nearly two days since he'd spent any real time with them.

As he roared through the empty country roads of Flackwell Heath towards the town centre, Townsend angrily slammed his fist against the leather steering wheel of his car. The frustration had been building and building, but now, with King summoning him to Maureen Allen's murder scene, it was threatening to overflow.

All he wanted to do was head back home, put his arms around his family, and tell them unequivocally that nothing meant more to him.

But he was needed elsewhere.

And what made his guilt even stronger, was that both his incredible wife and his beautiful daughter completely understood.

Which meant he couldn't give up now.

Otherwise, what was the point?

As Townsend sped past the police station and then turned down the dead-end road towards the town centre, he pulled his car in behind an ambulance that had shunted up onto the curb. The quiet street was illuminated with blue flashing lights as uniformed officers patrolled the cordon, doing their best to usher away any morbid curiosity of the early-rising public. Townsend stepped out of the car and could see King standing in the centre of the crime scene, her eyes fixed on a tall, wooden frame that had been placed in the middle of the town square, just opposite the Eden Shopping Centre.

The chill of spring was heavy in the night sky, and Townsend pulled his long coat together and yanked up the zip, and his footsteps seemed to echo loudly, drowning out the voices of the crime scene that was in full flow.

Above the surrounding shops, residents twitched their curtains, no doubt mortified by what they saw below.

SOCO were swarming, doing their best to erect a white tent over the scene to preserve and shield the horror from the public.

Beyond them, the Guildhall building stood on its impressive pillars, with a few officers patrolling through the archways to chase away any spectators. Opposite, the equally impressive Cornmarket building stood, its pointed spire shooting up into the night sky.

The feeling of failure became concrete.

The look on King's face as she welcomed him with a silent glance told him that she felt the same.

The wooden structure that had been erected was two solid beams, connected by a thick, bloodstained wooden panel at its base.

A razor-sharp blade was embedded in the top of the panel, the metal also covered in spatters of blood.

On one side of the panel, Maureen Allen lay slumped, chest first, into the wood, blood pooling around the sheet that covered her body.

On the other side, a few feet away, Townsend's eyes followed the spatter of blood to where another sheet was draped over what Townsend already knew was her severed head.

The SCU had failed.

Maureen Allen had been executed by guillotine.

CHAPTER SIXTEEN

'This is a fucking disaster.'

DSI Hall slammed his fist down onto his desk, rattling the laptop and scattered stationery. King sat opposite, hands on her lap, refusing to break eye contact with her superior.

He was right.

It was a disaster.

Not only had the SCU failed in finding and saving Maureen Allen from her pre-announced execution, the masked murderer had carried it out in the most public of places. The town centre was a five-minute walk from the High Wycombe Police Station, and the Executioner had shown no fear in carrying out their despicable plan so close to their hunters.

It was a slap in the face to the Thames Valley Police.

The ramifications would be severe.

There was a thunderous knock on the door, and Hall snapped for them to enter. DCI Lowe stepped in, looking as tired as the rest of them, and he greeted his ex-wife with a curt nod. Then he turned to their superior.

'Sir, we have CCTV of the incident.'

'Lock it down,' Hall demanded. 'Share it with SCU immediately, then ensure it doesn't leak. We can't have this going viral.'

'Yes, sir.' Lowe went to leave and then turned to King. 'Shall I send it through to Hannon?'

'Send it to Michelle,' King said. 'Hannon's on her way in, but at this hour, there won't be too many people about. Michelle can get to work seeing where that bastard went. I'll get Jack's eyes on it as well.'

Lowe gave a loose thumbs up and then marched out, closing the door behind him, and locking King in with her furious boss. She blew out her cheeks and turned to Hall, who was furiously rubbing his eyes with the palms of his hands.

'Sir, I know I—'

Hall cut her off by raising a hand. King obliged, sinking into her chair and having a horrible series of flashbacks.

Back to the time that, due to the increasingly toxic atmosphere created by her divorce from DCI Lowe, Hall tried to convince her that the SCU was a good move for her.

Back to the time where Hall told her, as a friend, that her drinking was becoming a problem that she needed to face.

And back to the time, after Baycroft had just brutally murdered his fifth victim, that Hall questioned whether King was the right person to lead the investigation.

As she waited for Hall to read her the riot act, King straightened herself up, set her shoulders, and was ready to take all the criticism coming her way.

She'd protect her team.

Take full responsibility.

Then Hall surprised her.

'I'm sorry, Izzy,' he said weakly as he continued to rub his eyes. 'This isn't your fault.'

'I appreciate that, sir. But another person is dead and—'

'And you did everything you could.' Hall sighed and lowered his hands. He offered King an understanding smile. 'Over the past year, you and your team have done some quite excellent work. Baycroft. Miller. Townsend proved himself a supremely capable detective with his work alongside Lowe in the Beckford murder. Did you know Lowe requested Townsend join his team?'

'I did.' King managed a smile. 'I believe Townsend told him to shove it where the sun don't shine.'

Hall chuckled.

'Something like that.' Hall's smile faded. 'I have faith in you, Izzy. I have faith in your team. But in…' Hall checked his watch. 'Christ…it's only four in the morning. In thirteen hours, that crazy bastard is going to show the world what he did. How he waltzed into the middle of our town and executed an innocent woman. And what's worse, he gave us fair warning.'

'You think the killer is a he?'

'It's an educated guess. Carrying deadweight bodies. The size and shape of the person on the video,' Hall mused. 'But we need to know for sure. Which means, Izzy, I'll take whatever shitstorm is coming, and believe me, it's going to be biblical. Press. Local governors. Hell, I expect a call from our MP once this video goes live.'

'*If* this video goes live…' King said hopefully. Hall didn't seem in the mood for hope.

'I'm big enough and certainly ugly enough to take it. But I need you and your team to get to work,' Hall said, snapping out of his pity party and back to authority. 'Find a link. Find what connects Asif Khalid to Maureen Allen, find the sick fuck who's doing this, and for god's sake, find out quickly.'

'Yes, sir.' King stood, the pep talk eradicating her fatigue.

'Every resource,' Hall stated. 'We've got some outside help coming in this morning. Get him up to speed.'

'Sir?' King's eyebrow raised.

'That will be all,' Hall said, dismissing her query, and he turned to the mobile phone on his desk that was buzzing to life. He waved her to the door, and King left him to take the call. As she closed the door to his office, she took a moment to collect herself.

She was tired.

She was angry.

She was craving a drink.

The voice behind her would do little to negate that feeling.

'This shit's really hitting the fan, huh?' Lowe said with a small hint of irritation. King turned, her patience waning, and she glared at her ex-husband.

'If you're looking to piss me off, Marcus, I'd highly suggest you rethink it.'

Being called by his first name at the office seemed to trigger a response, and Lowe's brow furrowed.

'I've got my team working round the fucking clock to support your investigation. I've got to go to court tomorrow to see a young kid have his life thrown away and don't for one second think that you're the only person Hall is chasing for results,' he said angrily before straightening his tie. 'Funnily enough, Izzy, not everything I do is a move against you. So before this goes any further, the CCTV footage is with your team.'

King took a second.

It sickened her when Lowe was right.

It sickened her even more when he knew that she knew it, too.

'Fine.' She waved him off and stepped past him. 'Thanks for your help.'

'Thanks for your help *sir*,' he stated coldly, and King sighed. She knew he wasn't looking for her to repeat. He was just, once again, underlining their places in the hierarchy. As Lowe ventured back into the CID office, King headed back down the stairs towards her own team, annoyed that she'd allowed her pettiness to once again give Lowe the upper hand. Despite his seemingly lighter approach towards her and her team, King knew that there would always be an underlying animosity between them, and her being the one to instigate it left a sour taste in her mouth. She swiftly bypassed the SCU office, nipped into the staff canteen for a coffee, and headed outside to enjoy it with a vape.

Hopefully, it would wash that taste out before she got back to her team. Five minutes later, as she pushed open the door to the SCU, she greeted her team with a forced smile. Hannon had arrived, and much to King's admiration, had seemingly taken charge of the CCTV search.

They were, as usual, huddled around Hannon's desk, and they all turned to her.

Beyond them, on the wall, the clock was still ticking.

It wasn't even 5 a.m. yet, but it meant they had less than thirteen hours before the video Hannon had paused on her screen was shared with the world.

Well, a version of it.

The one the Executioner would have filmed themselves.

'Guv, we've got the—'

'I know.' King cut Townsend off. 'Lowe said. Show me.'

Townsend stepped aside, and King stood, arms folded,

as Hannon clicked *play* on the silent video. It was one of the same cameras they'd watched when hunting down Lauren Grainger's killer, and the familiarity of the street sent a shudder down King's spine.

She'd walked through that clearing between the buildings more times than she cared to remember.

But now, as the footage rolled, she felt an anger build within her as the van pulled up. The masked killer stepped out and marched purposefully to the back of the van.

'You've run the plates?' she asked, not taking her eyes from the screen.

'Yup,' Hannon replied. 'They belong to a Honda Civic in Hazelmere—'

'So stolen,' King cut in.

The conversation died on the spot as the Executioner swiftly pulled out the wooden structure King had seen earlier, and then impressively constructed it in the middle of the town.

Just up the road.

Townsend stood beside King, staring at the screen as the Executioner hoisted up the blade that they'd slotted between the beams, and then returned for the tripod. With the camera fixed in place, a ring light illuminated the guillotine in a deathly glow.

Then they saw Maureen.

The terrified woman was bound at the wrists and the ankles, and the masked maniac hauled her roughly to her knees, and then pushed her neck down onto the wooden panel beneath the blade.

'Jesus,' Swaby uttered under her breath.

Hannon looked a deathly pale.

'We're about to witness a murder,' King warned, and sure enough, the Executioner released the blade. The devastation was instant, and Townsend felt his stomach turn as the woman's head separated from her body, hit the concrete and rolled a few feet, leaving behind a visible stream of blood. The poor woman's body slumped down the other side of the murderous apparatus, and the entire SCU watched as the masked man turned to their own camera, revelling in their work and ensuring the terrifying cross of their mask was on display.

Then the Executioner packed away the camera, returned to the van, and headed off, leaving behind a haunting murder scene like they'd just dropped off an Amazon package.

The entire team took a moment, grimacing at the heinous crime they'd just witnessed. King moved first, turning with her arms folded as she approached the murder board. Soon, it would also include images of Maureen Allen's horrific death.

More evidence of a killer who was firmly in control.

'You all right, guv?' Townsend asked as he approached.

'No, Jack,' she said with a quiet rage. 'I'm pretty far from okay. We need to find this bastard. Once forensics has everything in evidence, get a full report on the equipment used for that guillotine. The type of wood, the type of blade. Anything and everything and start searching where someone can locate those materials and then run through any recent purchases.'

'There's a good chance they spread it across a number of stores,' Townsend mused. 'I'll also run a check on local merchants as well. They might work in the trade.'

'Good shout.' King nodded.

Before Townsend could continue the conversation, there was a knock at the door. The two detectives turned to the tall, handsome man who was stood in the doorway. He had light-brown skin, with short black hair and a neat, trimmed stubble that ran across a solid jaw. While not particularly broad, the man had a lean physique underneath a dark blazer and navy turtleneck. Over his shoulder was a leather satchel.

Affixed to one of the lapels of his jacket was a small metal pin of a yellow smiley face.

Around his neck was a *police visitor* pass.

His brown eyes locked onto King from behind his glasses, and they held hers for just a second too long that King felt a little surge of attraction.

'Can we help you?' Townsend asked, his gruffness the complete opposite of the well-groomed man before them.

'I'm looking for Detective Inspector King?' The man was softly spoken.

'You've found her.' King stepped forward and began to extend her hand. 'This is DS Jack Townsend.'

The man took King's hand and shook it, and then likewise with Townsend. He was stronger than he looked.

'I'm Dr Elliott Manning.' He smiled. 'Criminal psychologist.'

Townsend and King looked at each other, and King quickly connected the dots.

'You're the outside help,' King said to herself more than anyone. 'We're fine.'

Her dismissal didn't seem to offend.

'I specialise in the thought process and psyche of killers,' he said proudly, and then pointed at the horrific still of the crime scene still on Hannon's laptop. 'And it looks like you've got yourself one.'

CHAPTER SEVENTEEN

'So...' Manning began, his arms folded across his chest, as he gazed up at the murder board. 'Where are we at?'

It was past midday, and the entire room was on edge. The team had been hunting through everything they could to piece together what had happened to Maureen Allen, while King had brought Manning up to speed with the investigation so far. The early start was taking its toll, and despite the cups of coffee and mediocre food from the staff canteen, King knew her team was flagging.

But they didn't show it.

Wouldn't show it.

The clock was ticking until the Executioner planned to share Maureen Allen's grisly death with the world. Hannon was at her desk, running background checks on all the staff who'd been at the supermarket the day of Maureen's abduction. The rest of the team had gathered around Manning. King stood to the side, next to DSI Hall, while Townsend was perched on the edge of his own desk. In one hand was the last mouthful of a chicken wrap he'd snagged from the canteen. Swaby sat in her chair, one leg over the other, with a pad and pen at the ready.

Behind her, and making no effort to hide his boredom, was DCI Lowe. He himself decided to answer.

'Stuck in here with this crap when we should be out kicking down doors,' he said dryly, drawing a scowl from Hall. Manning didn't rise to the bait and simply turned to face Lowe with a warm smile.

'That's one tactic,' Manning said thoughtfully. 'Although, given the preparation and execution, pardon the turn of phrase, of the crimes so far, do you really think he'd allow you to find that door?'

'So, you're certain it's a he?' Swaby spoke up, scribbling on her pad.

'I am.' Manning looked back at the board and then tapped the recently added photos from the town square. 'Judging by the size, body shape, and physical strength displayed, I'd say our killer is a male. Yes.'

'Oh, come on,' Lowe said loudly. He turned to an increasingly irate Hall. 'I could have told you that. Sir, this is a waste of time.'

'DCI Lowe,' Hall snapped, his tone sharp. 'Dr Manning is a widely respected criminal psychologist and has been kind enough to assist our investigation. Show some damned respect.'

Manning held up a hand.

'Elliott is fine.' He turned to Lowe. 'I understand your frustrations, DCI Lowe, but this is not a waste of time. Right now, this killer is, I'd say, a good three steps ahead of you. So, any potential help, no matter how obvious it may be, is crucial. Unless, of course, DCI Lowe, you know more than the rest of the team?'

All heads turned, and all eyes landed on Lowe, whose lips turned up in a snarl. It was clear to the room that Lowe was trying his usual alpha routine on Manning, who was simply refusing to rise to the bait. Townsend watched on as he finished his unsatisfying lunch, impressed with how Manning could handle such aggression. It was the polar opposite to Townsend, who had cleaned Lowe's clock with a well-timed right hook nearly a year ago.

Judging from the smirk on King's face, she was also enjoying her ex-husband being riled up by this mysterious stranger.

'Well, DCI Lowe?' Hall chimed in, clearly eager to back the psychologist he'd brought in.

Lowe fell back into his chair and folded his arms across his broad chest.

'What's the current theory?' Manning turned to King with another smile.

Were they reserved for her alone?

King shook off the thought and stepped toward the board.

'We were looking into anyone who may have had an issue with Dr Khalid to begin with. Past patients, that sort of thing. We found one recent appointment which piqued our interest, but she had a watertight alibi. We eliminated the idea of racism when Maureen Allen went missing.'

'I see,' Manning said, his eyes on the board and his thumb and index finger around his chin.

'Now, we're focusing on finding a link between Maureen Allen and Dr Asif Khalid.' King made a point of tapping both their pictures on the board. 'So far, there's nothing.'

'I spoke with the FLO currently with her husband,' Townsend chimed in. 'He couldn't think of a single person who had a reason to do this to his wife. Also, he'd never heard of Dr Khalid until he read about him in the local newspaper the day before. She said that he's, understandably, devastated.'

A small, silent moment of failure was shared amongst the team. Detective Superintendent Hall cleared his throat before speaking.

'Right now it's imperative we find that link between Maureen Allen and Dr Khalid before we get another murder on our hands.'

'These are not murders,' Manning interjected, turning from the board. 'They're executions.'

'Same difference.' Lowe huffed.

'Not quite, sir.' Manning pointed back to the pictures. 'A murder can be for a number of reasons. Passion. Revenge. Money. Anything. Usually, these amount to an erratic and frenzied attack. But this…this is cold. It's calculated. Well-planned.'

'Sounds like you admire this crazy bastard.' Lowe sneered.

'In a way, I do.' Manning nodded. 'I neither condone, nor agree with what he's doing, but I can admire the precision with which he works. But I think the biggest hurdle you clearly need to overcome is thinking that this individual is crazy.'

'That's kind of hard to do when there's a beheaded woman on the board,' Townsend said. Lowe gave him an approving nod, and Townsend instantly felt uncomfortable.

He didn't want to be thought of as being a disruption, too.

If Manning had seen the nod or not, he didn't acknowledge it, but he turned to Townsend with a smile.

'I can appreciate that. And the lengths this killer is going to to make his point does border on the psychotic. But to dismiss this individual as not of sound mind would be a mistake.' Manning walked back to the board and tapped the crime scene photos. 'Meticulously planned. Clean, concise. Look at the footage of Mrs Allen's murder. The know-how to build such an apparatus. The swiftness of how it's put together. The Executioner may well be a dangerous individual, but he's certainly not crazy.'

Townsend nodded along, impressed by the doctor. Everyone seemed to be.

Apart from Lowe, who slapped his thighs and stood.

'Thank you, doctor,' he said smugly. 'Our dangerous serial killer is, in fact, a dangerous serial killer. I'll be sure to tell the rest of my team.' Lowe turned to Hall, who looked furious. 'Sorry, sir. I have a team briefing to get to.'

'We'll speak later,' Hall said sternly.

'Thank you for your time,' Manning said politely, waiting patiently for the interruption to end.

'Thank you for wasting mine.' Lowe sneered and then stormed out of the room. Hall shook his head, and King rolled her eyes.

'Is he always like that?' Manning asked, once Lowe had slammed the door to the SCU behind him.

'A prick?' King quipped. 'Every day, without fail.'

'DI King,' Hall cut in, although his lip did reveal a slight smirk. He looked back to Manning. 'Apologies.'

Manning held up a hand and shook his head.

'There are two aspects of these crimes that have drawn my interest.' He tapped the photo of the Executioner. 'The mask. Why does our killer wear a mask?'

'To hide his identity,' Hannon offered. King nodded her agreement.

'It looks homemade.' She turned to the team. 'If not, hunt down where someone can buy that mask. If it is, look into any shops in the local area that sell leather and get a list of recent purchases. Same goes for white thread. Any sales of specialist sewing kits and machines. Everything.'

'On it, Guv,' Townsend said, making a note for his line of enquiry.

'I mean, if he wants to hide his face, he could just wear a balaclava?' Swaby mused. Manning waggled his finger.

'Possibly. But the white stitching across the front, and the fact that he wants it seen means—'

'It's a symbol.' King was on the same wavelength. 'He wants people to associate his acts with his mask.'

'Precisely,' Manning agreed. 'A symbol can be anything. If you put enough power and enough meaning behind it. People will associate what the killer is trying to do with the symbol.'

'Which is?' Townsend asked.

'Justice.' Manning tapped the crime scene photos, and Hannon made a note to laminate them soon. 'Or rather, the Executioner's perceived definition of justice. These killings not only show a remarkable amount of planning, but they're symbolic by their very nature. Firing post. Beheading. These were forms of capital punishment and the message on the videos has made it clear that both Asif Khalid and Maureen Allen had escaped justice.'

'For what?' Swaby asked.

'That's the million-dollar question,' Manning said. 'We can look at what links Maureen Allen to Asif Khalid, or we could look at what either of them has done that could have made them a target.'

'They have no criminal records,' Townsend said wearily. 'From what we've gathered so far, they're as clean as a whistle and nobody would want to harm a hair on their heads.'

'Well, someone has,' Manning said abruptly. 'One with a bullet, one with a blade. This is not a random murderer celebrating themselves in the public eye. This Executioner, he's trying to send a message. One that undercuts the very principles that this police service stands for. If we can understand what the perceived injustice is, then maybe we can…'

Manning's words trailed off at the morbid thought they were all sharing. Hall stepped forward and clasped his hands together.

'Maybe we can catch him before he executes another

innocent person,' he said firmly. 'Thank you, Dr Manning. I have an office set up for you upstairs and—'

'He can use mine,' King said suddenly. All eyes fell on her. 'I'm in and out most of the day anyway, and all the investigation is here. Plus, will give him a quiet space to work.'

'Excellent idea.' Hall nodded. 'We've got a few hours before another video hits the web, and a shitstorm like no other hammers down on this station. More specifically, you guys. Which, irritatingly, means me. So, let's get to work.'

Hall's pep talk did the trick, and King and Townsend pushed themselves up before Manning spoke.

'One last thing.' He frowned in contemplation. 'I don't want to cast aspersions or cause any trouble, but there is one detail we haven't discussed.'

'Which is?' Hall said, eyebrow raised.

'Upon reviewing the videos, and the notes on the crime scenes, the Executioner seems very astute in ensuring he leaves nothing for the police.' Manning took a breath. 'Little things like the angles of CCTV cameras, the entrance and exit routes. The lack of any DNA.'

'So he's clever?' King nodded. 'We got that already.'

'I think it's more than that.' Manning rubbed his stubbled chin. 'I think whoever's behind that mask has an intimate knowledge of how a crime scene works.'

The SCU all shared a look of worry.

Hall's was a look of frustration.

'Meaning?' the DSI grumpily demanded.

Manning looked at them sorrowfully.

'Meaning there's a good chance that our killer has a forensic background.'

CHAPTER EIGHTEEN

Fifteen minutes.

That was all that was left before Maureen Allen's execution was made public, and the tension within the High Wycombe Police Station was palpable. Hannon had been glued to her desk, ignoring the stiffening in her damaged spine, as she ran through CCTV footage, trying her level best to track the van that had delivered Maureen and the tools for her execution. They'd tracked it to the train station, where it had sat for an age, but nobody had batted an eyelash.

Hidden in plain sight.

What angered Townsend even more, was that the police station was just five minutes away.

The Executioner was mocking them.

As Manning had made himself comfortable in King's office, Townsend and King had ventured out into the town, hunting down their own respective leads and tying them off. King had returned to Khalid's practice, going over a few finer financial details with Jenine Carlisle, who was able to provide the answers to end several lines of enquiry. Townsend had returned to the farm with questions about access to the premises and the damage done to the fence. Again, the farmers were more than cooperative, and Townsend was able to draw a line underneath that potential lead. On the drive back, King called, and ten minutes later, he and King took five minutes to stand in the carpark of the enormous Starbucks, take in a little of the fresh air and discuss the case. As they recounted the dead-ends they'd just successfully run into, King changed the subject.

'What do you think about Manning?' King had asked, alternating between sips of her coffee and pulls on her vape.

'I think he likes you,' Townsend said with a smirk.

'Behave,' King snapped back playfully.

'I'm a pretty good detective, Guv,' Townsend joked. 'I can see sparks flying and…listen…'

He held a finger up to his ear.

King leant in to listen and scowled.

'What is it?' she finally asked.

'Wedding bells.' The two of them laughed. A brief moment of levity during a trying few days.

'Oh, fuck off.' King shook her head. 'I'm not going down that path again. That arsehole ruined that for me.'

Townsend ended the rib. Despite being more tolerable in recent months, Lowe's ego had once again reared its ugly head in their briefing with Manning, and Townsend was sure that the next time they crossed paths, Lowe would be back to his old self.

All hands to the pumps.

Lowe throwing his toys out of the pram just made things a little harder.

'I meant…' King continued. 'What did you make of his analysis? Do you think our killer's a cop?'

'Maybe.' Townsend shrugged. 'It's a theory. But like you always say, Guv…fol—'

'Follow the evidence.' King finished his sentence and smiled. 'You're a good lad, Jack.'

'Thanks.' Townsend nodded. They stood in comfortable silence for a few moments. 'How you getting on, anyway?'

King took a considered puff on her vape and then tucked it into her coat.

'You know me.' She shrugged. 'Day by day.'

That was all that was needed.

Townsend wouldn't pry any further, and King appreciated that. She also appreciated the genuine care that he had for her, and she felt a twinge of guilt that once again, the job was pulling him away from his home life.

But this was the job.

The other part of the job was the relentless pursuit of leads. Hannon was wading through the CCTV footage and running every check possible to locate the van. Swaby spent the day investigating the charity and the event where Khalid was snatched, working her way through the names of attendees and striking them off the list, while also confirming the level of involvement that Khalid held. She'd also compiled a detailed dossier on his and the surgery's financial situation, although none of it seemed to raise any red flags. Townsend focused on the supermarket staff. He checked them against the PNC for any previous records and then cross-referenced them with the patient list at Khalid's surgery, in a hope that someone, somewhere would provide a connection.

Everywhere they turned seemed to be bricked off.

But sifting through the chaff was necessary to get to the wheat.

But all they had were two dead bodies, a terrified public, an angry mob growing online, and a ticking clock.

With an hour before the deadline, King had once again gathered them round the murder board, walking through what they knew and what they could eliminate. While they were able to close off a few avenues of enquiry, the harsh reality was they were unlikely to stop the video airing.

And the likelihood was, they'd be unable to stop the next victim from being murdered.

Manning was right.

The Executioner was seemingly three steps ahead, meaning they were already preparing their next execution while the police were playing catch-up with the previous victims.

The cycle of violence seemed endless.

Townsend blew out his cheeks as the timer on the wall ran past the fourteen-minute mark and he stepped out of the office. He marched through the halls of the station to the gents, relieved himself and then approached the sink to wash his hands. As he did, he splashed water on his face and then stared at himself in the mirror, trying to will the answer to the case into his mind.

'Fuck,' he uttered under his breath, and then headed back out, almost colliding with PC Boyd as he did.

'Whoa,' Boyd said, stepping round him. 'Easy, fella.'

'I know, I'm sorry,' Townsend said sincerely. 'It's been a long few days.'

'Tell me about it.' Boyd shrugged. 'Still, all this overtime. Suits me down to the ground.'

'Does your wife not mind?' Townsend probed.

'Mind? She practically begs me to do it.' Boyd chuckled. His voice was raspy and suited his rough look. 'Still, that's what happens when you marry a woman who insists on two fucking holidays a year.'

Townsend chuckled politely.

He couldn't remember the last time he'd been on holiday.

'Walshy doesn't have that problem.' Boyd cut through

Townsend's thoughts. 'Lucky fucker is at home sleeping. He doesn't need the overtime.'

'We could still use the manpower,' Townsend said.

'Yeah, you been in the game as long as me and Walshy have, son, you'll get your sleep when and where you can.' Boyd joked. 'Right, I've got a hot date with a lukewarm pizza in the canteen. See you around, Scouse.'

Boyd trudged away, and Townsend watched him leave, his own stomach grumbling. It was nearly time for his tea, but in all likelihood, it wouldn't be spent around the table with his family.

Again.

Another missed meal.

Another day of absence.

With the usual guilt, Townsend typed out his apology to Mandy, knowing full well she'd understand. But Boyd's words had broken through, and when Mandy's message of encouragement did pop up on his phone, it was interrupting his search for a week-long holiday for him and his family.

A chance to show them that he didn't take them for granted.

It was two minutes to five, and Townsend paused his search, pocketed his phone, and then jogged briskly back down the corridors to the office.

Everyone was gathered around the computer.

Like so many others across the country, no doubt.

The clock hit five, and Lowe dipped in. The look on his face told them that there was no tracing the video.

Mauren Allen's execution was going to be shown.

Maureen Allen's decisions have led her to this point. The court of law cannot be trusted...

Therefore, there will be no judge...

No jury...

The air seemed to leave the room of the SCU office.

Just execution…

The footage wasn't anything they hadn't already seen before. Shot from street level as opposed to the overhanging CCTV. The phone's microphone picked up the scrapes of footsteps and the terrified groans of Maureen, adding a layer of raw fear to the footage. The Executioner revelled in front of the camera, ensuring their mask was seen clearly before they coldly marched to the guillotine and dropped the blade.

Hannon turned away.

Lowe grunted with anger.

King glowered at the screen.

The thud of the sharp blade as it ripped through flesh and bone was stomach churning, and after Maureen Allen's head cracked against the cold concrete, the Executioner stood for a few moments, admiring their harrowing handiwork, before they stormed towards the camera and let the footage linger on the X across their leather-clad face.

Letting their symbol resonate a few moments longer.

Then the footage cut to black.

Justice has been served…

Townsend felt his stomach turn. But it wasn't from hunger.

Nor was it from guilt.

As a man who'd grown up on one of the toughest estates in the country, he'd spent years undercover with some of the most dangerous criminals and had successfully faced off against two violent serial killers, Townsend was considered by many to be as tough as they came.

But his stomach was turning for one reason only.

Fear.

CHAPTER NINETEEN

The ripple effects of Maureen Allen's execution were far-reaching. More so than those of Khalid's. Not because she was a woman, nor the fact she was white, although King did say both of those factors would raise the alert level with the public, but due to the fact she was second.

It meant this was becoming a killing spree, and as the national news had now usurped the local journalists in front of Hall when he gave a statement to hammer home their efforts, the feeling was that the situation wasn't just spiralling out of control.

It was completely off the rails.

King and Townsend both stood to the side of the press room, a place where eight months ago, Hall had gone to bat for King when rumours of her alcoholism had begun to spread online. The internet was a breeding ground for misinformation and libel, and things had the propensity to spread faster than a cold in a nursery. Now, as Hall defiantly told the press that his team would bring the Executioner to justice, King couldn't help but feel a few subtle digs in his speech.

Despite my team's best efforts.

We have brought in specialists to assist our investigation.
I will be taking a hands-on role.

At face value, Hall was just trying to assure the public that the Thames Valley Police were doing everything in their power, but she couldn't help but read into the underlying message.

They needed to do better.

As Hall wrapped it up and marched towards the two of them, ignoring the sea of follow-up questions, he told both of them to walk with him.

'We need to get hold of this situation,' Hall ordered.

'I know, sir,' King offered. 'We are working round the clock to…'

He waved her off.

'I know,' he said softly. 'And don't think it hasn't been noticed. All over time will be signed off, you can guarantee that.'

'We're not doing it for the money,' Townsend said. Hall glared at him. 'Sir.'

'Again. I know.' Hall stopped and sighed. The corridor was empty, and up ahead, through the open door to the SCU, they could hear Hannon tapping away on her keyboard. 'Look, I make it a priority to look after my officers. And right now, our best hasn't been enough. So, I'm bringing in DCI Lowe to—'

'Sir,' King spat. He held up a hand.

'Let me finish…I'm bringing in Lowe to support. I know CID have been helping, but I want everything shared between the teams.' He could see King's eyes glowering with fury. 'This is still your case, Izzy. But it's bigger than that now, do you understand?'

King shuffled on the spot.

'Yes, sir.'

'Good.' Hall's phone buzzed, and he sighed. 'Right,

I've got our MP ready to shove my job description up my arse, so if you'll excuse me?'

The two respectfully stepped to the side, allowing the detective superintendent to head off to his presumed bollocking, and Townsend turned to King.

'You all right, guv?'

'No.' She shook her head.

'Look, we've faced this before.' Townsend tried to sound positive. 'And we came through both times.'

'This feels different.' King pulled her vape from her pocket and did a quick scan of the corridor. She took a pull and blew the vapour downwards in a lame attempt to hide it. 'Too many cooks.'

She was referring to the additions of Lowe and Manning, who was sitting in her private office as they entered the SCU. Hannon and Swaby were at their desks, and to King's annoyance, DCI Lowe was standing in front of the murder board. He had his broad back to them and his arms folded across his chest as he scanned the breadcrumbs they'd been following.

'DCI Lowe,' King said by way of a greeting.

'DI King.' He turned and saw Townsend, too. 'Scouse.'

'Sir,' Townsend replied. Despite their mutual respect, Townsend still knew Lowe was a stickler for hierarchy.

'I take it Hall told you—'

'Yep,' King cut Lowe off. 'Was probably pretty easy to worm your way into this one considering how little we have to go on.'

'First of all, I didn't ask for it,' Lowe said calmly, probably to irritate her. 'We've got a guy publicly executing people and you guys need all the help you can get. And second, you do have stuff to go on.'

He nodded to the board.

'We've run through that board countless times,' King said with a sigh. It was time to play nice. 'Every connection we can try to make between the two has come back empty.'

'Well, what about your new boyfriend?' Lowe said sarcastically. Whatever riot act Hall had read him for his earlier behaviour clearly hadn't registered. 'Has he not cracked the case yet?'

King looked beyond the board to her office, where Manning was standing, leaning over a desk full of case files, and deep in thought.

'I guess we'll find out,' King replied, and then made her way to the office. Lowe watched as his ex-wife and the psychologist exchanged pleasantries, and he shook his head.

'We don't need a fucking shrink,' Lowe said to Townsend. 'We need more men on the street knocking down doors.'

Townsend didn't like the idea of Lowe being too pally with him. It felt like a betrayal.

'I guess DSI Hall thinks it will help.' Townsend gestured to the board. 'All hands to the pump, remember?'

'Have we established how our killer knew where to find these people?' Lowe asked, looking back to the board. 'How did he know when and where both of these people would be at those times?'

'He followed them,' Hannon said, interrupting their conversation. Lowe waggled his finger. 'I've pulled all the CCTV from the surgery, supermarket and town centre from the past few weeks. I've been going through it looking for any possible matches to our van and the possible driver and then run the plates. Literally, I'm starting to see the whole world as if it was CCTV footage. I've gathered about 1000 hours' worth from various sources, times and angles that need checking.'

'That's a lot of film…get some of my guys to help,' Lowe said. 'And book yourself in for an eye test after.'

Lowe flashed his handsome smile, but Hannon just rolled her eyes. Lowe was either unaware or unconcerned by her orientation.

'Swaby, any luck on finding the actual registration?' Lowe turned to his old colleague, who shook her head as she looked up from her screen.

'Nothing. Was a long shot.'

'We need to take all the shots we can.' Lowe breathed out, placing his hands on his hips. Townsend looked over to King's office, wondering if she could see her ex-husband taking control of her case.

She couldn't.

She was deep in conversation with Manning.

Lowe continued his conversation with Swaby, their old repertoire reignited.

'How's Rich? You know…after everything.'

'He's doing okay.' Swaby shrugged. The loss of her father-in-law had hit her husband and her two sons pretty hard. 'Time heals and all that.'

'Well, send him my best.' Lowe nodded with a smile and then headed for the door.

'Sir,' Townsend called after him. 'Guv' was reserved for King, and King alone. 'What next?'

'For you?' Lowe raised an eyebrow. 'You get yourself home, Scouse. We've got court in the morning.'

'With all due respect, sir, I'm needed here.'

Lowe's demeanour changed.

'And with all due respect to you, this isn't the only thing going on right now. Tyler Davis is looking at life in prison, and you need to get some kip. Because you can rest assured, giving a character statement for a young boy headed to prison will take it out of you.'

Townsend held his tongue.

'Go home, Scouse.' Lowe offered him a genuine smile. 'That's an order.'

Lowe marched out of the SCU and headed back to the CID office one storey up, and Townsend stood on the spot. No matter what he tried to do, everything came with a side order of guilt.

If he stayed, he'd be away from his family again.

If he left, his team would have to carry the burden.

A rock and a hard place.

Swaby's voice of reason cut through his thought process.

'Hey, Jack. When someone gifts you an evening with your family in this job, it's worth taking with both hands.' Her smile was warm, as always. 'We've got this.'

Townsend reluctantly agreed, and as he gathered up his jacket and his notes on the Tyler Davis case, he looked back to the office to wave to King.

She was busy.

Engrossed by the handsome psychologist who was gesticulating as he spoke to her.

He'd leave them to it.

He had a day in court, where he got to provide evidence to ensure a young man was sent to prison for the majority of his life because he wanted to protect his mum.

Townsend could help himself to another plate of that guilt, only this time from a different tray.

As he headed to his car, Townsend tried to shake the thought from his mind and focus on Swaby's words.

He was heading home to his family.

With what was to come, he needed to make the most of it.

CHAPTER TWENTY

It took a particular set of skills to get DI King to lower her guard so quickly, but Dr Manning seemed to have the entire set. As she sat at the desk in her office, looking at the avalanche of emails that had landed in her inbox, she looked across the room to the man who she'd invited in. He was handsome, but that wasn't what King had found herself being drawn to almost instantly.

It was his nature.

Her marriage to DCI Lowe had, for a time, been just as exciting as the job they shared. He was spontaneous, romantic and adventurous, but it was ultimately undercut by one thing.

He was DCI Lowe.

The arrogance of the man, who in effect justified his infidelity by her inability to have children, was something that had exacerbated her drinking and had seen her spend the past few years on her own. In the initial heartbreak, she'd tried to fight fire with fire and had taken a few guys home to try to work out her problems.

It didn't help.

As Lowe seemingly moved on with his life guilt free,

King found more solace in the bottle than in the arms of another man and over the past year or so, the whole concept of romance had completely abandoned her. But her impulse to offer her office to Manning, while it made sense, was because she wanted to spend more time with him.

He was calm.

Kind.

Articulate.

Almost the polar opposite to Lowe, and while her mind was completely taken with the rapidly escalating case, it was nice to have a modicum of pleasure in her day.

'Everything okay?'

His voice cut through her train of thought, and King shook herself back into the room and turned to him.

'Sorry?'

'I asked if you were okay?' Manning said, looking at her over his glasses. 'You kind of zoned out there.'

'Oh, sorry.' King randomly moved and clicked her mouse. 'Just emails.'

'Okay.' He didn't seem to buy it. 'So what do you think?'

'Think?'

'About what I just said?'

King looked at him blankly, and just as she went to answer, she saw the corner of his mouth curl into a smile.

'Okay, fine. I wasn't listening.' She pushed herself off her chair and stretched her back. 'It's been a long few days.'

'I can imagine.' Manning turned back to the paperwork that had been spread over the table. 'I was just theorising that perhaps we're looking outwards instead of inwards.'

'Excuse me?' King said as she stepped around her desk and approached him.

'Our killer. We're working so heavily to find out what connects Dr Khalid to Mrs Allen, but maybe that's the wrong direction.' Manning shuffled a few sheets on the desk. 'Maybe, what connects them is in fact our killer?'

King looked across the evidence laid out on the desk, and then through the window that looked out to the rest of the SCU. Hannon was still tapping away, and it had been over an hour since she'd told Lowe to send Townsend home. Her eyes fell on the murder board, and the faces of the latest two deaths that had fallen into her lap.

'Maybe.' She humoured him. 'But that doesn't help us when we don't know who the killer is.'

'True.' Manning brought a thoughtful hand to his chin. 'But if we can find a point in time where both Dr Khalid and Maureen Allen could have possibly intersected, we could, theoretically, begin to build a picture of our killer and his mission.'

'It's a mission now?' King said, a little too jovially. She scolded herself. Manning just flashed her a smile.

'I'd say so. Or a crusade. Whatever you fancy. But this isn't simply a killing spree. If it was, it wouldn't have the pageantry.'

'The mask. The name,' King confirmed his view. 'The public killing.'

'Precisely.' Manning took a seat and blew out his cheeks. 'Without more actual evidence, I couldn't even begin to build a narrative as to what brought him to this point. But given what we've seen so far, this won't stop until either you stop him or—'

'He finishes his mission...whatever that might mean,' King said with a worried tone. She looked out to the SCU again, just as Hannon was easing herself from her chair and reaching for her jacket. King waved goodbye and then checked her watch.

Christ.

It was nearly half eight.

Clearly, the concern that had laced her words had eked out across her expression.

'You have a good team,' Manning said. 'They seem very determined.'

'They are,' King replied, not taking her eyes from Hannon who disappeared out of the SCU. 'The amount they've given and sacrificed over the past year is too much. But they'll never complain. Never make me feel bad about it but…'

Her voice trailed off.

Manning was still observing her with intrigue.

'But you do, right? You feel responsible for them.'

'I am responsible for them.' She finally turned to him. His eyes were intensely staring into hers. 'They're good people, and no matter how bad these situations get, they show up. Day in and day out. They all have lives. Kids, or in Hannon's case, a dog. And yet I know each one of them will be thinking of nothing but the horrors of this case while they force a smile to their loved ones.'

'That's not your fault. You understand that, right?'

King suddenly felt very under the microscope and turned to him and folded her arms.

'What about you, doctor? What brings you to my neck of the woods?'

He jokingly splayed his hands towards the paper covered desk.

'The case. Obviously.' They chuckled. 'But to be perfectly honest with you, I just needed a change. I've been working up in Manchester for the past few years. Had a house. Had a fiancée. You know…'

'Sort of.'

'Well, things went a bit pear-shaped, and I decided to move back down to London. It's where I studied, and I know people around there. I've been contracting for the past few months with the Met, when the request for support came in from Hall…'

'Ah, so you're not a local boy, then?'

'Oh no.'

'Funny, I transferred here from the Met, too. A few years ago, now. Moved with my husband at the time, but you don't need to know the details on that.' King shook her head. 'Let's just say you already understand why that marriage didn't last.'

The doctor connected the dots quickly.

'Lowe?' He raised his eyebrows. 'That must have been…challenging.'

'It still is.' She clasped her hands together. 'Why do I feel like I'm being analysed?'

'I don't know. Insecurity?' He smiled. 'Or maybe, I just want to know you a bit better.'

King turned away to stop Manning from seeing the smile trying its hardest to break across her face. She pushed open the door to the office and stepped out into the now-empty SCU. All three of her team had wrapped up for the day, their desks as neat as a pin, although she often wondered why Townsend even had a desk, given he rarely used it.

She looked up at the murder board, at the victims whose families were depending on them to find justice.

Looked at the picture of the Executioner who was belittling them with his own brand of it.

Head in the game, Izzy.

She heard footsteps behind her, and Manning stepped out, following her eyeline to the board.

'I just need something to make sense,' she said, a hint of desperation in her voice.

Her stomach rumbled.

'Well, there is one question we haven't answered if we're going to make some progress here.'

King turned to him.

'What's that?'

Manning was swiping on his phone with a smile on his face.

'Are there any decent Thai restaurants around here that deliver?'

She didn't know if he'd heard her stomach or read her mind.

CHAPTER TWENTY-ONE

It felt somewhat of a luxury to be heading home in the early evening, and Townsend knew that in his profession, looking a gift horse in the mouth was a foolish move. But as he headed up the hill towards 'Millionaire's Row', he couldn't help but feel the magnetic pull of the case pulling him back.

The Executioner had left two bodies for the world to see and marvelled in his handiwork.

Townsend knew he was needed at home, but he was needed in the office, too.

But orders were orders, and with Tyler's court date looming in the morning, he knew Lowe was right.

Townsend couldn't do everything at once.

Tomorrow, justice would be served, albeit in a way that would see a young kid's life thrown away.

As he whipped through the country roads that would soon give way to Flackwell Heath, he tried to refocus his mind.

He couldn't remember the last time he'd sat down with his family for a meal during the week.

Helped Eve with her homework.

Read her a bedtime story.

Sat and actually had a chat with Mandy about her day at work, even though he still wasn't entirely clear what her job was. That signalled another twinge of guilt, although his wife would just laugh it off as Townsend not having the required headspace to understand.

When he'd called Mandy to say he was coming home, his heart fluttered at the delight in her voice, and when he pulled into the driveway of their home, the door opened instantly.

Eve.

Standing in the doorway, still in her school uniform, was his daughter, who was shuffling on the spot. Before Townsend had closed the car door behind him, she rushed down the two steps and threw her arms around his waist, burying her face in his solid stomach.

'Whoa, Pickle.' He reached down and with considerable effort, hoisted her up. 'You're getting strong.'

He stood for a moment in the pleasant evening breeze and buried his head into her neck. When he lifted his head, Mandy was watching from the doorway.

'Hey, babe,' he said with a grin, as he walked towards the house with his daughter clinging to him like a koala. He leant in and gave his wife a kiss.

'Ewww.' Eve sneered, before dropping down and disappearing into the house.

'I think she was talking about you,' Townsend joked, and Mandy playfully slapped him on the arm.

'Get in, you,' she said with a grin. 'Tea's nearly ready.'

The evening played out just how Townsend had hoped, with his wife serving up a massive bowl of spaghetti bolognese, along with too much garlic bread that the three of them devoured with delight. As they ate, and the chilled music from Radio 2 played in the background, Townsend had quizzed Eve about school, and she excitedly ran him through the events of the day in extreme detail.

As she began another story, Townsend raised an eyebrow.

'Who's George?' Townsend asked, catching his daughter cold. She looked a little perturbed.

'Huh?'

'George,' Townsend repeated with a smile. 'Who is he?'

'Just a boy in my class.' Eve looked a little shy.

'It's just you keep mentioning him.' Townsend looked to Mandy, who shook her head playfully.

'Do I?'

'Yup.' Townsend smirked.

'Ignore him, babe,' Mandy said, before turning to her daughter. 'It's not your fault you're super in love with George!'

'Mum!' Eve yelled, and she scowled at her parents who were giggling like the kids in her class.

Mandy de-escalated the situation quickly with three bowls of ice cream, and Townsend tucked into his beside his daughter as he observed her doing her homework. It startled him the level of comprehension she had for some of the maths problems in her book and was secretly relieved that she hadn't asked him to help.

As the clock ticked towards Eve's bedtime, Mandy took their daughter upstairs to oversee her getting ready for bed, allowing her the independence to brush her teeth, sort her clothes out for the morning and pick her pyjamas. Townsend went to work clearing up the kitchen, as he loaded up the dishwasher and wiped down the sides. Then, he joined the giggling from upstairs and plonked himself down next to Eve who handed him her book.

Harry Potter and the Prisoner of Azkaban.

Mandy and Eve had already cleared a third of the

book, and Townsend offered to allow them to continue together.

But Eve was adamant that he read to her.

Mandy was non-plussed.

Like Townsend, the world of Hogwarts wasn't something she held dear, but their daughter seemed enthralled by the magical stories.

Townsend got through about twenty pages before he turned to find his daughter fast asleep. Carefully, he bookmarked the page, planted a gentle kiss on her forehead, and then shut off the lamp as he exited.

Mandy was on the sofa, half a cold beer in her hand and a full bottle on the side table for her husband. As he dropped down on the sofa beside her, he made an audible groan.

'Getting old, Jack?' she joked.

'I think so.' He took a swig of his beer. 'Either that or I need a new job.'

'Oh, come on now.' She nuzzled into him as he wrapped an arm over her shoulder. 'Where else would you get violent criminals and ungodly hours?'

Townsend took a thoughtful sip.

'Primark?'

His answer caused her to laugh out loud, and the two of them sat for the next twenty minutes, enjoying their drink and time together as Mandy spoke about her day. The meetings she'd attended and the arrangements she had to make for her boss's week ahead.

Townsend did his best to push everything else from his mind.

The case.

Tyler.

The white cross of the Executioner that had been goading them for the past few days.

His focus was on Mandy, and as she spoke, he looked at

her lovingly. She was still as beautiful as the day he'd met her, and although her blonde hair was now darkening a little, and her face showed a few wise lines of age, she was still as far out of his league as he could imagine. She'd have scolded him for thinking it and would have undoubtedly reiterated that he was a handsome man with a good heart, but Townsend would never agree.

Finding Mandy had been one of the greatest things to ever happen to him.

Getting her to fall in love with him was his greatest achievement.

Eventually, Mandy finished her beer and headed to the kitchen. Townsend sat, blew out his cheeks, and checked his phone.

No messages from work.

No updates.

Thankfully, no more abductions or death.

He opened his internet browser, and the holiday website reintroduced itself. As he began to read the specifics of the package, Mandy re-entered the room with another cold beer and the files he'd retrieved from his car just before dinner. She placed both on the side table beside them, leant in, and gave her husband a kiss.

'Figured you'd want this.'

'I don't *want* it.' Townsend sighed as he picked up the files. Mandy gently pressed the back of her hand to his cheek.

'Do what you have to do, babe,' she said with a nod of confirmation. 'I need to wash my hair, anyway. I'm in the office again tomorrow.'

'You have an office?' Townsend joked, and Mandy stuck her tongue out as she left the room. He watched her leave, his eyes appreciating every movement, and he promised himself he'd go over what he needed and then join her in bed.

Fall asleep together for the first time that week.

But as he opened the files, he was greeted with the photo of Jamal Beckford lying on the rain-soaked concrete, a pool of blood pumping from the open wound that slashed across his throat.

Tomorrow, he would take the stand and give his account of events to a judge on how a teenage boy had murdered the man who'd assaulted his mum.

Tyler Davis would get sent to prison.

And justice, despite the horrible ramifications for the boy and his despairing mother, would have been served.

As he leant forward and began to read the notes, Townsend sunk his beer quickly and then retrieved another.

All in the hope that he'd be able to drown out the voice that perhaps, on some level, the Executioner was right.

That sometimes the system failed.

CHAPTER TWENTY-TWO

It's surprisingly easy to follow someone.

Years ago, people learnt from a young age to be street smart. Their youth spent playing outside, knocking for their friends and just living in the real world. But over the years, the insidious reliance on the internet provided people with access to all their needs at the click of a button. From necessities like groceries, or more carnal desires such as pornography, everything was available at the click of a button.

Delivered to your door.

Addiction to screens meant generations now grew up with their heads down, eyes unfocused on what was around them, and it meant that despite people being afraid of their own shadows, let alone a friendly stranger, the majority of them were oblivious to the world around them.

Dale Ainsworth was one such person.

Seeing him for the first time in almost a decade, the Executioner had to do a double take.

Gone was the long, sweeping fringe that had plastered the man's forehead all those years ago. As was the earring and the tuft of hair he'd mistakenly thought had looked good below his lower lip. Father Time had taken his fair share from Dale, and the man had clearly given up the fight years ago as his shiny head was shaved to the scalp. It was counterbalanced by the impressive, thick beard that ran from ear to ear, and Dale's face wore the tired wrinkles of a man with young kids.

He was bigger now. Much bigger.

Back then, Dale wore the slim build of a man who was fresh out of uni and had based his entire look on whatever indie band was popular at that moment in time. Now, Dale looked every inch the plumber he was, with a muscular frame that had started to sag slightly due to the demands of being a one-man business and a busy father. His powerful arms pulled tight against the branded polo shirt he wore, with both arms covered in tattoos that bled out across the backs of his hands.

He'd be hard to move.

But not impossible.

It had been a few weeks since the Executioner had begun following Dale, the 'Ainsworth Plumbing' emblazoned van had become a familiar sight, and thankfully for him, Dale had landed a big job on a series of new builds that were obliterating the rolling fields just outside Flackwell Heath. Over one hundred new and 'affordable' homes, each one the same as the other and meant if you drove down the newly made streets for more than ten seconds, it felt like you were in a time loop.

But Dale was there from six until six, and every morning and evening, the Executioner adjusted his own routine and would swing by to ensure Dale was where he needed him to be.

When the mask wasn't on, the Executioner slipped seamlessly into his normal life.

Punctual to work.

Reasonably polite and cooperative with the people he faced.

Not a foot out of place.

A façade of a real life that nobody would ever question.

For nearly a decade now, that life felt like the cover. It was only when the mask was put on, or when the wheels of his grand design were in motion, did he feel anything close to normality.

He was only truly living when the art of killing was at hand.

Dr Khalid had been easy. The middle-aged doctor had proven just as gutless as he had a decade ago, and leading him to his execution had only been a strain due to the man's weight. Maureen Allen had been even easier, and although there could be little pleasure in brutally slaying an old-age pensioner, the cause outweighed the Executioner's moral compass.

But Dale Ainsworth might have proved a problem had the man not given the Executioner countless opportunities to scope the perfect spot.

All the Executioner had to do was to sit and wait.

The van was newly rented. The other one had been returned with their original number plates securely fastened. A different van from a different company from a different town meant the police, who were searching for the grey van that had been in full view during Maureen's execution, would be chasing a ghost. With the work underway on the next wave of houses, Transit vans were ten-a-penny across the new man-made roads, and nobody would bat an eyelid at another one parked up on one of the many curbs.

He waited.

Sure enough, a little after six, a fatigued-looking Dale emerged from the shell of a home he'd been working in, his tool bag swinging in his meaty hand, and he headed to the back of his own van. With the tools secured, he stepped round to the side, leant against the vehicle and took a cigarette out from his pocket and lit up. A few minutes of peace and quiet before returning home for his other full-time job.

Only he wouldn't be making it home tonight.

Nor again.

As Dale leisurely pulled on his cigarette, he thumbed through his phone, unaware of the eyes that were on him.

It was so easy to follow people.

Like clockwork, Dale flicked his cigarette, started up the van, and headed out of the repetitive streets and turned right, heading back towards High Wycombe, before he indicated and turned left, following the long country road that would eventually lead to Marlow, and then on to Bisham where Dale's family would be waiting. The rush-hour traffic was just starting to thin slightly, and the Executioner fell in behind Dale, a few cars back, but he knew where he was heading.

He'd stop off at the mini market opposite the Bisham Abbey National Sports Centre, where, as per usual, he'd pull his van into the small car park round the back. The majority of the customers were the local community, and with the pleasant warmth of spring descending upon the evening, many would arrive on foot.

There was always a space in the car park.

There was also one solitary CCTV camera.

As the Executioner turned into the car park, he watched as Dale walked around the side of the building, another cigarette in hand and making the most of his 'quiet time'. The research of the man's routine never extended to the contents of his shop, but it did allow for the Executioner to know where to park to ensure the camera didn't pick up his face. Swiftly, he pulled off a three-point turn, then reversed the van, so it was parked across the back of Dale's van, blocking him completely in his space. By turning his own van around, it meant the Executioner stepped out and was shielded by his vehicle. He then went to the back, opened both doors, sat and waited.

It wouldn't take long for Dale to return and, quite reasonably, ask what the hell he was doing.

He only had to wait two minutes.

'What the fuck?' Dale exclaimed loudly, his voice coarser and deeper than he remembered.

'Sorry, mate,' the Executioner called out, not moving from his spot. 'Won't be a sec.'

'You've blocked me in, mate.' It wasn't a statement so much as a threat. 'What you playin' at?'

There was nobody else around.

'Actually, could you give me a hand?' he called out. He pushed himself up and readied the chloroform onto the rag held by his side, out of view.

'Fuck's sake,' Dale uttered, and he dumped his shopping bag in his own front seat and then stomped round to the back of the Executioner's van. He didn't return the polite smile that greeted him. 'What's going on, mate? I need to get home.'

'Can you help me with this?' The Executioner pointed into the van. Dale turned and looked.

It was empty.

'What the fuc—'

A rag fell across his face, pressed down with considerable force that surprised him given the man's age. Another powerful arm wrapped around his neck like a python, and despite his best efforts to fight him off, the fumes from the rag soon took hold.

He faded quickly, and the last thing he saw before his world turned black was the dirty, wooden floor of the back of the van.

That, and the faces of his wife and kids.

Dale crashed hard into the back of the van, and with a grunt of exertion, the Executioner hoisted the man's limp legs off the ground and pushed him further into the vehicle. He took the man's phone from his pocket, turned the power off, tossed it towards the now abandoned work van and then closed the doors.

It was a short drive to the lock-up, and he'd bind him properly then.

Or make him bind himself at gunpoint if he managed to stir.

Either way, he needed to move, and he swiftly slammed the doors shut, locked them, and then moved to the driver's side. With his head down, he got in, pulled away, and left Dale's van, and his shopping, for the police to find.

It was easy to follow people.

Surprisingly, so was kidnap.

And knowing what Dale Ainsworth was responsible for, along with Maureen Allen and Asif Khallid, killing him would be even easier.

CHAPTER TWENTY-THREE

'You ready?'

Townsend looked up at DCI Lowe, who was immaculate in his suit. With the eyes of the public ready for him, Lowe had clearly taken time out of the current investigation for a quick trim. Townsend, on the other hand, was sporting a seven-day-old stubble, that had now passed the point of trendy. He knew he looked a little scraggy, something Mandy had been all too keen to point out, but his own appearance hardly seemed high on the list of priorities. His dark hair, swept in a loose side parting, was also in need of a tune-up.

At least he'd ironed his shirt.

As the DCI waited for his answer, Townsend wondered if the solicitor had asked the same thing to Tyler Davis moments before they marched him out to the chambers to make him relive the decision that had changed his life. Aylesbury Crown Court was tucked just outside the town centre, a short walk down from the Waterside Theatre and the parade of restaurants and the Odeon cinema.

That morning, Lowe had been waiting for Townsend in the car park of the High Wycombe Police Station, and had beeped his horn when Townsend had been heading into the station. Townsend had protested that he wanted to check in on the case before they headed out, but Lowe had made it clear that today's priority was to do right by Tyler.

The SCU would be fine without Townsend for half a day or so, and when Townsend said he just needed to run it by King, Lowe took it as a personal afront and ordered Townsend into the car. After that, Lowe's mood changed, and their drive from High Wycombe to Aylesbury had been mainly in silence. Townsend had looked out of the window of Lowe's luxury Audi sports car, and he watched as the springtime countryside rolled alongside them. The fields were filled with sheep and other farmyard animals, and Townsend spotted a few farmers out in the sun, working hard for the months ahead. He wanted nothing more than to appreciate the quaint, beautiful view as they drove towards the day he'd dreaded ever since he'd taken Lowe to Tyler's house. It had been the day after he'd faced Gemma Miller, saving DS Swaby from her death at the hands of another person just trying to protect their parent.

However, Tyler was different.

He'd never sat opposite Townsend, refusing to see the wrong in his actions. Unlike Gemma Miller, who'd revelled in her revenge with a murderous twinkle in her wild eyes.

The same murderous glint that was entirely absent when Townsend walked into the room and Tyler Davis turned to face him.

The young man seemed smaller.

He was sitting within a glass holding cell at the back of the court, overlooking the rows of benches beneath him like he'd been put on display. In a way, he was; presented to the room like a zoo animal as two highly skilled and overpaid solicitors fought to either ruin his life, or cover up a severe crime.

The evidence was damning.

Tyler himself had already confessed to the murder of his stepfather, Jamal Beckford, last winter. Lowe had made the arrest, but it had been Townsend who'd connected the dots. All he'd ever wanted to be was a good cop, just like his father before him, and since his relocation to Buckinghamshire, Townsend had caught three killers.

Only this was the one that hadn't felt satisfying.

This was the only one that made him question whether he'd done the right thing.

As he and Lowe moved down through the courtroom towards their designated seats, Lowe turned back to Tyler, who watched in awe. The teenager lifted a feeble hand and waved to Lowe, who waved back. He mouthed 'are you okay?', to which Tyler nodded, seemingly straighten his shoulders and lifting his chin. Lowe watched, smiled with a hint of pride, and offered the young man a comforting nod. It was little moments like that, these tiny pockets of genuine care, that would often undercut the reputation Lowe seemed keen to cultivate.

It was why Townsend was more willing to give Lowe a chance than the rest of the SCU.

'How's he doing?' Townsend whispered to Lowe.

'He's a tough kid,' Lowe responded. There was no follow up.

Townsend looked around the room. Important-looking people, dressed in gowns and oversized wigs, were busying themselves at their tables, while the public began to filter through into the viewing stalls. As Townsend looked around, his eyes met with Tyler's mother, Simone Beckford, and the rage was apparent by a small flare of the nostril. The woman had been heartbroken when he'd informed her of her husband's death.

Her world collapsed entirely when Townsend returned, alongside Lowe, to arrest her son for the crime.

Simone Beckford hated every fibre of Townsend's being, and he didn't blame her.

The door at the back of the room opened, and a regal man in his mid-fifties emerged, a slightly more elaborate gown and a slightly more ridiculous wig.

'Here we go,' Lowe uttered under his breath, and he, along with everyone else, stood out of respect for the judge as he took his seat and began to introduce the room to the reason they were there and proceedings to follow. Along the left-hand side of the room, where twelve empty seats, laid out in two rows of six. With Tyler already confessing to the murder, there was no case to present to the jury, just the painstaking formality of the young man's sentencing.

It would save the circus of a trial.

It also meant that any hope or doubt would be eliminated.

The jury were just twelve people, picked at random from an electoral register, to decide whether the prosecution or the defence were telling the truth.

Had Tyler not faced up to what he'd done, then twelve people, with little to no training or knowledge of the British legal system, without access to the full story of the case beyond what was either presented or debunked in front of them, would decide the fate of a sixteen-year-old kid, who'd been placed in a glass display case like a museum artifact.

For the second time in as many days, Townsend began to question the justice system.

The entire morning felt like it went along at a crawl, as the prosecution meticulously went through their case, with the evidence and the confession laid out and examined with a fine-toothed comb. The judge listened thoughtfully, interrupting with the odd question or request for clarification, each of which was answered swiftly and in great detail.

DCI Lowe was called to present a character statement on behalf of Tyler. Townsend couldn't help but roll his eyes as they laid out Lowe's credentials, as if he was accepting a lifetime achievement award, and Lowe was happy to confirm them. But as the seasoned detective who'd led the investigation, Lowe answered smoothly and in detail. As he confirmed Davis confessed to the murder, he looked at the young man and once again offered him an assuring nod.

Despite hammering one of the nails in Tyler's coffin, Lowe still cared.

Still gave a damn.

Townsend was up next and following Lowe instantly made him scrutinise his own appearance. With his thick Scouse accent and slightly more dishevelled look, Townsend instantly felt less credible in the eyes of the courtroom. He was glad there was no jury, not wanting twelve strangers, all without the training he had, to listen to his responses, critique his work, and decide whether he'd done a good job.

The whole concept felt flawed.

Townsend took the stand, and he felt a sickening feeling in the pit of his stomach as he recounted his steps to proving Tyler's guilt. How he'd realised that Tyler's coat was wet the night of the murder, despite his insistence on being in his room on his Xbox. He then explained how the game that Tyler played tracked in-game activity and upon accessing those activity logs, they could confirm that while Tyler had logged into the lobby of the game, he wasn't actually playing.

His answers seemed to fly over a few of the more senior heads in the room, but all in all, he seemed to do a pretty good job. Lowe gave him an encouraging wink as he stepped down, but as Townsend looked up at the young man on trial, Townsend could feel the hammer and the nail in his hands.

He turned to look at Simone, but she sat stoically, staring ahead, refusing to give Townsend any eye contact or the shed of a tear.

The sentencing wrapped by mid-afternoon, and the judge summarised what had been laid out before him, leaving no detail out of his account, before delivering the agreed upon verdict.

Guilty.

As the judge asked for order through the audible gasps and Tyler's sobbing, he began to read the young man his sentence, taking into account the young boy's age, and the reasons behind his actions. Therefore, he would spend the next two years in a juvenile correction facility, before beginning a minimum eight-year sentence at HMP Grendon Springhill upon his eighteenth birthday. Lowe turned to face Tyler, encouraging him to keep his chin up, and Tyler did so. There was no doubt in Townsend's mind that Lowe would do anything and everything to help the teenager through his sentence that the judge was bestowing upon him.

Townsend knew it had been the right thing to do. The young boy had killed a man in cold blood.

But it was Townsend who felt guilty.

And as Simone wept uncontrollably for her son, as Tyler stood, lip quivering and legs shaking, and Lowe watched on, grimacing at the system he helped to uphold, Townsend looked towards the empty seats of the jury, wondering how things would have played out had this had gone to trial.

Would twelve strangers have sent a young kid to prison for the rest of his life?

A decision that would bind them for the rest of their lives.

By the time Townsend finally made it out of the crown court, he was almost running, telling the annoyed Lowe that they needed to get back to the SCU as fast as possible.

CHAPTER TWENTY-FOUR

The call had woken King a little after three that morning, and she'd pushed herself up from her bed and groggily reached for her phone. She was still in her clothes, with the events of the past few days hitting her as she stepped through her front door, and she'd collapsed onto her bed and had fallen asleep before she scrambled to her pillow.

We have another missing person report.

That sat her bolt upright, like she'd just been seared with a cattle prod, and within minutes, she was showered, teeth brushed and was pulling on one of the many pant suits that lined her in-built wardrobe. Despite everything racing through her mind, the undoubted panic that was washing through the station, the terrified family she'd have to speak to, the shitstorm that Hall would bring to her door, she found herself wondering what colour jacket Elliott Manning might find most attractive.

Come on, Izzy. Head in the fucking game.

As she rushed from her home in Marlow to her car, under the cool spring breeze that swept through the darkness, she tried her best to get the criminal expert out of her head.

But it was proving difficult.

The past few years had been traumatic in ways she'd truly yet to unpack. Her primary focus, beyond the cases that had come through the SCU, had been either to her job or her sobriety. Her assignment to the SCU had been part of the fallout of her divorce from DCI Lowe, who had used his political sway to push her from CID when he took the reins. The SCU was meant to be a dead end for her, seemingly the first of several steps that would have eventually pushed her out of the Thames Valley Police. But she'd thrived, taking a team of underappreciated assets and moulding an effective and tightly-knit team that had already solved a few cases.

The other part of the fallout had been the drinking, which had seen King's dependency on a glass of wine turn to two, which in turn had lead to bottles. It was only when her addiction had been held up in front of her by a murderous priest did she finally take the necessary steps.

Got sober.

Stayed sober.

At no point during the past eight months, which she took day by day, did the idea of romance enter her mind.

But as she brought her car to life, pulled away and headed to High Wycombe, she had to make a concerted effort to shift Manning from her mind and put the missing person front and centre. It had only been four hours since she'd left the office, and when she returned and flicked on the lights, the murder board she and Manning had spent ages walking through stood proudly in the glow of the halogen bulbs above. An aroma of their Thai food still clung to the room, so King pushed open the windows for some fresh air. As always, they opened only a few inches. Another stark reminder that the job could take a severe toll on the officers, and giving them access to open windows was seen as a potential risk.

King had left messages with both Hannon and Swaby, informing them of Dale Ainsworth's disappearance, hoping they'd hit the ground running when they arrived at their usual time.

Her heart fluttered with pride, when both of them strode through the door an hour later, even if Hannon was complaining she had to make do with the machine coffee. King satisfied Hannon with the promise of a coffee and croissant from her favourite shop.

There was no call to Townsend.

He'd be pissed, King knew, but he had an important day in court to tie a bow on the Jamal Beckford murder, and hopefully, it would pull Townsend a little further away from Lowe. Her ex-husband had a magnetism that drew people towards him, and given that he'd shown a surprising amount of empathy for Townsend and Tyler Davis, King did worry that Townsend would soon fall under his spell.

She didn't want him to start thinking about moving along to CID.

Not yet, anyway. The truth was, Townsend was a natural detective, somehow balancing his eye for detail with his street smarts to bring a fresh perspective to any investigation. Her insistence that they follow the evidence was rooted in thorough police training and was the bedrock of any investigation. But a rogue thinker like Townsend was always worth their weight in gold.

Today, he and his mind needed to be elsewhere.

'Nic, I need you on CCTV,' King said as she clasped her hands together. 'Dale Ainsworth messaged his wife to say he was stopping off to pick up a few things on the way home. He was working out near Flackwell Heath, so trace his movements. I want a clear picture when we get back.'

'We?' Hannon asked, eyebrow raised. King turned to Swaby.

'We've got to go see the wife.'

Swaby never made a fuss. Whatever was required, she did with the utmost professionalism and her genuine, motherly nature would help when it came to dealing with terrified family members. A FLO was already in situ, and the drive from the police station to Bisham had been traffic free at that time of the morning. King and Swaby were greeted by the FLO, a DS Sam Matthews who King had known for a few years. DS Matthews had her hair pulled back in a loose ponytail, and her usually bright smile was also battling against the early start.

Eleanor Ainsworth was a jittery mess, and King let Swaby take the lead when it came to reassuring her that they were doing everything they could to find her husband. Taking the role that Townsend usually slotted into, King began asking the usual questions and Eleanor answered.

Dale sometimes headed out from work to a local pub.

Usually, he'd call ahead, but if he hadn't charged his phone, it might be tricky. And she'd tried countless times, but the phone wasn't even ringing, which led Swaby and King to share a knowing glance that the Executioner had likely switched it off.

Eleanor had become worried when it got near to eleven and called the police. They'd told her not to worry.

King was furious at that and made a note to read somebody the riot act when she returned to the station.

The marriage seemed like a normal, healthy one that had its ups and downs, but no jilted ex-lovers or extra-marital affairs to note.

No issues with neighbours or friends or ex-customers who had an axe to grind with Dale or the family.

The only thing of note was that he'd been having a few issues with the property developers, who'd been late with some payments and Dale had threatened to take legal action against them.

Something for them to look into.

When Swaby ran the names of Dr Asif Khalid and Maureen Allen by her, Eleanor's only knowledge of them was from what she had seen on the news. The mere whiff of a connection shook Eleanor to the core, as her terror took hold.

They were with Eleanor for a little over forty minutes, and by the time they were saying their goodbyes, her two boys, Joshua and Teddy, were still sound asleep. Her mother, Angela, arrived to help her through the tough time and King made the usual promise that they would do everything they could to find him.

'Is it him?' Eleanor had asked at the door. 'The killer in the mask?'

King and Swaby shared a concerned glance, enough to make Eleanor shudder slightly and skip a breath. King reached out and placed a calming hand on her elbow.

'We can't assume that,' she said warmly. 'But we'll do everything we can to find your husband, Mrs Ainsworth. If you need anything, please let DS Matthews know. We'll be in touch soon.'

The drive back to the station had been filled with dread, with Swaby calling the accountancy firm that held the accounts for Dale's business, and asking for the names of all the companies and people who had paid invoices so she could run her own checks on them. Although it was a necessary step, King couldn't help but feel it would be down a pathway that lead to nowhere. And another step closer to what the Executioner wanted.

Another kidnapping was going to send the station and the public into overdrive.

Another murder might just give Detective Superintendent Hall a heart attack.

By the time they returned to High Wycombe, the first wave of early commuters had awoken, and King stopped off at Hannon's favourite coffee shop to fulfil her promise. As she and Swaby re-entered the SCU office, Hannon's face lit up as she turned from her screen.

'Thanks, guv,' she said as King handed her the coffee and pastry. 'How was it?'

'Awful,' Swaby answered first. 'That poor woman.'

'She's understandably terrified,' King confirmed. 'How are you getting on?'

'Well, good news and bad news,' Hannon said, as the croissant crumbled from her lips. 'Good news is, I was able to track Dale's van the whole way to the mini market just opposite the sports centre. The bad news is, he has definitely been kidnapped.'

'Fuck.' King shook her head and then she and Swaby watched the harrowing footage. Dale arrived, headed into the store, while the same van that Hannon had tracked from his work site strategically blocked him in. Through the grainy CCTV footage, they watched Dale return, get lured to the back of the van, and then he was never seen again.

The man got behind the wheel and drove off.

'Have you been able to track the van?' King asked.

'A little,' Hannon said, pulling up another video. 'But we lose it when it gets towards Cookham.'

'Not much CCTV round there.' Swaby sighed.

'Dale's van?' King asked.

'I sent Boyd and Walsh to secure it. Figured we'd want to keep it where it was until—'

'I'll get it sorted,' King cut in. 'Good work, Nic.'

The young detective constable tried, but failed, to hide her smile.

'Michelle, can you look into those issues between Dale and the property developers?' King continued as she approached the murder board. 'I want to know who they are, their previous projects, and every single piece of communication between them and Dale.'

'On it, guv,' Swaby said, turning towards her laptop with the usual promise of efficiency.

'Nic, I need you to look back through Dale's previous jobs. See if there are any links to either Maureen Allen and or Dr Khalid. Also, see if there were any issues with late payments or any amendments made to invoices.' King pulled her hair back into a ponytail as she headed to the door. 'Anything that could have caused an issue. And get Boyd or Walsh to organise for that van to be brought back here.'

'Will do,' Nic said, slurping her coffee. 'You okay, guv?'

'Yeah. Just wish me luck?'

'Luck?'

'I have to go and tell Hall that an even bigger lump of shit is about to hit the fan.'

CHAPTER TWENTY-FIVE

'Jury duty!'

Townsend yelled out as he burst back into the SCU late that afternoon, followed by Lowe who seemed just as caught up in the excitement as the Scouse detective. Hannon spun in her chair in confusion, and Swaby looked up from her desk, equally puzzled. King and Manning emerged from her office, and Lowe instantly rolled his eyes upon seeing the doctor.

'Come again?' Hannon asked.

'Jury duty,' Townsend repeated as he headed towards the murder board.

'Jack, if you're telling me you need a week off in the middle of an investigation then I'm afraid I need to remind you that you're exempt from jury duty,' King said as she met him by the board. 'I've already had a new arsehole torn by Hall this morning, and we've got another missing person to find.'

'I know.' Townsend said glumly. 'But I—'

'—but you had something to take care of.' King looked to Lowe. Townsend did as well, and the DCI shrugged.

'I needed you on your game, Scouse,' he offered.

'How did it go?' King asked either of them.

'Eight years. Six at Grendon,' Lowe said with a sigh. 'I'll make sure I get round to see Tyler within his first few days at Aylesbury. Make sure he settles in okay.'

The team all shared a perplexed look, as Lowe's caring side wasn't one they saw often. Manning stepped forward to join King and Townsend and nodded to Lowe.

'You're full of surprises, Detective Chief Inspector.'

'Yeah? I've got another one for you.' Lowe dipped his hand into his pocket and returned it with a middle finger. Townsend had to suppress his smirk as Manning shook his head. 'But Scouse has something.'

'What is it?' King asked, ignoring Lowe's childish antics and turning to Townsend.

'We're looking for something that connects these people, right?' Townsend tapped the photos of Asif Khalid and Maureen Allen. A new photo, labelled *Dale Ainsworth* had also been added. 'What if they were on jury duty together?'

King looked to the board and then to Townsend.

'Based on?'

'A hunch,' Townsend said with clarity. 'What if the reason we can't connect these lives together is that they don't connect? We're so busy looking at what connects these people personally, but what if they're connected by circumstance? What was it the Executioner put in the video? *Their decisions* led them to this point?'

'Bingo,' Swaby clarified from her desk.

'I sat and watched a young kid get sentenced to prison today, and all I could think about was what would a jury have made of it all. And that got me to thinking…if my hunch is correct…' Townsend pointed to the Executioner. 'What if they made a decision that this guy didn't agree with?'

'And what if he's trying to put that right?' King said, joining Townsend's train of thought. 'Nic, can you—'

'Already on it, guv,' Hannon said, her eyes on the screen. She'd already reached out for access to the jury duty database, a constantly updated archive that logged which civilians had been called up for their civic duty. King turned back to the gathering around the board, and then, to Lowe's bafflement, turned to Manning. 'What do you think?'

'I think it's plausible,' Manning mused, as he rubbed his chin thoughtfully. 'The Executioner's words do pertain to a perceived lack of justice that he's trying to put right. That would also explain the dedication to capital punishment...'

King nodded along, but Townsend was now looking at Dale Ainsworth's photo.

'When was he taken?'

'Yesterday evening,' King informed him. 'His wife called it in late last night when he didn't get home from work. We've already tracked his last known location to the mini market in Bisham. CCTV shows him being taken in a van in the car park—'

'Same van?' Lowe asked, having invited himself to the conversation. King sighed. During the riot act that Hall had read her earlier that day, he'd made it very clear that Lowe and his team were now involved in the investigation.

All hands to the pump.

That was how it was sold to her, and although she knew that Lowe and CID's input would intensify the investigation, she was loath to admit to her ex-husband that they needed his help. Considering the way he'd just joined their briefing, she got the impression that Hall had already informed him.

'Different make and model,' King added.

'All likelihood, he switched it up,' Swaby added from her desk. 'The Maureen Allen murder—'

'Execution,' Manning interrupted.

'Execution...' Swaby continued '...was smack bang in the middle of town. Even with fake plates, he must have known we'd be all over that van like a rash.'

'And you reckon he has a police background?' Lowe said accusingly to Manning.

'I'd say, the way he handles the crime scenes, and the way Ainsworth was taken in a way that shielded our abductor from view...I'd say it's a strong possibility.'

'Where's the van, now?' Lowe asked, seemingly take control of the discussion.

'It's in the lot,' King said with authority. 'Forensics have been over it, but nothing immediate. No prints. No hair.'

'Clean as a whistle,' Townsend said to himself with a shake of the head.

'Dale's wife, Eleanor, gave us some information pertaining to some issues with the property developer Dale was working for. We're heading there in a second, Jack, so get ready.'

Townsend gave the thumbs up when Hannon clicked her fingers in the air but didn't look up from her screen.

'I've got it.' Her voice was high with excitement. 'Jack, you fucking genius.'

The entire team, along with Lowe and Manning, swiftly gathered around her computer, and Hannon clicked a few times and then pulled the document onto her larger screen.

'Nice one, Scouse,' Lowe said approvingly.

Townsend didn't want the kudos.

He was hellbent on finding the Executioner, especially as another life was on the line. But the document confirmed that Townsend's hunch had been correct. A case from a decade ago that went to Aylesbury Crown

Court. Hannon had scrolled and enlarged the jury names present for the hearing of a Phillip Myers.

Dale Ainsworth
Maureen Allen
Asif Khalid

All three were present, along with nine others whom King made very clear, were in serious danger. Hannon and Swaby were tasked with finding and contacting them.

Manning was needed elsewhere and made his apologies and left.

King and Townsend had a visit to a property developer who had no clue he was about to have a shit afternoon. As they all snapped into action, and King and Townsend marched through the High Wycombe Police Station, there was an energy that had been missing from the investigation now pulsing through the entire team.

There was still a man's life hanging in the balance.

Still a violent and meticulous killer at large.

A myriad of dots still to connect.

But as the entire SCU cracked on, and as King and Townsend pulled out of the station to head towards the development a few miles from Townsend's house, they couldn't help but feel that Townsend had just connected a major one.

CHAPTER TWENTY-SIX

'Right on your doorstep, huh?'

King gave Townsend a wry smile as they turned off 'Millionaires Row', turning left at the roundabout. Continuing over the roundabout for another few moments would have taken them into Flackwell Heath, and as they approached the large sign welcoming them to *Peach Trees: The Homes Of Tomorrow*, Townsend couldn't have been happier that she was wrong. While developing new homes was never a bad thing, the extortionate prices for the two-, three- or four-bedroom homes meant that the developers were hardly interested in 'affordable housing'. The first few streets had been completed at haste to provide any prospective buyers with a look at what the finished article would look like, and Townsend was struck at how dull it all seemed.

Every house the same as the next.

Identikit builds, all with the orange brickwork, grey front doors, and a patch of fake grass beside the driveways.

Everything built to look pristine, but on the smallest budget imaginable. But given High Wycombe's transport links with London, as well as its proximity to major motorways, it meant that every single one had sold, and those yet to be built had a long waiting list.

In essence, the developer had made a mint for as little as they could possibly manage.

As they cruised through the identical streets, the houses turned from fully inhabited to empty shells wrapped in scaffolding, and Townsend wondered how excited Dale Ainsworth would have been to have landed such a lucrative job. But based on what Dale's terrified wife had told them, things hadn't been going smoothly.

Late payments.

Arguments.

Hostilities.

As King pulled the car into the prospective buyer's car park, she looked at Townsend and could practically read his mind based on the stern look on his face. It had been another long and stressful day, and with the guilt of Tyler's still weighing heavily, Townsend was clearly desperate for something to fall into place.

'It might not be the Executioner,' she posed. 'We haven't had any word from him yet, and we have to—'

'Chase down every lead,' Townsend finished her sentence for her. He responded to her proud smile with one of his own. 'Eliminate all possibilities, right?'

'I'll make a detective out of you yet, Jack.'

As the two of them stepped out of the car and into the warm, spring afternoon, a burly man in an ill-fitting suit emerged from the sales office, which was nothing more than a makeshift hut put in at minimal expense.

'Welcome,' the man boomed, trying his best to shield his Eastern European accent. 'My name is Yuri. How can I help you fine people today?'

As King cast her eye over the vast construction sites, she took a lazy pull on her vape. Townsend took charge in responding to the salesman by flashing his warrant card.

'DS Jack Townsend. This is Detective Inspector King.'

The welcome quickly soured.

'What can I do for you?' Yuri's tone had shifted to almost non-compliant.

'We'd like to talk to you.' Townsend gestured to the hut. 'Shall we go inside?'

'I have nothing to say to the police.' The man was clearly anxious. 'I have filed all correct paperwork. We have been over this already.'

'We've never met, Mr Yuri,' King said as she stepped forward and showed her warrant card as well.

'Not you. Others.' He waved his hand dismissively. 'I am clean.'

'Well, personal hygiene aside, we have some questions for you about one of the contractors you have working on this site,' King continued approaching, seizing the authority. 'Mr Dale Ainsworth.'

'Plumber?' Yuri shrugged. 'He isn't here. No phone call. Nothing. At the amount he charges, he should be here every fucking day.'

'That's why we're here.' Townsend gestured to the hut once more, but Yuri's refusal to move meant they were having this conversation *al fresco*. 'His wife reported him missing late last night.'

Yuri's thick brow furrowed.

'Missing?' He snorted. 'The man is lazy. Probably drunk somewhere he doesn't want his wife to know about.'

Yuri smirked at King, who made it quite clear she didn't appreciate the joke. King turned, hands on hips, and surveyed the construction of the houses.

'How many properties do you own, Mr Yuri?'

'It's Mr Zerkhov,' Yuri said firmly. 'But you may call me Yuri.'

'How kind of you.'

'We have forty-six houses already occupied upon

arrival.' He waved towards the houses they'd passed. 'And another thirty-four in stages of construction, with planning for another forty next year.'

'Wow.' King faked her enthusiasm. 'That's a big job.'

'I am a big businessman, detective.' There was no humility as he pulled on the lapels of his tight jacket. 'And I am very busy. You find plumber, you tell him he is not to get paid today.'

'Well, that seems to be a running theme, doesn't it?' Townsend snapped, drawing the man's attention. 'Because we've been made aware of some payment disputes between yourself and Mr Ainsworth.'

'Says who?' The bravado was slipping.

'Says his wife. The person who reported him missing and as you can imagine, is worried sick.' Townsend stood tall, seizing control of the conversation. 'Now, we know that Mr Ainsworth was abducted because we have CCTV footage of him being thrown in the back of a van a few miles from here last night. So what would be helpful, Mr Zerkhov, is if you could give us your whereabouts yesterday evening at about six thirty?'

The man's eyes widened with anger. The team had already PNCed Yuri, and the men employed by his company, and beyond one DUI charge, it had come back clean. Swaby was trawling through Companies House and HMRC for any further information, but the fact that she hadn't reached out told King it had been clean enough.

Still, Yuri Zerkhov didn't need to know that.

'I did nothing.'

'Well, this will be straightforward then, won't it?' Townsend looked around at the huge construction project. 'Or, we could take you down to the station and we can go through every single detail of your company until we find what we need. Up to you.'

King followed Townsend's glare at the man, impressed

by his authority, and Yuri stood for a few moments, weighing up his options. Finally, with a sigh of resignation, he motioned for the detectives to follow him, and the trio headed towards the hut across the gravelled car park. The office was neatly furnished, with a comfy sofa area that surrounded a marble coffee table, which was coated in brochures of the 'luxury' homes on offer. Yuri walked past the shelving units that were decorated with random ornaments and classic books that Townsend was certain the man hadn't read. Yuri took a seat behind his plush desk and started trawling through the computer. Townsend and King stood, ignoring the offer to take a seat, and eventually, Yuri turned his screen to face them.

'I was here last night.'

But he wasn't alone. King rolled her eyes slightly, as the CCTV camera for the office showed footage of Yuri sitting at his desk, while a young lady's head was buried in his crotch. Townsend focused on the timestamp.

There was no way that Yuri could have been in two places at once.

'I take it that young lady won't want a visit from the police?' King said through gritted teeth. Yuri sheepishly shook his head and shut the video down.

'I am busy man. I have needs.'

'Get the vehicle registrations,' King said to Townsend as she headed to the door. 'I can't say it's been a pleasure, Mr Zerkov.'

King stepped out, and Townsend watched her head back to the car amid plumes of vapour. He turned back to Yuri, who shrugged.

'You know how it is,' Yuri said with a cheeky grin.

'Vehicle registrations. Now.'

Ten minutes later, Townsend emerged from the hut with printouts for all the vehicles registered or hired by the company over the past six months. As he crunched across the gravel towards King's car, he shot a glance back to Yuri, who watched them leave with interest.

'What a charming man,' King said dryly as Townsend joined her in the car.

'You think he's involved?' Townsend asked already knowing the answer.

'Nope.' King started the engine. 'But we have to be sure.'

When they arrived back at the station, they had all the confirmation they needed that Dale Ainsworth had been taken by the Executioner, and Townsend's theory about jury service gained more weight.

Hannon greeted them at the door to the office.

'We have another message.'

Her voice was shrouded in misery. King and Townsend stepped in, their gaze reaching beyond Swaby, Dr Manning, and the increasingly busy murder board, to the screen on the wall.

A new message had been sent by the Executioner, but they both knew what it would say before they read it.

The execution of Dale Ainsworth will premiere at 5 p.m. tomorrow.

By the hand of The Executioner.

CHAPTER TWENTY-SEVEN

Darkness.

As Dale slowly regained consciousness, he opened his eyes and a mild panic set in. As he blinked, nothing came into focus, and as the effects of the chloroform seeped away, his memory came flooding back.

The van that had blocked him in.

The rugged man who'd called him for help at the back.

The struggle.

And now, darkness.

He tried to take a deep breath, but the texture of the fabric that had been wrapped over his head clung to his face, and he began to panic. He groaned, forcing the sound to eek out around the cloth bound across his mouth and as he reached for it, he felt his hands press against the base of his spine.

They were tied.

So were his ankles.

Wherever he was, he wasn't going anywhere, and with no clue as to where he was, he began to thrash his body, his ribs slamming against the cold, solid concrete below. As his muffled groans of pain intensified, he heard the sound of a metal shutter clanking in its bracket before it slammed down with considerable force. The impact echoed throughout the room, and Dale felt his entire body stiffen as the sound of heavy boots grew louder as they approached him. Fingers spread out across the top of his head, and in one sharp pull, the black hood was removed and the blinding lights of the room hit him.

Dale had to squint, blinking through the initial daze, and then, as his sight fell more into focus, he felt his body freeze in fear once again.

His own morbid curiosity had led him to the videos on social media, of the final moments of a few names that he thought he recognised. Faces he felt were vaguely familiar. Hideous footage of a man shot in the head while strapped to a post.

The haunting imagery of an elderly woman, decapitated by a guillotine.

In both, he'd seen the black leather mask, and the unforgettable white cross that was stitched from corner to corner.

The same mask that now stared him right in the face.

Bound and gagged, Dale tried his best to control his breathing, and he arched his neck from side to side to take in his surroundings. It was a dank lock-up, floodlit by a few bulbs that had been hung from wooden beams that ran across the ceiling. The exposed brickwork was old and chipped, and beyond the masked man who squatted before him, he could see the same van that had trapped him in the car park.

The realisation began to set in.

He'd been targeted.

He'd been fooled.

And he'd been taken.

On the far wall, a wooden workbench was illuminated by another lamp, and Dale could see numerous chains piled up messily, with some of them hanging down over the rough, splintered edges. Hanging on the wall were a collection of tools, along with a map of High Wycombe, which had numerous lines scrawled across it in red marker pen.

The Executioner didn't move, his muscular forearms hanging over his knees as he seemed to be watching his captor struggle. Slowly, with a gloved hand, he reached out towards Dale, whose fight or flight kicked in and he began to struggle, arching his head away from the outstretched fingers that began to claw at his face.

The gag was removed.

'What the fuck do you want with me?' Dale spat angrily, writhing on his side, trying to summon the strength to break the plastic ties that were now drawing blood from his wrists.

The Executioner lifted a finger to where his lips might have been.

Dale ignored him.

'Help!' he shouted as loud as he could, tensing his body for the expected blow from the killer.

Nothing.

He peered back at the Executioner, who once again lifted a finger to his mask.

'Fuck you!' Spat Dale and then arched his head in the direction of the metal shutter. 'Help me. Somebody!'

As he screamed, the Executioner stood, rummaged on his workbench, and then squatted back down beside Dale.

In his hand, he held his phone.

It stopped Dale dead.

The image on the screen was of his wife Eleanor, leaning into the car to help their youngest, Teddy, with his seat belt. Like his younger brother, Joshua was in his school uniform. It was taken within the last few days, but the message was immediately clear. The Executioner had access to the people who Dale held dear, and if he continued to make noise, they would be in danger.

Dale fell quiet, and despite challenging himself to hold his nerve, he felt a tear loop over his eyelid and slide down his cheek.

Two hands wrenched hold of his shoulders and sat him up, and Dale looked around, in hope of an exit he knew wasn't there. The local media had been awash over the past few days with reports on how the masked killer had been several steps ahead of the police, and how there seemed little chance of stopping him from striking again.

Dale was beginning to lose all hope.

Hope that he would see his family again.

Hope that he would survive the night.

Surprisingly, the Executioner lifted a bottle of water and unscrewed the cap, then held it to his lips. Greedily, Dale guzzled as much as he could. Once he'd done, the Executioner unpacked a store-bought sandwich and crammed one of them into Dale's mouth. It was bland, but he hadn't realised how hungry he was. As Dale chomped down on the food, the Executioner lifted a leather clad device and held it to Dale's throat. Without latching it around his prisoner's neck, the Executioner dropped it back onto the bench and then waited patiently for Dale to finish eating.

As he swallowed the last few remnants, Dale looked up at his captor, his eyes watering and his voice breaking.

'You're not going to let me live, are you?' he asked feebly.

The Executioner shook his head.

Dale wept.

'If I stay quiet, will you promise me you won't hurt my family?'

Dale's head was down, and he was now weeping uncontrollably, as the full realisation that he was heading into his final hours took hold. The Executioner took a step forward, and once again squatted down before him. He reached out and gathered the gag and the black hood in his hands before he turned to Dale, who looked at him with resignation.

'Your family will be safe,' the gruff voice spoke. Then, to Dale's shock, he pulled off his mask and fixed Dale with a furious glare. 'You, however, will pay for what you've done.'

Before Dale could respond, the man roughly fitted the gag back around Dale's mouth, securing it tightly at the back of his skull. Dale struggled and wriggled, but a swift swing of a heavy boot to his stomach soon calmed him down. As he balled up and gasped for air, Dale felt the hood slide over his head, and everything went black.

Then, he felt the prick of a syringe in his neck, and as the world began to fade, and his consciousness began to slip from his skull, he held onto one worrying thought.

He should have thought about his family.

Eleanor.

Joshua.

Teddy.

But as his world went blurry, and he slumped unconsciously to the concrete, he clung on to one final thought.

He had no idea who the man under the mask was.

CHAPTER TWENTY-EIGHT

Dale Ainsworth was found dead at six thirty-five that morning.

The entire SCU had worked diligently through the evening into the early hours of the morning, with one eye pointlessly on the ticking clock posted to the untraceable link. Manning had told them it was a pointless endeavour.

'The pattern has formed,' he said coldly. 'This isn't a game of cat and mouse. It isn't a serial killer out to prove that they're smarter than the police. For all intents and purposes, they don't seem to care how you react. No clues. No hints. No rubbing it in your face.'

'I'd say beheading someone down the fucking road from us is rubbing it on our faces,' King had quipped.

'True. Our killer is brazen. I'll give him that.'

While Townsend had gone through the painstaking job of investigating every registered or hired vehicle that had been used by Yuri Zerkhov, King had tasked Swaby with going through all the contractors who'd been involved with the project. Most of them were legitimate businesses, run proudly by the owners who were just happy being their own bosses. A few were a little harder to trace, preferring a more cash-in-hand approach.

Even still, none of them had anything, other than where they currently worked, that linked them to Dale Ainsworth.

Nobody with a grudge.

Nobody who would want him dead.

None of the registered or hired vans met the specifics of the one from the mini market car park, and although they'd traced the plates to a car registered in a neighbouring second-hand car lot, they had nothing to go on.

No trace of Dale Ainsworth or where the Executioner had taken him.

And less than a day before his murder was displayed for the world to see.

And, given the pattern of the executions so far, it meant even less time before Dale himself would meet his maker.

Hannon had been doing her best to hunt down the files pertaining to the case that all three had been jurors for, but as always, speed bumps appeared in what should have been a flat road. The past eight years had been digitalised, uploaded onto the new network of the court system, but nothing stretching back a decade. As Hannon relentlessly harried the administration department for their location, King saw her eyes getting heavy, so she sent her home. The team was working round the clock, but they needed to rest. With the additional support from Lowe's team, they were able to continue the investigation throughout the night and pick things up in the morning.

She told them she'd see them bright and early.

Only, they'd hoped it would have been in the SCU office.

King had received the call the moment the body had been found, and she'd called her team with the location.

One by one, they arrived, waved through the tape by PC Walsh who'd drawn the short straw of working the police cordon, which this time was surrounded by the eager journalists who were hardly containing their excitement at a murder investigation that was snowballing out of control.

'Morning,' Townsend had said glumly as he lowered his window on approach. The beefy officer approached.

'We any closer to catch this bastard?' Walsh said with anger.

'We're working on it.'

That was all Townsend could muster. Because Walsh's question wasn't without merit. As a man who'd worked his entire career in the heart of the nation's capital, Walsh had probably expected to see out his final years in the sleepier town of High Wycombe. Yet here he was, his third murder of the week, and like so many others, was clearly losing faith in the SCU.

The business park in Loudwater was less than a few miles from Flackwell Heath, and Townsend waited for Walsh to move the police tape that blocked off the entrance and he wondered how much flack Hall would get from the managers of the large stores that comprised its residency. A hardware store, a carpet shop and a home furnishing franchise all had outrageously large outlets, none of which would be open for at least the day.

A life had been taken.

Yet people's own lives would still take precedence.

Townsend parked up next to Hannon's car, and stepped out, where he could see her and King looking up at the horrendous final presentation of Dale Ainsworth.

The body was swaying ever so slightly, the skin drained of its colour. A good six feet from the ground, the dead body was suspended in the air by the thick leather collar that had been strapped tightly around his neck. From the back of it, a chain ran up, looping over the low hanging street lights that had been selected to add a 'touch of class' to the run-down park. The chain pulled tightly back, where it had been affixed to a trolley barrier in thick loops, with a padlock holding it in place.

Dale Ainsworth had been executed by hanging.

As the three of them looked up at the body, King tried and failed to stifle a yawn. Behind them, Swaby arrived, guiding her car around the corner and into the business park. At least the murder scene was a little less public than Maureen Allen's.

Small victory.

But none of them felt anything more than a failure.

'We need to go and speak to Eleanor,' King said as she lifted her phone. 'And we need to find this fucker before we run out of FLOs.'

As King stepped away, vape in one hand, phone pushed to her ear with the other, Townsend turned to Hannon, who stood with her arms wrapped around her slight frame. Hannon was a great detective, but the darker side of the job never sat well with her. Put her in front of a computer and ask her to find a needle in a haystack, and she'd devise a magnet. But looking up at the murdered man, had turned her as white as a sheet.

'You okay?' Townsend asked, slipping into his role as her makeshift older brother.

'Not really.' Hannon looked up at Ainsworth and then looked away. 'You know, I always wanted to be a police officer. From like, the age of twelve.'

'Same.' Townsend nodded. She looked at him in disbelief, and he shrugged. 'My father was one. All I ever wanted to be the moment I saw him put on his uniform.'

'Ah. I just wanted to help people. I would watch those TV shows, you know, not the ones that glamourise the job. The twenty-four hours, the ones that show you the shit that we all go through, day in and day out.'

Townsend scoffed.

'And that made you want to get involved?'

'I just saw people who needed help. And I saw good people trying to do their best and fighting a losing battle.' Hannon looked over to King, who had finished her call and was updating Swaby who, as always, was a picture of calm. 'This feels like that.'

'Like what?'

'A losing battle.'

Townsend regarded Hannon, who seemed trapped in a spiral of self-doubt. Ever since she'd been attacked while on the beat, resulting in a permanent injury to her spine, it didn't take much for her to question her role.

Townsend never would.

'Hey. Nic.' He waited for her to look at him. 'We're all feeling it. Okay? This killer, they are good. But we've faced this before and we came through, okay? So why don't you go and grab a coffee, head back to base, and keep digging on that court case? I'll stick around here.'

Hannon took a minute and then reached out and squeezed Townsend's arm.

'Thanks, Jack.' She forced a smile. 'You just don't want to order my coffee, do you?'

'He gives me a weird look every time.'

Hannon chuckled and headed off, offering a wave to King and Swaby as she headed to her car. King wouldn't question the decision to send her back. The longer they worked together, the more King was entrusting Townsend with authority. Swaby joked that she was grooming him, but there was certainly some truth in it. When King returned to his side, with Swaby in tow, they said their goodbyes to head off to inform a terrified woman that her husband, the father of her kids, and the main breadwinner of their household had been brutally murdered.

'This is the job.' King shrugged, as Townsend wished

them luck. The four words the team used whenever they thought things might get too heavy.

They had all signed up for this.

All of them wanted to make a difference, and the only way they could now was to manage the fallout of another murder and throw everything behind catching the killer.

The Executioner.

Always three steps ahead.

As if they knew what and where the team would be looking.

Manning's theory of them being of a police background was starting to gain weight, and Townsend wondered how heavy it would get before they started looking inward, rather than outward.

And that thought process intensified when his eye caught something on the ground, a few feet from the railing that was wrapped in the murderous chains. Carefully, he squatted down, and with his pen, he shifted it over.

It was a metal pin.

And as he turned it over, Townsend felt his heart sink.

And his rage grow.

CHAPTER TWENTY-NINE

Although Townsend parked in his usual spot behind High Wycombe Police Station, he didn't enter the building. Instead, he made the perilous trip across the 'Magic Roundabout' on foot, crossing three of the six miniature roundabouts at considerable risk. Despite each one of them offering a safe path via a zebra crossing, Townsend was aware of the strange panic that flooded through drivers, unfamiliar with the concept. As he dashed across the third one, he headed up the slight incline, into the entrance of High Wycombe Hospital, and made his way towards the morgue. It wasn't lost on him how upsetting it was that he'd visited on a number of occasions.

However, the beaming smile of Dr Mitchell lightened the dark feeling.

'Well, well, well,' she said as she opened the secure door from the inside. 'What a treat.'

Townsend smiled politely. King had assured him that her 'interest' was just a bit of fun to add a little levity to what must have been heavy day after heavy day, but sometimes, Townsend did wonder if that was true.

'How are you?' he asked as he followed her in, walking

through the brightly lit corridors that felt like they were overcompensating for the darkness that lay ahead.

'Oh, you know me,' Mitchell said, her white lab coat swaying behind her as she walked. 'Rooting around in dead bodies. Cracking case after case. The usual.'

'Sounds fun,' Townsend smirked.

'Oh, you have no idea.'

Mitchell pressed her security pass to the reader, and a harsh buzz signalled the unlocking of the thick security doors to the morgue. As they entered, she ran off the usual health and safety protocols with such ease it was like she was reciting the alphabet. She led Townsend through, and his eye was instantly drawn to the metal table where a body was covered by a sheet.

'Maureen,' he said with a sigh. Townsend had been at the crime scene, and Mitchell clearly knew that.

'I've sewn the head back on.' She assured him and then drew her lips into a thin line. 'It was pretty grim, but we can at least hide it with a scarf for the family. Very unpleasant, though.'

'I know. I was there,' Townsend said with authority, and then motioned for her to lift the sheet. She hadn't been lying. 'Anything you can tell me besides the obvious?'

'What, that she died by decapitation?' Mitchell half-joked and then pointed to the decimated neck. 'She was drugged. Thankfully, the blade wasn't a few inches lower otherwise we wouldn't have found the puncture mark here. We'll get the full tox reports back soon but I'd wager it's the same as what we found in Dr Khalid's body.'

'Any…' Townsend began and Mitchell read his mind.

'No signs of any sexual assault. No signs of any assault really, besides the…you know…beheading.' Mitchell had her ways. 'A little light bruising on one arm, which would suggest she'd been lying on a hard surface for a while.

Some other sporadic bruises, most likely from being in the back of the van.'

'Any DNA traces?' Townsend was keen to get back to the station.

'None. No skin under the nails, no random hairs.' Mitchell blew out her cheeks. 'Just like Dr Khalid, the body is clean. Whoever did this was careful. Prepared.'

'Knowledgeable,' Townsend added with a grimace. 'I'd wager the same when Ainsworth arrives.'

'Ainsworth?' Mitchell looked up; eyebrow raised.

'Body number three.' Townsend shook his head. 'Found hanging this morning. Have you not been told?'

'It's been crazy here.' She blew out her cheeks in exasperation. 'Hanged? Jesus Christ.'

'I think we're going to need more than religion for this one,' Townsend said. 'Thanks, doctor. Can you send everything through?'

'Will do.' She called out after Townsend as he headed towards the exit, 'And, Jack…'

He turned to look at her.

'…Be careful out there, all right? All of you.'

Dr Mitchell had two settings. When there was a body on the table, she was as professional as anything. In conversation, she was a ball of energy with a quick wit and a devilish tongue. So, hearing her speak with such genuine fear and compassion caught Townsend slightly off guard.

He gave her a reassuring smile.

'You know me.'

'Exactly.' Mitchell mirrored his smile. 'Which is why I'm saying it.'

As he headed back towards the station, Townsend reached into his jacket and ran his fingers over the evidence bag that contained what he'd found at the scene. His stomach flipped, hoping it wasn't true, but he had to follow the evidence. That's what King had always made clear, and even if it eliminated the smallest possibility, it was still part of the investigation.

Still a win.

DS Swaby often joked that if the detective shows on TV were really on the money, then nobody would watch it. They'd be put to sleep within one episode, as there was only so much red tape, paperwork and blind alleys people could devote their attention to.

But all of it was important.

Every visit to a suspect.

Every file they read.

Every hunch they followed.

People were dying, and as Townsend headed through the side door of High Wycombe Police Station, he knew that if there was even a sliver of a chance that he was right about this, then he had to see it through.

It could save someone's life.

Townsend stepped into the SCU office, where Hannon, as always, had her eyes glued to the screen and her fingers clacking keys. She nodded to his desk.

'It's probably cold now.'

The coffee she'd bought him was lukewarm to the touch, something Townsend didn't mind, and he took a sip and smiled.

'It's fine.'

'You're gross,' Hannon joked. 'I thought you'd be back a little sooner.'

'I had to stop in at the hospital. Maureen.'

'I bet Dr Mitchell loved that.' Hannon chuckled. The pathologist's seeming attraction to Townsend was a source of humour in the office. 'Anything?'

'Well, she confirmed that Maureen Allen died by decapitation.' Townsend perched on his desk and sipped his coffee again. 'Beyond that, nothing. Just like Khalid. A perfect execution.'

Townsend glared at the murder board, visualising where the photos of Ainsworth's demise would be placed. He didn't realise he was frowning.

'You okay, Jack?'

'Something's not right.' He was talking to both her and himself. 'There's planning, but then there's knowing. Think of Baycroft. Think of Miller. They'd planned their kills for months, maybe years in Miller's case.'

'Don't remind me.' Hannon shuddered at the thought.

'But they weren't this good. This clean.' Townsend pushed off from the desk and lazily approached the board, his eyes scouring the collage of evidence. 'It's like the Executioner knows exactly what tiny mistakes people make that allow us to catch them.'

'You think Manning is right?' Hannon asked, leaning back against the support of her chair. 'They have police training?'

Townsend ran his fingers over the metal pin in his pocket.

'Or knowledge,' Townsend said with gritted teeth. 'You heard from the guv?'

'Not yet.' Hannon returned to her screen. 'She's still with Eleanor Ainsworth. That poor family. Being told that their whole world has just been destroyed.'

'This is the job,' Townsend said glumly, and then arched his neck to peer into King's office at the far end of the room. 'Where's Dr Manning?'

'Dunno.' Hannon shrugged. 'Wasn't here when I got in.'

Townsend left it. The early starts and late nights made it feel like the days were just melting together, and the concept of time, beyond watching the countdown clock of a murder, had fallen by the wayside. Manning was a paid consultant, most likely expensive, meaning his hours were more precious to Detective Superintendent Hall than the rest of the team. So far, Manning had been an asset, not just in helping them build a psychological profile on the Executioner and the potential reasons for his rampage, but also in the office.

He'd integrated well with the team and had seemed to have a soft spot for DI King, which the rest of them had noticed. Despite her pushback, King did seem to have a spring in her step.

It also didn't hurt his chances that he'd dealt with DCI Lowe's ego pretty well, too.

'What do you think of him?' Townsend asked, turning back to Hannon. 'Manning.'

'He's pretty cool.' Hannon looked up. 'The guv clearly likes him. So does Hall, come to think of it. And he's been on the money so far.'

'He has, hasn't he?' Townsend said, a hint of suspicion in his voice. Before Hannon could question it, he reached into his jacket, pulled out the evidence bag and placed it on her desk. Hannon picked it up, took a few seconds to glance over it and then looked up at Townsend with a confused frown.

'What's this?'

'I found it this morning. I had forensics log it at the murder scene and told them I needed it right now.'

A penny dropped in Hannon's brain so visually, Townsend was shocked he didn't hear it too.

'Have you told the guv?'

'Not yet,' Townsend said, retrieving the item and pocketing it again. 'But I can't sit on this.'

Hannon agreed, and Townsend looked back to King's office, and then to the murder board.

He was going to follow his hunch.

And he wasn't sure if he wanted to be right.

CHAPTER THIRTY

Guilt was for the guilty.

That had always been DCI Lowe's viewpoint throughout his stellar career. Although he may have bent the rules on the odd occasion, there had always been a righteous end to justify the means. But bending the law was different to breaking it, and that was something that Lowe had stood by.

Guilty people were eventually caught, tried and sent to their punishment.

Tyler Davis was guilty.

The teenager had watched his mother being abused by the man she'd chosen to marry, and in the end, Tyler decided to use extreme measures to protect her. Measures that would see him spend a minimum of eight years in prison. Only two of them would be spent in juvie, and it meant by the time Tyler got out, he'd begin his adult life in his mid-twenties with untold horrors behind him.

There would be little waiting for him on the outside, and Lowe had made a vow to both Tyler and his mother that he'd do everything he could to be there for Tyler throughout it all.

Even though Tyler had confessed to killing Jamal Beckford, it was Lowe who was racked with guilt.

He gazed out through the glass wall at his office, watching as the CID unit was in full flow, with his detectives working as diligently as he demanded to try to bring down the Executioner. Since the first message had been posted by the killer, he'd been leaning on Hall to let him take the case. It had nothing to do with his history with King.

That was just that. History.

It had been fun for a while to needle her, but in truth, it was easier to deal with the shame of his infidelity by trying his best to push her out of the team. Looking at her reminded him of his failings, and he tried his best to mask those by leaning into the bravado that seemed to hold significant charm over the rest of the team. They rallied behind him, and despite King being the one who had been betrayed, he'd managed to paint her out to be the villain.

Another thing he wasn't proud of.

But what really had got to him over the past year was how swiftly his ex-wife had turned her life around.

The SCU was supposed to be a dumping ground for CID and the rest of the Thames Valley Police. A storage facility for capable detectives who just didn't fit the status quo.

DC Hannon was as bright a detective as Lowe had come across, but her physical limitations and crippling self-doubt meant she was better placed in a team that would have minimal impact.

DS Townsend was an outsider who'd been awarded his position as an apology for his time spent undercover. Although the man was tougher than beaten leather, and Lowe knew firsthand that the man possessed a hammer of a right hook, he'd pushed Townsend to the SCU as he didn't want to babysit a novice.

And King, she wasn't only a constant reminder of his own faults, but she had plenty of her own, and by pushing her into the professional abyss would just push her deeper into the bottle.

But she'd turned it around.

King had given up the drink, that much was clear, and her clarity of thought and the freshness in her skin meant she glowed when she walked into a room. She'd sparked a confidence in Hannon that had seen the young detective flourish, and her eye for detail and technical skills put most of cybercrime to shame.

Much to Lowe's envy, Townsend and Hannon were loyal to King, and Lowe often wondered if there were any members of his team who'd run through walls for him like King's team would for her. Even DS Swaby, a woman who'd been part of the CID furniture for years, had made the full-time switch from his command to King's.

Because despite the horrors they'd faced over the past year, and the obstacles they had to scale, the SCU had delivered.

That was why Hall had given them the case. And despite Lowe's insistence, it was why it would remain with them.

Feeling agitated, Lowe pushed his bulky frame from his chair, adjusted his tie and ambled out of his office, casting his eye over his team. One of the younger detectives noticed and sat up.

'Everything all right, guv?'

'How's the investigation into Yuri Zerkhov going?'

'It's going,' the detective said, gesturing to his screen. 'I mean, he's got a few links to some shady people, but nothing that really screams masked murderer.'

'Well, keep going. If we can scratch his name off the list, then we've done a good job.' Lowe spoke with authority. 'And besides, if you dig enough shit up, we can nail him for some of it.'

The young detective dived back into his work with a renewed vigour, and Lowe glanced over at CID's own version of the Executioner murder board. It was smaller, had a little less detail than the SCU's, and it wasn't lost on Lowe that his team was the one doing the 'busy work'.

But all help was help, and when there was a killer on the loose, one as methodical as the Executioner was turning out to be, then Lowe would toe the line and play his part. He glanced down at the expensive watch around his wrist.

It was only ten past ten.

The days just melted together, and Lowe had become accustomed to the comfort of the sofa in his office most nights.

The rest of the Thames Valley Police could question his attitude, or his macho persona, but one thing they never could, was his commitment to the cause.

With a dramatic yawn, Lowe asked the team if any of them wanted a coffee, and after taking down a few orders, he grabbed his jacket and headed out for some fresh air. It wasn't much, but the gesture of getting his team a 'treat' would boost morale. As he marched past the SCU door, he almost collided with another sturdy detective.

'Jesus, Scouse,' Lowe said with a slight startle. 'Where's the fire?'

Townsend didn't offer anything resembling a polite smile. If anything, he looked anxious.

'You got a minute?' Townsend asked. Lowe looked interested. 'Sir?'

'Up for a walk?' Lowe nodded to the stairwell. 'Coffee's on me.'

Townsend fell instep alongside the DCI, but he waited

to speak until they were outside the station itself. Lowe turned and headed towards the town centre, but on Townsend's recommendation, headed to the coffee shop just up the hill.

'So...what's up?' Lowe asked. 'You've rethought my offer?'

Lowe knew that wasn't the case, but if it wasn't worth a try, it would at least lighten the atmosphere.

'A little busy to be thinking about my career right now,' Townsend replied.

'I know. A third body.' Lowe shook his head. 'If it helps, we're getting nowhere with Zerkhov. The man might be a criminal, but it's looking unlikely he's our guy.'

Townsend shifted uncomfortably as they stopped outside the coffee shop. Lowe threw out his arms in frustration.

'Scouse. Stop pussyfooting around. What is it?'

'You know Manning theorised the killer might have a forensic background?'

Lowe rolled his eyes. Townsend wasn't sure if it was Manning's calm intellect or obvious attraction to the man's ex-wife that irked Lowe most.

'Oh, yes. The expert. Hall's paying that man through the teeth to theorise that our killer is a *dangerous man*?' Lowe shook his head. 'So what, you think he's right?'

Townsend gave a few anxious looks around, checking that the coast was clear, before he reached into his jacket pocket. As the warm, spring morning settled across the town, and the sun cast a bright glow across the surrounding buildings, he placed the evidence bag in the Lowe's hand.

'I think he might be.'

Like Hannon, it took Lowe a few seconds to recognise what he'd been handed. The penny dropping was louder, and instead of the apprehension that accompanied Hannon's realisation, Lowe's was awash with excitement.

'Well, fuck me.'

Lowe was already marching back towards the station with Townsend, aware that he owed a few members of his team a cup of coffee at some point, but when he told them why, they'd have no choice but to understand...

CHAPTER THIRTY-ONE

Being dropped into a well-oiled machine was always the trickiest part of the job, which was saying something. Manning had studied for years, interviewed some of the most dangerous people in the country, and written thesis after thesis on some of the most depraved and stomach-churning acts of violence humanity had ever know. It was his job to understand how the mind of a killer worked, to try to not only understand, but to empathise with their viewpoint, and in doing so, subjected himself to both verbal and mental abuse.

But getting to grips with a team dynamic always held more apprehension, especially in an environment as tightly coiled as a police station. In all industries, there were numerous personalities that would undoubtedly collide, and it was one of the few real-world lessons young people were taught as they made their way towards adult life. By getting a job, you would be thrust into a daily situation where your performance was monitored, results were expected and the people you would spend more time with than your own family, could well be the worst type of people to spend your time with.

Introverts mixing with extroverts.

Egos clashing.

The day-to-day life of secondary school prepared the attendees more for adult life than any subject lesson could.

Manning had always been a pretty open-minded and easy-going person, but he'd witnessed countless times someone being forced to stand up in front of a group to present something, despite it clearly not being in their wheelhouse.

It would be labelled as 'development'.

But in the workplace, 'development' usually meant that you do as you're asked and be thankful for the opportunity.

For Manning, being his own boss meant the opportunities that came his way were ones he'd selected or put his name forward for, and the chance to work alongside the Specialist Crimes Unit in the Thames Valley Police was one that he'd desired. Despite their humble attitude, the SCU had a burgeoning reputation for bringing down two serial killers over the past year, and that had echoed throughout the justice sector. When Gordon Baycroft had been apprehended, Manning had been working for the Met, helping them build a portfolio of potential profiles for them to dip into when needed.

During the cold winter, and Gemma Miller's vengeful rampage, Manning had been running a series of guest lectures at Nottingham University and had followed the case via the news and his connections, with interest. When the opportunity was thrown out by DSI Hall to assist the team, Manning had jumped at the chance. Hall was a firm hand with a soft touch and was keen to avoid what had essentially happened.

The situation was spiralling out of control, and Hall had numerous reasons, beyond the safety of the public, to bring the Executioner's reign of terror to an end. A man of his experience and savvy meant he was a few moves away from an even more senior role within the Thames Valley Police, and currying favour with the likes of the Mayor and other influential people would only help his cause.

The last thing he needed was another long list of murders under his watch, and Manning had been drafted in to try to stop that from happening.

And Hall was just one of the powerful characters that had been thrown into the blender that was the High Wycombe Police Station.

DCI Lowe was the archetypal alpha, a man who matched his broad physique with the need to be the biggest and loudest personality in the room. It clearly had its merits, and despite Manning's assumptions that the man wasn't particularly liked, he could see that Lowe was respected by many.

And he seemed to know it.

Townsend was an intriguing man. Clearly, he was a more than capable detective and carried with him an understated notion of menace. He was big, muscular, and had just enough gravel in his voice to convince you that he was as tough as he looked. King had mentioned he'd been undercover, and when Manning watched Townsend work, he found the detective's methods unique. He asked questions most wouldn't, would accept what he couldn't change, but seemed determined to try, anyway.

Then there was King.

Just as his mind began to wander, Manning snapped himself out of it and stepped into the SCU office. Unlike the team itself, he wasn't on call, and Hannon quickly brought him up to speed.

Another body found that morning.

King and Swaby were with the recently widowed.

Townsend had gone to chase a lead.

Manning was playing catch up, but he could sense a

little apprehension in Hannon, who kept strangely flicking her attention to his jacket. She was trying to be subtle, but failed, but Manning couldn't place why.

'I have my database access now,' he told her with a warm smile. 'Send through the crime scene write up and I'll start building my notes.'

Hannon agreed, and then awkwardly returned to her screen. Manning was an expert in his field, and he would have been able to pick up on her change in attitude towards him even if she'd been good at hiding it.

'Everything okay, DC Hannon?' he asked softly.

She forced a smile. It clearly wasn't. But she lied all the same.

'Just a heavy morning.'

Manning accepted he wouldn't get the truth, and gave her another smile.

'Well, I'm here if you need me.'

That was the end of that, and as he made himself comfortable in King's office, he wondered what was truly going on. Hannon was usually a ray of sunshine in the gloom of the investigation, but the morning's events had darkened that cloud. But Manning could sense it was his presence, and as he logged into the database with his guest credentials, he made a note to speak to King about it.

They needed to talk.

Footsteps from outside drew his attention, and his excitement at his office buddy's return was quickly trampled when he saw the burly sight of DCI Lowe marching across the office towards him, followed by a more reserved Townsend. Not wanting to escalate the apparent confrontation, Manning sat back in his chair and politely greeted them both as they stepped in.

'Morning, gents.' He looked up at them. 'Busy morning, I hear?'

Townsend closed the door behind him. Lowe looked excited.

'It has been, hasn't it?' Lowe said with clear snark.

'I appreciate you've been at a crime scene, but Hall has insisted that my hours are adhered to and spent here where I would be more productive.' Manning looked past the glaring Lowe to Townsend. 'What's going on?'

'We need to have a chat.' Townsend seemed almost regretful. 'Might be best if we went somewhere a little quieter.'

'Like an interview room,' Lowe added.

Manning looked at them in confusion.

'Can I ask what this is about?'

'By all means.' Lowe motioned for him to get up. 'Although, I'd rather not cuff you and march you through the office. I'm a prick, but I'm not that much of a prick.'

'I don't understand.' Manning now stood on the defensive. 'What the hell is going on?'

'Come with us, Doctor,' Townsend said a little more calmly.

'Not until you tell me what the hell this is about?'

Townsend reached into his jacket pocket as Lowe stood, arms folded, clearly as a show of how physically bigger he was than Manning. As the doctor looked on in a mixture of panic and annoyance, Townsend placed the evidence bag on the desk.

Manning looked down, his eyes widened, and then he quickly began searching his own jacket.

'DS Townsend here found that at the crime scene this morning.'

Manning searched every part of the jacket, double checking the pockets, not realising that it was missing.

But here it was, collected from the crime scene of a brutal murder.

His metal pin.

The smiling face peering up at him through the see-through plastic with its mocking grin. Clearly shaken, Manning looked at both men.

'I still don't understand.'

Townsend stepped forward, controlling the situation as Lowe watched on.

'Like I said, doctor. I think we need to have a chat.'

CHAPTER THIRTY-TWO

Manning had been cooperative, which was the first sign to Townsend that maybe everything wasn't as it had seemed. The shock and terror that had exploded from the man when they'd presented him with the pin had felt genuine, and now, as the doctor sat opposite them on the other side of the table, Townsend could see the confusion spread across him like a mask.

'This is some kind of mistake.' Was all Manning could offer them, as the silence in the room became unsettling.

'Then, make it make sense,' Townsend said, a hint of hope in his voice. He'd tried to call King once they'd secured Manning in the interview room, but she hadn't answered. Townsend didn't want to arrest the doctor, not yet anyway, and he certainly didn't want to do that without King's approval.

Behind him, Lowe was leant against the wall of the interview room like a bouncer, making it clear that if Manning made any doomed attempt to rush for the door, he'd be in his way in a second. But nothing about Manning's demeanour gave Townsend any impression that he'd try anything like that.

He seemed genuinely confused.

And he didn't seem to have any answer to Townsend's statement.

Lowe cleared his throat.

'We might not have as many degrees as you, doc. And Detective Superintendent Hall might not think the sun shines out of our arses.' Lowe stepped forward. 'But we're good at our jobs. Now, we get a body turn up, Khalid, and then suddenly you're here on the scene. Then, more bodies start turning up, and instead of us doing what we should be doing and kicking down doors and following the evidence trail, you're filling King and Hall's head with theories, sitting us down for story time and getting in the way.'

'I'm doing my job,' Manning said curtly.

'Really?' Lowe sat lounging in his chair and clearly enjoying himself. 'Tell me, doc, what is it you have actually done to help this investigation?'

'I have been helping to collate a profile on the killer to try to help you figure out his next steps.'

'That's a pretty good position to be in if those next steps belong to you, right?'

'Am I under arrest, DCI Lowe?' Manning seemed to find a little confidence. 'Should I have some legal representation here with me?'

'You tell me,' Lowe snapped back. The two men were locked in an intense stare.

'Look.' Townsend interjected. 'Our job is to follow the evidence. And I need to know how your pin ended up at the murder scene? It is your pin, right?'

'Well, I can't seem to find mine.'

'Convenient.' Lowe scoffed. Townsend frowned.

'So yes, detective. I would make an educated assumption that that pin is mine.' Manning shrugged. 'But how it got to the crime scene, I don't know.'

'When did you notice it was missing?'

'When you blindsided me.' Manning was clearly uncomfortable. 'Look, it was just a badge my nephew gave me a year or so ago, and I just wear it as a way to add a little levity when I meet people.'

'Levity?' Lowe sneered, looking for any attempt to needle.

'Yes, detective. Levity. You should try it sometime.' He turned back to Townsend. 'I'm usually brought into situations that aren't exactly the most enjoyable. So that stupid little smiley face is just a marginal gain to getting people to lower their walls.'

Once again, Lowe sighed, shaking his head. Townsend, however, kept on.

'And you didn't notice it was missing?'

'No. Did you?' Manning replied.

'You're not the one asking questions here, mate.' Lowe interjected.

'I'm not your mate,' Manning said with contempt. 'And I think, given that I haven't been arrested and you are insinuating that I have something to do with these murders, then I think I'm well within my rights to ask some questions.'

'Fine.' Lowe stood, pulling a pair of cuffs from his belt and stepping round the table. Townsend quickly leant forward and placed a hand on Lowe's arm.

'Let's just stay calm, shall we?' Townsend insisted. Again, Lowe and Manning stared each other down, and Lowe relented, sat down, and then jabbed his finger onto the table.

'Make this make sense, doc.' Lowe's voice was laced with impatience. 'Now.'

Manning seemed lost for an answer. His usually calm, controlled manner had deserted him and he looked feebly to Townsend for help.

'I didn't do this.' Was all he could offer.

Lowe smirked.

Townsend leant forward and abruptly angered his colleague.

'I believe you, doc. I do.' Townsend held up a hand to stop Lowe's interruption. 'But I have to follow the evidence. And the only piece I have that could link anyone to the crime, someone who has access to police methods and more worryingly, our investigation itself, is this.' He tapped the pin in the evidence bag.

'Scouse. A word,' Lowe said through gritted teeth as he stood. He looked at Manning. 'Don't move.'

As Lowe headed to the door, Townsend lifted himself out of the chair to follow. Manning looked at the badge on the table and then to Townsend.

'It's someone from this station,' Manning blurted out.

'Excuse me?' Lowe was incensed.

'If someone had access to remove that pin from my jacket, then they had access to the SCU.' Manning looked up at the two detectives, immediately understanding only one of them was giving his theory any credence. 'Which means whoever took that pin is fully aware of your investigation.'

Lowe's brow furrowed so heavily Townsend was worried the man would topple over.

'If I were you, doc, I'd keep my mouth shut. Because the next time we speak, you're going to need some legal fucking representation.'

Lowe threw open the door and marched out, and Townsend followed, pulling it closed behind him. He went to speak, but Lowe slammed his hand against the wall with frustration.

'You believe him?' It was more of an accusation. 'Fucking hell, Scouse. You can't say that to him. He's a fucking suspect.'

Townsend held his ground. They'd done this dance before, and Townsend knew that giving Lowe even half an inch was quickly converted into a mile.

'I'm trying to get him to talk, sir. I don't think belittling him and treating him like shit just because he hurt your ego the other day is helping.'

'Careful. Remember your rank, DS Townsend.' Lowe pointed to the door. 'He has access to our files. Knows everything we're doing, and we found his personal item at the scene. Right now, beyond any shadow of a fucking doubt, he's our prime suspect.'

'Maybe,' Townsend said defiantly. 'But if he didn't do it, then he's right, isn't he? Whoever took his pin would have taken it from here, which means everyone with access to this case is a suspect.'

Before the two men could collide, the thumping sound of DI King marching down the corridor drew their attention. As she approached, she glared at Lowe and then turned to Townsend with just as much suspicion.

'You want to tell me what the hell is going on?'

'I tried to call you, guv…'

'Hannon said you were interrogating Manning?' She threw her arms up. 'What the hell are you thinking?'

'I found his pin at the crime scene and Lowe wanted…'

'I bet he did.' King turned and shot a glare at Lowe who seemed non-plussed. 'But this isn't his investigation, is it? And besides, there is no way that Manning murdered Dale Ainsworth last night.'

'We don't know that,' Lowe said firmly.

'Yes, I do.' King sighed. She took a moment, a deep breath and then looked up at both detectives. 'Because he was with me all of last night.'

CHAPTER THIRTY-THREE

Sitting opposite another person who'd been relying on her to save their spouse was starting to scratch away at the hard surface DI King was proud of. For the third time in a week, King had sat and taken all the anger and the blame on her shoulders, allowing the recently widowed their moment to expel some of their grief.

Eleanor Ainsworth was no different, screaming at both King and DS Swaby that they were 'fucking useless' and that her husband deserved better.

She was right on one count.

There was no point in going over just how many hours had been put in, how many stones were overturned, and how many blind alleys had been run down.

Because none of it mattered.

What mattered was the cold, hard fact that the Executioner had promised he would execute Dale Ainsworth, and unlike the SCU who had promised they would do their best to stop him, the Executioner had delivered.

The FLO wasn't someone who DI King was all too familiar with, and the young man seemed a little out of his depth. DC Josh Norton looked fresh out of training, and

King wondered if he was in fact half her age, and if the ink on his promotion to detective was still drying. Thankfully for him, and for King herself, Swaby's in-built maternal instincts kicked in and she soon managed to get through to the grieving Eleanor and eventually calmed her down.

There would be statements to be taken, a body to be identified, and arrangements to be made, and carefully and thoughtfully, Swaby walked her through all the options. As DC Norton made himself busy by making them all a cup of tea, King addressed the issue of Ainsworth's employer.

'Mr Zerkhov wasn't the man who abducted your husband,' she said with authority. 'We have video footage of him being elsewhere at the time of the abduction.'

'Well, he could have had one of his men do it,' Eleanor said with anger. 'Dale said he saw enough shifty people going in and out of that site.'

'We're still looking into his business practices,' King assured her. 'We'll make sure if he is doing anything out of line, we'll nab him for it.'

'Can you make sure we get paid?' Eleanor asked, and then the realisation that her husband's business was now likely to fold hit her. Swaby intercepted.

'We'll do whatever we can.' She held Eleanor's hand softly, and placed her other over the top of it. 'And we'll put you in touch with people who can help you with the next steps.'

'I'll have to sell the house.' Eleanor began to weep, collapsing her head forward into the palm of her other hand.

'I appreciate this is an incredibly difficult time for you, Mrs Ainsworth,' King began. 'But we need to find the person who did this to your husband, as based on previous, he's likely to do it again. Can I ask, nearly a decade ago, your husband did jury service, yes?'

Eleanor looked up, frowning.

'I think so.' She shook her head. 'I mean, we'd just gotten together at the time.'

'Do you remember if he spoke about it at all?'

'We've been married and had kids since then, detective,' Eleanor said dryly. 'So no, I don't really remember if he fucking enjoyed jury duty. Sorry.'

King held an apologetic hand up, then looked to Swaby and nodded to the door. Just as the two detectives stood, DC Norton stumbled in with four teas on a tray and his face dropped when he realised it was for nothing. King wondered if this was his first ever successful cup of tea.

'We'll be in touch, Eleanor,' Swaby said with care. 'If you need anything, DC Norton is right here.'

As Swaby and King made their own way to the door, Eleanor called out to them but she didn't look up.

'He said it was messed up.'

'Excuse me?' King stopped. Eleanor now lifted her head, staring at King with bloodshot eyes.

The look wasn't one of anger or hate.

It was a look that told King that she'd failed.

'The jury duty,' Eleanor said, wiping her eyes with a tissue. 'I think he said it was messed up. That the whole thing fucked with his head. Something about kids…'

'Did he ever go into detail?'

Eleanor shot King a cold glare.

'Do you have children, detective?' The question caught King cold, unlocking a dark folder in her mind that she tried to slam shut. All she could muster was a shake of the head. 'Then you'll never understand that when you have kids, the idea of anything happening to that innocence sticks with you. That's why he hated thinking about it. Because…'

Her voice trailed off.

'Because of what?' King said, swallowing her own

sadness and reasserting herself. 'Please, Eleanor…it could be important.'

'Because he thought that they made a mistake.'

Despite pushing the widow for more information, there was non-forthcoming. Either she didn't know or was holding back, so King and Swaby departed. Nothing would be achieved by them pushing her at this point – no matter how important it could be. They'd leave Norton to do his job so the two detectives made their necessary calls from the car. The two of them had worked alongside each other in CID during the more palatable days and although King was now Swaby's superior in rank, the two women were still friends.

Swaby knew the reason Lowe had eventually ruined his and King's marriage.

And she knew King wouldn't want to talk about it.

'Let's just hope the others haven't burnt the office down,' King said glumly as they pulled into the car park.

As soon as they entered the office, Hannon span in her chair, anxious to discuss the blazing inferno.

'It's Manning,' she said accusingly.

'What are you talking about?' King snapped back. How did she know?

'At the crime scene.' Hannon quickly steered in a different direction. 'Jack. He found his pin. You know that little smiley face one?'

'At the crime scene?' Swaby clarified. Hannon nodded.

'Where…' King began heading back out of the office.

'Townsend and Lowe took him to an interview room and…'

'Fuck,' King barked, and she was off, jogging down the hall, and making no attempt to move out of anyone's way. As a few officers sidestepped her, she took the stairs two at a time, until she rounded the corner to the interview rooms. Her eyes quickly landed on Townsend and her ex-husband, who were exchanging heated words. As King approached, they both turned to her, both men keen to explain to her what was going on.

They did.

And, swallowing her embarrassment, she confessed that she and Manning had spent the night together.

Townsend looked away, as if he'd just caught her cheating.

Lowe laughed.

'Him?' He jabbed a thumb back towards the door. 'You're fucking Albert Einstein in there?'

'Not that it's any of your business, DCI Lowe.' King refused to feel embarrassed for her personal life anymore. Especially not to her arsehole of an ex-husband. 'But no, we didn't fuck as you so gracefully put it.'

'Too boring, is he?' Lowe looked to Townsend for support but found none.

'No. It's just having to put up with a prick like you kind of puts a woman off.'

Lowe sneered and pushed open the door. King and Townsend followed him in, and Manning stood, confused and clearly scared.

'Izzy…' he began, then realised where he was. 'DI King.'

'It's okay, Loverboy,' Lowe said with a little jealousy. 'Izzy here has vouched that you were with her. I assume you can prove that?'

'Ummm…' He looked to King in desperation.

'There's CCTV at the end of my street. Neighbourhood Watch,' King said curtly. 'It'll show us returning to mine last night, and most likely, Dr Manning leaving this morning after I did.'

Lowe looked back and forth between the two of them, taking a few deep breaths as he struggled to find something to say.

Someway of getting out of it looking like the victor.

'Hall is going to fucking love this.' He eventually sneered, before walking off, not even looking at Townsend who had stood patiently to the side. Once the DCI had disappeared around the corner, Manning reached out and put a hand on King's shoulder.

'Thank you.'

She shrugged it off.

'Don't.' King shook her head. 'You need to tell me how that pin got at that murder scene?'

'I don't know.' Manning looked lost. Townsend stepped up.

'We're surmising that whoever planted it there must have had access to it and knew we'd look into Manning. Meaning...'

'Meaning they *are* in this station,' King said quietly, under her breath. 'Right, we keep the circle tight, we get back to the office, and we go through the court case our victims were on the jury for.'

'Guv?' Townsend called after her as she led them back up the corridor. 'What's going on?'

'If what Eleanor Ainsworth told me is true about jury duty...' She shot a look back over her shoulder to Townsend without breaking stride. 'Your hunch might be bang on the money.'

The three of them headed back upstairs, stepped back into the SCU, and King made sure she slammed the door shut.

CHAPTER THIRTY-FOUR

Detective Superintendent Hall had barged into the SCU not long after lunchtime, the scowl on his face informing all of them that his patience had been eradicated during a morning of difficult phone calls and constant questioning of his ability. It wasn't something he was accustomed to, and by the sharp tone in his voice, it was something he was prepared to take out on his subordinates.

'Right. This better be something,' he snapped, arms folded across his protruding gut, that pulled his uniform tight. DI King stood, hands on hips, in front of the murder board, which was now overflowing with information. Images of the gruesome crime scenes were pinned alongside happier pictures of the victims, and countless titbits of information were either written in white pen on the glass or stuck to the screen on Post-it notes. All of it building their investigation, and all of it orbiting one photo in the middle of the display.

The terrifying mask of the Executioner.

Hannon and Swaby were sitting at their desks, while Townsend and Manning had taken up a semi-comfortable position against the far wall. At the back of the room, Lowe had slunk in, but his face made it quite clear his mood hadn't changed. A few other uniformed officers, including PC Boyd, were also present for the briefing. He nodded to Townsend as he entered, and Townsend couldn't help but think that the man looked shattered.

Just seeing the tired police constable reminded him that the tab for holidays was still open on his phone.

King brought his train of thought back to the room.

'Just under ten years ago, Phillip Myers was arrested for the rape of twelve-year-old Amanda Swann.' King pointed to the dated pictures of the two people that had been recently added to the board. 'The case went to Aylesbury Crown Court, where after a lengthy trial, Myers was acquitted of the charge.'

'I recall it. Vaguely,' Hall said with a frown.

'Scrolling through the press coverage at the time, it seemed that the verdict wasn't a particularly popular one. Since then, Myers has been a ghost, missing numerous meetings that were set up to monitor his behaviour. In fact, there is nothing on the man for nearly eight years.'

'The man hasn't so much as paid for a Netflix subscription since then,' Townsend added, who was standing against the far wall alongside Dr Manning.

'Connect the dots,' Hall ordered.

'Dr Asif Khalid. Maureen Allen. Dale Ainsworth. Three people of varying ages, backgrounds and professions. All of them living in different parts of Buckinghamshire. Not one shred of a connection.' King then tapped the photo of Phillip Myers. 'Except that they were all on the jury who acquitted this man.'

Hall's eyebrows shot up. King continued.

'Working through the other list, two of the other jurists have since passed away from natural causes – one of old age, the other, bowel cancer – while another two have relocated. One to Newcastle and one migrated to Australia three years ago.'

'We've reached out to their local law enforcement agencies and have confirmed their safety,' Swaby added.

'That leaves five more,' Hall said.

'And so far, we've been able to make contact with four of them,' King said firmly. 'Uniform have been assigned to them for the time being.'

'And the fifth?'

'Anne-Louise Mulligan.' King tapped her photo, which had been lifted from her social media. 'Her last registered phone number has been disconnected, and her family hasn't been too forthcoming with information. Her father mentioned drugs, so we're currently running checks through local rehab facilities as well as leaning on any informants we have…'

'Find her,' Hall said firmly.

'Yes, sir.' King turned to Boyd and the other officers. 'Swaby has a few hotspots and…'

'We know 'em,' Boyd said glumly, but still obediently took the sheet. 'We're on it.'

With his seniority anointing him as the voice of command, Boyd led the uniformed officers out of the SCU office, and those who remained waited until the door was closed before they continued.

It was Lowe who broke the silence.

'Where are we on Myers?'

'His last known address was in Pangbourne,' King said confidently. 'Townsend's been in contact with our friends in Berkshire who are looking into it.'

'I know a DCI in Reading CID,' Lowe said, surprisingly not boasting. 'Want me to get in touch?'

'Get down there,' Hall commanded. 'They'll be just as busy as we are, so you using your…how should I put this…charm, will kick things into gear.'

'On it, sir.' Lowe made for the door. He turned to speak, but Hall beat him to it.

'Swaby, you're with Lowe.' Hall turned to Swaby. 'You know the case inside out, and the more information we can overload them with, the quicker we can root him out.'

'Yes, sir.' She started to gather her things and then offered a smile to King. Lowe and Swaby headed through the door, and Hall then turned back to the room.

'Good work,' he said firmly. He meant it.

'Sir, do you know a DI Gavin Thorpe?' DS Townsend asked, approaching the board. 'He was the lead detective on the case.'

'Thorpe…' Hall scanned through a memory that held a lot of information. 'Yes. Good man. Thorough.'

'It seems he left the service not long after the verdict came in. We've got a few instances on file of drunken behaviour, and a stint in therapy provided by Thames Valley Police. But then the trail goes cold…'

'He'd have a motive,' Manning added, but received a scowl from Hall. He pushed through it. 'The entire crusade so far has been predicated on a perceived lack of justice being carried out by those who made the decision to acquit Myers of his crimes.'

'Makes sense,' Hall agreed. 'Townsend, call HR, get them to give you everything they have on Thorpe. If they give you any shit, tell them to call me.'

'Yes, sir.'

'And Amanda Swann?' Hall asked, looking to each person in the room. 'Have we looked into her? Her parents?'

'Yes, sir,' King said, looking back with heartbreak at the innocent face of a twelve-year-old girl pinned to the board. 'They moved to Leeds not long after the verdict, and Amanda is now living in Edinburgh, having graduated from uni last year. She has a job, and more importantly, several alibis for the dates of the murders.'

'And her parents?'

'Same. Well, they're still in Leeds, but they've been in Lanzarote for the past ten days on holiday.'

'Lucky bastards,' Hall moaned.

'We're starting a deep dive into their finances as soon as we finish up to ensure they couldn't have funded it,' Townsend added. 'We'll see what shakes out.'

The mood in the room shifted as Hall took a few steps closer, and Hannon lowered her head, returning to her search for Anne-Louise. Townsend began to gather his things from his desk, mentally preparing himself for his call to HR, who seemed to have anointed themselves the actual bosses of the Thames Valley Police. Hall approached Manning and King.

'I don't want anything impeding this investigation.' He looked at them both sternly. The message was clear. 'Is that understood?'

'Yes, sir,' King replied. 'Just to be clear, Dr Manning and I didn't…'

Hall raised a hand and waved it off.

'You two are both adults, and to be perfectly honest, I couldn't give a shit if the sex lives of my team involved S&M and a safe word.' He turned to Manning. 'Who had access to your jacket?'

Hall had clearly been briefed, most likely by Lowe, on the incident this morning.

'Anyone with access to, or who has been in, this room.' Manning shrugged. 'Beyond a trip to the bathroom and the canteen, this is the only part of the station I've been in.'

'Well, we'll look into it.' Hall gave them both another firm look. 'But right now, clear this up and bring that masked bastard in.'

'Yes, sir,' they said in unison. As Hall turned to head to the door, Townsend beat him to it, and showing his respect of rank, he held it open and stood to attention.

Hannon piped up enthusiastically.

'I've found her,' she said quickly. 'Anne-Louise. She's in Recovery Housing Project in Thame.'

'Address?' Townsend asked, pulling his jacket on. HR could wait. King was also racing for hers.

'Just sent it.'

'Call in uniform, too,' Hall ordered King, as she hurried past.

'Will do. Hannon, try to make contact with her and tell her to stay put.' She dashed past Townsend who was still holding the door open. 'Let's go.'

The duo hurried through the corridors of the station, knowing Hall would be expecting their first result of the case so far.

They'd identified the potential next victim.

Now, they had to hope they could get to her in time.

CHAPTER THIRTY-FIVE

It felt like the first time they were on the front foot, and Townsend could feel the adrenaline pumping through his veins as he sped through High Wycombe. King had punched the address into the in-built navigation system of his car, and as they passed the petrol station where Irena Roslova was murdered last summer, Townsend hit the roundabout at full speed, zipping past a turning car that thanked him with an aggressive blast of the horn and a window full of obscenities.

'We need to get there alive, Jack,' King said.

They thundered up the long, winding country road that took them through the picturesque Saunderton, before they approached Princess Risborough. The idyllic little town reminded Townsend of his own slice of High Wycombe, as Princess Risborough was similar to Flackwell Heath in a number of ways. It had the same winding roads that splintered off into quaint, quiet residential streets, and a deceptively full high street that was dominated by coffee shops and restaurants. A number of cosy looking pubs were dotted in intervals throughout the town, offering a surprisingly heavy pub crawl.

'On at the next roundabout,' King directed, pointing through the windscreen at the large roundabout ahead. To the right, the road led towards Aylesbury, and the left-hand turn filtered car after car into a large supermarket.

Townsend saw the gap and sped through, angering another driver as he put his foot to the floor and sped across the roundabout, past the petrol station and thundered past the sign that told him Thame was only a few miles away. As he shifted through the gears, King was on the phone, confirming the uniform support who were already en route. As she hung up her phone, she glanced at her vape but thought better of it.

Townsend used the control panel on his own door to lower the passenger window, and King thanked him with a smile.

'Any luck with the Housing Project?' he asked. King took a puff and shook her head.

'Not yet. No word.' King blew the vapour out of the car. 'But Hannon is trying them on repeat until we get there.'

'She might not be there.' Townsend offered.

'That's true.' King's eyes narrowed. 'But if she is, and we can get to her, then we have a chance of keeping her safe.'

They approached the 'Welcome to Thame' sign on the side of the country road, but they zipped past it too fast to see which obscure French town it was twinned with. The rolling fields soon gave way to rows upon rows of pristine looking houses, and Townsend felt like they had looped back and were cruising through Princess Risborough again. All these small towns and villages were almost indistinguishable, but all held their own charm and allure. With the continuously soaring house prices in London, it was no surprise that more and more people were heading out to such places, especially with the transport links back to the city. Thame couldn't have been further from the grim, narrow streets of the nation's capital, and the houses were half the price. Yet, within forty-five minutes, you could be stepping off the train in London Marylebone.

Townsend passed the train station, then followed the blue arrow on his screen through a number of back roads, each one more affluent than the next. Even King, who lived in the popular town of Marlow let out an impressed whistle at some of the properties. As he turned one final time, King pointed to the large building at the end of the road.

'There it is.'

The neat brick work and well-maintained flower beds of the Recovery Housing Project soon came into view, and the entire venue looked more like a plush retirement home than a rehab facility. There were three police cars already in the car park, with two near the front and one further down, no doubt, with their eyes on the backdoor. Townsend swung the car in front of the squad cars and killed the engine, and he and King stepped out in sync. King immediately took control of the scene, ordering a few of the officers to cover the exits and another few to come with her and Townsend as they marched towards the entrance. A few visitors stood by their cars, a clear look of confusion on their faces as well as a hope the police weren't there for their loved one. As they approached the front door, Townsend saw PC Simon Walsh across the car park and offered him a wave.

The gruff police constable returned a grumpy nod.

At least he wasn't sleeping today.

Townsend chuckled to himself, and kept his eye out for Boyd, but they were soon standing in the reception of the facility, where the young receptionist looked overawed by the police presence and the severity of the situation.

Anne-Louise Mulligan was on her third bout of rehab

with the Recovery Housing Project, and one of the senior recovery workers arrived to greet and assist them. As they ventured deeper into the facility, the stern man described Anne-Louise as a troubled young woman who, despite his best efforts, never seemed to fully embrace the idea of getting better. Clearly passionate about his work, the man answered all King's questions as they climbed two sets of stairs, with the two uniformed officers stationed at the bottom just in case.

Yes, Anne-Marie was in the building.

No, she didn't have regular visitors.

No, there hadn't been any incidents of attempted break ins.

The place was secure, and although there was limited CCTV to protect the privacy of their patients, all of them were required to check in at various times throughout the day.

Anne-Louise had checked in less than two hours ago.

Which meant, when the recovery worker gently wrapped on her door and called her name, he expected her to answer. When he gave forewarning that he was unlocking the door and coming in, he expected her to be asleep in her bed.

But the room was empty.

King and Townsend stepped in. Although there was little in the way of furniture or personal affects, the room was neat as a pin. No signs of struggle. Townsend noted the mobile phone that was still in the room.

More worryingly, no signs of life.

King put a warning through the radio to the officers that Anne-Louise wasn't in her room and to keep their eyes open. Stop everyone and anyone trying to leave the site. They checked the function room, where a number of residents, all in various stages of rehabilitation from various ailments, were sitting, engaging in board games, television or just simply some time spent with others.

Time spent within the feeling of not being on their own.

But no Anne-Louise.

With their pace quickening and a sense of dread beginning to creep in, King and Townsend swiftly checked the canteen area, as well as all the bathrooms in the facility.

Nothing.

Patients weren't allowed access to other patients' rooms, but King insisted that the senior worker take two police officers and search all eighty-eight resident rooms for the woman. King and Townsend accompanied the senior care worker to the management office to trawl through the CCTV.

If she was there, they needed to find her.

They needed to bring Anne-Louise in and keep her safe.

But the footage only caught a glimpse of her walking through the corridor roughly fifteen minutes before, and as the uniformed officers continued their searches of the rooms, Townsend and King went outside to once again search the ground. Neither one of them wanting to verbalise what they were thinking.

The notion they were too late would have been awful, but the idea that whoever knew they were heading to the Recovery Housing Project beat them to the punch would only confirm that whoever was behind the mask was certainly involved in the investigation.

As they searched, with the spring sunshine beaming down on them, and a constant stream of 'she's not here' cackling through the radio, King and Townsend were losing faith that they would be able to save the young woman.

And, as she was over three miles away, drugged and shrouded in the darkness of a car boot, that faith would soon dissipate completely.

CHAPTER THIRTY-SIX

It's surprisingly easy to avenge someone.

Over the years, the notion of vengeance had been consigned to fantasy. There was the odd story that would filter through, though. The outrageous tale of Sam Pope raging a crusade through Europe and beyond to avenge whatever justification he gave for his need to kill people. Years ago, the Met hunted a murderous husband called Lucas Cole, who targeted a notorious crime family after the death of his wife.

But true vengeance was something the world was missing.

A world that would rather cancel someone for saying the wrong thing than take others to task for their heinous crimes.

Politicians who'd lied through their teeth and fattened their pockets, while thousands of people died alone and afraid. CEOs of huge companies who destroyed pockets of the planet to appease shareholders.

These people were allowed to walk away, because the world was as too busy dealing with the inconsequential as it was too scared to do anything of consequence.

But nothing was more broken than the justice system.

And those who'd been betrayed by it, those who'd dedicated their life to it, only to have it turned and spat back in their face, those were the ones who deserved vengeance.

And that was the vengeance the Executioner was hell bent on delivering.

Like those before her, Anne-Louise Mulligan had been complicit in aiding the broken system to continue spinning its wheels. She, like Asif Khalid, Maureen Allen and Dale Ainsworth, were just as responsible for what happened as Phillip Myers was.

If not, even more so.

Myers had been sick. The repulsive nature of his crimes would haunt the Executioner until his dying day, which would pale in comparison to the lifelong damage the man had inflicted upon poor Amanda Swann. The details of the case were nightmare fuel, and when the prosecutor laid out how he'd tied the twelve-year-old to a bed and raped her, the jury had, quite rightly, squirmed in their seats.

Myers was a paedophile. A man who needed to be stricken from the streets and chemically neutered.

The chance for justice had been right there, in the palms of twelve hands, but it was thrown away.

A decision that rendered the entire justice system obsolete, and one that had sparked a chain of events which now saw Anne-Louise Mulligan being driven to her death sentence. She was motionless in the boot of the car, and she wouldn't wake until long after he'd stored her away in his sanctuary. Ironically, as he drove back through the quaint country roads of Buckinghamshire, the Executioner knew that nobody would bat an eyelid.

They would see the uniform and instantly assume safety.

How ironic, that to him, the uniform was the mask.

The black and white leather he would proudly adorn when he put an end to Mulligan's life was his real face.

It was what he had become.

Years had passed, and he'd watched as his friend had been battered and broken by a decision that had not only crushed the notion of justice but also whatever spirit his friend had had left.

Detective Inspector Gavin Thorpe had been a man of principal. A mentor whose vision of right and wrong was twenty-twenty. Ten years ago, as he'd hunted down Myers, Thorpe had been a force of life that could have powered the entire county. But it had cost him his marriage, and the verdict had cost him his sanity.

Drinking became a necessity.

The job, like his family, soon saw a life that was better off without him.

Drinking morphed into other addictions.

Now, a man who the Executioner had seen as a beacon of integrity, had been reduced to nothing more than a junkie.

A good friend turned into a ghost.

All because twelve unqualified people decided that the evidence wasn't clear enough. All because a system put in place to protect people like Amanda Swann, driven by good people like DI Thorpe, was fundamentally broken.

As he returned to High Wycombe, the Executioner guided the car through some of the narrow streets that led to Desborough Business Park. The run-down row of businesses was secluded from the main road by narrow houses, as well as a line of trees that belonged to a neglected sports field. The business park was home to a printing specialists, an MMA gym which the Executioner frequented, along with a courier service that specialised in large goods. As always, an articulated lorry was parked up, and the driver was going through the painstaking process of unloading one large container at a time via his tediously slow lift.

The Executioner pulled into the small car park afforded to the storage facility that offered ten lock-ups at *reasonable prices*. The owner, whose name and country of origin he'd forgotten, was happy to accept cash and ask no further questions.

Thankfully, nobody was watching as he pulled the car in close to the metal shutter, and quickly, the Executioner hopped out, shunted it open and then swiftly moved to the back of the car. It took just five seconds to move the cargo from the back to the cold, hard concrete beside his van, and the Executioner bound her wrists and ankles, slipped a gag over her motionless head, and then left her in the dark.

She'd be out for at least another hour, and if she woke before he returned, she'd make minimal noise.

But he'd be back soon.

He needed to be.

Everyone would be looking for Anne-Louise Mulligan, and he'd be expected to help.

The net was closing, and DI King and DS Townsend in particular were like dogs with bones. It was actually rather impressive, and he knew that were Gavin Thorpe of sound mind, he'd have seen himself in the two detectives.

They seemed to care.

To give a shit.

But stopping him wouldn't achieve anywhere near the same level of justice as he'd deliver, and he needed to keep them at arm's length until the final kill. The misdirect with the shrink's pin hadn't worked as planned, and now, with all twelve names splattered across the board he'd seen in the briefing, he knew there would only be one more kill after Mulligan.

A name that hadn't been uttered once.

And that kill…that would be his masterpiece.

Until then, he would continue as planned, return the car to the station, say all the things he needed to say and do all the things he'd be expected to do.

Then he would return.

He would prepare everything he needed.

He would execute Anne-Louise Mulligan.

And he would let the world watch as the very system his uniform dictated he upheld would come crashing down around them.

CHAPTER THIRTY-SEVEN

The entire time, the Executioner had been three steps ahead of them. With Anne-Louise Mulligan, they finally had the opportunity to get ahead of the masked murderer, but they'd failed. And that failure presented itself as a tense silence on the drive back from Thame, as Townsend kept his eyes on the road, as headlights after headlights passed him by. The beautiful, scenic views of the rolling countryside were now cloaked in darkness, along with a fine drizzle that had fallen across the country, and Townsend didn't want to think about the inevitable.

Neither did King.

Anne-Louise Mulligan had been at the Recovery Housing Project before they'd left the station, but somehow, in the thirty-minute drive from High Wycombe, she'd been abducted.

The reality that someone within their ranks was working with the Executioner, or even worse, was behind the mask, was growing with every passing headlight, and Townsend could feel his knuckles whitening on the steering wheel.

They had done everything they were supposed to.

They had followed the evidence.

They had eliminated suspects.

But the entire time, they were playing catch up.

Now, as their one hope of protecting Anne-Louise drifted further and further away from them, Townsend could feel a sense of hopelessness, exacerbated by the likely late night full of blind alleys. It was one thing knowing who the Executioner was targeting next. It was a completely different thing to know how and where he would carry out his plan.

As they returned to the station, King turned to her detective with a sigh.

'Head on home, Jack.' She started getting out of the car. 'Get some rest.'

'With all due respect, guv. I won't rest. Not when this is going on.'

King admired his sternness, something they had in common, and as she led him back towards the SCU office, they stopped off at the canteen for whatever lukewarm "specials" were on offer. Back in the SCU office, Hannon was locked to her screen, and Townsend and King approached the murder board. Swaby was still out with DCI Lowe, and her usually unshakable positivity was missed.

'DI Thorpe.' King tapped his photo. 'All the people who've been killed or taken were the ones who let Myers walk all those years ago. If anyone had a grudge to bear...'

'It would be him.' Townsend nodded; arms folded.

'We need to find him.'

Townsend got to it, and King yawned, stretched and then headed to her office, where a sheepish-looking Manning greeted her with an awkward smile.

'How you doing?' he asked. His tone told her that he'd heard how things had gone.

'Not great.' She shrugged. 'I take it you heard...'

'I did,' Manning said thoughtfully. 'Hannon's going through the CCTV of the surrounding areas, trying to pinpoint any similar vans. You never know…we might get lucky…'

Manning's words were hopeful, but his tone wasn't, and King dropped down into the seat at her desk and rubbed her eyes. She was shattered; it had been another long and ultimately fruitless day, in what was becoming a series of them. No doubt soon, she'd get another rocket up her arse from Hall, who seemed to be running out of patience and undoubtedly, DCI Lowe would be there to pick up the pieces of her broken case. King tapped her credentials into her laptop and was greeted with a software update.

Perfect timing.

As she waited, she broke the rules of the station once more by pulling out her vape.

'I couldn't tempt you with a mediocre coffee from the canteen, could I?' Manning turned, his handsome face pulled into his perfect smile. 'My treat.'

King scoffed and nodded, and then followed the doctor out of the office. As they walked quietly through the station, her mind went back to last night. They'd spent hours talking, and when Manning had ventured the idea of going for a drink, King knew that the attraction was mutual. For a long time, the idea of a physical relationship with anyone had been alien to her, but there was something about Manning's calmness that she found comfort in, and before she could stop herself, she told him that she was a recovering alcoholic.

She had regretted it instantly.

But she needn't have.

Manning just thoughtfully took her by the hand, led her past the pubs, and took her to a late-night diner on the edge of the town centre where the two of them indulged in a ridiculously sugary milkshake. The conversation flowed like the wine would have, and King found herself opening up to Manning about everything.

Her alcoholism.

Her disastrous marriage to Lowe.

Her constant feeling of failure.

The man was a hell of a psychologist, and King had never felt so comfortable expressing her genuine feelings. She had been a closed book for so long, she'd forgotten what chapter of her own story she was on. When she invited him back to hers, she had the very real intention of crossing the line, and probably pissing off Hall, but when the moment came, and the two of them were inches away from one another, she'd pulled back.

She wasn't ready.

Manning didn't question it at all, made them a cup of tea, and they sat opposite each other on the sofa, talking throughout the night.

The details of their 'night together' had already washed through the station, but King didn't care. She knew her truth, was proud of herself for it, and as Manning handed her the sludge that passed as coffee, she smiled at him.

'Thanks.' She lifted the cup. 'I feel spoilt.'

'Well…second date…thought I'd splash out.'

'Is that what this is?' King smirked, and the Manning took a seat at one of the canteen tables. He turned back to King, who agitated from foot to foot.

'You tell me.' Manning smirked. 'Although, a woman being abducted probably wasn't the run up I'd have liked.'

'And that has to take priority,' King said firmly. She could tell Manning was disappointed, but made no attempt to show it. 'This is the job.'

The two shared a smile once more.

A flicker of a spark emanated from between them.

The moment was interrupted by the thumping of footsteps, as Townsend appeared, bursting through the canteen doors. He scanned the room, all eyes on him, until he landed on King and Manning and dashed across.

'Guv.'

'What is it, Jack?' She stood.

'I found Thorpe.' Townsend looked at Manning and then back at King. 'He's in an assisted living complex in Slough.'

King was already heading for the door.

'Get the nearest available unit to sit on the door. Another to follow us.'

'Yes, guv.'

King stopped and turned on her heel back to Manning, who was sipping his coffee. She mouthed 'sorry' to him, but he just gently tilted his cup.

'Go get 'em,' he said, accompanied by his charming smile.

King bounded after Townsend with an extra spring in her step.

In a week that had been overflowing with darkness, it was nice to have one ray of sunshine to cling to.

CHAPTER THIRTY-EIGHT

The Millrose House Assisted Living Centre was a few minutes outside of the Slough Trading estate, the largest privately owned industrial estate in Europe. An expanse of tall buildings, each of them emblazoned with their business name, were lined along the wide roads, and looming, unattractive fuel towers jutted up into the spring evening sky like jagged fingers. Despite the numerous businesses taking residence, the entire estate felt run down, as every building was stuck in various stages of decline and each road or car park was signified by a faded sign.

Once they'd navigated their way through the maze of the estate, Townsend pulled down the side road that took them towards Millrose House, the aesthetic of the building matching the sadness of its residence within. In essence, it was a medical facility, designed to offer sanctuary for those who needed support for their declining physical or mental health. The brickwork was old and crumbling, and what little effort had gone in to maintaining the front garden hadn't been rediscovered after the bitter winter months. Townsend pulled the car into a parking spot beside a flower bed, which had been overrun with weeds.

'Looks nice,' King said drably.

The two detectives stepped out into the car park, which was lit from above by the street lights, and from below by a few bulbs that had been placed into the now neglected flower beds. There was a police car already situated by the door, and the two officers from the Slough arm of the force greeted them. Pulling into another vacant spot was PC Boyd and PC Walsh, both looking as grumpy as usual. Townsend cast an eye around the desolate car park.

Not a place that seemed to be frequented by many visitors.

Boyd and Walsh approached the four of them by the door, and Boyd greeted the other officers with a hearty shake, while Walsh, as had become his custom, offered a half-hearted grunt.

'Boyd, Walsh. Stay here. Eyes on the front,' King ordered and then turned to the two other officers. 'You two, cover the back entrance. I don't want Thorpe getting away if he sees us coming. We know he's here, so eyes open.'

With Mulligan's abduction fresh in her mind, King wasn't taking any chances, and the four officers headed to their respective posts as King and Townsend marched through the automatic door, which slid to the side obediently. The reception area was as welcoming as the dilapidated garden outside, and behind the wooden reception desk, a mousey woman with glasses and greying hair greeted them.

'Hello,' she said nervously as they approached the desk. The two of them displayed their identification.

'DS Jack Townsend. This is DI King.' He offered his warmest smile. 'I called ahead.'

'Ah yes. I remember your accent. I'm Helen.' She was busily shuffling stuff for no apparent reason. 'Gavin Thorpe.'

'Yes. He's still here, right?' King asked, her voice low as if it was a secret.

'Oh, yes.' The woman waved it off. 'Gavin doesn't do much. He's in his room. Follow me.'

King and Townsend shared a resigned glance, and they followed Helen who shuffled down the nearest hallway. As they followed, they passed what was intended to be a communal room, which consisted of two tatty sofas and a TV on the wall. They were soon headed down a corridor that they could have mistaken for a chain hotel until they stopped at room number twenty-three. She stopped and turned to them.

'It's hard to get him to talk at the best of times,' Helen warned them. 'He might be tired, so...I'll be right here just in case.'

'Thank you,' Townsend replied, and the woman then gave a gentle knock on the door, warned Gavin they were entering, and then used her security pass to unlock the door. They were greeted with a stale smell, a clear indication that the room was occupied almost constantly. The room was painted a dreary grey colour, which was only interrupted by a few framed pictures of unidentified coastal towns. A cramped bathroom was just off to the left, the shower unit stuffed in the corner beside the toilet and a small basin. The room was barely furnished, with a rickety-looking wardrobe pushed into the far corner, opposite a well-made double bed, and a bedside table adorned with a lamp and a book.

At the end of the room was a bay window, with the curtains open, overlooking the unkempt grounds of the facility. In front of the glass was a chair.

And in it, motionless, was Gavin Thorpe.

It was a depressing sight for two reasons.

One, the man looked entirely alone. Slouched in the chair and wrapped in a worn dressing gown, the man's vacant eyes glared out from his gaunt face, transfixed on the darkness beyond the window. He looked fragile, but worse than that, he looked like he didn't even know he had company. His skin was a deathly pale, and his thinning, grey hair swirled around his skull like mist. A decade ago, Gavin Thorpe had been a senior detective within the Thames Valley Police, a man of stature and respect. But ten years was a long time, and whatever spiral he'd fallen down had been a steep and dark journey.

The second reason, and one that King and Townsend acknowledged to each other with a shared nod, was that there was no way that the husk of a man sitting before them could have been the killer.

'Gavin,' King said softly as she approached the chair. 'Gavin.'

The man took a few moments, but then lazily turned to look at her.

'I'm DI King.' She squatted down to his eye level. 'I'm from the Thames Valley Police.'

He murmured something inaudible and then turned his attention back to the window.

'This is my colleague, DS Townsend,' she continued. It was falling on deaf ears. 'We were hoping to ask you some questions about a case you worked a decade ago.'

The man didn't move.

Didn't make a sound.

King was wondering how much was getting through.

'We believe it could help us with an ongoing investigation,' she said hopefully. Still nothing. 'Gavin?'

King stood and turned to Townsend, who shared her concern. They both returned to the entrance to the room, where the woman was waiting.

'Is this usual behaviour?' Townsend asked her.

'Unfortunately, yes,' Helen said sadly. 'Gavin came to us a few years back. He suffered a mental breakdown nearly a decade ago, and then turned, as many do, to substance abuse to counteract it. Eventually, his brother intervened, and about two years ago, maybe three, I'd have to check, he was brought to us.'

'By his brother?' King asked, her interest peaked. 'Do you have his name?'

'Jimmy. I think.' She was waffling a little. 'Or James. Anyway, his brother helped him move in and sorted everything out for him.'.'

'Does his brother pay for him?' Townsend asked, clearly on the same train of thought as King.

'I believe it's set up to come from his police pension. Gavin was a detective like you are. Although, we don't have much on that. His brother never says much when he's here.'

They closed the door gently, locking the broken ex-detective in with his vague thoughts, and Townsend and King followed the helpful woman back to the reception area. She quickly returned to the sanctuary of her desk and then looked across to them both.

'Sorry if this hasn't been much help.'

'The brother…' King cut her off. 'Do you have anything on Gavin's file about him? A contact number or an address?'

'Not an address,' she said sadly. 'But we do have him as an emergency contact, but we've never had to call him. Here, let me get the number up for you.'

Helen pulled up the number, and Townsend sent it Hannon to trace. Unsurprisingly, it came back as out of service – a disused number for a delivery firm.

'Surprise,' Townsend said dryly when he got off the phone with Nic.

'It's not my place to say, but he isn't the nicest man,' Helen offered. 'He doesn't offer any greetings. He doesn't even take his hood down when he comes inside.'

'What does he look like?' Townsend asked.

'White. Oldish. Pretty rough,' Helen said thoughtfully. 'Like I said, I don't want to cast aspersions, but he doesn't seem like the nicest person. It feels like when he visits Gavin, it's more out of necessity.'

'At least he visits,' King offered. 'When did he last come?'

'Now let me see...' Helen made a show of pulling the log in book from the desk and began thumbing through the pages. With each page she turned, the chances of finding him were dwindling. 'Ah, here we go. Just after Christmas.'

She turned the book and handed it to Townsend.

'Do you have CCTV of that day?' King asked.

'I'm afraid not. Our CCTV only holds the past thirty days of footage.'

'Is there a back-up server?' Townsend asked. Judging by her reaction, he may as well have asked it in Russian.

'I don't know. I'm not really a techy person.'

'Can you give me the name of the security service you use, please?' King said, putting her at ease. 'We can direct our enquiries straight to them if that helps?'

'I'll have to speak to my boss,' Helen replied. 'I don't have authority to do that, I'm afraid.'

King sighed at the continuous frustration of hierarchy, but Townsend stepped in and encouraged her to do that. As Townsend waited patiently for Helen to make the necessary calls, King stepped out, pulled out her vape and approached Boyd and Walsh.

'Any luck?' Boyd asked. King blew out a cloud of smoke and shook her head. 'Bollocks.'

'Maybe,' King said. 'Anything and everything is useful.'

'Anything you need us to do, guv?' Walsh asked.

'We're done here.' King nodded. 'You guys head on back, try to find out where the hell this bastard has Anne-Louise Mulligan.'

The two burly officers grunted their goodbyes, and headed back to their squad car as King watched a Townsend strode through the doors, his phone pressed to his ear and his face was rife with confusion. King arrived at the tail end of his call.

'You're certain…okay. Thanks, Nic. We'll be back in a bit.'

He disconnected the call and turned to King, a jolt of excitement in his body.

'How's she getting on?' King asked.

'She's working through the files HR sent through on Gavin Thorpe.' Townsend pocketed his phone and yanked open the driver's door of his car. 'Hunting for his brother.'

'We got him?' King said hopefully.

'That's the thing, guv.' Townsend looked across the car to her, the morose building that housed a once prominent detective loitering in the background. 'Gavin Thorpe doesn't have a brother.'

CHAPTER THIRTY-NINE

The following morning, the energy around finding Gavin Thorpe's 'brother' was brought to a harsh stop by the death of Anne-Louise Mulligan. King and Townsend had returned from Slough with a spring in their step, and although the rest of the team, and Manning, had departed the office, the two detectives had spent the evening hunting through Thorpe's career, looking for the smallest breadcrumb they could to form a trail to the "brother". As the evening melted into another late night, King ordered in a reasonably tasty pizza to try and rid them of the taste of failure.

Lowe had even joined them for a slice, and despite the odd barbed comment batted back and forth between him and King, it didn't take long to get him on board with their hunt for the 'brother'.

Whoever was posing as Thorpe's brother was most likely the man behind the mask.

The question was, who?

King had hit the pillow a little after one o'clock that morning, but her alarm had her showering and brushing her teeth just after five. Adrenaline had replaced tiredness as her dominant force, and as she pulled into the station car park at six, she stopped and took a moment to take stock.

Armed with a homemade coffee – because it was better than the sludge in the office – in one hand, and a vape in the other, she looked around at her surroundings, as the pink hue of the sun was beginning to cut through the clouds to signal its arrival.

The roads were quiet, and beyond the 'Magic Roundabout', she could see the Rye. The stretch of trees that reached beyond her line of sight were gently rustling in the spring breeze, and a paddle of ducks were swooping down gracefully onto the lake itself. She'd come close to death on those grounds, but now, as was always the case when they were on the right track, she felt more alive than ever.

The net was closing in on the Executioner.

And Isabella King would be the one to tie it shut.

Across the road, the High Wycombe Council Offices loomed large, set back from the road by a car park that offered minimal parking at outrageous costs. Along with the post office, the town hall and the police station itself, the council office was another reason why the road was seen as the life source of the town. As with nearly all towns and cities, the residents would complain about the decisions made by those elected to make them, but King had found High Wycombe to be, on the whole, a pretty nice place to try to rebuild her life.

In the concrete forecourt, which was hidden from the roundabout by bulbous bushes, a homeless person was draped across a bench.

It wasn't always perfect.

But she knew that most people ended up on the streets due to circumstances she couldn't comprehend, and as much as she would have wanted to help them, there was a missing girl to find. With a silent apology, King headed into the office. Townsend made the same mistake, although he didn't notice the prone body practically on their doorstep. His mind was wrapped up in the case.

In fact, it wasn't until a road sweeper by the name of Jeremy Hilson had trundled by on his rounds that anyone paid her any real heed.

Anne-Louise Mulligan was sprawled across the bench like a drunk, her eyes closed, but her mouth slightly open. Around her lips was a thick coating of white foam, which was illuminated by the deathly pale shade of her skin. Jeremy had tried a few times to rouse her, even prodding her leg with his broom. She was clearly unresponsive in the non-drunk way he usually found people here, so he'd rushed across the now-busy road to the station and informed the front desk. Two uniformed officers took less than a minute to call it in, and what had started as a morning of hopeful progression, given their discovery of Thorpe's mysterious 'brother', swiftly turned into another stark reminder of failure. King and Townsend were back outside when Swaby and Hannon arrived within minutes of each other, and as the traffic and footfall began to grow, so did the interest. Uniform had begun to tape off the roads, redirecting the morning rush hour away from one of the busiest roads of the town, and bearing the brunt of the anger it inevitably caused. Cordons were set up across all potential access points to the road, where more uniformed officers were shooing away nosey civilians who'd already cottoned on to what had happened.

Townsend summed it up succinctly when Swaby and Hannon joined him and King.

'This is a kick in the bollocks.'

SOCO had been deployed to quickly erect a partition to block the body of Anne-Louise from the public eye, and they were doing their best to try to secure the crime scene. But there wasn't much to go on.

A dead body.

That was it.

But a dead body, presumably alive when first delivered a few metres away from their front door, which meant the Thames Valley Police had literally been seconds away from being able to save her. The optics would be painful, and the fallout even worse, which Lowe had pointed out when he trudged across the road, his hands stuffed in his pockets and a similar look of failure on his face.

'Hannon's on CCTV,' he informed King, after she'd sent the youngest member of the team into the office. 'If anyone can find something, it's her.'

'It's unlikely,' King said. 'Our guy isn't sloppy.'

'He's ballsy.' Lowe sighed. 'Killing someone right on our fucking doorstep.'

'Didn't you give Manning shit for admiring this guy?' Townsend asked. Lowe turned with an authoritative raise of the eyebrow.

'Maybe he was right?' Lowe shrugged. 'Just don't tell him I said it.'

A voice interrupted them and they turned to see the handsome psychologist approaching. The glasses, turtleneck and blazer only feeding into his aura of intelligence.

'Don't worry, DCI Lowe. I heard it.' Manning offered them his smile. 'But I won't say anything.'

King brought everybody back into the conversation.

'This woman died, alone and in the dark. Because we couldn't find her.'

'That's not fair, guv,' Townsend said. 'We were this close…'

'But not close enough.' King shook her head. 'And now we need to tell her family what happened.'

King pulled out her phone to make a call and began to turn back towards the car park.

'Want me to come with you?' Townsend asked. King shook her head.

'Stay here until we've moved the body. If our killer is this brazen, he could still be out here. You get even a hint of suspicion, you bring them in. Then I need you upstairs, hunting down Thorpe's brother. I'll be back as soon as I can.'

Before Townsend could respond, King's call connected, and she asked Swaby to send her through the details of Anne-Louise's parents, as she prepared for another tough day ahead. Townsend sighed and turned back to the crime scene before him. It wouldn't take long for them to wrap it up. Unlike the other murders, this one hadn't required impressive apparatus or any moving parts.

This one had been cold. Heartless.

Dr Mitchell would do her job, but chances were, she'd confirm that it wasn't painless.

'Overdose,' Manning mused, drawing Lowe and Townsend's attention. 'Or…in our killer's case…lethal injection.'

'It tracks,' Lowe agreed. 'And despite her past, I doubt it was anything she was familiar with. Get this cleared as soon as, okay, Scouse?'

Lowe gave Townsend one of his needlessly powerful slaps on the back and then turned and headed back towards the station. Townsend barely felt it. His eyes were locked on the motionless, pale body of the woman they'd failed.

Four dead.

Brutally executed.

But what was worse, was that in less than twelve hours, the world would get to see it happen. The Executioner hadn't announced their next video, but it was only a matter of time. And when the world saw that it happened on their doorstep, an avalanche was heading his and the SCU's way.

It was a theory shared by Detective Superintendent Hall, who soon joined them within the cordon, and frowned as he surveyed the anarchy of the situation. Car horns blared a constant rhythm, causing a dull and continuous echo of anger throughout the town. Every road surrounding their failure was bumper to bumper with angry travellers. At each cordon, more and more people were lining up to complain to the uniformed officer, to let them know that their best wasn't good enough.

Discovering Thorpe's 'brother' felt like a lifetime ago, and Townsend couldn't allow another death to pull them away from their investigation.

It needed to be a catalyst.

They needed to find the killer.

But when Hall stood beside him, hands on his hips and his brow furrowed so angrily it almost shut his eyes, Townsend couldn't help but agree with his superior. Hall would be the barrier for the SCU, from the tidal wave of calls from the Mayor, councillors, business owners, scared citizens – anyone and everyone effected by the murder and the subsequent road closures – all of whom would be furious as the situation once again escalated beyond their control.

The Executioner had not only killed again, but this time, had sent a clear message by doing it right on their doorstep.

With his long career behind him, and his sharp mind working overtime, Hall summed it up better than Townsend could.

'This is the biggest fucking slap in the face the Thames Valley Police has ever had.'

CHAPTER FORTY

People wanted answers.

Detective Superintendent Hall had been screening calls since the news broke of a fourth body, as anyone and everyone of influence with access to his number wanted an explanation.

Local committees.

Senior police figures.

The Mayor of High Wycombe.

The local MPs.

For the third time in just under a year, the town of High Wycombe, and the surrounding county of Buckinghamshire was in the grip of a serial killer. Baycroft's killing spree had been ruthless and swift, a man battling the tumbling grains of sand in his hourglass as he sort to punish those who had, in his mind, turned their backs on the second chance the Lord had given them. Gemma Miller's had been routed in revenge, infiltrating the very school where the events had been set in motion to take her vengeance on those who had driven her father to suicide.

But this was different.

Neither Baycroft nor Miller had been as cunning or as

methodical as the Executioner. Nor had they been as antagonistic.

The public executions had been a symbol of what the Executioner had perceived to be a lack of justice, but their proximity to the police station stank of a challenge to the police themselves.

One they hadn't been able to rise to.

As he sat in the press room of the High Wycombe Police Station, flanked by DI King and an irritating member of the PR Department, who knew more about social influencing than police procedure. Hall had been here many times before, had faced down more than his fair share of eager journalists with the poise and sharp tongue that had seen him rise through the ranks.

But this morning, he was on the back foot.

And the journalist, from one of the bigger online media outlets, knew it.

'The body was found less than twenty metres away from the front door. Is this a sign that the killer has little to no fear of the Thames Valley Police?'

It wasn't so much a question as an insult, and Hall regarded the meek, smirking journalist with the respect he and his question deserved.

'Let me ask you a question…'

'Oscar,' the man said confidently. 'Oscar Simmons.'

'Mr Simmons,' Hall said it with a bitter twist to his words. 'Do you smoke?'

'Excuse me?'

'Do you smoke? As in cigarettes.' Hall guided every set of eyes in the room onto the man in question. Hall already knew the answer to his loaded question.

'Err…yeah,' Oscar said with a hint of shame.

'And when you buy your cigarettes, they have a 'smoking kills' or a 'smoking increases lung cancer' warning on them, yes?'

'Yes.' Oscar nodded feebly, shrinking into himself.

'Yet, you still do it.' Hall waved him off. 'The bottom line is, whether the Executioner killed the person twenty feet or twenty miles from the front door isn't relevant. He has no fear of the Thames Valley Police, as he has no fear or seemingly any regard for the law that keeps us as a society. So while the unfortunate death this morning, the identity of whom will remain hidden until further notice, was a bitter pill to swallow, my team worked tirelessly to prevent it from happening.'

'But how can we have confidence in the police's capacity to stop these murders when they happen so close to home?' Another question. A sterner, more world-weary man at the end of it.

'Because we've done it before. And because right now, the net is closing. We have firm leads on who's behind the mask and who they'll target next.' Hall commanded the room with authority. 'We've taken steps to ensure their safety and will bring this killer to justice. DI King and her team turned over every stone in their pursuit of this man, and to deliver peace to the families and friends affected.'

A hand shot up.

The PR woman, in an attempt to provide some value to the conference, pointed to the owner of it.

'DI King. Do you believe that, given your past indiscretions, those families will have confidence in your ability to—'

'Sorry. What past indiscretions?' Hall interrupted. Irate.

'Well, it was only last summer that a trail of bodies was left through this town, while DI King was all over the internet with several bottles of wine in tow.'

King felt a shiver of shame slide down her back. At her lowest point, as the body of Irina Roslova had been shipped off to Dr Mitchell, the fourth and final victim of

Gordon Baycroft's murderous rampage, photos had spread online of her buying her usual two bottles of wine from her local shop. The coverage of the murders at the time had thrust her into the limelight, and with a town terrified as the body count rose, she had become the focus of their anger.

The messages had been heartbreaking.

What a disgrace.

Those poor girls deserve better.

DI Drunk on the case.

It had been her lowest ebb, and the final push came when Baycroft, hands bound by cuffs and admitting his guilt, berated her for her weakness. But the push wasn't to the bottom of a bottle. It was towards sobriety.

Hall fixed the journalist with a haunting stare.

'DI King is one of the finest detectives that the Thames Valley Police has seen, certainly in the long career that I have had. Whatever perceived 'indiscretions' you are alluding to, in an attempt to undermine her authority or ability, does more to disturb the case than they do. So if you don't mind, we shall finish it there, because some of us…have actual work to do.'

The cutting line drew a wary silence from the onlooking gaggle of journalists, and the target of Hall's sharp tongue sank in his seat. King looked to Hall, who offered her a reassuring nod, and she mouthed 'thank you' to him as they stood from their seats. As they began heading towards the door, a wave of excitement washed across the room, and through the noise, titbits of information slipped through.

'He's messaged again!'

'Oh dear, not another one.'

'At five o'clock again!'

'Surely they can't let this one air…'

Sure enough, as King checked her messages, Hall's

phone began to buzz. Answers would be demanded, and Hall, ignoring the background noise, turned to King who confirmed with a shake of the head.

'He's posted. This evening at five.'

'I see,' Hall said grimly.

He looked back out to the journalists who all stared at him as if he himself was the man under the mask.

As if a serial killer running riot under his watch carried just the same amount of responsibility. In a way, he did, but unlike the Executioner, he wouldn't hide his face from it.

The snarky journalist, who seemed pleased that Hall's failings were being posted on the internet, piped up once more.

'I guess you'll be watching like the rest of us then?'

Hall turned, his eyes burning a hole right through the pompous man and making him squirm in his seat.

'Not if we can stop it,' Hall said with authority. 'But unlike you, I won't be trying to piggyback off it for a cheap payday. I, and the rest of the Thames Valley Police, will be doing our best to stop it. So…as you can imagine…we have work to do.'

Hall marched towards the door, his back straight and his shoulders set. Thankfully for him, and the rest of the officers under his eye, they were broad enough to carry the can, and as his phone buzzed again, King appreciated just how many plates a man in his position had to spin. As they stepped through the door to the relative safety of the station corridor, the PR representative tried to reprimand him for being curt with the journalist.

Hall waved her off and turned to King.

'That should take the heat off you for a little bit.'

'Sir, I'm a big girl,' King said defiantly. 'I can handle a hack journalist looking for a retweet.'

'I know, Izzy.' Hall, despite the pressure, still found a

warm smile. 'But you're a part of my team. So I'll protect you. All of you. But there is only so long I can keep the wolves from the door. Understood?'

She did.

Clearly.

'Yes, sir.'

'So use Lowe. Use Manning. Use Townsend. Hell, send every uniformed officer you can find to kick in every door in the fucking town if need be.' Hall looked down at his phone again, seeing the word 'MAYOR' flashing for what felt like the hundredth time. As he lifted his phone to his ear, he looked at King one last time. 'Just find this guy. Today.'

Hall marched off, phone to his ear, absorbing whatever anger he had to. King watched him leave, amazed at his composure under such circumstances.

A fourth body in a little over a week.

This one on the front fucking doorstep.

The whole town, media and senior figures baying for blood.

Yet he stood tall.

Made himself accountable.

Lead by example.

With the case spiralling beyond any semblance of control, King knew she had a dedicated team upstairs, a number of other professionals, all of whom were working round the clock to bring this to an end.

They needed King to lead by example.

In the secrecy of the corridor, she took a puff on her vape for courage, and then headed upstairs to the SCU, promising them all, and herself, that she would.

CHAPTER FORTY-ONE

Hannon and Swaby had combed through the CCTV footage from the night before, and as expected, the Executioner had picked a blind spot for the kill. The bench was just a few metres out of the range of the camera that covered the entrance to the police station, while the council office's own recording equipment only extended to the expensive parking spaces directly outside.

Once again, due diligence had been done.

Townsend had spent the better part of the morning trying to follow the path of Phillip Myers, the man whose escape from conviction had seemingly been the catalyst for the entire murder spree. Based on the angered expressions he kept making at his screen, or the way he slammed down his phone after a call, King ascertained it wasn't going too well.

Sitting at her desk, King had been subjected to an 'urgent procedural review', where she, Hall and Lowe all logged onto the video call to have their failings repeated countless times by people who weren't actually in the weeds of the case. Phrases like 'public interest' and 'organisational reputation' were batted about, but together, the trio stressed what a waste of time it was.

There was still a killer to catch.

Thankfully, a message from Dr Emma Mitchell gave King a valid excuse to sign off from the call, and Manning offered her his sympathies. He'd only heard her side of it, but hearing her having to defend herself and her team on more than one occasion gave him the basic gist of it.

'Don't let them get to you,' he'd offered.

'I don't.'

And King meant it.

Her focus was solely on catching the masked man pinned to the middle of the murder board and finding justice for the four people whose photos surrounded him.

'Jack, let's go,' she said as she walked into the main office. Without further information needed, Townsend leapt from his desk, eager to abandon his fruitless morning. He slipped his muscular frame into his bomber jacket.

'Where we going?'

'Mitchell called,' King said, approaching the team. 'Apparently, she already has some news on Anne-Louise. And she requested you specifically.'

Hannon and Swaby chuckled. Mitchell's flirtation, whether in jest or not, was a constant source of amusement in the team. Townsend was one of the toughest men all three of them had met. But seeing him squirm under Mitchell's jovial compliments was the only time any of them saw him in a flap.

'Oh, goody,' Townsend responded dryly, and then followed his boss out of the office and through the station. The atmosphere had morphed once more, descending beyond panic into an almost permanent state of unrest. Everyone walked with an extra step. Every conversation was uttered with a little more angst.

A dead body always set off a chain reaction that echoed through the station. A serial killer amplified it.

Townsend and King both knew that, having hunted down Gordon Baycroft and Gemma Miller.

But having a woman murdered within a stone's throw of the front door had sent a stark reminder to everyone, whether in a uniform or not, that they were steps behind a killer who seemed to know every move they were making.

Ultimately, the overwhelming feeling throughout the station was suspicion.

King and Townsend had kept the circle small since it became clear that somehow, the Executioner had access to them. It was evident from Manning's pin being planted at one of the murder scenes. It was evident from the Executioner somehow getting to the now deceased Anne-Louise Mulligan just moments before they arrived to save her.

Townsend had hoped that stepping out into the brisk, late-morning, spring air would clear his mind, but the immediate image of the SOCO tent, along with the strips of police tape that blocked off the road outside the station, was another stark reminder of the severity of the situation.

He and King walked through the town centre to the hospital and then made their way to the morgue. King buzzed to signal their arrival.

Townsend waved into the camera above the door to speed up their entry.

'I would say this is a nice surprise...' Mitchell greeted them with a smile. 'But I did invite you.'

She led them through the familiar corridor, past her neat and tidy office and through to the main room, where a white sheet clung to a body on one of the metal tables like a ghost. The bodies of Asif Khalid, Maureen Allen and Dale Ainsworth were all now preserved in storage. As Townsend ventured further into the room, he could see

Anne-Louise's head poking out from beneath the sheet, her skin almost as pale as the fabric that covered her.

She was a deathly pale.

Townsend shuddered. Surprisingly, his relocation down to Buckinghamshire had seen him quickly acclimatise to being around dead bodies. More so than he or his family would have expected. He'd seen some gruesome deaths, from Baycroft's murderous, rage fuelled stabbings, to Gemma Miller's staged suicides. All the way up to Maureen Allen's beheading.

The acts of violence themselves didn't unsettle him.

But the state of the body afterwards, the vacancy of death. That always sent a chill down his spine.

'So...' King said, stopping a few feet from the metal table as Mitchell went through her usual routine of putting on her latex gloves. 'What do you have?'

'Same, really,' Mitchell said with a sigh. 'No signs of struggle. No signs of sexual abuse. No signs of penetration.'

'Just the kill,' Townsend said coldly. Mitchell nodded.

'Yup. Straight to the point,' Mitchell said as she adjusted the sheet on the body.

'Cause of death?' King asked.

'Cardiac arrest,' Mitchell replied. 'Enforced, I might add. No, this young lady, despite her addictions, had pretty decent organs, truth be told.'

'But this could have been natural?' Townsend threw it out there. 'Or, induced through the Executioner's actions?'

'Oh, I'd say that's a certainty,' Mitchell said. 'But this isn't manslaughter. No. Considering the amount of potassium chloride that's been pumped into her, I'd say she was very much murdered.'

'Potassium chloride?' King repeated. 'As in...'

'As in a lethal injection.' Mitchell nodded.

'That's what Manning suggested,' Townsend added. 'Said it fit the narrative of capital punishment.'

'Anything else in her system?' King asked. Mitchell looked at her notes, but it was more for show.

'We'll get full tox back later today. Unsurprisingly, this has jumped the queue. But I can tell you what's not in her body. Zero traces of Midazolam and zero traces of Bromide.'

King stood still.

Townsend looked to her and then back at Mitchell, who raised her thin eyebrow at him.

'Sorry, doc,' he said sheepishly. 'I didn't do well in science at school.'

'It means she felt it all,' King answered for Mitchell, her eyes thin with rage and her voice low and vengeful.

'Usually, a death-row inmate would be sedated, medically paralyzed, and then they would inject the potassium chloride,' Mitchell explained. 'But without the first two steps...it would be fucking torture.'

'Jesus,' Townsend said, running a hand through his scruffy, dark hair.

'Her chest would have been on fire, but her heart would have been overloaded. Whatever panic she suffered would have been drowned out in agony.' Mitchell seemed genuinely upset. 'There's a reason they won't even do that to those on death row.'

'It's barbaric,' King uttered. She then snapped herself out of it. 'Can you send everything across?'

'Yup. Tox reports as soon as they come in and I cast my eye over them.'

'Thanks, Em,' King said as she headed to the door.

'Thanks, Doc,' Townsend offered.

'You know, DS Townsend. I do wish you'd come and visit me more often.' She smirked. 'You don't just have to wait for a dead body, you know?'

For once, Mitchell's joke fell a little flat, but she was thankfully rescued by Townsend's phone buzzing. He scarpered from the morgue to the outside world, boosting his signal as the voice on the other end of the line brutally cut off one of his lines of enquiry. By the time DI King had caught up, and emerged through the doors and out into the sunshine, Townsend was already off the phone, his hands on his hips and his head hung.

'Jack?'

'They found Phillip Myers,' he said glumly. The man who'd been found not guilty of the rape of a twelve-year-old girl.

That moment of perceived injustice, seemingly the reason for all that had happened.

'And?' King asked, already suspecting they'd be slamming into a brick wall.

'He's been under sedated supervision for the last four years in a mental health facility in Wiltshire.' Townsend clenched his fist with anger. 'Bottom line—'

'He's not our guy,' King said. Townsend nodded. 'Well, Jack…just another name to tick off the list.'

And that was what they had to do.

Keep searching.

Keep ticking.

Until they finally found the name that counted.

The name of the Executioner.

CHAPTER FORTY-TWO

The same morbid sense of failure hung over the rest of the SCU like a storm cloud, and Hannon and Swaby were waist deep in the mire of shifting through the physical and digital evidence. The usual positivity that batted back and forth between them was absent, and the SCU office, much like the rest of the building, felt like it was in mourning.

The radio wasn't on.

There was no friendly chatter.

Just eyes on screens and heads in files, as the reality of the morning had bled into the rest of the day.

A troubled young woman, one who'd spent the past decade battling substance abuse, was brutally slain by a man who was now openly mocking them.

They had been tasked with finding him.

Yet, it was starting to feel like they had led him to her.

With King and Townsend at the hospital, and Manning in King's office, Hannon and Swaby sat, their desks connected, as they hunted down whatever they could to take them one step closer to bringing it all to a close.

Just one breadcrumb.

Just the faint shimmer of a needle.

Swaby was leaning back in her chair, a headset clasped around her mousey blonde hair that she always wore in a ponytail. Knowing it was going to be a long, arduous morning of phone calls, she'd pinched a headset from the IT department to allow her the freedom of her hands. She'd been with the Thames Valley Police for nearly two decades, having joined in her early twenties, and she still had a charming 'old school' way of working.

Transcribing meetings or calls was done by hand.

Phone usually held to her head.

Watching her fumble with the headset configuration before the calls began was a small, jovial moment for Hannon in one that already hung heavy with regret. Eventually, Swaby connected the headset, and as her call with the manager of the Recovery Housing Project began, Hannon decided to venture out of the office, up the hill to her usual coffee shop. Shilpa often gave her stick about her addiction to coffee, often posing the idea that with the amount she spent on it, she could probably buy a barista machine. But Hannon's counterpoint was that she could buy herself a canvas and a paintbrush, but it didn't mean she could paint the *Mona Lisa*. Also, stepping out for some fresh air was good for her. It gave her eyes a rest from the screen, it allowed her to stretch her back and gave her the headspace she needed, especially on days like this.

Days when she didn't feel good enough.

The immediate image of the crime scene as she stepped out of the station didn't help with that. Her police ID would allow her passage through, and by the time she'd bought the two coffees and wandered back down the hill, the SOCO team were starting to clear away.

Hannon doubted they would have found anything.

The other three crime scenes had been as clean as a whistle, beyond a tactfully placed pin that had been planted to waste their time.

Again, it felt like the Executioner was not so much as challenging the justice system as he was openly mocking the Police Service.

When she got back into the office, Hannon handed Swaby the coffee, and she smiled her thanks. On the screen, the serious-looking woman, who Hannon assumed was the manager, was gesticulating as she spoke. Hannon couldn't hear a word and so she plugged her own ear buds in, set her favourite playlist on, and began to shuffle through the CCTV footage from the crime scene, as well as the Recovery Housing Project.

Between the two of them, Swaby and Hannon would piece together the minor details that helped build the foundations of their investigation. King and Townsend would be out and about, thumping on doors and chasing down leads. Hannon admired King more than either of them realised, and her fierce resilience could power not just the SCU alone, but the entire High Wycombe Police Station itself. The woman wasn't without her demons, and Hannon admired King's bravery in sharing her alcoholism with them, but she never let it be an excuse.

Never used it as a reason to lower her own expectations.

Townsend had seamlessly blended into the team over the past eight months, proving his worth and his loyalty by running headfirst into trouble to protect his team. Hannon's longstanding fear of 'the beat' was routed in the violent attack she'd suffered as a uniformed officer, a harrowing experience that flashed into her mind whenever her back seized up.

But with Townsend by her side, she never felt worried.

They joked that he was her 'big brother', and considering she was an only child, Hannon appreciated the feeling.

As Swaby sat, lightly drumming her pen on her pad as

she listened intently, Hannon wondered if the woman had ever ignored an order. In any industry, in any public service, there were always standout members of teams. Those who shone brighter than most, and those who took responsibility in their stride and pushed themselves to the centre of attention. But teams only functioned seamlessly when the cogs behind the scenes were turning, and Swaby was the most consistent cog in the Thames Valley Police. There was no task too menial, no job too dull or laborious.

Swaby was a grinder, and it was telling that for all the arrogance and ego of DCI Lowe, he only ever spoke to Swaby with respect. In fact, he'd even offered her a more senior role in CID when she transferred through to the SCU.

Everyone had their role, and Hannon knew hers.

She was the 'whizz kid'. She was the one who could tackle the case from the comfort of her chair and her fingers on her keyboard, but so far, there had been little reward. Yes, she had managed to pinpoint the vehicle the killer used, and yes, she'd dug out the information on the Myers case all those years ago.

Booting up the CCTV footage from the multiple crime scenes, and arranging them across her multiple screens, Hannon sipped her coffee, took a breath and began to trawl through the footage. An hour flew past like a minute, and Swaby disconnected from her call, removed the headset and slumped back in her seat.

'I need some chocolate,' she said dryly.

'Can I interest you in a Digestive?' Hannon shrugged, rolling her the half open packet of biscuits on her desk. Swaby gratefully took one. Just as she did, the SCU door opened, and DCI Lowe stepped, his shirt sleeves rolled up and his tie loosened.

Like them, he was working tirelessly, and his usual

panache had been squashed under the boot of today's murder.

'You both okay?' he asked. His sincerity catching Hannon a little by surprise.

'As well as we can be,' Swaby replied. 'I just had a long chat with Millrose House. I spoke with the staff, one at a time, to discuss Gavin Thorpe's 'non' brother.'

'Any luck?'

'So...' Swaby sighed. 'Our 'mystery brother' isn't much of a talker, which would make sense. But on the occasions he has been there, he's always had either his hood up or a hat on. Small detail, but it means he's doing whatever he can to try to hide his face from the CCTV cameras.'

'Moot point considering they don't have back-ups,' Lowe added.

'Maybe.' Swaby took a bite of the biscuit and waited until she'd swallowed before continuing. 'But we've made a request to their security supplier to see if they're able to retrieve it from some back-up network somewhere. Beyond that, they all gave a vague description. Early to mid-fifties. Pretty rough looking. Apparently, he would just sign in, go to the room and sit with Gavin.'

'And they never second guessed him?' Lowe asked.

'Would you?' Swaby offered. 'I mean, they're underfunded and understaffed as it is. They did say Thorpe recognised the man and would at least show a little more life when he was there, so an easy thing to believe.'

'Well...good work,' Lowe said with a sigh.

'I have a few other staff who aren't on shift until this afternoon to speak with,' Swaby said as she stood and stretched her back. 'So I'm going to go stretch my legs and get some lunch.'

Swaby said her goodbyes and headed out, and Lowe stood for a while, arms folded, his eyes glued to the murder board as Hannon continued with her own investigation.

Eventually, her concentration was interrupted by Lowe's voice.

'And how are you?'

'Me?' She seemed surprised.

'Yes. You.' Lowe looked around and then shunted a thumb towards King's office. 'I don't give a shit how that book worm is doing.'

'Oh. I'm okay,' Hannon said, unconvincingly.

'You sure?' Lowe stepped to her desk.

'I just feel like I'm going in circles.' Hannon sighed. 'I mean, the CCTV coverage on the street outside gives us nothing we don't already know about what happened to Anne-Louise this morning, and I'm going through the CCTV footage from the Housing Project, but there isn't much to go on.'

'No sign of Anne-Louise?'

'Nope.' Hannon shook her head. 'The only camera on the front of the building is for the entrance gate to the car park, and she doesn't pass through the barrier or the pedestrian gate.'

'She could have jumped the fence?' Lowe posed.

'Maybe. But someone would have seen that.' Hannon clicked her mouse a few times. 'There was one car that left the car park before King and Townsend arrived, but I was able to corroborate their visit with the Housing Project and speak to the owner. They were seeing a friend currently going through rehab, and I was also able to verify that they went shopping in Aylesbury not long after. CCTV of the Waterside car park shows them arriving and staying for a few hours. Beyond that, the only vehicles in and out are police cars and King and Townsend.'

'So why the glum face?'

'What do you mean?'

It wasn't often that people completely took Hannon by surprise. This was one of those moments.

'What you've just done is brilliant police work,' Lowe said firmly. 'It might not have slapped the cuffs on our guy, but you have shut down a number of possible avenues that we could have run blindly down. You've also proven one thing.'

'What's that?'

'That it's quite likely she left in a police car,' Lowe said, a hint of anger in his voice. 'Give yourself some credit, DC Hannon.'

'I dunno…' Hannon shrugged. 'Sometimes…I just…'

'People take this job for a number of reasons. And we're all built for this in different ways.' Lowe offered her a genuine smile. 'You'd do well to remember that.'

Lowe turned and headed to the door, and as he yanked it open, Hannon finally responded.

'Thank you, sir.'

'No worries.' He looked up and nodded to the countdown on the screen on the wall. 'Besides…in a few hours, we won't need the CCTV from outside the Housing Project. That sick bastard will show us all what he did to that poor girl.'

Lowe closed the door behind him, and once the shudder ran down Hannon's busted spine and leapt off, she turned back to her screen. With Lowe's encouragement still echoing in her mind, she opened the internal database and began to follow her hunch.

We're all built for this in different ways.

She hoped he was right.

CHAPTER FORTY-THREE

'Here we go.'

Lowe said it with the same apprehension that everyone was feeling, and sure enough, as the time on the clock hit zero, the feed burst into life. King felt her muscles tighten as the white mask of the Executioner erupted onto the screen in front of them, the white cross now a symbol of chaos that they couldn't contain. The visual filled the entire frame, shot once again from a tripod, only this time, there was no piercing ring light illuminating the shot. A smart move, Townsend pointed out, as a random bright ring would have been spotted by someone from the station across the road.

This time, the Executioner would depend only on the street lights that were staggered down the Queen Victoria Road, and as he stepped to the side, the entire room held their collective breath.

Clear as day, in the background, the camera showed the High Wycombe Police Station, the logo more prominent as it was backlit against the darkness.

It wasn't the slap in the face Hall had predicted.

It was a kick between the legs.

In the foreground of the shot was a wooden bench, the thick wooden panels bolted to the stone legs that held it in place. On the bench, sitting motionless, was a woman. The angle only provided a sideways shot of her, but she was clearly unconscious, and the Executioner marched confidently around so he stood before her, in full view of the camera and in clear defiance of the building behind him. With time clearly of the essence in the face of the outrageous risk he was taking, the Executioner held up the syringe in his hand for the camera, and then plunged it forcefully into Anne-Louise Mulligan's arm.

Hannon held her breath.

Townsend shuffled on the spot, his arms folded tightly and his knuckles whitening.

The Executioner stepped out of shot, presumably to hide in the shadows provided by the thick bushes that stood between him and the street lamps. Based on Mitchell's discovery of the potassium chloride in Anne-Louise's blood, King wasn't expecting to wait very long and warned the group what was to come.

It happened swiftly.

Anne-Louise jolted in her seat and then began to shake violently, her head twisting to the side to reveal her terror-stricken face as the agony shooting through her chest roared her back to consciousness. She moaned and Swaby held a hand to her mouth as the young woman gasped for help, before she collapsed backwards onto the bench. Hidden behind the slats, Anne-Louise began to convulse, with the odd limb shooting up above the wood. Through the gaps of the bench, the team could see the young woman shaking as the cardiac arrest began to reach its natural conclusion and sure enough, the woman stopped moving.

Hannon took a breath.

Lowe grumbled something about lighting several rockets up cybercrimes' arse, and then marched out.

Manning shook his head solemnly, his eyes closed, and Townsend wondered if the man was saying a prayer for the young woman.

An eerie silence, one of respect and of grief, had filled the room and King broke it by reaching forward and switching off Hannon's monitor. Then, she marched to the centre of the room and slapped her hand on the board.

'Four people,' she said sternly. 'Four people have now been brutally executed by this man right here.'

She slammed her fist against the photo of the Executioner, making the entire board shake.

Townsend turned to Hannon.

'You all right, mate?' he asked softly.

'Yeah,' Hannon replied. She tried to find Lowe's uncharacteristic words of encouragement. 'I will be.'

Before anyone could proceed, the rattling of the SCU door slamming shut caused them all to spin, and their eyes landed on Detective Superintendent Hall, who stood, hands on his hips, and his brow almost touching the tip of his nose. Townsend stood to attention, and King stepped forward.

'Sir, before you say anything—'

'I'm not here to rip you all new ones, if that's what you're worried about?'

He scanned the room, and as expected, the entire SCU and Manning looked back in confusion.

'Sir?' King urged him to continue.

'I know I've been a little impatient with this investigation. Having to speak to the Mayor on a day-to-day basis is enough for anyone to blow their brains out, quite frankly.' He nodded to the board. It was packed from edge to edge with photos, Post-its, arrows and information.

A tapestry of dedication and excellent police work.

He continued.

'You've all gone above and beyond to try to find justice for these poor people and their families. It's been hard. It's been trying. I appreciate that. And from what you tell me, DI King, you are tightening the net?'

'Well…yes, sir,' King said. 'We've been able to account for almost all of the victim's families and co-workers, so we're now focusing our efforts on our strongest lead.'

'The "brother"?' Hall accompanied the word with air quotes and a hint of disdain in his voice.

'Yes, sir,' Townsend chipped in. Whether he accepted it or not, Townsend was becoming a senior figure in the team. 'We've eliminated Phillip Myers and the family of the young girl who he'd raped.'

Behind the conversation, Hannon had found Lowe's words and had switched her monitor back on. The feed had shut down, replaced with the usual black screen, only this time, there was another message.

Another warning from the Executioner.

Only not like the others.

'Oh shit,' Hannon said out loud. It drew Swaby's attention, whose reaction was noticed by the rest of the team. Soon, all of them, including Hall, had huddled round Hannon's desk, their eyes glued to the sinister warning.

This is not over.
Those who are afraid of true justice shall be educated.
The FINAL execution will be broadcast LIVE.
By the hand of The Executioner.

'What the hell does that mean?' Swaby said to break the silence.

'It means this is almost over,' Hall stated coldly. 'And I don't want that sick bastard to win. Speak to every police service you have been in contact with and tell them their potential targets are in imminent danger.'

'Yes, sir,' King replied and then turned to address her

team. 'Get them questioning family members, journalists, any witnesses that acted even slightly strange. Have them push on the Myers case. Did anyone protest the decision? Anything and everything could be useful.'

Hall nodded approvingly as he followed on.

'I know it might not be within our town or our jurisdiction, but if he is going for a grand finale, we need to make sure he can't get to his target.'

A sense of urgency began to pump through the room, and Hall shot a confident glance to every person in it.

This was heading down its final avenue, and nobody wanted more blood to be spilled.

'If I may, sir...' Manning piped up. He'd been stationed on the periphery of the room, allowing the team to work. But now, in his customary, thoughtful approach, he stepped forward. 'We need to look at why this is now his final act.'

'What do you mean?' King asked. Manning couldn't help but smile at her.

'Well, as you discovered, there are a number of people who were, in his mind, culpable for the miscarriage of justice all those years ago. So why is he stopping now?' Manning rubbed his jaw. 'Why is this now coming to an end?'

Townsend gestured to the board.

'It doesn't matter,' he began. 'We've got eyes on the potential targets and...'

He trailed off as the penny dropped, and he turned and looked to King and Hall, who seemed to be on the same wavelength. Manning's eyebrows raised slightly as he shrugged.

'If they know that you know who the next targets are, then...'

'That fucker knows our investigation,' Hall spat with anger. He scratched his head and looked at the board. The theory of it being an inside job wasn't one he'd ignored, rather than one he didn't want to entertain.

But combined with Manning's missing pin, the spotless crime scenes and being a step ahead the entire time, Hall had no other option but to confront the fact.

He looked towards the closed door to the office and then clasped his hands to draw all attention.

'Right. From now on, this investigation stays within this room. I can assign manpower where needed, but I don't want anyone outside of you five to know what our next move is.'

King scoffed.

'Yeah, tell that to Lowe.'

'I will. And he will have to like it,' Hall said with authority. 'No more sharing with other teams. No more briefings. If the killer is someone from this building, then I want to know who the fuck it is.'

'Yes, sir,' the entire team said in unison.

'DI King.' He turned to her. 'We need someone in here round the clock. Divide the shifts up between your team, ideally two to a shift. Whatever overtime, I'll sign it off. Bottom line, I don't want anyone outside of those currently in this room to step foot in here again until this bastard is in cuffs. Understood?'

'Yes, sir,' King said. She looked to her team, knowing none of them would object.

They were all in this to the end.

It filled her with pride.

Before Hall could take his leave, Manning once again spoke up from his corner, his incredible mind clearly overturning another stone.

'There is another question we need to look at.'

They all turned to him.

'What is it?' Hall asked for them.

'If the Executioner is privy to all this information and

knows that you've tightened the net around the other jurors…' Manning shot a concerned glance to the board. 'Then who's the final target?'

It was another question they needed to answer.

One that was quite literally the difference between life and death.

CHAPTER FORTY-FOUR

Glancing through the window of her chambers, the Honourable Mrs Justice Holloway grimaced at the thought of the rush hour traffic. It had been another busy day at the Aylesbury Crown Court, and as the most senior of the High Court judges, she was looked upon by many for advice and direction. After nearly forty years of law experience, and over two decades as a High Court Judge, Claire Holloway knew that she was seen as a maternal figure to the younger judges. Not only that, but numerous solicitors and prosecutors sought her advice on a number of key issues.

All in all, she was a pillar of the UK justice system, and although her remit was within the fine county of Buckinghamshire, it wasn't a rare event for her experience to be required elsewhere. In a week's time, she would be a key speaker on a panel set up by an anti-knife charity in London, followed by an event for another charity, this time tackling homelessness, that she was a trustee of.

Despite the busy calendar, she was champing at the bit to leave the office and head home. Her loving and understanding husband, Liam, had taken a few days off from his job as a marketing director for a media company to bring their son, Harry, back home from university. It had been nearly three months since she'd seen him.

Harry was in his third year at Newcastle Law School, and her heart fluttered with pride that her son was following her into law.

He said he wanted to be a judge like her, and considering the grades he was getting and his incredible understanding of how the system worked, she didn't doubt he would.

In fact, she was sure he would surpass her.

Claire's PA ducked her head in through the office door to say her goodbyes, and Claire waved her off before skimming over the final few documents of the day. Her current case, an attempted murder by a spurned spouse had eaten up the past eight days, but with the result now sitting with the jury, she was positive that tomorrow she would be able to draw a line under it.

One way or another.

Because that was what the justice system was about. Ensuring every person accused of a crime was given a fair trial, a chance to defend themselves and for a panel of unconnected people be presented with the facts and come to a unanimous decision. All under her careful and knowledgeable eye. Outside the court, the traffic was beginning to fade in tune with the sun setting, and with an eager spring in her step, she began to pack away her documents.

Knock. Knock.

She glanced up to the door, where once again, her PA's head popped through.

'Kelly, I thought you'd left?' she said with the stern manner of a headmistress.

'Sorry, ma'am.' Kelly almost curtseyed. 'But the police are here to see you?'

'See me?' She frowned and placed her glasses back on

to look at the calendar on her screen. 'There's nothing in the diary.'

It wasn't unusual for the police to seek her advice, but it was unusual to be calling at this hour.

'He says it's an emergency. He's waiting outside.'

'I'm on my way out now,' Claire said with a wave of the hand. 'Head on home, and I'll speak with them on the way out.'

Kelly nodded and disappeared, and a few minutes later, with her spring jacket looped over her arm, and her laptop swinging in the satchel she clung to, Claire Holloway headed to the exit. The courts had been closed for a few hours, and the only sound that interrupted the silence of the corridor was her own footsteps. As she made her way to the reception, she saw the policeman standing on the steps beyond the glass doors, his eyes locked on the emptying road before him. The evening security guard wasn't at his post, although she often saw him sneaking out back for a cigarette.

She had even joined him for a few, and the thought of a nice cigarette and a glass of wine in the spring breeze became very appealing. With a resigned sigh, Claire pushed open the doors and stepped out into the cool evening.

'Good evening, officer,' she said, struggling to hide the inconvenience in her voice. 'Can I help you?'

The officer introduced himself with a gruff voice and a rather curt manner. He wasn't the tallest, but he was sturdy and Claire got the impression that he could more than handle himself. Just in the way he moved, the years of experience in his voice and the sigh he gave as he showed her his identification.

'I'm sorry, ma'am, but in light of the current murders in High Wycombe, we believe that your life may be in danger.'

'Excuse me?' Her eyes widened. 'I have no idea what you're talking about.'

'The Executioner, ma'am,' the officer stated. 'We believe those murders are linked to a trial from a decade ago, one which you presided over.'

'I see.' Holloway paused for thought. She'd been following the investigation on the local news. 'And how does it link back to one of my trials?'

'Ma'am, four members of the jury have been murdered over the past two weeks.' He took a step toward her. His body language verged on threatening. 'I've been asked to escort you home safely and wait outside until a detective is available to speak to you.'

'Right,' Claire said with a slightly worried nod. 'I have plans this evening with my family. So if you don't mind, can we please get home and get this sorted as quickly as possible?'

She turned to head towards the car park, but the officer stepped in her way.

'I have strict orders to escort you home, ma'am. I'm parked round the back, if you could follow me, please.' The officer was almost speaking through gritted teeth. He kept flicking his eyes above her.

Why?

Claire sighed and shook her head.

'Let's go. I'm also parked round the back, and I'd rather not leave the car here overnight.' The officer agreed and fell in step behind her.

As she strode briskly around the large building, Claire was adamant that she wouldn't let the man's intrusion or quite confrontational behaviour ruin her mood. She hadn't seen her son in so long, and returning home with a face like thunder and a grievance to air would just ruin the evening. Besides, she'd spent decades dealing with the police, and knew full well that usually when an officer is being snappy, it's because they've had a worse day than most people could contemplate.

They were just expected to get on with it.

Dealing with the shit that nobody wants to think about.

Considering the officer who was following her was roughly the same age as her, she'd imagined he's seen his fair share of that shit in his lifetime.

He was just doing his job. And if their concerns held merit, he was putting himself in the line of some pretty heinous fire.

As she thought about turning and apologising to the officer, she almost collided with the security guard. He apologised profusely, but she just chuckled, wished him a pleasant evening and continued to the car park that was tucked away behind the court itself. As she rounded the corner, she got a waft of the smoke that the security guard had left behind, and once again allowed her mind to wander to the packet of cigarettes in her study desk, and the pleasant evening that lay ahead.

Hopefully, the detective that would arrive at some point wouldn't disrupt the evening too much, and by then, her police escort would have cheered up a little.

Or better yet, been told to go home.

As she entered the car park itself, she tried to connect the dots on how the Executioner could be targeting her, and as she did, she walked past a grey van.

Behind her, the footsteps grew quicker.

It was only then, as she looked out to the vacant spaces, that she realised that apart from the van behind her, hers was the only car in the car park.

There was no police vehicle in sight.

Instinctively, she turned, ready for confrontation, but immediately, she felt the firm grip of a hand latch across her face like a muzzle, pressing the soaked rag to her nose and lips.

As she felt her airways fill with pungent fumes, the world around her began to spin and fade.

The last thing she remembered was the contorted scowl of the officer as he pulled her towards the back of the van with his powerful arms.

Her last vision was of his eyes, bulging with rage as he sapped away her consciousness.

Eyes filled with murderous hate.

CHAPTER FORTY-FIVE

No matter how long or how trying the day had been, walking into the house while Mandy and Eve were still awake quickly wiped the slate clean. After the premier of the haunting execution of Anne-Louise Mulligan, Townsend and the team went about finding who the next target could be. Dr Manning had made a prescient point that if the killer was a copper, then they'd know that jury members were now accounted for.

Safe.

But not long after Hall had told King to keep the investigation within the confines of the SCU, King had sent Swaby and Townsend home. They both protested, but King underscored the order from Hall that he wanted them on it twenty-four seven. They would now be working in overlapping shifts, but Townsend knew King would most likely be there for the duration. He was just as dedicated, but King pointed out that both Swaby and Townsend had children waiting for them at home.

So when he opened the door to his home, the thundering footsteps that approached were welcome. As was the lunging hug from his daughter that almost drove the air from his lungs.

'Hello, Pickle,' he said with a smile, tightly squeezing the girl who clung to him like a koala. 'How are you?'

'I'm fine,' she said with a smile. 'It's the Easter holiday soon.'

'Ah, yes,' Townsend said, more to himself than her.

A reminder.

Mandy appeared in the doorway to the kitchen.

'Hello, babe,' she said with a grin. Townsend managed to wriggle free from the clutches of his adoring daughter and met his wife for a passionate kiss. Eve made a puking noise.

'What's the matter?' Townsend turned to his daughter, his arm still around his wife's waist.

'That's gross,' Eve stated.

'What? This?' Townsend turned and planted another kiss on his wife's lips. Eve protested, and Mandy chuckled as the three of them made their way into the kitchen.

'Beer?' she asked, practically reading his mind. He nodded, and she took two bottles from the fridge, popped the caps off and handed him one. 'Cheers.'

'Cheers,' he echoed and took a swig. 'How was work?'

'Not bad.' Mandy slid into one of the chairs by the kitchen table as Eve situated herself between the two of them, her workbook open before her. 'I have to go into the office next week for a client meeting…'

Townsend nodded along.

'That's good, right?'

'Well, it's my first one.' She shrugged. 'But I'm just there for support, really. I think they want me doing a little more than just EA work, but I'm not too keen on the extra hours for a few quid extra.'

'What do you want to do?' Townsend asked. The question seemed to catch Mandy completely off guard.

'What do you mean?'

'I mean what do you want to do?' He took a thoughtful sip of his drink. 'I mean, if you love your job, then great. But you said to me last year this was your introduction back into the workplace, and we both know you're too smart to be running round after someone else.'

Mandy couldn't hide her flattered grin.

'I haven't really thought about it. You know, with your job being the way it is, I just figured having something steady was an easier fit for us.'

Townsend shrugged and had another swig.

'Give it some thought. It'd be nice if one of us had a good day at work from time to time.'

His comment was laced with sadness, but Mandy knew better than to ask about it in front of Eve. Their daughter was now nine years old, but Townsend was still keen to shield her from the finer details of his job. She knew he was a detective and understood that his job could call to him at any time. She also understood that he dedicated that time to stopping bad people from doing bad things, and whenever she spoke of his job, she did so with pride.

And she would never understand just how much that meant to him.

'What do you fancy for dinner?' Mandy asked, changing the subject.

'I don't know.' Townsend turned to his daughter and pressed his index finger into her side, causing her to wriggle. 'What do you fancy, Pickle?'

'PIZZA!' Eve roared, pumping both fists into the air.

With the decision made, Townsend ordered in from a local pizza restaurant, and within the hour, their kitchen table was covered in pizza boxes. As always, they'd ordered too much, but whatever was left over would be fine for the next day or so.

'Cold pizza?' Eve turned her nose up at the thought.

'You don't know what you're missing, kiddo,' Townsend said, pulling another slice from the box and making a show of lapping at the stringy cheese, much to his daughter's delight. Mandy called him a pig, but couldn't stifle her own laughter. After they'd all eaten too much, they collapsed on the sofa, and Eve cuddled into Townsend as they watched some of her favourite film. As the time ticked towards eight o'clock, Mandy began running Eve a bath, and Townsend tidied up the kitchen as his wife got their daughter washed and ready for bed. When he finally made his way up the stairs, Eve was already sitting up in her bed, her legs covered with the duvet, and she waggled her Harry Potter book at him.

'Mummy and I have read loads since you last did,' she said with a grin.

'Oh, really?' Townsend looked to his wife. 'I bet she loved that.'

Mandy rolled her eyes, kissed their daughter goodnight, and left them to it. Although Townsend had never been one for Potter, he found himself enjoying it more than he'd thought. Possibly because his daughter seemed enchanted by the magical world, and that she could relate to the insecurities and problems that children faced.

Somewhere in the house, he could hear a low, dull rumbling sound.

He read on.

As the pages turned and the story unfolded, Townsend looked down at his daughter, who had fallen asleep with her head on his chest. Carefully, he placed the book on the nightstand, lowered her to the pillow, and gently placed a kiss on her forehead.

'Goodnight, Pickle,' he said softly, clicking off the bedside lamp and shuffling quietly out of the bedroom. Townsend made his way down to the kitchen, eager for another beer and to switch off with a TV show of his wife's choosing. According to her, they were behind on watching some of the hottest shows on TV, but Townsend didn't see that as a fatal flaw of their marriage.

But as he pulled open the fridge, he heard the rumbling once more, this time much louder, and he turned to see his mobile shunting across the wood of their kitchen table. Mandy was sitting at the other end, still nursing her beer and flicking through her phone.

'That's the third time it's rung, babe,' she said with a sigh of acceptance.

Townsend felt the pizza in his stomach flip over.

As the incoming call sprang the phone into life once more, he knew who it was before he looked at the screen.

DI King.

He knew why she was calling before he had even reached for the phone.

'Answer it, babe.' Mandy nodded encouragingly. Townsend shook his head, and Mandy stood and purposefully snatched up the phone and approached him. 'Answer it.'

Townsend pulled her in close, breathing her in.

'I really don't want to,' he said, meaning every word.

'I know.' She stepped back and once again held out the phone. 'But this will only stop when you catch this bastard.'

Townsend took a breath, looking deep into the stunning, beep blue eyes of his wife. Everything about her made his heart beat faster, and with a resigned look, he took the phone and answered the call.

'Guv.'

He listened intently and his brow furrowed.

'On my way.'

Townsend turned, kissed his wife, grabbed his coat, and rushed out of the door. Within seconds he was pulling off the driveway, once again being pulled away from

Mandy, and what he had hoped would have been a pleasant evening off.

But duty called.

A high court judge had been reported missing.

And Townsend didn't need to be a detective to work out which case she had presided over a decade ago.

CHAPTER FORTY-SIX

The country lane was shrouded in darkness, and the only lighting came from the tasteful spotlights that were dotted across the wall of the house. The Holloway family home oozed wealth and status, tucked away from the public eye behind well maintained trees and a thick, metal gate. Usually, the only cars that would be parked on the gravel laden driveway were the Honourable Mrs Justice Holloway's black 4x4, and her husband's dark-blue sports car.

But tonight, King had parked her own car beside the sports car, and two police cars were also in attendance.

Little Kimble was not so much a village as it was a stretch of country road, with large, expensive houses all designed and presented to the owners' tastes. The 'village' was an affluent hub between High Wycombe and Aylesbury, so much so that it demanded its own rail station which amounted to nothing more than a small building and two concrete platforms.

King had arrived ten minutes prior, liaising with the uniformed officers who she didn't know. They were based out in Aylesbury Police Station but were able to respond to

Liam Holloway's panicked call about his wife's abduction. In most cases, the man's terror would have been viewed with a dose of scepticism, especially as in most domestic cases, the answer is usually closer to home. But King knew in the pit of her stomach that this wasn't the work of an angry spouse trying to cover his tracks.

It was the work of the Executioner.

As she awaited Townsend's arrival, King spoke with two of the uniformed officers, who updated her on the chaos unfolding back in Aylesbury. Uniform were locking down the city in a one-mile radius, while CID were handling the courthouse. King had already reached out to the DS in charge of the search, informing him that she'd be there as soon as she'd spoken to Liam Holloway.

If the Executioner had wanted to ramp up the tension, he'd more than succeeded.

Soon, headlights appeared in the distance, navigating the winding road that snaked under the overhanging branches of the trees. The Holloways were clearly successful in their chosen professions, and that success meant being able to afford such a private residence. As the car fully came into view, King held up her hand to shield her eyes from brightness, and Townsend pulled the car through the open gate, and his tyres crunched the gravel before coming to a stop. King stepped forward as he hopped out of the car.

'Guv.'

'Sorry to pull you in.' King checked her watch. It was nearly half nine.

'Is he inside?' Townsend asked, ignoring her apology. It wasn't needed.

'Yep.' King turned and headed towards the door, where two of the unknown officers stood watch. They had their hands tucked into their stab proof vests, and were discussing the previous night's football. 'Excuse me, constables.'

The two fresh-faced young men stepped to the side and almost stood to attention. Townsend thanked them both as they knocked on the door, and it was quickly yanked open by a man no older than they were.

'Harry Holloway?' King asked. She'd spent the time waiting for Townsend to have Hannon dig up some information on the family. 'I'm DI King, and this is DS Townsend.'

'Come in, come in.' The boy beckoned, not even fussing about their identification. As they walked into the home, it took all of Townsend's power to not whistle at the impressive home.

High ceilings.

Wooden beams.

Plush, expensive furniture.

They followed the young man through to the kitchen, where the father, Liam, was seated. He was a carbon copy of his son, just with a half a decade more wear and tear on the skin, and an unsuccessful battle with his hairline. Liam was seated at the marble topped island that stood proudly in the middle of the kitchen. As his bloodshot eyes fell upon the detectives, he stood respectfully. King and Townsend introduced themselves again, shaking the man's hand and gesturing for him to sit.

'When did you realise that your wife was missing?' King kicked things off. Liam Holloway was every bit the corporate director that his job professed, and he spoke clearly and thoughtfully.

'Claire works late. A lot,' he insisted. 'Sometimes I won't hear from her until gone nine on a busy day.'

King checked her watch.

'It's not even ten,' King she said. 'Are you sure she's missing?'

He nodded.

'Yes, because I spent the day bringing that young man right there back from uni in Newcastle. It's all she's been talking about all week, and she promised she'd be home early this evening so we could all have dinner together. We even stopped on the way, as usually, she gets held up at work, and I knew she wanted to be home to welcome him.'

'Have you tried to contact her?' Townsend asked. He had to.

'Of course,' Liam replied, understanding the need to tick all boxes. 'But her phone's off. It was ringing out for about , now it just goes straight to voicemail.'

King already knew that the man wouldn't be able to offer much. None of the families had been able to so far, on account of them not expecting what was coming. None of the other jurors would have more than a vague recollection of the other faces in the room, or the names of their peers from over a decade ago. Life moves on and life moves fast, and the brain is on a constant archiving process to keep people going.

Forgetting pointless information from years ago was always the first port of call.

For Claire Holloway, she had overseen hundreds of cases in her career, and as a high court judge, all of them carried with them a level of severity and undoubtedly, morbid details. If she was able to forget some of the atrocities she'd been subjected to, she would have.

King wished she could do the same.

When it became apparent that Liam had no information of use, Townsend was able to clarify the man's alibi of being on the motorway when the Executioner had struck. He had a receipt for a Costa Coffee just off of the M1 near Dunstable, and the time of payment put him miles away from where his wife was taken.

King then explained the widespread search for Claire

that was already underway, and that the safe return of the judge was the number one priority for the entire Thames Valley Police. Every available unit from both Aylesbury and High Wycombe had been pulled in, and King assured them that they were doing everything within their remit to find her. With their presence required at the courthouse, King and Townsend thanked Liam for his time, made promises of trying their best to bring his wife home, but stopped short of guaranteeing it, much to the son's dismay.

'They can't promise that, Harry,' Liam had snapped, the situation clearly getting to him. 'But they'll do what they can.'

'Everything we can,' Townsend emphasised, and minutes later, he and King were racing each other towards the locked-down courthouse, pushing their pedals to the floor to get there as fast as possible. The late night offered them open roads, and as they passed through Stoke Mandeville, they saw the first police blockade, which had slowed a number of cars to a crawl. King angrily punched her horn, drawing an irate officer to her window who soon changed his attitude when she presented her credentials. Swiftly, he waved both King and Townsend through and at King's insistence, radioed their license plates to any blockades on their path ahead.

Every major road that connected to a way out of Aylesbury was now awash with blue flashing lights, and a sense of panic felt like it was being carried on the late-night breeze. Townsend recognised the dual carriageway that led up towards the crown court from his visit earlier in the week, and the entire building was lit up with the same blue lights that now painted the streets. As they approached, one of the uniformed officers waved them through the cordon, and both King and Townsend pulled right up to the front of the building. As King stepped out, a haggard-looking man in an ill-fitting suit approached her with an extended hand.

'DI King?' he asked, and she nodded, taking the hand. 'DS Wilder.'

'What's the update?' King asked. The man had clearly been informed she was SIO.

'We've done a search of the building, but found nothing.' He sighed. 'We've spoken to her assistant, Kelly Porter, who confirmed that a police officer had arrived at the end of the day to speak to the judge.'

'Did she get his name?' Townsend asked, joining the conversation. He held out his hand. 'DS Townsend.'

'No, she didn't.' Wilder shook the hand. 'Well, she couldn't remember. She said he was white, middle-aged. According to her, he "looked like a cop".'

'Where is she now?' King asked, walking towards the glass doors to the courthouse and peering through.

'We have uniform bringing her to Aylesbury station. Do you want to speak to her?'

'Not right now,' King said. 'But I need someone to dig up every photo on file we have of every white, male police officer, over the age of thirty, who's currently serving in the TVP and have her go through them. She could identify our guy.'

The detective looked a little confused.

'You think she's been taken by a police officer?' He looked a little flummoxed, and King remembered he wasn't privy to the same information that she was.

'It's a possibility. But if that's not the case, then that police officer was the last person to see her before she was taken, and we need to speak with them.' King pointed through the glass. 'Is that the security guard?'

'Yes.' Wilder was already on his phone. 'Hassan will let you through.'

King and Townsend thanked the detective, who began

making the necessary calls, and they hurried towards the entrance. PC Hassan was a large man with a thick, black beard, and after checking their identification, he showed them through and introduced them to the security guard, who seemed guilt-ridden at what had happened.

'I saw her,' he said. 'I just popped out for a quick smoke. You know, at that time…there are only a few people left in the building. The courthouse was closed to the public.'

'When was this?' Townsend asked.

'About six-ish. Maybe half past.' He blushed. 'She was with one of your lot. I didn't need to look after her…'

'And were you aware of why the police had made contact with Mrs Holloway?'

'No, I wasn't.' He seemed almost embarrassed. 'But we get police in here all the time. Only…usually, they sign in. You know? Come to the reception desk.' He pulled the logbook from behind the counter. 'I know I was outside for a few minutes, but our man didn't sign the book. He didn't even come into the building.'

'Where's the CCTV outside the building?' Townsend asked.

'Just one camera out there.' He pointed to the doorway. 'And another overlooking the car park. I had a look at the footage before we sent it across. He's hardly in either of the videos.'

'He knew where they were,' King surmised out loud. There was no reason to doubt the man, but she'd have Hannon corroborate it swiftly. 'And the vehicle?'

'It was a van. Grey.' The security guard let out a deep breath. 'I thought it was a bit strange when I saw the uniform but no marked car. They usually stick out like a sore thumb.'

'Did you recognise the man?' Townsend said. He held back from saying officer.

'We get a lot of your lot in here. Every day. I couldn't tell you his name. He was white. Short…like shaved…grey hair. Pretty grumpy looking.' The security guard shrugged. 'That's all, really.'

King saw Detective Superintendent Hall arriving and left Townsend to wrap up the conversation with the security guard. They'd need the names of everyone who'd visited the courthouse yesterday, along with every sign in of an officer from the past few weeks. PNCing them was a job for Swaby, who would diligently eliminate anyone who was there for a true reason. Through the glass, King could see Hall asserting his authority across the crime scene, and as she emerged back out into the cool night, Hall was finishing his discussion with DS Wilder and turned to face her.

'You okay, sir?' King asked, as Wilder turned to follow whatever order Hall had just given him.

'No. Far from it,' Hall groaned. 'We *cannot* allow this maniac to execute a judge, King. It would be biblical.'

'Yes, sir. Townsend's just finishing up with the guard, Hannon's on the CCTV back at HQ, and once we have copies of the logbooks, Swaby will go through every visitor in that building for the past few weeks.'

Hall's brow furrowed.

'I've just had Commissioner Powell on the phone on the drive up here.' Hall looked around the street, at the police cordons and the flashing lights. 'She's making her way into Aylesbury station as we speak. I need to debrief her, and then I need *everyone* back at HQ for a proper briefing. We need to find Judge Holloway.'

'Understood, sir,' King said

Hall stood up straight, a pillar of authority.

'So whatever you need to do. Do it. Don't worry about the red tape. I'll handle that and any fucker who gives you trouble. You understand me? The clock is ticking on this one, Izzy. We need to find that bastard. And you and your team are the best shot that she has of making this out alive. So dig deep, and get your team to do whatever it is they need to do.'

'Yes, sir,' King said with conviction. Hall offered her an encouraging smile, and then headed back to his car, offering encouragement to the officers who were standing watch. King blew out her cheeks and turned back to the glass doors, where Townsend trudged out, holding the thick logbook in his arms. King raised an eyebrow.

'I couldn't be arsed waiting for him to shift through it. I'll do it myself back at the station.'

As Townsend steadied himself, King glanced up and across the stretch of bricks above to the CCTV camera. It was high up, designed to offer a clear and widespread view of the entire outside area. The officer would most likely be visible, but not identifiable. Same with the car park camera.

King could feel a sense of dread sweeping through her body.

He'd have planned his movements carefully.

Targeting the jurors had felt like a quest of vengeance, dressed up as a noble crusade.

But to execute an honourable judge, live on the internet, would send the Executioner's message global. The national interest in the case was growing by the day, but international media outlets wouldn't be able to ignore such a story.

The clock was ticking, and King felt in her gut that the Executioner was building to a violent crescendo.

As they reached their cars, King stopped, opened the door for Townsend, who dumped the logbooks on his passenger seat.

'I'm just going to speak to DS Wilder. Make sure we're

all aligned,' King stated. 'Head back to the station and start going through those names with Swaby.'

'No worries,' Townsend said and then offered her a half-hearted smile. 'We'll find her, guv.'

King looked out across the street. The uniformed officers were standing by their cars, intermittently illuminated by blue lights that warned off any late-night drivers. Somewhere out there, Claire Holloway was being held against her will, taken by a man she should have trusted and was now on the likely countdown to her death.

They couldn't let that happen.

Knowing her team, and the rest of the Thames Valley Police would be working tirelessly through the night, King willed the fatigue from her body and looked back to Townsend.

'I hope so. For all our sakes.'

CHAPTER FORTY-SEVEN

'Do you remember me?'

The gruff voice called to Claire Holliday from somewhere behind her, and she felt her entire body tighten with fear. The restraints around her wrist were cutting into the skin and had locked her hands behind the back of the chair she had been forced into. The tightly pulled cables that pinned her arms to her side and her body to the seat threatened to impact her strained, panicked breathing.

She couldn't answer.

The gag that had been wrapped around her jaw had been knotted at the base of her skull, pulling the fabric taut against her mouth. Her feet were also bound, each one strapped to a front leg of the chair, meaning she was locked in place.

She wasn't going anywhere.

What was worse was she couldn't see a thing.

When she had roused from her slumber, she'd tried to piece together what had happened.

She recalled getting ready to leave her chambers, a spring in her step at the thought of the reunion with Harry. Her pride and joy was on his way back for the Easter break, and she had been champing at the bit to spend some time with him.

Kelly had interrupted her.

A policeman was there to escort her home.

Her recollection was fuzzy, the remnants of the chloroform presented her memories in a haze. Everything was slightly out of sync, but she remembers the officer waiting for her on the steps to the crown court. He'd been curt.

What had he warned her?

That she was a target?

She could remember the fresh air as she'd stepped out of the building, and for some reason, the smell of smoke as she headed to the car park. Had someone else been there? Or were her own nicotine cravings jumping to the fore due to her perilous position?

There'd been a van.

Then blackness.

And when she'd finally roused and opened her eyes, there was nothing but blackness again. At first, she'd been terrified that she'd lost her sight, but once she'd managed to find something resembling calm, she took stock of the situation. Her paralysis wasn't physical. She'd been bound to the chair she was sitting in. And the stuffiness that clogged her nose was due to the bag that had been placed over her head.

The officer had been right.

She was a target.

And now, in a location that she didn't know nor could she see, in a seat that she couldn't escape from, a man's voice that she didn't recognise boomed from behind her.

She tried to respond, but her voice was muffled.

Her captor spoke again.

'How rude of me.'

His voice carried an air of superiority, as if he was enjoying his position. She felt a powerful hand latch onto her shoulder; the grip digging into her muscles causing her body to jerk in pain. He pulled up the cloth that was covering her head, rolling it up so it rested on the tip of her nose. Then he violently wrenched the gag from her mouth.

Claire gasped for air.

She tried to speak through her sharp breaths.

'Please. Let. Me. Go.'

She felt hopeless, but it was all she could muster. Despite her vision still being obscured, she could feel the presence of the man in front of her.

'I don't expect you to remember me.' He returned to his previous train of thought. 'Why would you? It wasn't *my* case you railroaded.'

She tried to place the voice. Tried to connect the dots.

Nothing.

'We can sort this out.' She tried to remain calm. 'Whatever the problem, this is not the right way to go about sorting it.'

Her captor laughed.

'And what would the right way be?' he asked. 'For this to go through the proper channels? For whatever sense of injustice I feel has occurred, it deserves an investigation and a fair trial? Don't make me laugh. There's no such thing as a justice system. *You* made that very clear to me a long time ago.'

Claire tried and failed to struggle against her restraints. Her fear was slowly being replaced with defiance, as if it was her last throw of the dice.

'How did I make that clear?' She spat. 'I don't even know who you are.'

She heard a ruffling sound a few inches from her face, and then the rough hands clamped onto her head and pulled the hood clean off. The brightness of the room hit her like a cold slap to the face, and she instantly squinted through the brightness. Slowly, as her vision returned, the person before her came into focus.

She froze with fear.

A few inches from her was a leather-clad face, with dark eyes burning through the eyeholes. Across the mask itself, there was a white cross, crudely stitched from corner to corner.

It was a symbol she'd been following with interest in the news.

The Executioner.

Instantly, her mind snapped back to her last conscious moment, the passage of time had escaped her a while ago. She had no idea how long she'd been held captive, and no clue where they were. But she recalled the words of the police officer who'd been sent to protect her.

'The Executioner, ma'am. We believe these murders are linked to a case from a decade ago, one in which you presided over.'

Just like her vision, her mind suddenly fell back into clarity. She'd been abducted by a violent serial killer who'd been raging a horrifying campaign against what they had perceived as a broken justice system. Whatever pathways this troubled individual had taken, they'd led him to her.

And now she was at his mercy.

She thought of Harry. Of Liam.

How long had she been missing? Did they know? Were they worried?

Were the police searching for her?

All those questions were begging to be asked, but in her terror, as she gazed into the unblinking stare of the man who meant to kill her, she could only muster a few words.

'I-I-I'm sorry.'

The Executioner didn't move.

Didn't blink.

She looked beyond him and around at the small, modestly furnished living room of the home she'd been taken to. On the coffee table before her was a toolbox, some metal brackets and rolls of elasticated chord. There was nothing that signalled a family, nor anything resembling a happy home.

It was as vacant as the look in her captor's eyes.

'There is no apology you can offer.' He finally spoke. His words were heavy with hatred. 'A decade ago, you were presented with the facts. DI Gavin Thorpe had dedicated months of his life to prove that Phillip Myers had raped twelve-year-old Amanda Swann. It cost him everything. His marriage. His sobriety. His sanity. Yet this system we have…this broken system…allowed twelve uneducated people to undo his work. Twelve people, none of whom knew the law nor the way it worked the way we do…the way DI Thorpe knew…were allowed to pick holes in his investigation. To question the work he'd done.'

'Everyone deserves a fair trial,' Claire said meekly.

The Executioner rocked her in her seat as he connected with a brisk slap with his gloved hand.

'Fair?' His voice rose. 'Justice should have seen Myers rot in a fucking cell for the rest of his life. But instead, you allowed the verdict of not guilty to stand. You were presented with the same facts. You looked into the eyes of a rapist and upheld the uneducated verdict. You…Mrs Honourable Justice…were just as culpable.'

Claire was crying. The sting from the slap was still burning within her cheek, but it was the realisation that had drawn tears.

Four people had been executed by this man.

For the world to see.

And she was next. As she wept in her seat, and trembled in terror, it was as if the Executioner could read her mind.

'True justice would have seen Phillip Myers being locked away, and a good friend of mine know that his sacrifices hadn't been for nothing.' He stood, and then to her horror, revealed a jagged blade that shimmered under the light above. 'But this isn't a *just* world. This system didn't allow that. So I'm here to restore that balance. And you...you will be the final representation of that act.'

He leant down, his mask less than an inch from her face. She flinched as he held the blade up to her face, pressing the flat metal against her cheek.

'You will be executed for your dereliction of duty. And when your blood is shed, and the country sees what I've done...then maybe they will understand the need to fix this.'

The Executioner stepped back, withdrawing the blade, and Claire gave a sigh of relief. The Executioner regarded her for a few more moments, and then, despite her protests, wrenched the gag back into her mouth and cloaked her in darkness once more.

Then he turned to the laptop, knowing that the following message would send the Thames Valley Police into overdrive.

He would be lowering his defences.

Once the message was typed out, he hit send, uploading it to the feed that he'd worked so hard to keep untraceable.

The execution of Mrs Honourable Justice Holliday will be shown LIVE tonight.

By the hand of The Executioner.

There wasn't any way he'd be able to block the live feed from their surveillance.

They would come for him.

For the judge.

But The Executioner was willing to die for his cause if needed.

CHAPTER FORTY-EIGHT

'So we know what the plan is.'

Hall stood at the front of the briefing room, his shoulders set and his authority undeniable. Behind him, the murder board had been wheeled in, and every inch of it was covered. All four victims were pinned in a row across the top, surrounded by Post-its and crime scene photos, and the unnerving face of the Executioner. To the side of the board stood Townsend and King, watching as the packed-out briefing room had locked their eyes on Hall. DS Swaby was sitting in the front row, alongside Manning who'd insisted on joining the team for the night-long quest to find the judge. Hannon had been excused from the briefing, as she continued to lead the search of the van from the CCTV footage. DCI Lowe was standing at the back of the room, arms folded, alongside a few of his team. Rows of uniformed officers were crammed together on seats, all of them sitting to attention despite the crushing weight of fatigue. Boyd and Walsh were among them, both looking as tired as Townsend felt.

Hall gave a sharp look to the board and pointed at the picture of the masked murderer.

'In the early hours of this morning, that man right there announced that tonight, he would murder judge Claire Holloway live on the internet.' He let the very real threat hang in the room for a moment. 'That cannot happen. I know how hard everyone in this room is working to ensure we find Mrs Holloway, and that most of you have been here all night. But we cannot stop now. So, eyes and ears, and DI King will lead us through what we know so far.'

Hall stepped to the other side of the murder board, allowing DI King to take the floor. With a sense of authority, King stepped up, and tapped the photo of DI Gavin Thorpe on the board.

'Ten years ago, DI Gavin Thorpe was a pillar of this very police station. He arrested this man, Phillip Myers, for the rape of this young girl, Amanda Swan.' King pointed to the photos on the board. 'A long, and gruelling investigation, that ultimately ended with a not-guilty verdict. Thorpe soon left the force, and his life fell apart, and he is now in an assisted-living complex in Slough after multiple mental breakdowns and struggles with addiction. The Swann family has all been accounted for, as has Phillip Myers,' King continued. 'Asif Khalid, Maureen Allen, Dale Ainsworth, and Anne-Louise Mulligan all served on the jury that came to that verdict, and Claire Holloway was the judge who oversaw it.'

Before her, officers were scribbling notes and nodding along, all of them locked in. Townsend stepped forward.

'We've spoken to everyone with access to the farm where the execution of Dr Khalid took place,' he began. 'We've also cross-checked every patient that Khalid had seen over the past six months with our own database, and the few that pinged had been accounted for. Likewise, DS Swaby went through all the guests who attended the charity event where Dr Khalid was taken, and all of them have been cleared from the investigation.'

King noted the pause and naturally continued.

'DS Townsend's been trying to locate the murder weapons, which have yet to be found.' King then moved to the photo of Maureen Allen. 'Like with Dr Khalid, we have eliminated all of Maureen Allen's co-workers from the investigation, and our investigation into the acquisition of the materials used to build the guillotine have so far been unsuccessful.'

'Our killer knows what they're doing,' Townsend added. 'They know every single avenue that we would look in to.'

Hall spoke from the side of the room.

'DCI Lowe.' All heads turned to the back of the room. 'I believe your team found the same when looking into the noose used to murder Dale Ainsworth?'

'Yes, sir.' Lowe nodded firmly. Hall turned back to King, signalling for her to continue.

'So, we need to focus on what we do know. And we know that by targeting these four unconnected people, and now the judge, that the quest for what the Executioner perceives as justice, is based on this trial. The other jurors have all been accounted for and are safe, but this all leads back to DI Gavin Thorpe. And more specifically, the man posing as his brother.'

A few officers shared confused glances, and Townsend once again took the lead.

'At the living complex where Thorpe now lives, he is regularly visited by a man posing as his brother. Now, Gavin Thorpe has a sister, but no brother, and according to the staff, he's visited Thorpe since he moved in. The emergency contact number is a dud, and they have no other means of contacting him. Both DC Hannon and DS Swaby have spoken with the staff, although there is one member of staff still speak to which DC Hannon will be doing today.'

'But we can't wait until then,' Hall said, stepping back to the front of the room. 'We need to find Claire Holloway, and I don't want it to be after she's butchered in front of the watching world. Now, DCI Lowe has the cyber team ready to trace the link the second it goes live, and we should then be able to locate this bastard. But until that link goes live, we need to be out there, hunting every god damn lead we have and following every fucking hunch that comes our way. Understood?'

A united agreement echoed from the crowd of officers, and Hall dismissed them with a thanks. As they filed out, he turned to King and Townsend, who were eager to join them.

'Good work. All of you.' He turned to Swaby and Manning, also. 'We've got until that link goes live, and…'

'Yeah, that doesn't feel right to me,' Townsend cut in. Hall turned to him. 'Sir.'

'None of this feels right, DS Townsend,' Hall replied.

'I know, but if, as we believe, this man has knowledge of how these investigations work, then he will know that the second he begins that feed, we'll be on him like a hawk.'

'So we'll be quick,' Hall assured him. 'I have an Armed Response Unit already on site. They're ready to go at a moment's notice.'

'But that's the point I'm making,' Townsend said, looking around the group. 'It feels like he's inviting us.'

Manning nodded, clearly in agreement.

'I think DS Townsend might be right,' he offered. 'What better way for his crusade to end than to be made a martyr for his cause?'

Hall's phone began to buzz, and he pulled it from his jacket and frowned.

'His cause isn't the priority. Finding Claire Holloway and bringing her back alive is. Now, all of you…go do what you do best. Find that poor woman and catch that bastard.'

Hall marched out, phone pressed to the side of his skull and already in what sounded like a heated conversation. The Executioner hadn't just gripped the entire town in fear, he'd caused chaos with his abduction of the judge. The lockdown of Aylesbury town centre had wreaked havoc with the morning traffic, and Hall would likely bear the brunt of that anger.

As the final few officers filtered out through the door, Lowe stepped away from the wall and approached the team.

'Whatever you guys need support with, send it through to my team. More hands and all that.'

'Thank you,' King said. And she meant it. Just then, her phone buzzed, and she frowned. 'It's Nic.'

As she stepped away to take the call, Townsend and Swaby began to shift the murder board, to return it back into their office. They'd rolled it only a couple of feet when they heard King excitedly praise Hannon, before she went rushing towards the door.

'Guv?' Townsend called after her. King slowed and stopped at the doorway.

'Jack, leave that. Nic's located the van.'

That was enough, and Townsend hurried after King, but as he turned to head towards the exit of the station, King went hurtling up the stairs. Townsend rushed to the bottom step and called after her.

'Where are you going?' Townsend asked. 'Just get Nic to ping us the address.'

'I'll meet you by your car,' she said, and a glint of excitement shone through her tired eyes. 'I need to speak to Hall about that Armed Response Unit.'

CHAPTER FORTY-NINE

Hannon had been glued to her screen since the moment the CCTV footage had come in. Everything else had fallen to the periphery, and the sound of the radio, Swaby's phone calls and Manning's arrival had become nothing more than background noise. Beyond the walls of the SCU, she could hear the palpable panic as the search for the abducted judge intensified. The rest of the team were in and out, making urgent phone calls and having heated discussions.

But Hannon was locked in.

She was determined to track down the Executioner.

Driven to saving Claire Holliday.

The footage from the front of the courthouse offered a wide view of the street and the parallel road, which by that time, had started to fall under the glare of the streetlights as the day turned to evening. The tail end of the rush hour traffic that usually brought the one-way system of Aylesbury to a standstill had begun to calm.

Hannon saw the police officer, but cleverly, he approached from underneath the camera, keeping his face out of shot. From the height of the footage, along with the glare of the street lights, it was hard to distinguish any features.

He was white.

Medium height.

That was about it.

A tense conversation played out between him and the unsuspecting judge, who then turned and marched away from the camera with the officer in tow. As they rounded the corner, a security guard emerged, just passing them on route.

Hannon switched to the CCTV that overlooked the car park, one that didn't hold a police car.

But there was a van.

Hannon felt her muscles tighten with apprehension as the judge and officer disappeared behind the parked van, and then didn't emerge from the other side. He'd snatched her, and she saw one of the back doors fly open, then slam shut, and then the officer swiftly enter the vehicle and drive away. She clocked the license plate number.

She fed it to Swaby, who ran a search, and quickly surmised that it belonged to a red Ford Fiesta that was registered to an address in the neighbouring Wendover.

But Hannon followed the van through the CCTV footage provided by the roads out of the town, heading back towards High Wycombe until the footage finished as he approached the country roads. Swiftly, she transitioned to the cameras dotted around Princes Risborough, and married up the time that she lost track of the car. She sped the footage up, and twenty-two minutes after she'd lost sight of the van, it emerged on the main roundabout of Princes Risborough. She followed it through the main roads that circled the village, following it all the way through until it shot down the country lane towards Wycombe.

She picked it up again as it arrived back in West

Wycombe, and followed it as it took the West Wycombe Road, heading back towards the town centre.

'Where are you going?' she said out loud.

The traffic lights that split the road towards either Downley or Sands had a traffic camera mounted, and she flicked to the footage. The van had gone.

She'd lost it.

But she traced back to the last image of the van and then looked through the surrounding areas.

Desborough Business Park was a business park only in name, as it amounted to nothing much more than a few small businesses, a spit and sawdust gym, and more interestingly, a garage lock up. There were no barriers to the business park itself, and unlikely there would be any CCTV, but Hannon then checked the footage of the traffic lights at the end of the only other possible route the van could have taken.

It never emerged.

Hannon whipped out her phone, interrupted King's briefing, and after she'd told her boss what she's found, she sat back in her seat, exhilarated.

She might very well have located the judge and more importantly the killer.

But as she left King and Townsend to lead the charge, to return to her next part of investigation.

She may have found the location.

But her hunch, she hoped, would now lead her to the man behind the mask.

As soon as King had burst into his office, Hall had authorised the Armed Response Unit immediately, telling her to be careful. He had a number of escalating fires to try to put out but would join her and Townsend at the business park once he was finished. King then raced to the car park, thankful to find Townsend already behind the wheel and the engine running. Adrenaline was kicking in, and although Townsend had been in perilous situations while undercover and had run headfirst into two serial killers over the past few months, he'd never been involved with the Armed Response Unit. As they arrived at Desborough Business Park, Townsend pulled the car into a narrow parking space on the residential road a few yards down from the entrance. Moments later, King spotted the unmarked Armed Response Van parked just a little further up the road.

'Wait here,' she said to Townsend, and exited the car and approached the ARV. The Senior AFO stepped out, kitted out in his bulletproof attire, and Townsend watched them with interest. Whatever King was saying was agreeable, and when she returned to the car, her determination was infectious.

'Right, pull into the business park and park up. I'll deal with the storage facility staff. You go and inform the other businesses that nobody is to leave the premises without our say so.'

'On it,' Townsend said, whipping the car through the open gate and into the first vacant spot. As the two detectives split to take care of the matters at hand, Townsend saw the ARV pull through the gate and park directly in front of the small cul-de-sac that comprised the storage facilities. There were twelve in total, all of them locked, and King would soon find which ones were in use. Townsend ducked into the neighbouring businesses, flashed his identification, and warned them not to leave until further instruction. A few gym goers were argumentative, but he shut them down with a stern word and a sterner tone.

Then he raced back across the uneven car park, where King was standing next to the Senior AFO.

'Facilities five, six, nine and eleven are currently occupied.' King pointed as she spoke. She then handed the keys over to the AFO. 'They've asked us to keep the damage to a minimum.'

'Understood,' the man grunted from under his visor. He had the look and stature of a soldier, and Townsend watched as he marched to the back of the van and rattled his gloved fist against it. The doors flew open, and eight identically dressed officers leapt out, falling into formation as they huddled close to the main building for cover. King and Townsend stepped to the side, watching as they were led towards the garage doors, their Heckler & Koch MP5s in hand. They moved in synchronicity, keeping their eyes open and their weapons ready, and the Senior AFO approached gate five. With a click of the key, he unlocked it, and two other officers shunted the shutter up as quickly as possible.

Two men stepped forward, guns trained on the opening, and then slowly, the team approached, expertly covering all angles until they cleared the lock-up.

It took a matter of seconds.

The same process played out in lock-up six, and Townsend could see faces pressed to the windows of the surrounding buildings.

For some reason, that feeling had returned to the pit of his stomach.

Something wasn't right.

The unit moved in unison to the ninth shutter, and as per the previous two, they had their guns trained on the metal as the senior AFO unlocked it.

Even from their position, Townsend and King could see the grey van, which had been reversed into the lock-up. The armed team swept in, their guns drawn, and

Townsend could hear them barking instructions. They checked around and under the vehicle, and then beyond, searching under the tool bench which was stacked with tools, wooden beams and chains. Their boots crunched on empty packets of bland supermarket food and empty water bottles.

The entire garage hung heavy with the stench of urine, sweat and fear.

Two officers peaked through the windows of the vehicle, and those on the back door of the van, giving it the all clear.

The senior AFO turned to King and Townsend and beckoned them forward. As they approached the open shutter, three of the armed officers trotted out, a sense of disappointment encompassing every step.

They'd found the van.

But there was no action for them here today.

'This is it,' King said with some certainty.

She and Townsend stepped forward, approaching the threshold of the facility, when one of the armed officers pulled open the backdoor of the van, as another one covered him.

As it swung open, a metal pin was ripped from the grenade taped inside the door.

The bright light snapped through the garage like a camera flash, followed by an explosion that rocked the entire business park to its foundation.

Townsend and King were blasted clean off their feet.

And as Townsend hit the ground, the last thing he could hear was the terrified yells of the surviving unit, before he fell into unconsciousness.

CHAPTER FIFTY

News filtered through to the High Wycombe Police Station of an explosion at the Desborough Business Park, and suddenly, the emergency services were inundated with calls. Firefighters were dispatched, along with paramedics and as many available police officers in the vicinity.

The Senior AFO reported in that the lock-up had been rigged and two officers were down.

Swaby was up, rushing to her car to get down.

Hannon felt numb.

She'd been the one who'd tracked the van to the storage facility and directed everyone right to it. She tried to call, but neither of them were picking up.

Two officers down.

Was it King and Townsend?

She felt sick to her stomach.

Every day was a threat. That was what Hannon had been told by her trainer all those years ago, when she'd been wide-eyed cadet, adamant she could make a difference as a police officer. All her friends said she was mad for wanting to join, warning her that she'd see a side of the world that would change her immeasurably. But she'd been young and naïve, so when the trainer had said that every person who wears the badge or puts on the uniform is putting their life at risk, she didn't want to believe it. It had only become true to her when, on a routine call, she'd been jumped by a group of drunken louts, beaten to the ground and stamped on.

It had damaged her spine as well as her psychological state.

But now she'd sent her closest colleagues, along with a team of brave officers who were willing to fire a gun in the name of the law, to a building that had turned out to be a death trap.

Two officers down.

Hannon could feel the tears building in the corner of her eyes, as she held the phone to her ear, begging for King to pick up.

Nothing.

She tried Townsend and again, got only a voicemail message.

'Pick up!' she yelled, before slamming her phone down on her desk and burying her head on her hands.

'DC Hannon?' A familiar voice rose from behind her. 'You okay?'

DCI Lowe.

Hannon sat up and took a deep breath, trying her best to maintain her composure.

'Not really.' She groaned.

Lowe parked himself on the sliver of her desk that wasn't covered in paperwork.

'You know, I've been doing this job for a long old time. Back when I was in the Met, I worked with this guy, DCI Alfie Staunton. Well, he weren't a DCI back then. Neither of us were.' Lowe folded his arms. 'Anyway, we headed up an operation to bring down a gang that were flooding the streets with knives. Nasty fuckers. Basically pouring gasoline onto the problem in the city.'

Hannon looked up at him, eyebrow raised. He continued.

'Anyways, DI King, back when she worked with us, she was on the team as well. And one night, we smashed the door in of their base, and it was fucking chaos.' Lowe shook his head, reminiscing. 'We had riot police with us, and fuck me, I think I got a few stitches from that night. Anyways, Staunton is a mean fucker, and he battered one of the ringleaders who came at him with a knife. Proper went to stab him. Anyways, Staunton dealt with him, and afterwards, we all went for a drink.'

Hannon was clearly lost.

'Sorry, sir. I don't follow.'

Lowe smiled.

'Sitting there with a beer, do you know what Staunton said was the scariest part of the whole thing?' He looked to her, waiting for the expected shake of the head. 'Watching DI King run headfirst into the leader of the group and put him on the fucking ground like he was nothing.'

Hannon sat back in her chair, impressed. Behind Lowe, Manning shuffled into view, and for once, Lowe didn't greet him with a condescending comment. He reached out and patted Hannon on the shoulder.

'Take it from me. There's nobody tougher in this station than DI King. Scouse ain't a soft shit either. They'll be fine.' Lowe stood and turned to Manning. 'I'll let you both know when I hear anything. Until then, let's keep working. We've got a few hours until that feed goes live.'

Lowe's speech seemed to do its trick, and Hannon blew out her cheeks and turned back to her screen. As she did, Lowe met Manning by the board.

'Nice speech,' Manning said with an approving nod. 'Surprising. But nice.'

'I'm a soft touch, really,' Lowe said with a smile. Whatever animosity had existed between them was dissipating. 'How are you holding up?'

'Excuse me?' The question caught Manning by surprise.

'Izzy will be fine. Trust me.'

'Oh, we're not...'

'None of my business.' Lowe held his hands up. 'Just, don't worry is all I'm saying.'

'Well...thank you.'

'Any thoughts or headway?' He nodded to the board, and the collage of evidence surrounding the masked murderer.

'I feel like we're coming to an end of the crusade, for lack of a better word,' Manning said, his thoughtful gaze resting on the investigation board. 'We've accounted for the rest of the jury, the defendant is under twenty-four-hour supervision, and saving a senior figure like a judge for last makes sense.'

'Makes sense how?' Lowe asked.

'This whole mission has been about more than revenge. It's been about "fixing" the justice system.' Manning provided the air quotes with his fingers. 'By executing those he perceived to have been responsible for a miscarriage of justice, he wanted to right those wrongs. And when the details of this emerge, there'll be some who'll agree with his motives, if not his methods. A judge is a gatekeeper for the system, therefore, executing one who he deems corrupt would be his *piece de resistance*.'

'And doing it live as opposed to recording? That just adds weight to it.'

'Or brings it to a close.' Manning turned to the detective. 'Think about it. If our man is someone from within this service, then he knows what will happen next. Two officers have been injured or worse. There'll be no leniency, will there? When that feed goes live, armed officers will swarm the location as soon as possible. What do you think the chances are that our man doesn't comply with their orders?'

Lowe drew a hand across his mouth and rubbed his beard.

'He'll make himself a martyr.'

'Quite possibly.' Manning nodded. 'And if he is killed, live on the internet, by the very system he's been preaching is corrupt, then…'

'The fucker wins.' Lowe grunted. He then looked to the doctor and scoffed. 'Not bad.'

'Well, if you recall, DCI Lowe…I'm a well-respected expert in my field.'

Lowe turned and headed back across the SCU and, as he passed Hannon's desk, he assured her once more that he'd let her know the second he had an update. As he left, Hannon spent a small second to contemplate a world where DCI was always a complete dick, and then returned to her screen, just as an email came in that made her drop everything.

CHAPTER FIFTY-ONE

The rain began to lash down and stirred Townsend back into consciousness. As his eyes flickered open, he tried to lift himself up but failed. His skull weighed a thousand pounds, and as he looked around at the chaos, muffled voices failed to puncture the high-pitched ringing in his ear. Through gritted teeth, he got up onto his elbow and dabbed a hand to the back of his skull. A little blood trickled across his fingers, no doubt from the hard impact of the concrete when he was thrown.

There'd been an explosion.

The cobwebs began to clear, and he managed to get to his feet, woozily stumbling until one of the AFOs steadied him.

'Are you okay, sir?'

Townsend waved him off, looking through the pandemonium until his eyes landed on King, who was lying motionless a few feet away from him, a concerned AFO knelt beside her. Like his, her white shirt was smeared with black stains, and her eyebrow was trickling blood down her face.

Beyond her, smoke was billowing out of the lock-up,

and a few of the AFOs were doing their best to peer through, screaming the names of the two officers who had been caught in the blast zone. In the distance, Townsend could hear a multitude of sirens, as the various arms of the emergency services descended upon them.

Townsend bent down to King and checked her for any serious injuries.

'Guv,' he called over the noise. 'Guv, can you hear me?'

King's eyelids fluttered, and like Townsend himself, she emerged into a confused haze. After a few moments, clarity seemed to grip her, and she turned to Townsend, her eyes wide.

'The bomb…' she said, snapping her head towards the lock-up as she sat. Her words trailed off as she surveyed the mayhem around her, and the smoke billowing through the metal shutter. The van was ablaze, wiping away any significant evidence along with it, along with the rest of the damage the fire and smoke would do to the Executioner's lair.

But worse still, there were two officers in there.

As Townsend extended his hand for King to pull herself up, a fire engine burst into the business park, and as the firefighters got to work, the AFOs regrouped by their van, visibly shaken. Terrified faces were pressed against every window of the surrounding building.

Five minutes ago, Townsend was ready to bring the Executioner's reign of terror to an end.

Now, it had spread like a virus.

An ambulance soon arrived, its sirens wailing, followed by two police cars. Uniformed officers swarmed out, and King, with blood slithering down her face, gave them orders to keep the peace within the buildings, and to cordon off the entrance to the business park. They got to work without a second to spare.

'Fuck me, guv,' Townsend finally said as the two of

them surveyed the chaos before them. 'Those poor officers…'

King's eyes narrowed with anger.

'We'll get him, Jack.' She didn't break her stare. 'I promise you, we will fucking nail this guy.'

As Townsend looked around the business park, he saw Boyd in deep discussion with the manager of the gym. The officer on the cordon at the entrance moved the tape, to allow Swaby to come running in, the relief on her face evident as she approached the two of them.

'Oh, thank God,' she said out loud. To Townsend's surprise, she threw her arms around him. 'We were worried sick. We heard there were two officers down and…'

'There are,' King said sadly, and Swaby followed her gaze to the inferno the firefighters were working to put out. Swaby looked away in horror.

'Fuck,' she said, a rare curse.

'Yeah. Fuck.' King spat, and then angrily puffed on her vape as the brave firemen brought the blaze under control. The senior AFO was the first one in, followed by the paramedics. He emerged swiftly, his fists clenched and then he hurled his helmet in anger across the parking lot.

His men were dead.

The Executioner had killed two police officers.

Everyone in the business park felt a shift, as a hurricane of grief swept through as they mourned the loss of their comrades. As the morbid silence took hold, Swaby tried her best to break it.

'I'm going to call Nic,' she said, fishing her phone from her pocket. 'She was worried sick you were…we all were.'

Townsend gave her a nod and Swaby stepped away to make the call. Another ambulance soon arrived, and King and Townsend watched as the paramedics spoke to the distraught survivors of the Armed Response Unit.

Another paramedic approached King.

'Let me look you over, ma'am,' he said. He was half their age and looked it.

'I'm fine.' King waved him off.

'That's a pretty nasty cut,' he replied.

'I said I'm fine,' King snapped.

'He's just doing his job.'

The voice boomed behind them, and Detective Superintendent Hall approached, taking purposeful strides through the rain. He carried an air of authority, but the devastation was plastered to his face like a Halloween mask.

'I'm fine, sir,' King said defiantly.

'I don't doubt that for a second, Izzy,' Hall said as he stopped before them. 'But you know the protocol. Jesus... two of our own killed.'

'We'll get him, sir,' Townsend said.

'You two won't.' Hall snapped back. 'You both need to get your arses to the hospital. You're both covered in blood, and you need to be checked over.'

'Sir, I have to disagree...' King began.

'That is an order.' Hall snapped. He took a moment to collect himself. 'Swaby can stay here and will be on hand for if and when the feed goes live.'

'But sir...' King began. Hall held up a sorrowful hand.

'Please. I know how much all of you have given to this case. I do.' He looked over at the burnt-out lock-up. The remaining members of the Armed Response Unit stood, heads down, hands to their front, in a mournful salute to their fallen comrades. 'Some more than others. Above all, your safety is my priority. We will see this through to the end, you have my word. But for now, I need you both to go to the hospital. Understood?'

'Yes, sir,' Townsend replied. King didn't say anything. She took one more glance over to the dead bodies, turned on her heel and then marched towards Townsend's car.

Before he followed, he turned back to Hall, who was watching the events unfold.

'Are you okay, sir?'

The question caught Hall by surprise, and he turned to Townsend and offered him a thankful smile.

'No, son. I'm not okay.' His eyes glowered with fury. 'But I will feel better when we bury the fucker who did this.'

Townsend patted Hall on the shoulder, and then trudged through the rain to the car, where King was leaning, puffing away her frustrations.

He knew she was contemplating breaking her sobriety.

Knew even more that she wouldn't let it happen.

As they got into the car, both of them sat for a moment, contemplating the failure of the raid.

Two good officers dead.

All the evidence burnt and destroyed.

Now, they'd spend the rest of the day at the hospital, not seeing the case through to the end.

Townsend went to offer King a word of encouragement, anything to rein in her anger, but thought against it.

It would be hypocritical.

Because he was just as fucking furious as she was.

They'd been so close.

Right on the cusp of catching the killer, but as had been the case the entire way through, they'd been a few steps behind. Only this time, those steps had been fatal. In the eyes of the Executioner, the blood he'd spilt up until this point had been in the name of a deluded campaign against the justice system.

What was the rationale behind spilling the blood of the police?

And if Manning was right, if it was a police officer, then the blood of a comrade?

All of them knew that whenever they stepped out for another day of work, they were putting their lives on the line. They ran towards danger when most people would run away.

That was the job.

But the danger wasn't supposed to come from within.

If the man behind the mask was also a man who stood behind the badge, Townsend would make damn sure to get some retribution for the two officers who were being loaded into the back of the ambulances in body bags.

He'd happily serve a suspension for it.

Judging by the look on King's bloodstained face, she would too.

As he pulled out of the business park and turned towards the city centre, the downpour continued to lash against the windscreen, and the street lights began to flicker to life. An afternoon of devastation was turning into an evening of potential horror, and neither Townsend nor King would be a part of it.

Townsend's knuckles tightened as he gripped the steering wheel with frustration. There only hope now was to track the live link and hope that Hannon and Swaby could piece it all together in time.

But then DI King's phone rang, and everything changed.

CHAPTER FIFTY-TWO

'They're both okay, Nic. A little shaken and heading to hospital, but they're okay.'

Swaby's soothing voice relayed the message to Hannon, calming her nerves but doing little to lighten her mood.

Although her two colleagues, and friends, hadn't been killed by the blast that had obliterated the garage she'd sent them to, two other brave officers had been.

It was time to dig deep and push on.

And Hannon had been digging.

While the rest of the team were out chasing down the leads, investigating crime scenes and interviewing suspects, Hannon had been locked in her seat, her fingers on the keyboard and her eyes on the screen. The guilt she felt for the two officers who'd been killed in the blast was unheralded, but she still needed to compartmentalise and store that away for a night on the sofa with Shilpa and a bottle of wine.

Now it was time to dig in.

And she had been.

King's request for her to investigate the officers who shared the same halls as they did was one that had made her a little uncomfortable, but it needed doing. The evidence had stacked up that someone within the building was, at the very least, aiding the Executioner with their crusade. The attainment and placement of Manning's pin could have happened outside the office but would have required the intimate knowledge that they'd make the connection.

Being a few steps ahead of the investigation meant they were at least privy to where the SCU was heading.

And snatching Anne-Louise Mulligan within the time frame of the team locating her and arriving to her location had sent it over the edge.

It had to be one of their own.

Hannon hated the idea that somebody who'd taken the oath would then shed blood across it and she'd compiled a list of everyone who potentially had access to the information.

It was a long list.

Senior figures like Hall and DCI Lowe had been checked first and she'd investigated Lowe's history within the Met, as DI Gavin Thorpe had been in the same investigation. It surprised Hannon when she was able to clear him. For over the past year, he'd been one of the few things she hated about her job, and his constant belittling and confrontational behaviour with King had built a resentment. But since he'd been on the receiving end of a right hook from Townsend, he'd seemingly turned a corner.

In fact, she was worried that she might actually becoming a little fond of him.

We're all built for this in different ways.

His words had struck a chord with her and as she went through the list, her hunch began to grow. It started out as something small – a name that she would have expected to see at a crime scene but didn't. And she'd kept digging, and soon, the connection to the Metropolitan Police began to wave a red flag like the beginning of a Formula One race.

They'd worked together on a few operations during their respective stints in London before Thorpe had relocated to Buckinghamshire.

The email from the Millrose House manager confirmed a video call between Hannon and the two staff members who hadn't been present for the original interviews. Hannon took a breath and joined the call. As she did, she was greeted by two women, both of whom looked pretty nervous. One was Black, in her-mid fifties and the other was an Eastern European woman who Hannon guessed was the same age as she was.

'Hello. I'm Detective Constable Nicola Hannon.' Hannon smiled. She'd ensured her police lanyard was visible. 'Thank you very much for taking the time to speak to me.'

'Are we in trouble?' the older woman, Martha, asked.

'Not at all.' Hannon shook her head. 'We are currently in the middle of an investigation, and I could use your assistance.'

Both women shared a worried glance.

Hannon continued.

'It has been a few months, but your resident, Gavin Thorpe, is often visited by his brother.' Hannon watched them carefully. 'We are trying to contact him but we do not have any means to do so. His name is James Thorpe. Or you may know him as Jimmy?'

A flicker of recognition sparkled in Martha's eye.

'He hasn't been here for a few months now.'

'We are aware,' Hannon said softly. She took a breath. 'We do not have any contact details for him, but I was wondering if you could help me identify him?'

Hannon held up a picture.

It wouldn't have been one they would have been

familiar with. This one was a man, standing proudly in his police uniform. His shoulders straight and his chin up. Martha pointed to it and smiled.

'Yes. That's him. Jimmy.' She nodded.

Hannon felt her heartbeat quicken. She quickly thanked the two women for their help and then shut down the call. Then she turned and looked at the photo in her hand.

PC Simon Walsh.

Hannon didn't know the man too well but had spoken to him a few times. The odd grunt in the canteen or a dry, grumpy comment at a crime scene. He'd always seemed like the run-of-the-mill veteran who was counting down his days until retirement. He was quiet, seemed to have a decent rapport with PC Boyd, but beyond that, had seemed content to see out his final few years of service away from the mayhem policing the capital city.

Hannon looked up.

The office was empty.

There was less than an hour left on the clock before the Executioner's feed went live, and a senior judge would be murdered in front of the watching world. Quickly, she shifted through the previous shift logs for the uniformed officers. Townsend had noted he'd seen Walsh at the Recovery Housing Project in Thame as one of the first officers on sight as they had rushed to reach Anne-Louise Mulligan before she'd been taken.

Walsh wasn't down to work that day.

Hannon returned to the CCTV footage from that afternoon. They'd been stumped by the women's disappearance, and Hannon herself had followed down the only car to leave the location and cleared it from the investigation. But moments after King and Townsend arrived, a police car did leave the car park.

'Jesus,' Hannon said, reaching for her phone.

The entire station was in a frenzy, with the rising body count and now the death of two AFO's rattling through each corridor like a sinister echo. She quickly called the sergeant on duty, who confirmed that PC Walsh wasn't working this afternoon or evening. When they questioned why, Hannon quickly ended the call.

Then she called King.

'Come on…come on…' Hannon uttered impatiently until finally the call connected. 'Guv…'

'Nic. Look, we're okay—'

'It's Walsh,' Hannon interrupted.

'What?'

'The Executioner. It's Walsh.' Hannon stared at the evidence on her screen and the papers around her desk. 'He was at the Housing Project, but he wasn't on shift. He's been at all the briefings. And one of the staff at Millrose House has identified him as Thorpe's brother.'

'You're kidding me?' King spat. 'I'll call Hall now. Get everything together.'

'Yes, guv.'

'And Nic…' King said before disconnecting. 'Great work.'

The call ended, and Hannon felt a smile curl across her lips. She lifted her phone again, hoping to get through to the detective superintendent who'd put everything in place to bring PC Simon Walsh to justice. As she waited for the call to connect, she took one more glance up at the clock.

Time was ticking away.

But there was a chance that the Executioner's time was running out.

CHAPTER FIFTY-THREE

For the past six years, Detective Superintendent Hall had achieved incredible things for the Thames Valley Police. As one of its most tenured and respected figures, he'd implemented a number of key initiatives, delivered exemplary results under budget and had overseen numerous successful investigations. All from either behind the desk of his private office, or around meeting room tables in the company of other powerful peers.

It had been a long time since he was at the forefront of an arrest, let alone an investigation.

But the adrenaline came swooping back with a vengeance, coursing through his aging body like he'd been struck by lightning. With the spring shower turning into a full-on storm, that wasn't out of the question.

As a figure of authority, he'd stayed and ignored the rain, overseeing the clear up of the tragic bombing at Desborough Park, as well as organising for the Explosive Ordnance Disposal unit to conduct a thorough sweep of the remaining lock ups. Unlike the Met, the Thames Valley Police service didn't have the means for a dedicated arm to deal with such a threat and therefore relied on the EOD to interject where needed. Formed and managed by former military bomb disposal operators, the EOD were at the cutting edge of bomb safety. Something that Hall needed in abundance.

As the EOD went to work, the rest of the Armed Response Unit began to filter back into their van, while DS Swaby and the senior AFO were engaging in a rain-soaked debrief.

'What a mess,' Hall uttered under his breath. His attention was stolen by the vibration of his phone. He pulled it from his pocket.

DI King.

With a roll of his eyes, he took the call.

'You better be at the hospital, Izzy, otherwise...'

'Sir, it's PC Simon Walsh,' King's voice carried an equal amount of excitement and clarity. 'DC Hannon has had a positive ID that he's the one visiting DI Gavin Thorpe.'

Hall looked around the crime scene.

Several uniformed officers were ignoring the elements to fulfil their duties. Two of them were stationed at the entrance to the business park. Walsh's running buddy, PC Boyd, was maintaining his post across the car park by the gym.

Walsh was nowhere to be seen.

Had he even been at the crime scene?

'Are we certain?' Hall's voice carried a threat. 'Because if we kick down the door of one of our own, we need to be fucking sure it's for a good reason.'

'DS Townsend saw him at the Recovery Housing Project when Anne-Louise was taken. He made the easy assumption he was responding to our call.'

Hall nodded. He couldn't take Townsend to task for not knowing the shift patterns of the uniformed officers.

'Walsh isn't on shift. We can be at his home in...'

'You'll do no such thing.' Hall felt his chest puff. 'You two have strict orders to undergo medical protocol. Swaby and I will get there straight away.'

'But sir…'

'I will be in touch.'

Hall hung up the phone and then marched across the car park to Swaby's conversation. As he approached, both she and the senior AFO stood to attention.

'Sir?' Swaby turned. Her hair was plastered against her soaked skull.

'We have a potential lead,' Hall said, careful to keep the name quiet. 'DS Swaby, you'll come with me. Sergeant Roberts, I'll send you the address. I'll need your team on hand to ensure a safe arrest.'

'Yes, sir,' Roberts said, turning back to the van to relay the information to the rest of his team. As he did, Hall made a quick call to Hannon to have her forward the address to himself and to Sergeant Roberts. He then called in a request for a bomb squad to meet them at the same location. Swaby fell in-step behind him, and the two of them soon hopped into Hall's car and pulled off. Minutes later, the AFO van followed.

On the drive across town, Hall relayed the information to DS Swaby. They'd known each other for nearly two decades, but their work lives had always been on the fringes of each other. By the time Swaby had moved up from a PC to join CID as a DC, Hall was already on the political climb. He'd swapped his desk in CID for one in the higher offices, but had watched as Swaby had risen into a dependable cornerstone of CID.

When she'd requested to transfer across to the SCU after successfully helping the team apprehend Gordon Baycroft last summer, Hall had signed it off without hesitation.

'The live feed hasn't activated yet,' Hall said, his eyes

locked on the road ahead. 'Which means we can assume that Judge Holliday is still alive.'

'We have a little under thirty minutes,' Swaby said, checking her watch.

Despite the early evening, the clouds had darkened and painted a dull, grey tinge across the town. They passed through the town centre and past the Rye, then bypassed the turnoff to Micklefield before turning off down Cock Lane and making their way towards Penn. The small village was almost equidistant between High Wycombe and Beaconsfield, and offered some stunning country walks that befitted its inclusion in the Chiltern Area of Natural Beauty. As they turned off into the village, they passed a few of the popular country pubs, unsurprisingly sporting names such as The Crown and The Red Lion.

With his windscreen wipers working overtime, Hall pulled onto Walsh's street, and then pulled the car to a stop on the side of the road. A few moments later, the AFO van shot past and pulled up directly in front of Walsh's house.

Hall stepped out into the rain, followed by Swaby, and watched as the armed unit swiftly got into position. The bomb squad arrived moments later, and got to work quickly.

Fourteen minutes.

They could still save Judge Holliday.

Expertly, the unit got into position, and after the bomb squad safely ascertained there was no trap on the door Sergeant Roberts gave the order for them to breach the property. As the team filtered in, their guns drawn, Hall could hear the cries of 'Armed Police' echoing from the property. Curtains on the street were twitching, and he stepped forward to usher the old lady in the neighbouring house back inside.

They could hear the cries of 'Clear' from within the house.

The thudding of boots as the ARU swept through PC Simon Walsh's home with the lethal efficiency of a military raid.

But there were no gunshots.

No cries of surrender.

With the rain lashing against his furrowed brow, Hall checked his watch once more, watching as the grains of sand in Claire Holliday's hourglass continued to fall.

As Sergeant Roberts emerged through the busted front door, with his Heckler & Koch MP5 safely hanging from its strap, Hall felt a knot in his stomach tighten. The sergeant called both him and Swaby to the house with a gloved hand.

But Hall didn't need to enter to house to be shown what he already knew.

Judging by the look on Swaby's face, she knew it as well.

The two of them were squelching through the rain to an empty house.

This wasn't the location.

Simon Walsh was still at large.

CHAPTER FIFTY-FOUR

'My wife's gonna be ragin',' Townsend said with a cruel grin, and the young doctor who was bandaging the back of his head let out a chuckle.

It was half said in jest, but the truth was, Townsend knew that Mandy wouldn't be thrilled that he'd ended up with another trip to the hospital. Over the past year, he'd taken a strike from a bouncer in a chase through the woods, and the past Christmas, had a scalpel embedded into his shoulder. He brushed both off as risks of the job, but Mandy was quick to remind him that he had another job at home.

That he needed to be careful.

In truth, even though there was little he could have done or known about the bomb, Mandy was still likely to read him the riot act.

'There you go,' the young doctor said as he finished the bandage that was stuck to the back of his head with medical tape. 'The stitches should dissolve nicely. Might be a bit sore, but no signs of a concussion right now. But we'll need to do a more thorough check.'

'Great. Can't wait.'

Townsend sighed as he lifted himself from the hospital bed and followed the man back out into the waiting area. King was waiting, herself the proud new owner of a set of stitches that were holding her eyebrow together.

'Is this the queue for the concussion train?' Townsend asked, pointing to the seat beside her. She patted it.

'Hop aboard.'

Townsend sat and grimaced slightly.

'If I wanted a headache, I could have just gone home.'

'Well, if I want another one after this, I could pop round. Am sure Mandy will be thrilled that I put you in harm's way.'

'I'm a big boy. I make my own decisions.' Townsend joked. 'Any news from Hall?'

'Nope,' King said glumly. They looked at the clock.

Two minutes until five.

Almost time.

'Fuckin' Walsh, eh?' Townsend said with a shake of the head. 'I saw him there. Right there when we went to get Anne-Louise. I should have said something.'

King sat back in her chair.

'You weren't to know, Jack. None of us did. So don't you dare start placing any blame on your shoulders, okay? You've worked too damn hard to stop this to think that you failed.'

The two sat quietly in the corridor, as a couple of nurses walked by, seemingly impervious to the constant pressure that pulsed through any hospital.

'Thanks, guv,' Townsend said.

King went to respond, but her phone buzzed.

Swaby.

She answered it swiftly.

'Michelle—' King began, but was cut off. By the way her eyes bulged, Townsend knew the news wasn't good.

'Fuck. Right...tell Hall we...'

She turned and shot a glance to Townsend, before a deeper voice echoed in her ear.

'Sir, we are fine…yes, sir.' King hung up the phone and slammed it down on her lap.

'No luck?'

'The house was empty.' King winced as she shook her head. Despite her insistence to the contrary, the rattling in her skull was causing some discomfort. 'Hall says they're turning the house upside down, but no sign of him.'

Townsend looked up as the clock turned to five.

'It's go time.' He nodded towards it, and both of them looked up at the clock with a sense of failure.

King's phone buzzed again.

Hannon.

'Nic, talk to me.'

'He's at a location near Handycross.' She spoke quickly. 'I've tracked the feed and it's to an Airbnb about three hundred yards away from the roundabout. Shall I send it to you?'

'I'm still at the hospital. Send it to Hall,' King ordered, her other hand balling into a frustrated fist. 'He's with the ARU. They'll be there as soon as possible. Get uniform on it now.'

'Yes, guv.' There was panic in her voice. 'Jesus Christ, guv. He's got her strapped up somewhere. We need to stop this.'

'Now! Nic!' King yelled and then hung up the phone. 'The fucker is up the hill.'

'What, up Marlow Hill?' Townsend pointed. It was part of his route to work. He knew it well. It was steep, but a decent pace could get you up it in five minutes.

'Yeah. Some Airbnb,' King said, finding Swaby's number and lifting the phone. 'They need to get uniform there quickly.'

'You calling it in?'

'Hannon is. I need to let Michelle know. Get her to get Hall and the ARU round there right now.'

Townsend looked around. There were no windows in view, but he was certain that the roads surrounding the hospital would be thick with traffic. Marlow Hill was the steep hill that connected the town centre to the massive Handycross Roundabout, which was a gateway to multiple motorways. Anyone wanting to leave the town, in either direction, would head there, and as rush hour descended upon the town, it meant all roads to the location would be gridlocked. The road closures due to the explosion at Desborough Park meant every road would be log jammed, with no hope of cutting through the traffic.

Sirens or not.

Add in the torrential downpour, and it would be chaos.

And they didn't have time for it.

Townsend stood and messaged Hannon, demanding she sent him the address.

It pinged within seconds.

It was just over a mile away.

'Nope. Not having it,' Townsend said and stood. King looked up at him, her phone pressed to the side of her head as she waited to connect the call.

'Jack, what are you doing?'

Townsend was already marching towards the door that would lead back to the Emergency Room. His head was a little sore, but he was thinking clearly.

'I'm not going to sit here and do nothing, guv.'

'We have our orders from Hall…'

'Then he can fucking suspend me or fire me. Whatever.' Townsend frowned as he looked to the door and then to King. 'But I need to go right now. I can get there before they can.'

Townsend headed to the door and King called after him.

'Jack. Wait…'

'Guv…' He turned back, irritated. 'I'll say you ordered me to stay.'

King's call connected, but she hung it up before Swaby could say anything. With a grimace, she stood and pocketed her phone.

'No…wait…' King straightened her jacket and marched towards him. 'I'm coming with you.'

Side by side, the two detectives marched past the reception desk, where the young doctor who had tended to Townsend called after them to stop. They carried on through the emergency waiting area and towards the exit of the hospital. The dark clouds had cloaked the entire town in their shadow, and as Townsend had predicted, the surrounding roads were a sea of car headlights and angry car horns. For as far as he could see, cars were bumper to bumper, meaning any hope they had of making the mile by car was eliminated.

Townsend looked to King, then up at the steep hill.

The rain lashed down, adding a further challenge.

'You ready, guv?' he said as they stepped outside and past the hospital car park where his car was parked, racking up an extortionate fee.

'Let's go,' King said.

The two of them burst forward into a sprint, rounding the entrance wall of the hospital and then began the long, hard climb of the hill.

They ran as though a life depended on it.

Claire Holliday's life.

CHAPTER FIFTY-FIVE

This was the moment.

Years had passed since the moment when DI Gavin Thorpe's world had crashed around him, and since Simon Walsh saw the justice system for what it was. Nothing more than a series of rules and regulations, overseen by those in power, to keep people in check. There was no true sense of morality. No real sense of justice.

Nothing more than a concept.

It didn't matter what could be proven.

What mattered was who you could convince.

The jurors who'd been presented with the clear facts that Phillip Myers had raped a twelve-year-old girl were apparently unconvinced by the methods Thorpe himself had gone to. The defence, snivelling cretins who made their money by defending the undefendable, had laid traps in their questions, doing their level best to undercut Thorpe when he'd given his testimony. Walsh had watched from the balcony, squirming in unison with Thorpe as his case was picked apart.

That fickle justice system once more.

All the defence had to do was plant reasonable doubt

in the mind of an uneducated juror, and Myers walked, and Thorpe spiralled.

A man who had given Walsh his time and his energy; had shown an interest in his career and had taken him under his wing. A man who had dedicated his entire life to the law, only to have it spat back in his face.

It wasn't the law who was there for Thorpe when he had his first mental breakdown.

It wasn't the justice system who had found Thorpe in the midst of an overdose and brought him back from the dead.

It had been Walsh.

And as the months turned to years, and Thorpe's life crumbled around him, Walsh knew then that the only true sense of justice was to punish those who'd sent a good man down a bad path. It had taken years for Walsh to pluck up the courage to even think about what was needed, but soon, as that courage seeped into his psyche, a plan emerged.

It wouldn't have been enough to just kill those who had made the wrong decision.

That wasn't justice.

That was murder.

No, what was needed was something more. He needed to turn the mirror in on the system itself, and show not just those who held it up, but those who depended on it, that the entire thing was damaged.

It needed to be public.

It needed to be memorable.

It needed to be a cause that people would eventually get behind.

Years on the beat had not only hardened Walsh to the harsh realities of the world, but it had exposed him to it. The country, which was led by posh, rich people arguing in their magnificent chambers, was a lie. The rhetoric was that the country was a booming, thriving nation that was at the forefront of the world's next steps.

In reality, that future was only reserved for those who had the means to place their boots on the heads of the many.

Too many people were scrapping day to day, just to get by, and when they reached out for support, they were turned away or shamed for failure. The reality was that success was only available for a few, while many were expected to watch on with envy.

Walsh had seen it.

He'd been in the estates that 'successful' people avoided.

He'd seen what people with nothing were willing to do for just a crumb of something.

Those people, they'd been abandoned by the system the same way that Thorpe was.

They would need something to rally behind.

A symbol to be placed against the acts he'd committed to do.

With great pride, Walsh took a deep breath and fastened the leather mask over his face. The white cross would live long in the history of this country, when the final moments of his crusade would be seen by millions.

The Executioner.

The man who brought the UK justice system to its knees.

He knew it was a heavy cross to bear, but when the blood was shed, social media would do the work for him. The video would spread like a deadly virus, and those it infected would do their research. They'd find the other videos and see a figure of clarity in this murky world.

A man who was willing to kill those who'd broken the constructs designed to keep them safe.

A symbol that would force change where change was needed.

As he tightened the straps on the back of the mask, he peered through the eyeholes at the scene before him.

The Honourable Justice Claire Holliday was on her knees in the middle of the room, the gag still pulled tightly between her lips. Both of her arms were held aloft by the elasticated chords which had been tied to the brackets he'd embedded into opposite walls of the room. With her arms spread out, it looked like she was about to receive a gift.

In a way, she was.

The truth.

Throughout every execution, Walsh had been in complete control. Working under the anonymity of his mask, he knew the links had been untraceable. But the SCU was close, which meant the second he pressed the button, his location would be known to them.

In all likelihood, they would descend upon him before he'd reached the final moments of Holliday's death.

'The Blood Eagle' was the most artistic form of capital punishment he'd ever known, even if its legitimacy was questioned. The Norse method of severing the ribs from the spine, and pulling the lungs through the victim's back, was one of the most sensational forms of execution he'd ever heard of.

Firing Squad.

Beheading.

Hanging.

Lethal Injection.

The jurors had been eradicated in ways the public would be familiar. But for the judge? A woman who knew that she was looking at a paedophile but still allowed them to make their decision, her death would be one that would echo through eternity. In all likelihood, the police would arrive before he'd made it to the lungs, and they would kill him in front of the camera for the world to see.

But the damage he would do to her before then, would be enough to take her with him.

Walsh took one last breath and then reached for the scalpel that he'd laid out on the table just off camera, along with the circular saw and the hatchet.

'This will hurt,' he warned her.

Holliday screamed; her muffled cries being absorbed by the rag that was pulled tight across her face.

Outside, there wasn't anything but the sound of traffic and torrential rain.

Not a siren in the sky.

No hope of salvation.

The Executioner hit the button and set the time running, as his feed hit the internet. There were already five thousand people viewing, waiting patiently for his masterpiece.

The number began to grow and he stepped in front of the camera, allowing his mask to be seen by his public.

He turned to the woman before him, her pointless attempts to wriggle free only add to the theatre.

He grabbed the back of her shirt with a gloved hand and pierced it with the blade, before roughly ripping it open, allowing it to drape around her neck. He then unclipped her bra, allowing it ping forward and she groaned with fear.

Her bony spine was like a dotted line, and he held up his scalpel, and placed it to the base of her neck.

He pressed down.

Claire Holliday howled in agony as he drew blood.

Her screams were shielded by the rag, and by the downpour.

But what wasn't was the sound of a mighty crash from

behind them both, and panicked, the Executioner spun round as the door to the apartment caved in.

CHAPTER FIFTY-SIX

With his lungs screaming for mercy, Townsend kept one foot in front of the other, his shoes slapping the wet concrete as he raced up the Marlow Hill. The civilian walkway framed the dual carriageway, which was separated by a thick, metal barrier.

Either side of it was bumper to bumper, as the irate drivers impatiently crawled through the rain.

King kept in step, following Townsend a few feet behind, trying her best to ignore the pain in her skull which felt like it had been detached from its resting place. A few commuters honked their horns, mocking the two who looked like they had either been caught short in the downpour, or were involved in a slow motion foot race.

Either way, Townsend kept his head down and his feet steady.

Behind him, he heard a gasp of panic and a clatter and turned to help King from her knee after taking a slip. As he pulled her up, she tried to return to the same pace, but hobbled, she began to slow.

'Just keep going,' she yelled, her voice barely audible above the racket of their surroundings.

Townsend carried on.

His foot slipped just once, but he steadied himself and pushed on, eventually hitting the flat road atop the hill, opposite the Wycombe High School for Girls. The school rush had long since subsided, but a few late stragglers were huddled under the nearby bus stop, giggling round one of the girls phones. They looked at Townsend with worry, but he just carried on.

His own phone buzzed.

It was the address. Hannon had sent it through as a location, and he opened it, allowing his own phone to take control. The route to the Executioner's link was visible via a blue line, and he was four minutes away. He looked back, just as an exhausted King made her way to the top of the hill and took a few deep breaths as she arrived.

'This way, guv!' Townsend yelled, and the two of them set off once more, barrelling down the street and past the two rival petrol stations that sat on opposite sides of the Cressex Business Estate. With the roads gridlocked, they rushed across the busy junction, weaving through the gaps of the stationary cars, and then turned off down one of the side streets. Townsend looked down at the soaked screen, following the directions until they arrived at the street. King was about twenty yards behind him, but he darted down the street, counting down the numbers of the houses until he arrived at the location.

It was just a plain house, split into two flats, both of them offering a small bit of privacy, set back from the pavement by a tiny stone courtyard. Townsend lifted a hand to shield his eyes, peering at the building, trying his best to draw as much air into his burning lungs as possible.

The ground floor was occupied, but the light on in the front room was dulled by the drawn curtains. As he reached for the gate, King arrived next to him, limping badly but gritting her teeth to ignore it.

'Jack. Wait.'

'I can't wait, guv.'

'Back-up's coming,' she said through her short, sharp breaths. 'Plus, last time you ran into a house you ended up on the wrong end of a blade.'

Townsend glanced to his sodden shoulder, which still bore the scar of the scalpel that Gemma Miller had rammed into him. Every now and then, a shooting pain would emerge when he stretched it, but it was just a reminder of how close she'd been to her revenge.

To killing Michelle Swaby.

'You call Hall and tell him I ignored you.' Townsend leant in close. 'But I can't wait here.'

King knew it was futile, and she gave Townsend a firm nod.

One that told him they were in this together.

The door to reception area had two panels of frosted glass running through it, and Townsend drew his elbow back and drilled it into the bottom corner of one of the panels.

The glass shattered, dropping to the tiles below in broken shards, and he reached through and unlocked the door.

Two doors presented themselves, each one leading to a separate flat.

Light was creeping out from underneath one.

'Ready?' King asked, the rain dripping from the tip of her nose and chin. The run has disrupted her stitches, and a trickle of blood gently squirmed down her soaked face.

Townsend didn't respond.

He took a few steps back, and with the propulsion of an Olympic sprinter, he hurled himself shoulder first towards the door. His impressive bulk took the door straight out of its frame, and he crashed through, the wooden panels splintering as he burst through into the apartment.

He could hear a dull groaning sound.

The sound of metal scraping.

As he turned to enter the living room, a metal hatchet spun through the air towards him.

'Jack!' King called out, and she grabbed the back of his collar and pulled him back. It rocked him back a few inches, and the blade whipped by, just missing his nose by a few inches before it crunched into the plasterboard wall behind him.

Townsend turned and shot a thankful look to his boss.

The sound of a door slamming echoed beyond, and they both entered the living room, startling at the sight before them.

Claire Holliday was on her knees, her arms strapped up, and her back laid bare. Blood trickled down her spine from a nasty looking cut at the base of her neck, and she was screaming and struggling against her restraints. Townsend rushed in, dipping under one of the cables, and dropping to a knee before her.

'Claire!' he called loudly. 'I'm DS Jack Townsend. You're safe.'

He removed her gag, and she cried out with relief.

'He went that way.'

She nodded to the door to the kitchen, and Townsend wasted little time heading out after Walsh, as King quickly went about untying the woman. To preserve Claire's dignity, and to shut down the vile crusade of Simon Walsh, King approached the laptop in the corner, and her rain-soaked, blood-stained face would be the last image the watching world would see as she shut down the link.

King began to unfasten the chords that had strapped the judge into place for her execution, and when she'd loosened the second one, Claire threw her arms around King and began to sob.

King held her close.

The sound of sirens began to fill the air.

They had saved the woman.

Had stopped the Executioner.

But somewhere out in the downpour, Townsend was chasing a violent murderer.

And he was on his own.

CHAPTER FIFTY-SEVEN

Walsh was roaring with anger as he dashed through the small, well-maintained garden, and shoved one of the metal chairs over as he moved quickly to the back fence.

They weren't supposed to be there.

This wasn't supposed to go this way.

The live feed was always going to be a homing beacon, and although he'd still planned to butcher the dishonourable judge, he knew that taking a chest full of bullets from the Armed Response Unit live on the internet, would etch his mask and his deeds into legend.

How did they find him?

Despite the rain, his face was clammy with sweat, as the leather mask pulled tight against his skin. As he scaled the fence and dropped down into the alleyway behind, he ripped at the straps, yanking it from his face and then hurled it angrily against the opposite panels.

Footsteps in the garden.

Walsh wasn't going to be taken alive.

Without thinking twice, he broke out into a sprint, navigating the overgrown alleyway that would wrap around the next ten houses and return him to the street. It would be just enough of a head start.

As he thundered past a few of the houses, he heard the sound of someone colliding with the fence behind and arched his neck round to see.

Townsend was dropping down into the shadows.

'Walsh!' the Scouse detective roared through the rain. 'It's over.'

Walsh didn't respond.

He cleared the next few gardens and then turned sharply, racing through the weeds that ripped at him with their prickly fingers. The thorns ripped at his arms and legs, but he ignored them, his anger and adrenaline combining to push him onwards.

To take him to the only acceptable ending.

As he emerged onto the street, he could hear the cries of the sirens growing louder, and the far end of the street was beginning to reflect their blue lights. He turned and headed the opposite way, running as fast as he could towards the main road that would lead up to the Handycross Roundabout, which overlooked the motorways beneath like a large, concrete halo. Behind him, he could hear the footsteps of Townsend, the fucking boy scout who just couldn't let things lie. Despite the man's calls for him to stop, Walsh exploded out onto the main road, his anger exacerbated by the gridlocked traffic. As a last resort, throwing himself under a bus would have been an option, but with nothing moving, the only option he had was the roundabout.

He cut across the main road, evading an impatient driver who was trying to change lanes, and the driver angrily honked his horn and cursed from the window. Walsh ignored it, his eyes focused on the roundabout ahead. Every lane of it was packed, but he could hear the whip of cars racing down the motorways beneath.

Fifty yards.

Forty yards.

The high, metal barrier that ran alongside the pedestrian walkway was built to protect any chance of someone tumbling over it.

Thirty yards and Walsh would scale it and allow gravity and the cars racing beneath it to do their jobs.

Twenty yards.

Walsh got ready to leap, but as he passed the final car before the pedestrian sidewalk, he felt a sledgehammer collide into the centre of his spine, knocking him forward and off balance. As he stumbled forward, he collided shoulder first into the barrier, and turned to see Townsend standing with his fists clenched and rolling his shoulders. The driver of the car who'd seen the incident began to open their door, clearly thinking they could intervene. When Walsh scrambled to his feet, with his face scowling like a pit bull, they reconsidered.

'You ruined it!' Walsh screamed. 'You have no idea what you've done.'

Angry tears joined the rain that was rolling down his cheeks.

'It's over, Walsh,' Townsend said, stepping up onto the walkway, and the two men slowly circled. 'The judge is safe. This whole crusade of yours. It's over. Let's not make this harder than it needs to be.'

'There's only one way this ends, Scouse.' Walsh barked. His eyes flashed to the barrier. A few feet and he'd be done. 'Otherwise, it was for nothing.'

'Don't do anything stupid,' Townsend warned, holding his hand up.

From the direction they'd run, sirens were wailing, and the gridlocked traffic was trying to part to allow the backup to arrive. Townsend and Walsh kept their eyes locked on each other, both waiting on the other to try to close the few yards between them.

Walsh burst into life.

Instead of going for Townsend, he leapt to the barrier, but just as he was about to pull his significant weight over the threshold, Townsend wrapped an arm around his stomach and hauled both of them to the ground. A frenzied rage consumed Walsh, who swung wild elbows over Townsend's arm, until one connected with the detective's jaw. Dazed, Townsend loosened his grip, and Walsh spun, mounting Townsend and driving down furious fists to the shock of the watching motorists.

One of them opened their door and screamed for him to stop.

Townsend threw up a forearm, blocking the blows, but one snuck through and caught him flush on the nose. The pain was instant, and as he blinked through the tears, he saw Walsh lift both arms up to slam a final, clubbing blow.

Townsend threw up a fist, drilling his knuckles straight into Walsh's throat, and the murderous officer fell backwards, gasping for air.

The two men stood.

A few feet to the left was a chest-high barrier that protected them from the instant death below.

Walsh threw up his hands, slipping seamlessly into the stance of a seasoned boxer.

Townsend accepted the challenge, and as the ARU van finally made it through the traffic to the roundabout, Walsh threw a few jabs, but Townsend evaded them and then caught Walsh with a hard right to the kidney. Walsh grunted, but responded in kind, and then ducked Townsend's haymaker and charged. He buried his shoulder into Townsend's stomach and tried to lift him off his feet. Townsend leant forward, shifting his bodyweight, and then swung a few knees up into Walsh's unprotected face. Walsh loosened his grip, stumbled slightly, and then threw another right hook.

Townsend ducked and connected with a hard strike that sent Walsh stumbling onto the ground.

Armed officers began to weave between the parked cars, their rifles locked and loaded, and they held them up through the downpour.

Sergeant Roberts was at the forefront and held up a hand to bring them to a halt.

Walsh looked up at them.

There was no fear in his eyes. No worry at the idea of being shot dead.

All Townsend could see in the man's gaze was failure. Townsend wiped the blood from his nose and approached, hauling Walsh up, and spinning him round. He patted his jacket for his cuffs, and as he did, he began to read him his rights.

'Simon Walsh. I am arresting you for the murders of Asif Khalid, Maureen Allen, Dale Ainsworth, Anne-Louise Mulligan, Officers Tegan Whitworth and Justin Partridge, and the attempted murder of Claire Holliday. You do not have to say anything, but anything you do say may be used in evidence against you.'

'Fuck you, Scouse!' Walsh spat. 'You think you're doing good by stopping me?'

'I'm just doing my job.'

With the guns trained on him, Walsh turned and spat at Sergeant Roberts. Roberts startled slightly, and as the other officers retrained their weapons, Townsend lifted one hand and yelled at them to stop.

Beyond them, he could see King and Hall emerging from one of the cars.

With the grip loosened, Walsh struggled free of Townsend, turned and pounded the pavement towards the barricade.

Townsend yelled for him to stop.

Roberts readied his men to open fire.

But Walsh pushed up off the concrete, hit the base of his spine against the barrier and toppled over, inches away from Townsend's grasp.

As he plummeted towards the motorway below, Walsh closed his eyes and welcomed death.

CHAPTER FIFTY-EIGHT

'We can confirm that last night, Simon Walsh, the man who has been acting under the monicker of The Executioner, fell to his death yesterday evening, upon his attempted escape from police custody.'

The entire media room of the police station was packed to the walls, with local, national and even some international news networks represented by eager journalists holding their recording devices. The entire back wall was lined with cameramen, all of them aiming their lenses towards Detective Superintendent Geoff Hall, who stood behind the lectern, his uniform immaculate and his posture commanding. DI King stood off to the side, pressed against the doors, alongside the PR representative who was watching intently.

The entire evening before had flown by like a blur.

Panic had spread through the parked cars as the ARU had taken up their positions, and no matter how brave people thought they were, when trained officers with guns were in the vicinity, bravery quickly faded.

Hall had sent the word out to shut down the junction of the M40 that had been painted by Walsh's body, who upon examination, had shattered when he hit the ground and then been smeared by an articulated lorry that had ground him to paint.

The traffic was chaotic, causing further delays that had already brought the town to a halt.

The rain finally let up at around ten, but even by then, the sense of failure had drained the entire police force.

The Executioner had been stopped.

But Simon Walsh wouldn't face the system he'd violently tried to take down.

King had slept well that night, staving off the nagging need for a celebratory glass of wine and hadn't been surprised to see her team already in the office when she arrived this morning. They were there to wrap things up, and their dedication was something she was immensely proud of.

And judging from the tone in Detective Superintendent Hall's voice, he shared the same sentiment.

'Since the moment Asif Khalid was found on a farm in Cadmore End, the Specialist Crimes Unit, headed up by the Detective Inspector King, has worked tirelessly to bring this man to justice. Through incredible spirit, relentless effort and impeccable police work, King and her team were able to finally locate PC Simon Walsh and apprehend him before he was able to carry out another tragic murder.'

A hand shot up from the crowd of journalists, but Hall ignored it. There were to be no questions.

'Yes, people lost their lives. And every single one of us who wears this uniform mourns every one of them. Our thoughts and our apologies go out to their families, and we hope they know the effort that was expended to prevent such horrors. Let us not forget their names – Dr Asif Khalid, Maureen Allen, Dale Ainsworth and Anne-Louise Mulligan. All of whom were taken by the hand of a man who had turned his back on the system he'd sworn to uphold. In doing so, he also took the lives of two of our own, and Police Constables Tegan Whitworth and Justin Partridge, were also killed in the pursuit of this man. Their bravery will be honoured once the necessary arrangements have been made with their families.'

More flashes of cameras and more whispered voices spread through the journalists. King watched Hall, transfixed by how he held the room.

'The Thames Valley Police knows that the county of Buckinghamshire and the rest of the country have been held in a grip of fear over the past several days. As always, we strive to protect you and know that we can always do better. But were it not for DI King and her team, we would be here today mourning another murdered civilian, and the possibility that Simon Walsh would have walked free. Whatever it takes…justice will always conquer evil. Thank you for your time.'

The volume in the room rose exponentially, but Hall simply turned, straightened his shoulders, and marched with purpose towards the door, ignoring the questions being hurled his way. King opened the door for him, and followed, as the PR department swept towards the lectern to bring the conference to a close. As the door swung shut, the noise disappeared, and Hall turned to King with a sigh.

'This will take a long time to get over.' He nodded back to the room. 'For them and for us.'

'I know, sir.' She shook her head.

'And as for you, Izzy…' He fixed her with a glare. 'I gave very strict and clear orders for you and Townsend to head straight to hospital to receive medical attention. I made myself very clear that any information was to be passed to myself and DS Swaby. Not only did you fail both of those directives, you also ran into a hostile situation with a man under your command, putting yourselves both in mortal danger.'

'Sir, I know you're mad...' King began, but Hall lifted an abrupt hand to cut her off.

'And in doing so, Izzy, you saved Claire Holliday from a torturous death.' He smiled. 'You're a pain in the arse sometimes, you know that? Townsend, too. And I don't want you to make a habit of ignoring me, but had you not done so...this would have been a very different conference this morning.'

'Thank you, sir.' King smiled. 'It won't happen again.'

'Don't make promises you can't keep.' Hall chuckled and then continued walking. King fell in step with him.

'What now?' She asked.

'Now. I believe Townsend has put in for some well-deserved holiday, and you and your team have a shit ton of paperwork that should have been on my desk an hour ago.'

'On it, sir.' She smirked and headed up the stairs, as Hall continued his march towards the canteen. As she climbed a few, he called after her.

'Oh, and Izzy...' He smiled warmly. 'Great work.'

King nodded her appreciation and then climbed the rest of the stairs with an extra spring in her step. As she pushed open the SCU, she found the office empty. Hannon and Swaby had mentioned going for a coffee and had clearly seen it through. She'd wait until they returned to thank them once again for their efforts.

Across the room, through the glass of her own private office, she saw Elliott Manning shuffling papers into his satchel. She stopped in the doorway, watching as the handsome psychologist collected the last of his things.

'You not sticking around to celebrate?' she asked, stepping into the room. He greeted her appearance with a warm smile.

'I'm afraid not.' He slid his arms into his long, expensive jacket. 'I've just been assigned a case up in Leeds, and they want me there for a briefing this afternoon. So…'

'Right…' King tried to hide her disappointment. 'Do you need a lift?'

'The station is literally over there.' He pointed to the window. 'But thank you.'

'Oh, you're welcome. I mean…it's been fun, right? All the killing?' She shook her head and then looked up at him. 'Do you think your next case might be back this way?'

Manning took a tentative step towards her.

'That depends…' He gently reached up and slide a caressing hand across her cheek. 'You planning on chasing any more serial killers?'

King chuckled.

'I hope not.'

She pressed up on her tiptoes, and her lips met his, and for a few moments, the two of them lost themselves in a loving embrace. The attraction had been there from the moment their eyes had met, and the chemistry had grown with every waking second.

But the case, and the demons that King was trying to keep in the dust, had held her back.

But on the cusp of goodbye, the two of them knew what this was.

And what they were leaving in its wake.

Unfinished business.

Manning eventually pulled back, and gently stroked King's face again.

'You're a remarkable woman, Isabelle King,' he said as he looked into her eyes. 'Never forget that.'

Manning picked up his satchel, gently kissed her on the forehead, and then stepped out of the room and out of King's life. She watched him leave, feeling a sense of regret thumping where her heart should be, and then turned back to her desk.

She stopped.

She smiled.

Smiling right back up at her was a little yellow smiley face, and without thinking, King picked it up and pinned it to her jacket.

'You're a remarkable woman, Isabella King. Never forget that.'

King made a silent promise that she wouldn't.

CHAPTER FIFTY-NINE

By the time the weekend arrived, the weather had taken an upturn, casting a wonderful warm sunshine across the county of Buckinghamshire. The picture-esque countryside was illuminated by the glow, and as Hannon and Shilpa traversed the hill, Fudge scampered through the tall grass excitedly, chased by both of Swaby's children. A few steps behind, Swaby and her husband, Rich, were walking, taking in the breathtaking views and remarking how they needed to move away from Princes Risborough and head out this way.

'Come off it,' Hannon said over her shoulder. 'Your house is lush.'

The four adults chuckled, and Hannon felt Shilpa squeeze her arm tighter. Throughout the last year, Swaby and Hannon had forged a genuine friendship, and after the traumatic past few weeks, the two had agreed to escape the shackles of the SCU office and enjoy a day as just that.

Friends.

The walk through Wendover Woods was a popular one, with the kids' trails based around popular book characters a lucrative draw to the forest. Along with the café and cleverly plotted snack bars, the place was a gold mine. But the incredible walks it offered, either through the rolling hills or the deep woods, more than made up for it.

'I'll take the boys to the adventure playground,' Rich offered as they saw it loom in the distance.

'Wait up,' Shilpa said and then called for Fudge. The little Cavapoo proving the most obedient of the three. Hannon watched as her partner joined Swaby's husband, and they walked on, discussing their own work lives that were considerably less blood-soaked than her own.

'I like her.' Swaby interrupted her train of thought. 'Looks like things are going well now?'

Hannon smiled. It hadn't been too long since the discussions around starting a family had threatened to rip their relationship apart, but this past week had made her appreciate Shilpa even more.

'Really good.' Hannon eventually grinned.

The two walked slowly and silently, enjoying the company, and silently understanding that the past few weeks had taken its toll. Hannon eventually broke the silence.

'Jack's off tomorrow, isn't he?'

'Yeah, lucky bastard.'

'Where's he going, again?' Hannon asked.

'Corfu,' Swaby said with over-the-top envy. 'All right for some.'

'I mean…if anyone deserves it…'

'True.' Swaby chuckled. 'Although I do worry he'll find some dangerous situation to run headfirst into.'

'That's our Jack.'

The two began to laugh, and as they approached the adventure playground, Swaby nodded to the large, glass fronted café.

'Fancy a coffee?'

'When have I ever said no?'

Swaby broke free from linking Hannon's arm, and headed towards the glass door of the building, and Hannon stopped and took stock. After tying up the paperwork surrounding the Walsh case, King had brought her into her office for a debrief. In essence, it was ten minutes of King heaping praise on Hannon for all the work she had done and Hannon trying her hardest to control her blushing.

'Nic. Without you, Claire Holliday would have been killed. Walsh would have got away. You're a hell of a detective, and it's time this place recognises that.'

The words had been greatly appreciated, but as always, Hannon's crippling self-doubt began to rear its ugly head once more. It was always the same for her, and although she knew she'd done incredible work to track Walsh, she still clung to past failures like they were life floats.

Shilpa constantly tried to snap her out of it, reminding her of how much she meant to her and the incredible things she'd achieved already in her career.

The team had rallied around her countless times, and although King and Townsend were always on hand to compliment her work, she still second guessed her true worth to the team.

She needed someone to snap her out of it.

And as if she could read her mind, DI King's voice cut through her train of thought.

'Nic.'

King's voice echoed behind her, and she startled as her boss approached her. Seeing King in civilian clothes always took a moment to register.

'Guv.' She looked confused. 'What are you doing here?'

'Swaby invited me.' She looked around for the other member of her team.

'Oh, right. Swaby's inside.' She pointed to the café. 'If you hurry, you might catch her before she orders.'

'I'm fine.' She smiled. 'How are you?'

'I'm all good.'

'Really?' She looked at her sceptically. 'Because I spoke to DCI Lowe, and he said he was worried about you.'

'Hold up.' Hannon lifted her hand. 'You two talk now?'

'When we have to. That okay?'

'Well…yeah. It's just like being a child of divorce and seeing your folks getting along.'

King cracked a smile.

'Well, we weren't exactly putting the world to rights. Hall had a debrief and asked how the team were doing, and he said you were having a crisis of confidence. That you didn't think you were built for the job?'

Hannon looked to the ground. That self-doubt was creeping in and she knew King would read it the second it made its way to her facial features.

'It's just been a long week or so…'

'You know, when I told you that we wouldn't have caught Walsh without you, I meant it. What you did went beyond 'good' police work, Nic. It was exceptional.'

Hannon looked up at King, and her smile was as genuine as her words.

'Thank you, guv.'

'Trust me. Everyone has noticed,' King continued. 'Detective Superintendent Hall was incredibly impressed, and DCI Lowe…well, he was banging on about being low on head count and…'

'Well, he can keep my head out of his maths lesson,' Hannon quipped.

King smiled proudly.

'You are built for this, Nic. And one day, you'll make a hell of a DS.'

'I'm not that old, guv,' Hannon joked. But she was unable to stop the smile spreading across her face. 'Thank you.'

'Don't mention it,' King said, and the two of them began trundling across the muddy pathway towards the adventure playground. Swaby emerged from the glass doors, balancing a tray of coffees, and politely offered to go back for King.

'I'm fine, Michelle,' King said with a grin. 'You know, I've never been here before. It's gorgeous.'

'Yup,' Hannon agreed. 'Although it's an absolute nightmare when it's raining.'

The three detectives walked towards the adventure playground, where they could see Swaby's boys swinging recklessly on the climbing frame. Swaby sighed.

'I tell you what, these Easter holidays will run me ragged.' She took a sip of her coffee. 'Hopefully, we get another serial killer so I can get some time off.'

Hannon nearly spat out her coffee.

'Michelle,' King said in shock. 'That's an awful thing to say.'

'You could go on holiday?' Hannon suggested. 'Like Jack.'

'Oh yeah.' Swaby rolled her eyes. 'Who signed that off?'

'I didn't really have a choice.' King shrugged. 'I figured Mandy would have something to say if I didn't. I mean, I did promise her I wouldn't let him run into dangerous situations anymore…'

'Oh, come on now,' Hannon said dismissively. 'You've got as much chance of doing that as I have of stopping Fudge jumping on the sofa.'

'Jack's never going to change,' Swaby added with a wry smile. King could feel herself almost basking in the warmth of her team.

'Besides…he'll probably find something to run head-first into on holiday,' she joked.

Hannon joined in.

'Yeah. Probably a water slide. The lucky git.'

The three of them broke out into laughter again, and as the sunshine cut through the high trees, King was thrilled to see the world in a lighter glow.

It had been a long and torturous week or so, one shrouded in the darkness of vengeance and violence.

But they had made it through.

They had stopped Walsh from finishing his crusade.

They had delivered true justice for the lives he had taken and the subsequent one's he had destroyed.

And they had done it as a team.

CHAPTER SIXTY

It always baffled Townsend why people queued for the gate at the airport. The flight to Corfu wasn't yet ready to board, yet a row of at least fifteen various families and couples were already impatiently waiting. From his seat at the gate, Townsend wondered if they knew the plane wouldn't leave until everyone had boarded. When a portly middle-aged gentleman confronted one of the staff, claiming to have paid for 'Speedy Boarding', Townsend wondered if there was a bigger waste of money at the airport.

When Mandy and Eve returned from the shops, they answered it for him.

'Look what I've got, Daddy,' Eve said, waving a luminous pink neck cushion in his face. 'It's so I can relax on the plane.'

'You know the flight is only three and half hours, right?' Townsend chuckled. 'We're going to Greece, not Australia.'

'Still.' Eve shrugged. 'I like to be comfortable.'

Townsend shrugged and then glanced down at the price tag that was still attached to cushion.

'Sorry. How much?'

Mandy laughed and took the seat beside their daughter.

'We're on holiday, Jack,' she protested. Then pulled her own out of the bag. 'Besides, I like to be comfortable, too.'

Townsend chuckled and shook his head.

It had been a strange few days in their household.

The evening of Walsh's death, Townsend had traipsed through the front door a little after ten that evening, dripping wet and Mandy waiting to read him the riot act. Unbeknownst to him, he was famous.

The news of the Executioner's failure had spread, with the live feed being watched by thousands. The footage of the masked man being chased from the room, followed by the handsome detective giving chase had spread across all the news and media platforms, and Townsend was being heralded as a hero.

Mandy had seen it, and although her initial anger soon gave way to immense pride, she'd scolded Townsend for once again running headfirst into danger. When she replayed the footage for him, and paused it as the Executioner hurled the hatchet off camera, she demanded to know how close it had come to hitting him.

Townsend had joked that he was Neo from *The Matrix*, but it failed to land.

In truth, she was right.

Townsend had been centimetres away from death, and although his efforts saved Claire Holliday's life, he'd come perilously close to once again leaving Mandy and Eve on their own. He'd told her everything, including the fist fight he'd had with the desperate murderer, who'd eventually taken his own life.

Mandy had wept.

The job was the job, they both knew that, but the

thought of Townsend putting himself in such danger was something she despised.

Townsend knew he couldn't promise her he wouldn't do it again. He was who he was, and they both knew that even in the face of serious danger, he would always do the right thing.

By the time they had retired to their bed, she'd forgiven him, expressed her pride in having a brave and now, a seemingly famous hero for a husband, and the two of them had made love that night with a new appreciation for each other.

The following days were easier, with Townsend's time spent in a whole manner of different debriefs, while Mandy tied things up at her work before her two weeks off for the Easter Holiday's. Eve was hopping about with excitement at having time off school, and that excitement trebled when Townsend surprised them both with a holiday.

He'd found a last-minute deal to a lovely looking, four-star resort on the coast of Corfu, which offered three massive swimming pools, all-inclusive food and drink, evening entertainment and most importantly, access to the adjoining splash park.

Eve had never been on holiday.

During her early years, Townsend had been undercover in some of the most dangerous OCGs in the country, and since then, they'd had to spend time adjusting to the normality of family life.

Mandy had thrown her arms around him when he'd told her, and had spent the weekend updating her wardrobe.

The holiday was turning out to be more expensive than he'd envisioned.

But as he sat back in the uncomfortable chair, waiting

for the plane to board, he couldn't help but feel a sense of happiness wash over him.

They hadn't arrested Walsh, but his crusade was over.

They'd managed to stop a brutal murder from playing out live over the internet.

And here he was. Still alive. Still kicking. Ready for their first holiday as a family, and a chance to shut the world off and be present with them.

The thought made him smile, and as he met his wife's beautiful blue eyes, her face cracked into a beautiful grin. Clearly, she was thinking the same.

'When can we go?' Eve asked, not looking up from her tablet that she'd fished from the carry-on she'd insisted upon.

'They'll call our flight soon, Pickle.' Townsend said.

'Why are these people queueing then?' she asked, her youthful innocence verbalising Townsend's thoughts.

'Christ knows,' Mandy said.

Townsend chuckled, but before he could add to the conversation, his phone rumbled. He fetched it from his pocket, and Mandy cast a curious look in his direction.

King.

'One sec. Promise,' Townsend said, and Mandy nodded and turned her attention to their daughter. Townsend took the call and meandered through the gate.

'Guv.'

'Jack.' She sounded chipper. 'Just wanted to catch you before you left.'

'Hopefully any minute now,' he said dryly. 'What's up, Guv?'

'I just wanted to say have a great holiday. You deserve it. And bloody try to switch off.'

Townsend laughed out loud.

'I'll try, guv. I'll try.'

'That beautiful family of yours is better with you in it.'

King wasn't usually one for too much sentiment. 'So make sure you're in it. Whatever's going on here, we've got it covered.'

'I appreciate that, Guv.' Townsend shuffled uncomfortably. He thought back to that moment, as he burst into the Airbnb, and the Executioner hurled that hatchet in his direction. King had pulled him out of the way. 'And also… not sure if I said it…but thank you.'

'For what?'

'For saving my life back there.'

'Well…now we're even, huh?' King chuckled. 'Have a great holiday, Jack.'

'Thanks, Guv.'

'Oh, and keep track of how many people ask for an autograph. We've got a sweepstake going.'

'Ha ha,' Townsend said sarcastically, then hung up the phone. He took a beat, thinking of his team and everything they'd been through together.

Trials and traumas that bound people together in ways that only those in the job could understand. King. Hannon. Swaby. Hell, to some extent, even Hall and Lowe.

People who were in the trenches with him.

People who made sure he got back to his family.

With his heart full, Townsend turned and headed back towards his girls, just as the screen shifted and announced the boarding of their flight. Townsend met Mandy and Eve at the back of the impatient queue, and Eve was hopping with excitement.

'Let's go!' she yelled, her fist pumping into the air and drawing smiles from passersby. Townsend slid an arm around Mandy and planted a kiss on her cheek.

'Love you.'

'I love you, too,' she said, and then the three of them shuffled slowly towards the desk, ready to board their plane and head off on their holiday. Mandy joked that Townsend might have a fanbase in Greece, and he told her about the sweepstake.

But in truth, nobody would truly remember the face of the man who burst into the room and was on screen for a few seconds.

But someone did.

The last person who Townsend would want.

GET EXCLUSIVE ROBERT ENRIGHT MATERIAL

Hey there,

I really hope you enjoyed the book and I'd love for you to join my reader group. I send out regular updates, competitions and special offers as well as some cool free stuff. Sound good?

Well, if you do sign up to the reader group I'll send you FREE copies of THE RIGHT REASON and RAINFALL, two thrilling Sam Pope prequel novellas from my best-selling Sam Pope series. (RRP: £1.99/$2.99 each)

You can get your FREE books by signing up at www.robertenright.co.uk

BOOKS BY ROBERT ENRIGHT

For more information about the DS Jack Townsend series and other books by Robert Enright, please visit:

www.robertenright.co.uk

ABOUT THE AUTHOR

Robert lives in Buckinghamshire with his family, writing books and dreaming of getting a dog.

For more information:
www.robertenright.co.uk
robert@robertenright.co.uk

You can also connect with Robert on Social Media:

- facebook.com/robenrightauthor
- instagram.com/robert_enright_author

COPYRIGHT © ROBERT ENRIGHT, 2025

All rights reserved. No part of this publication may be reproduced, stored in a retrieval system, or transmitted in any form or by any means, electronic, photocopying, mechanical, recording, or otherwise, without the prior permission of the copyright owner.

All characters in this book are fictitious and any resemblance to actual persons living or dead is purely coincidental.

Cover by The Cover Collection

Edited by Emma Williamson

Proof Read by Martin Buck

Printed in Great Britain
by Amazon